Claimed by the Boss

BARBARA WALLACE

JENNIE ADAMS

KATRINA CUDMORE

MIX

Paper from
responsible sources

FSC

FSC C007454

This book is produced from independently certified FSC™ paper
to ensure responsible forest management.

For more information visit www.harpercollins.co.uk/green

Printed and bound in Spain
by CPI, Barcelona

MILLS & BOON

First Published in Great Britain 2020
By Mills & Boon, an imprint of HarperCollins*Publishers*
1 London Bridge Street, London, SE1 9GF

CLAIMED BY THE BOSS © 2020 Harlequin Books S.A.

Beauty and the Brooding Boss © 2011 Barbara Wallace
Nine-to-Five Bride © 2009 Jennifer Ann Ryan
Swept into the Rich Man's World © 2016 Katrina Cudmore

ISBN: 978-0-263-28085-2

0220

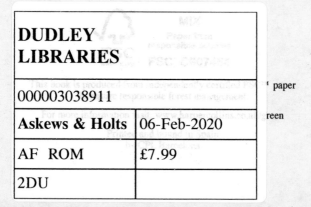

BEAUTY AND THE BROODING BOSS

BARBARA WALLACE

For Peter—
I couldn't do this without you.
And for the Moody Muses—the best support
group a gal could ask for.

CHAPTER ONE

ALEX Markoff WASN'T *really ugly.*

Nor was he scarred, horribly disfigured, or any of the other things Kelsey imagined a recluse to be. In fact, the man standing before her couldn't be described as anything less than stunning. He was tall, at least a half a foot taller than her, with a lanky athletic build that took up most of the door frame. Faded jeans hung low on narrow hips while a black golf shirt molded to expansive shoulders. With his right arm engulfed from biceps to fingers in a plaster cast, she wondered how he managed to put on such a well-fitting garment.

Storm-cloud-colored eyes bore down on her from above finely-honed cheekbones.

Nope, not ugly. But definitely unhappy to see her on his doorstep.

Other doorsteps and other unwelcome expressions threatened on the edge of her memory and she shook them away. This wasn't the same. Not at all.

Still, she couldn't stop that all-too-familiar uncertainty from creeping into her voice as she offered up a polite smile. "Hi. I'm Kelsey Albertelli."

When he didn't respond, she added, "Your new assistant."

Silence.

"From New York. Mr. Lefkowitz hired me to—"

"I know who you are."

His voice matched his physical stature. Kelsey nearly stepped back from its impact. *Or was it the barely veiled hostility?*

Driving up the Taconic Parkway with the windows rolled down had blown her topknot loose, and strands of brown hair were falling into her line of sight. She tucked a few of them behind her ear. "Good. For a moment, I thought maybe Mr. Lefkowitz's office forgot to close the loop."

"No, he closed it. Several times."

Kelsey nodded as an awkward silence settled between them. More strands of hair fell in her face. She tucked them back and waited to see what Markoff would say next.

The answer was nothing. He simply turned around and retreated into the house leaving her standing alone on the threshold.

Can't say you weren't warned. "Doubt you'll get much of a warm welcome," his editor had said. Clearly an understatement. "Just remember, he doesn't have a choice. You work for me, not him."

"Don't worry," she'd assured him. "I'm sure I'll be fine. Nothing I can't handle." *For the right price.* Thanks to Grandma Rosie, she was all about the paycheck these days. She'd have to work three or four jobs to earn what Mr. Lefkowitz offered. Besides, it wasn't as if she hadn't shown up unwanted on a doorstep before.

Coincidentally, that was thanks to Grandma Rosie too.

Since Markoff left the door open, she assumed he intended her to follow. By the time she realized and crossed the threshold, he was several paces ahead, and she had to rush to catch up.

"You're certainly tucked away up here," she said, reaching his shoulder. "You don't get too many sets of directions saying 'turn right at the big pine tree' in New York City. I think I turned right three times at three different trees."

"It's the one at the fork," he replied.

"I know that *now*." She emphasized the word. "Still, in most places when they give you a landmark, it's a building or a sign or something. Not a pine tree. I missed your driveway the first time driving by too. You can barely see your mailbox behind the bushes. But then, I imagine that's the point…."

Her sentence faded off. She was rambling. She hated rambling. Nervous chatter to fill up silence. Drove her insane. She'd had enough of it as a kid to last a lifetime. Got to the point, in fact, where she wanted to scream at the social workers to shut up. Yet here she was doing the same exact thing. Anxiously trying to break the ice with a man whose resentment at her presence poured off him in waves.

Still, she refused to feel intimidated. "Mr. Lefkowitz said you write all your drafts longhand. I assume that's what I'll be typing—your longhand draft, that is." Her gaze flickered to his plaster-encased arm. "I hope breaking your arm hasn't affected your progress."

No sooner did the words leave her mouth than he stopped short, turning his gray eyes on her. Kelsey found herself rooted to the spot by their intensity. "Did Stuart tell you to ask that?"

"I—I—" Kelsey honestly didn't know how to reply.

"You tell Stuart Lefkowitz he'll get his manuscript when he gets it. Bad enough he's foisted a damn typist on me—I don't need a babysitter too."

"I wasn't—that is, I'm not—" Scrambling to catch up once again, Kelsey found herself wishing she'd asked a few more questions during her job interview. *That's what you get for being motivated by money.*

When she first learned she'd be typing manuscript pages for Alex Markoff—the Alex Markoff—she thought the assignment sounded exotic. She'd been in high school when *Chase the Moon* debuted, but she remembered the book sitting on teachers' desks, and she remembered reading excerpts from it in literature class. Alex Markoff was The Author of the Decade. The one writer everyone clamored to read.

She stole another look at her new boss. Maybe she should have looked at a book jacket before arriving. His looks might not have caught her so off guard. It wasn't that he was stereotypically handsome—in profile some might consider the nose a tad long or his jaw too angular—but the strong features suited him. Hard to believe she imagined him disfigured. Then again, how else was she supposed to picture a man who went from bestselling author to hermit?

She really should have asked more questions during the interview.

Looking to her surroundings for answers, she could only see that Nuttingwood was as dark and masculine as its owner. It reminded her of an English cottage from some old black-and-white movie, all stone and ivy. The front room was similar in appearance, small with antique furniture and hunter green furnishings.

Turning the corner, however, Kelsey suddenly found herself thrust into a large space dominated by windows and French doors. Outside lay a sprawling garden awash with color so vivid it made both the dark wood interior and the green Berkshire mountains pale in comparison. Through the glass she could see birds darting back and forth amid the flowers, many of which she didn't recognize.

"Wow," she said under her breath. It was like standing in the New York Botanical Garden.

Footsteps pulled her from her reverie. Markoff had headed across the open space to a door on the opposite side. Following, Kelsey found herself in a room similar to the one she left, though smaller and with fewer windows. It was no less spectacular, however, thanks to a pair of French doors that opened onto a terraced rose garden. Adirondack chairs encouraged visitors outside, while inside a pair of plaid overstuffed rockers battled back with a comfortable invitation of their own. Clutter—mostly magazines, books and papers—littered the end tables and bookcases. A few crumpled balls of paper lay on the floor. For some strange reason, they seemed more like decorations than mess, complements to the room's lived-in atmosphere.

"Great office." In her mind, she could imagine him scribbling away by the window.

Markoff simply pointed to a large wooden desk tucked in the corner. "You can work here."

"No computer?" The desk was barren of electronics.

"You can use your own and save to a flash drive."

"Okay." Good thing she had brought a laptop. Wonder what else she'd need. "Do you get Internet up here on the mountain?"

"Why?" That laserlike intensity had returned to his eyes, and they now bore into her suspiciously, as if she'd asked him for the National Defense codes. "Why would you need Internet access?"

"So I can keep in contact with New York. Mr. Lefkowitz will want updates."

He made a noise in the back of his throat, a sort of quiet, guttural growl. Kelsey immediately recalled his babysitter comment. Just her luck to step into some sort of bad blood between editor and writer. "If you don't, I can find a place in town—"

"There's Internet."

"Great." She'd worry about access another time when he was in a better mood. *If he had a better mood.*

A stack of yellow notepads lay on the desk so

she turned her attention to them. "This is what I'm typing, I presume."

"Type exactly what's written," he replied. "Don't change a thing. Not a single word. If you can't read something, leave it blank. I'll fill in the word later."

Kelsey picked up the top notebook. Lines of gray masculine scrawl filled the page. Great. He wrote in pencil. And changed his mind a lot too. With all the arrows and slashes, the paper looked more like a sports play than a story. Looked like there would be a lot of blanks.

"Anything else?" she asked. One thing she learned as a temp was to learn an employer's quirks and rules upfront. Knowledge made adjusting to that much easier, and she figured Markoff's typing guidelines were merely the tip of the iceberg.

She was right. "I don't like loud noise," he continued. "No music, no loud voices. If you need to call your boyfriend or whoever—"

"I won't be calling anyone." Her quick answer must have caught him by surprise, because his stormy eyes blinked. "No boyfriend, no family." Why she felt the need to supply the information, she didn't know.

A shadow flickered across his face, momentarily quieting the turbulence in his eyes. The change threw her off balance. Without the glare, his face went from intense to downright arresting. It was most unsettling. Tucking her hair behind her ear, she looked away to the ground.

"Well, if you do need to make a call," she heard him say, "please go outside. Or better yet, wait until after work hours."

"Speaking of which, what hours did you have in mind? I mean, do you have a preference? So I don't disturb you?"

"Doesn't matter."

Because he didn't care or because she would disturb him no matter what? "Then if it's all right with you, I'm a morning person. I like to get an early start on the day."

"Fine."

Silence engulfed them once more, awkward and uneasy. Kelsey adjusted her appearance: her satchel, the hem of her T-shirt, anything rather than let Markoff's obvious displeasure get under her skin.

"Well then," she said, forcing a cheery note, "since we've covered where I'm working, what I'm working on and when, all that's left to settle is where you'd like me to sleep." Again, she found herself prodding his non-response. "Mr. Lefkowitz said you agreed to let me stay here." Amazingly.

"Upstairs," he replied. "The bedrooms are up-stairs."

"Is there a particular room...?"

"I don't care."

"As long as I don't steal yours, right?"

Her attempt at levity fell flat. More than flat, based on how his expression darkened.

"I appreciate you being so accommodating. The Berkshires are a popular spot apparently, because summer rooms are at a premium." She was babbling again. "Mr. Lefkowitz had his office call every hotel first."

"I'm sure he did."

Was that skepticism in his voice? What on earth? Did he think she chose to stay up here in the middle of nowhere? She took a deep breath and smoothed back her hair. "Look, Mr. Markoff, I know this arrangement wasn't your idea." She kept her voice as level and calm as possible. "And I'll be the first to admit the arrangements are less than ideal...."

"Or necessary."

"Be that as it may, I'm here for the summer. I promise I'll do my best to stay out of your way as much as possible."

"Good."

The blunt answer stung more than Kelsey expected. She tightened her smile, hiding the reaction. "It might help if we set some ground rules right now. For example, as far as meals go..."

"The kitchen's in the back. You're on your own for food."

Now why didn't that surprise her? "And the bathrooms?"

"The main one's upstairs, across from the guest rooms. You'll find towels and a tub. There's limited hot water."

"Guess that means I should catch the first shower."

He wasn't amused. Again, the reaction hurt. She chalked it up to a new location and old ghosts. *It's only for a summer,* she told herself. Any situation could be endured as long as it was short-term and she kept her personal distance.

"Don't worry," she amended. "I'm not one for lingering under the spray." Or anywhere she wasn't wanted, for that matter. Since he nodded in response, she assumed he approved the answer.

Meanwhile, she could tell Markoff was eager to end their meeting. So he could stomp off and rue her presence, no doubt. "My laptop is in the car. Why don't I go get it and start working. I'll print out the finished pages and leave them for your review."

As she spoke, she moved toward the door. Unfortunately, Markoff moved toward the desk at the same time and they inadvertently ended up in each other's personal space. The scent of wood and cloves drifted toward Kelsey. A warm earthy aroma that made her want to close her eyes and inhale deeply. Instead, she looked up to meet eyes that were stormier than ever.

Awareness, strong and instinctive, spread through her. "Sorry, I didn't realize you were..." For some reason her brain wiring had suddenly gone haywire, and she was having trouble putting words together. "I mean, I was heading..."

She slipped past him, into the vacant doorway. "Why don't I go get my laptop?"

Alex didn't respond. Good thing, since it took till she reached her car and some deep breaths of fresh air before the weird flustered sensation left her brain.

"Get a grip on yourself," she muttered to herself, unlocking the door. "You're going to be here all summer." Surely she wasn't going to spend the next three months rattled by her boss, was she?

When she returned a few minutes later she heard a voice coming from the office.

"For crying out loud, we're talking a couple extra months. Three tops. You can't wait an extra ninety days?"

Who couldn't wait? Markoff's voice was razor-sharp, cutting through not just the air, but her as well. "And I suppose I broke my arm on purpose too," she heard him say. "That why you sent the babysitter? To make sure I didn't hurl myself down another hill?"

Babysitter. He meant her. That meant he was talking to Stuart Lefkowitz. Trying to get rid of her perhaps?

Crossing the main space toward the doorway, she stopped shy of the entrance and peered through the crack. Markoff had his back to her. She could see his shoulder muscles rippling with tension beneath his shirt. When he turned, she saw a similar tautness playing across his profile.

"Did it ever occur to you," he said, "that I can't write with someone breathing down my neck twenty-four seven?"

Alex's jaw twitched while he listened to the voice on the other end. Suddenly, his eyes grew disbelieving. "What did you say? Yes, I know what 'breach of contract' means. You wouldn't…"

There was silence, followed by a slow controlled intake of breath. Incredulity had changed to outright fury. "Fine. You'll get your damn book."

Kelsey jumped as he slammed the cell phone on his desk. Breach of contract? They were threatening legal action? No wonder Mr. Lefkowitz had been so adamant about her staying. And no wonder Markoff resented her. He was right. She *was* a babysitter.

On the other side of the door, Alex let out a

frustrated groan, and she heard footsteps. Fearing discovery, she instinctively drew back, scrambling mentally for an explanation should she be confronted for eavesdropping. A second later, the banging of a door told her she was safe; that he'd left through the garden. Sure enough, looking outside, she could see him stomping off toward the woods.

With the angry conversation she heard fresh in her mind, she finally let out the sigh she'd been holding since her arrival.

This was going to be a long summer.

That night Kelsey unpacked, settling into the room that would be her home for the next three months. Since Alex never mentioned which bedroom would be hers, she selected one that looked like a guest room. Like the front of the house, the room she picked was dark and woodsy, draped in hunter green and brown. The only thing missing was a deer head hanging on the wall.

The aroma of cedar wafted from the closet, adding to the rustic appeal. As she unpacked her clothes, she tried to count the number of times she'd gone through this routine. And it was a routine. First came the bureau, taking up as little drawer space as possible—a throwback to sharing a room with multiple people—then the closet. The entire process seldom took more than fifteen minutes. She'd learned early to travel light and not get too settled, so all her worldly possessions fit into two large suitcases. This summer it was the most she'd ever packed, she noted. Then again, the two years she just spent subletting was the longest she'd ever spent in one place. Guess in sticking around, she'd acquired a few more things.

Closet done, she reached for her satchel, the final part of her ritual. Immediately, her fingers found her most prized possession. The ceramic mug was cool to the touch despite sitting in her bag all day long. Hard to believe that once upon a time, brightly painted flowers had circled its surface. They were nothing more than faded speckles of paint now. There was a crack along the top of the handle from too many washings. Smiling, Kelsey cradled the mug in her palm. She could picture the same mug, colors still bright, resting on a countertop, a female hand pouring coffee into it. If she tried really hard, she could picture her mother bringing the cup to her lips, though as time passed, that memory got harder and harder to conjure up.

All of a sudden she felt overwhelmingly small and alone, as if the simple act of remembering transported her back in time. For a moment, she wasn't a grown woman controlling her own destiny, but a little girl back in the system, gripping the last talisman she had from her old life. Living with her mother hadn't been great, but at least she'd been wanted. At least that's how she chose to remember those years.

She leaned against the headboard, knees drawn close, the mug pressed to her breast. This was part of the routine too, this momentary lapse into loneliness. She'd get over it soon enough. She always did. Soon as she familiarized herself with the surroundings. Although this time the feelings were stronger than usual. Hardly surprising given Alex's animosity.

She gave herself five more minutes of self-pity, then put the emotion back on the shelf and walked to the window. Her bedroom overlooked a less landscaped part of the garden, closer to the trees, increasing the feeling of isolation. Outside, through the tree line, she noticed the sky still bore traces of daylight even though it felt far later. "Country living," she mused, raising the sash. The greeting quiet was unsettling. Nothing but the rustle of leaves and a few intermittent high-pitched trills. How on earth would she sleep without the undercurrent of traffic? Or streetlights? Didn't Markoff believe in outdoor lighting?

Of course not, she answered with a roll of her eyes. Lights would ruin the whole "darkness" theme he had going.

To her right, a branch snapped. She leaned over the sill, half expecting—or maybe fully expecting—to see a wild animal dashing out from the trees. What she saw instead surprised her more. It was the silhouette of a man.

Markoff.

He was walking the perimeter of the property, just inside the tree line. Head down, he picked his way carefully, as if counting his steps. Kelsey watched him approach with a catch in her throat. He looked so alone. Not at all like the hostile man who had greeted her this afternoon. This man reminded her of a specter. That was the only word she could think to describe him. There but not there.

He came closer, and Kelsey drew back, not wanting to get caught watching. No sooner did she pull into the shadows than she noticed he'd stopped. His face slanted upward to her window. Kelsey stifled a gasp. What light remained hit his eyes just right, turning them to shining silver. Even from two stories up, she could see the emotion churning behind them, bright and unguarded. She couldn't name what emotion she saw, but whatever it was, it struck a familiar chord, pulling her in and making her insides twist. It felt like he was looking straight at her. Or rather, *inside* her. Which was silly, since he couldn't see her from where she stood.

Eventually he moved on, leaving the night air charged with his presence. Quietly, Kelsey lowered the shade. A few moments later, she heard footsteps on the stairs, followed by a bedroom door clicking shut.

His room was next to hers. She hadn't realized. Through the wall, she heard the scraping of a chair and she swore what sounded like a long, desolate sigh followed by another and another, each sounding more frustrated than the next. Suddenly there was the rattling rush of glass and paper punctuated by a groan. The door opened and footsteps, heavy, angry footsteps, sounded in the hall. Kelsey knew the front door would slam before she heard it.

Okay, so maybe she was wrong about the night-time quiet. But she was right about it being a long summer. Maybe she should have stayed in New York and worked those three jobs after all.

And be tied to Grandma Rosie's debt for even longer.

Letting out a long breath, she collapsed backwards on the bed. "Thanks a lot, Grandma," she muttered. Looked like Markoff wasn't the only one who didn't have a choice.

CHAPTER TWO

"ALL I can say is thank God for coffee. Especially—" Kelsey took a long sip "—fresh-ground Italian roast. I swear this stuff might be the only thing keeping me upright today."

Her companion, a large orange tabby, said nothing. Kelsey had found the furry critter dozing on the terrace when she arrived at dawn, and he'd been keeping her company ever since. She suspected the animal was a stray. Unless Alex had a hidden soft spot, she didn't see him as the pet-owning type.

Then again, those eyes she saw last night definitely hid something....

Forget it. He didn't deserve sympathetic thoughts. Not after the way he kept her up last night with his continual pacing and sighing.

"I thought writing was a sitting profession, not one that required moving across the floor all night long." She took another drink and waited for the caffeine to kick in. She was going to need to be alert if she was going to spend the day deciphering his handwriting. "I'll tell you one thing, Puddin'-cat, I don't care how brilliant a writer he is, the man definitely needs to improve his social skills. He acts like my being here is some kind of plague. How much you want to bet he's annoyed that I helped myself to the coffee this morning?"

The cat pulled a paw over its eyes in response.

"Exactly," Kelsey replied. "Though seems to me, if you're going to leave a fresh pot brewing at the crack of dawn, you shouldn't be surprised when people help themselves." The smell alone had been nirvana after a sleepless night. "Fair's fair, right?"

"Who are you talking to?"

Kelsey nearly jumped out of her skin. Standing at the edge of the terrace was a very dark and bothered Alex Markoff.

Immediately, her insides somersaulted. How was it he could look so intimidatingly perfect at this hour? He wore a navy blue T-shirt the same shade as his sling, the hem of which skimmed the waistband of his jeans. Jeans, she noted, that looked made to hug his hips. He'd been up and about from the looks of it. His skin glistened with perspiration, the moisture darkening the collar of his shirt. Dark curls peeked out from the back of his neck with the unruliness that only came from damp hair. Though it shouldn't, seeing them made her wonder what he might look like stepping from the shower.

"Good morning," she said once she caught her breath.

He stared at her with unreadable eyes. "You didn't answer my question. Who are you talking to?"

"Just the—" She pointed to the sunny spot on a terrace that was now deserted. "Myself."

"Do you always do that?"

"When there's no one else to talk with. What's that they say, 'You're your own best company'?"

"So I've always believed."

As she tucked her hair behind her ear, Kelsey swore he checked for an earpiece. Really, did he think she was lying? "Looks like I'm not the only morning person after all. I helped myself to the coffee, by the way."

"I heard."

Along with how much else? Quickly, she raised her mug, hoping he wouldn't notice her skin flushing. "Have you been up long?" she asked over the rim. "I would think after such a long night, you'd be sleeping in."

"Why do you think I had a long night?"

Why did he seem to scrutinize everything she

said as though she had a hidden meaning? Along with staring at her with those probing gray eyes?

"I heard you," she explained, resisting the urge to duck her head like a nervous teenager. "Kind of hard not to, actually. Old house, thin rooms. You sigh loudly."

"Oh."

Oh, indeed.

"I take it writing didn't go well last night?"

"Why do you want to know?"

"I don't know, to make conversation?" She shrugged. "Do I have to have a reason?"

"There's always a reason."

"Well, in this case, my reason was to be friendly. After all, we're going to spend the summer working together, we might as well be civil to one another, right?"

He gave her a long look. Gauging her sincerity? While she waited, the part of her not insulted used the standoff to study his face, catching the details she'd been too overwhelmed to notice before. Things like the tanned complexion, the faint scar on the bridge of his nose, the curve of his Cupid's bow.

And, of course, the emotion behind his eyes. Yet again it struck her that there was something sad and painful behind their turbulence. A kind of longing, perhaps.

Or loneliness.

What was his story? She really should have done some research before taking this job.

Her curiosity would have to go unexamined as the sound of crunching gravel on the other side of the house interrupted the standoff. Soon as he heard the noise, Alex's expression changed. Again. His shoulders straightened and a soft curse escaped his lips.

"What?" Kelsey was having trouble keeping up with his collection of abrupt moods. Naturally he didn't answer. Like yesterday, he simply turned and walked off leaving her to follow. She turned the corner in time to see a burly tree-trunk of a man step out of a green pickup with the words *Leafy Bean, Farley Grangerfield Prop.* painted on the side. The man looked from Alex to her with interest, but said nothing. Not surprising given the dark warning plastered all over Alex's face.

Continuing in silence, both men reached over the side of the truck bed and each grabbed two canvas bags laden with groceries. Alex, she noted, carried both with his good arm. As the stranger passed, he shot her another look. "Last two bags won't unload themselves."

Taking the hint, Kelsey hustled to the truck to see they'd, fortunately, left her what looked like the two lightest bags. She brought them into the kitchen where she found the two men wordlessly unpacking groceries and arranging them on the kitchen table. The door swung shut behind her, causing them to both look up.

"Where should I put these?" she asked.

"Counter," Alex replied. "That's not necessary," he added when she started unpacking.

"I don't mind." What else was she going to do, stand there and watch them? "You'll have to tell me where the stuff goes though. At least the first time. I'm pretty good at remembering where things go. Plus this way I'll see where there's space for my groceries."

Dammit, she was babbling again. It was quickly becoming a bad habit. But the quiet… It filled the room so completely. And those looks she kept feeling the grocer give her. Curious and full of implied innuendo. She had to say something just to hear something besides her own thoughts. Although the subsequent look Alex shot her made her wish she'd reconsidered.

"Bigger order'll cost you extra," commented the grocer shortly.

"Kelsey will be buying her groceries separately."

"Right," she said. After all, she was on her own for meals. Why would they do something as simple as combine grocery orders? "I'm Kelsey Albertelli,

by the way. Mr. Markoff's new assistant. I'm here to help while his arm's broken. Are you Farley?"

The lack of denial suggested he was. "Need three days' notice for delivery. You want your food sooner, you have to pick up your order yourself. Special orders take longer. And if I don't have the brand, I'll substitute. No complaining."

Was everyone in Berkshire County this brusque? At least Farley's silence felt different. Gruff though he was, he lacked the anger and wary defensiveness that surrounded her new boss. "Got order forms in the truck," he said when the last grocery item had been put away. They were the first words anyone had said in a few minutes. "You want some, follow me."

She did, feeling Alex's stare on her all the way to the drive. "Normal delivery's every ten days," the old man was telling her. "First four bags are free, after that you pay."

"I'll bear that in mind." Kelsey took the stack of tri-colored forms he handed her. "You been delivering to Nuttingwood long?" she asked.

"Long enough"

"And that's been…?"

"Three, four, five years. I don't keep a calendar."

She would have liked to have been surprised by the vague answer, but deep down she suspected that's all she'd get. Still, it was worth a shot. "Thanks again for the forms," she said, waving them in the air. "I'll see you soon."

Farley muttered something about having nothing better to do than drive around all day and shut the door. Kelsey stifled a smile. The answer was so grumpy and so over the top, she actually found it funny.

She waited until the truck disappeared round the tree-covered bend, then returned to the house. Where, she discovered, Alex hadn't moved. He stood flush against the kitchen sink, his eyes glued to the space beyond the window.

"Interesting character," she said, shutting the door. "Is that grumpy old man act for real?" *As opposed to yours, which I can't for the life of me understand?*

"I wouldn't know."

"Ever been to his store? The, uh," she looked at the forms in her hand, "Leafy Bean?"

"Once or twice."

"It as colorful as him?"

"The pastries are decent."

Coming from him, that was nothing short of a glowing recommendation. She made her way to the kitchen table where a few grocery items, mostly fresh produce, remained. Maybe she was imagining things, but Alex seemed pretty annoyed she'd crossed paths with Farley. Then again, surely he didn't expect, because he was apparently an anti-social hermit, that she avoid human contact too? Did he think she'd spend all summer alone with no one but him and a stray cat for company?

A strange, warm shiver ran down her spine at the notion.

Alex had switched his attention from outside the window to her. Eyes dark and murky, the scrutiny ignited another set of shivers. Aw, hell. Why not come right out and ask the question? "You don't like him knowing I'm here, do you?"

"I don't like people knowing my business."

"I hardly think you having a temporary assistant will be big news in town. If they even find out. Farley doesn't seem like the kind of guy who talks about anything let alone gossip."

"Everybody talks eventually, Miss Albertelli. I don't have to help them out." He pushed himself away from the counter. "And neither do you."

Everyone talks eventually.

She didn't know it at the time, but Alex's parting remark was the last she heard from him for two days. He disappeared Lord knows where shortly after, leaving her to wander Nuttingwood alone.

"I see you more often," she said to Puddin' the cat when he made his daily appearance on the terrace. "He's like a ghost, only showing up at night."

She knew he showed up then because she could hear him pacing the floor. Pacing and pacing.

"Maybe if he wrote something upbeat he'd be able to sleep." What pages she'd deciphered so far were darker than the man himself. Bitter too. Brilliant but bitter. About as far removed from *Chase the Moon* as you could get. "Like they were written by two different people," she told Puddin'. Maybe in a way they were.

With each passing hour she kicked herself a little harder for her lack of due diligence before taking this job. Instead of asking questions, she had let herself get distracted by the size of her impending paycheck. Sure the money was a priority, but why didn't she think to get a little more information about her boss? She'd really like to know what his story was. Why he seemed so angry at the world.

"I know, I know," she said to Puddin', "keep your head low and mind your business." That was the rule. "But if I knew why, then maybe I'd know if this disappearing act was going to play all summer."

It still wasn't too late to find out. Wasn't that what the Internet was for? Without giving it another thought, she rose from her seat, moving so fast Puddin' jumped too. Farley said he'd been delivering groceries between three and five years. *Chase the Moon* came out about six years ago.

Surely in six years there would have been some kind of news article written about Alex Markoff, right?

A dozen keystrokes later, she had her answer. The Actress and the Author: It's Love! screamed the tabloid headline.

Alex Markoff, in love with a movie star? Seemed incongruous if you asked her. But there was proof. A photo of Alex and a familiar blonde cozying up to each other over a cup of coffee. An odd kind of irritation settled over her as she read about their courtship. Apparently the starlet, Alyssa Davenport, met Alex at a book signing. A whirlwind romance followed and much to everyone's surprise the couple married and settled in Los Angeles where one of Alex's short stories was being made into a film. Alex's fame and her looks made them a favorite for the camera. A click of the mouse found dozens of photos. At fund-raisers. At movie premieres. On a producer's yacht. Of Alyssa's platinum-blond hair and perfectly formed features. In every photo Mrs. Markoff appeared lovingly perched on her husband's arm, her smile a glowing complement to Alex's somber, almost reluctant expression. Even living a fairy tale, he didn't smile.

Another click and the story changed. "What Went Wrong?" asked the headline superimposed over Alyssa's face. Other stories promised to reveal "Markoff's Dark Secrets."

Everyone talks eventually. And talk they did. Friends, acquaintances, even employees offered lurid "insider" details of the marriage, the breakup and the couple's intimate life.

"Did everyone who knew him give an interview?" she asked aloud.

"Short answer, yes."

Kelsey's stomach dropped. Slowly, she raised her eyes from the screen, coming face to face with Alex. Fury darkened his features. "What the hell are you doing?"

She tried to answer but the words stuck in her throat. Instead she ended up opening and closing her mouth like a fish gasping for air.

Meanwhile, Alex turned the laptop around and glared at the screen. Kelsey could feel the rage boiling up inside him. Which made his tightly controlled voice doubly scary.

"I'll ask again. What do you think you're doing?"

"I—I—" Tucking the hair behind her ear, she took a deep breath and steadied herself. A difficult task, what with the death stare Alex was throwing her way. "I'm sorry. I thought maybe if I knew more about you I could—"

"Could what, Miss Albertelli?"

The glare got worse, forcing her to look away. All of a sudden, her answer didn't sound so adequate. "Understand you better," she replied softly.

Apparently Alex didn't find the answer adequate either. His jaw muscle twitched as he looked from her to the screen and back. "You want to understand me better?" he asked finally, his voice even more maddeningly controlled than before. "Then understand this. My private life is that—*private*. You do not have the right to root around in my past, no matter what your reasons are."

I wouldn't have had to if you weren't such a mystery, Kelsey muttered inside her head. Still, she knew Alex was right. She dropped her gaze to her hands, feeling like a kid caught breaking house rules. It was a feeling she detested, although never so much as this particular moment, since she had no one to blame for her predicament but herself. "It won't happen again."

"Damn right it won't. Because you're leaving. Today."

Leaving? As in fired?

Stupid, stupid, stupid. Why didn't she listen to her own rules and mind her own business? No, she had to go poking around in Markoff's past and get herself fired. Fired as in out on the street with no reference. Who knows how long it would take her to find a new position? Images of collection notices flashed before her eyes. She was so screwed.

"Mr. Markoff, wait!"

Having issued his order, Alex had turned and marched out. Kelsey scrambled after him, catching him by the shoulder. "You need to reconsider."

He whirled around, lightning flashing in his stormy eyes. "I don't *need* to reconsider anything. I'm not the one who invaded my privacy."

"Please. I need this job." Lord, but she hated the pleading note in her voice. Another insult courtesy of Grandma Rosie.

"You should have thought of that before you went on Google."

"But—"

"Today, Miss Albertelli. Go pack your things."

Idiot. What was she going to do now? Maybe she could get Stuart Lefkowitz to intervene….

She didn't relish playing this gambit, but desperate times called for desperate measures, and if she had any hope of paying off Grandma Rosie's debt in a reasonable amount of time, she didn't have a choice. Alex was almost to the garden door. If he left, who knew how long he'd be gone.

"What about Mr. Lefkowitz? He's not going to be happy with another delay."

That stopped him. "Stuart's happiness isn't my

concern." He still sounded haughty, but a hint of wariness had crept in.

"I'm sure that's true," she replied, "but…"

His lips became a tight line. "But what?"

Now or never. Slowly, deliberately, she crossed the room, making sure her eyes stayed locked with his. It wasn't easy, what with the fluttering in her stomach that accompanied each step. "But you and I both know he doesn't want more delays."

He tried to disguise the hitch in his breath, but she heard it nonetheless. The cards were on the table. He knew that she knew about the breach of contract. For several seconds, the only sound in the entire house was the ticking of the hallway clock. Kelsey waited, holding both her ground and her breath.

Finally, he let out what sounded like a strangled groan. She recognized the noise as defeat. "Why won't the world just leave me alone," he muttered, jamming his fingers through his hair. "Is that so much to ask?"

The pain in his growl did little to ease her conscience as Kelsey watched him stomp away. Although he didn't say so, she knew she'd won the challenge. He wouldn't throw her out. This time anyway. She waited until she heard the front door slam before sinking to the sofa in relief. Relief accompanied by a hefty dose of guilt. Cursing, she smacked a nearby cushion.

So much for her getting on Alex Markoff's good side.

CHAPTER THREE

THAT night, Kelsey went out to eat. After the day's debacle, she wanted to put as much distance between her and Alex as possible. She ended up in town at the local inn. The two-hundred-year-old building featured a pub in the basement, so she tried drowning her guilt with a cheeseburger and Irish music. No such luck though. Her conscience still felt lousy. She could kick herself for being so nosy. Alex was right; his past was none of her business. After all, how would she feel if someone poked around in her life?

And yet, thanks to those shocking Web sites, here she was obsessing more than ever. There was something about the man she simply couldn't let go of. Something in the way he expressed his anger. In the way he begged the world to leave him alone. There was despair in those gray eyes of his that told her there was far more to Alex Markoff than some angry, mournful hermit.

What was he like before his divorce, she wondered. Carefree? Happy? She tried to picture him laughing and came up short.

How sad. Even she found occasion to laugh once in a while.

It was well past midnight when she returned to Nuttingwood. She might have arrived back earlier, but no sooner did she leave the restaurant than the sky erupted in a monstrous thunderstorm. Thanks to the torrential rain, the wind and the lack of streetlights, she couldn't see more than five feet in front of her on the drive home. As a result, she missed the fork with the pine tree and had to retrace her path.

Happily, Nuttingwood was dark when she pulled into the drive. Alex was, no doubt, avoiding her as well. She dashed to the front door, bumping her hip against the marble entranceway table the second she crossed the threshold. Cursing for not leaving a light on, she felt along the wall until she found the switch and flipped it upward.

Nothing happened.

She flipped the switch again. And again.

"You're wasting your time."

Lightning flashed, briefly illuminating the room and she caught sight of a dark silhouette at the great room window. "You're wasting your time,"

Alex repeated. "Lights went out thirty minutes ago."

Kelsey drew closer. Now that her eyes had adjusted, she could see Alex was doing more than simply standing at the window. He was kneading the muscles on the back on his neck. He wore a pair of loose-fitting sweatpants with no shirt. His hair was messed too. He must have been lying down when the storm hit. Seeing him so exposed felt queerly intimate, almost voyeuristic. For the first time since she moved in, Kelsey realized she shared a house in the woods with a flesh-and-blood man. A very handsome, very desirable man. The sudden awareness made part of her grow shaky while other parts became painfully awake.

"This happen often?" she asked. "Power outages, I mean." Nice to know how frequently they'd find themselves together in the dark. Because of a storm, that is.

"If the wind blows hard enough."

"And how often is that?" she asked, reaching his shoulder. He didn't turn around upon her approach, seemingly intent on studying the shadows in the garden. Lightning flashed, and she caught his reflection. His expression was much farther away than this room.

"Often enough. There's an emergency generator in the basement."

"You haven't turned it on yet?"

"I like the darkness."

Why am I not surprised?

"Did you say something?"

"Nothing important." She didn't realize she'd spoken aloud. Covering, she changed topics. "Lightning's putting on quite a show."

"Suppose."

"When I was little one of the other fost—other kids told me thunder and lightning were caused by alien attacks. Scared me so much I would hide under the covers." She could still remember cowering under the blanket, clutching her mother's cup to her chest like a talisman. "The stupid things kids fall for, huh?"

"Not only kids."

"What?" His voice was so soft, she missed part of his sentence, making it her turn to ask, "Did you say something?"

"Nothing important."

Intuition said otherwise, but she didn't press. He wouldn't admit the truth if she did. So instead, she stole what had to be the hundredth look at his profile. In the dark, she could only see the outline of his features. His expression was impossible to read. Even so, his magnetism was stronger than ever. Maybe because they were alone, or because the dark made everything that much more intimate, but she felt surrounded by him. There seemed no escaping his scent or the heat emanating from his body. She could even feel the rise and fall of his chest, his breathing strained as it filled his lungs. His desolation was palpable, so much so she hurt for him. She found herself wanting to reach out and soothe his pain.

"I'm sorry about this afternoon," she said softly. "I had no right to snoop behind your back."

"No, you didn't."

The corner of her mouth twitched upward with guilty amusement. "You don't believe in cutting people slack, do you?"

"If I cut slack to everyone who betrayed my privacy, I'd need a much larger supply of scissors."

She thought of the gossip articles and Web sites, and she understood. No one deserved to have their life splashed on the front page. "I'm sorry too, about your marriage."

"It was a long time ago."

"Still, you—"

"I don't want to talk about Alyssa, Miss Albertelli. Our marriage failed. End of story."

The myriad of emotions in his voice—anger, frustration, hurt—said otherwise, but seeing as how she was already treading on thin ice, Kelsey didn't push. "Did you say the generator was in the basement?"

"At the foot of the stairs." He sounded grateful for the change of subject.

"Mind if I turn it on? You can keep the lights out in this room, but I'd like to find my way upstairs without incident." Not to mention, shedding light might diminish the intimacy of their situation. Maybe, if she could see his usual stormy expression, she wouldn't feel his pull so intensely.

"Knock yourself out."

Finding her way to the kitchen in the dark was easier said than done. Nuttingwood was one of those houses that had been added onto over the years, leading to an abundance of twists and turns and unexpected corners. During the day, the eclectic layout gave the house character, but at night, in the pitch black, the layout became a pedestrian nightmare. Kelsey was certain she'd fall and break an arm too. Worse, she'd break some piece of furniture or irreplaceable family heirloom.

Eventually she reached the double-swing door leading to the kitchen, just in time to hear footsteps approach from behind.

"You'll need a flashlight," Alex said, giving the door a push. Kelsey followed in silence, trying not to think about how his body brushed against hers when he passed.

He moved around the dark kitchen with a grace to be admired. At least she assumed he moved with grace since she didn't hear any of the bumps or knocks that accompanied her own clumsy movements. The basement door was to the side, behind the farmer's table. She was walking cautiously in that direction when she heard the scraping of a chair being dragged across the floor.

"What are you doing?"

"The flashlight's in the back of the cupboard. With my cast, I can't reach it flatfooted."

"Then let me." Making her way back toward his silhouette, she took the chair from his grip. "It's pitch black in here. Break your other arm and I'll be here till Christmas."

"By all means then, be my guest. We wouldn't want that."

Even though he couldn't see her, Kelsey smirked in his direction and stepped up. A warm sturdy hand pressed to her back. "I'm steadying you," Alex said from behind.

Steadying, huh? Then why did her legs feel shaky? Why did her spine feel like it had an electrical current running up and down it?

"There a problem?"

"No problem." It was the dark, she decided. It heightened everything. Turning something innocent, like a simple touch or Alex's low-pitched voice, into something sensual. Once the lights came on, the illusion would disappear.

All of a sudden, a pitiful wail sounded in the kitchen.

"What on earth was that?" Alex asked.

"I'm not—" The wail sounded again and recognition dawned.

"Puddin'!" She'd wondered what kind of shelter the cat had found to ride out the storm. He must have heard her drive up and was crying to come in the house. "Poor thing must be drenched to the skin."

"Who's Puddin'?"

Jumping down from the chair, she hurried to the back door only to have a jet-propelled streak of water rush past her legs when she opened it. Loud meows filled the kitchen. There was a click, and Alex, who'd apparently retrieved the flashlight, focused the beam on the sopping orange mass shivering under the kitchen table.

"That," Kelsey said, "is Puddin'."

"It's a cat."

An extremely sarcastic retort jumped to the tip of her tongue, but Kelsey managed to bite it off. "A very wet one at that. Would you hand me the dish towel?"

"For what?"

"To dry him off, of course. Or would you rather he drip water all over the floor?" Alex sighed, but she heard him move toward the kitchen sink. All the while keeping the light shining on Puddin''s waterlogged form.

"Poor baby, he's trembling." She reached out her hand, letting the scared animal sniff her fingers. "You're okay now. I think he's been living in your garden. He showed up on the terrace the other morning and has been keeping me company since."

"You mean you've been encouraging him?"

Don't tell her, she broke another rule. Taking the towel Alex draped over her shoulder, she gently wrapped the stray up. The cat barely protested, an indication of how wet and miserable his state was. A low rumble sounded deep in his chest. "See, he's happier already," she said.

"Bully for him," Alex grumbled. "Now that he's happy, what are you going to do?"

"I—" Good question. She hadn't thought much further than rescuing the little guy. "Well, we can't very well put him back outdoors," she said.

"We can't?"

"Look outside. It's raining cats and dogs."

"Then he'll be right at home."

"Very funny. Why can't he stay the night in the house? He's not causing any trouble." She lifted Puddin' a little closer. The cat immediately curled into her, seeking warmth and attention. "See?"

Alex flashed the light at her. "He doesn't belong here."

His words pushed a button inside her. How many times had she heard that same disinterested tone? "Says who?"

"Says me, the owner of the house."

Didn't matter. She looked at Puddin' who was flexing his front paws, oblivious to the debate around him, and felt frustrated anger swelling in her chest. Suddenly this wasn't about keeping a cat dry; it was about being wanted. About having someone want you. "I'm not putting him outside in this weather. He'll catch cold."

"He's a cat, not a child."

"So what? He still has feelings. Don't you?" Looking up, she found herself staring directly into the flashlight beam. "Surely you don't hate the world so much you'd send a defenseless animal out to drown."

She could hear his exasperation, and while she couldn't see his face, she could picture the irritation clouding his expression. Okay, maybe that last remark crossed the line.

"The way I feel about the world, you're lucky I don't make both of you sleep in the rain."

Kelsey was pretty sure he meant what he said. She clutched Puddin' a little tighter.

Alex turned around, taking the light with

him. As she blinked the spots from her eyes, she heard the sound of a door opening and for a wild second, she wondered if he planned on carrying out his threat. That is, until she heard him heading downstairs.

"Just make sure he's gone by morning," he grumbled. "And if he leaves any kind of thank-you present on my doorstep, I'm holding you responsible."

A smile tugged the corner of her lips as she savored the moment of victory. A small victory, but a victory nonetheless. Maybe Alex Markoff wasn't as hardhearted as he'd like the world to believe.

While she may have won this particular battle for Puddin's rights, there were only so many times she could push her luck before Alex tossed her out, Stuart Lefkowitz's threats be damned. By her count, she'd already pushed twice. Three times if she counted using the breach of contract threat as leverage. Therefore, Kelsey made a point of bringing Puddin' to her room for the night, making sure the cat stayed out of Alex's way.

"The less he sees of you, my friend, the better," she told him. Puddin', naturally, didn't mind. He simply sprawled across her comforter and started bathing.

Next morning, she woke at the crack of dawn

and deposited the now indignant Puddin' on the doorstep before heading into town. The latest Grandma Rosie payment was due and she wanted to make sure the check went out registered mail. The storm had ended a few hours earlier, leaving only a few downed branches and puddles as evidence it existed. Pulling onto the main road, she saw a power truck restringing the line and was surprised at the small stab of disappointment. Surely she didn't want to spend another night in the dark with Alex, with its odd mixture of intimacy and mystery. Did she?

She pulled onto Main Street, grateful the early hour meant an abundance of parking. Stockbridge was one of those sleepy towns that exploded in summer. Once a Gilded Age playground, the area had reinvented itself as an arts center featuring everything from symphony orchestras to offbeat art galleries. City dwellers flocked to the region, eager to soak up the pastoral atmosphere even as they disturbed it. For the residents, she imagined the crowds were a double-edged sword, simultaneously welcome and disdained.

Except for Alex. He simply disdained.

A sign on the post office window told her she had another fifteen minutes so she made her way down the street to the Leafy Bean. Farley's grocery store captured the area's atmosphere in one eclectic building. Part grocery, part café, part gourmet haven, the place featured everything from imported almond oil to homemade pastries served with a healthy dose of local color. And, as Kelsey discovered when picking up her grocery order, the store boasted an amazing selection of brewed coffee.

A brass bell announced her arrival. Farley was behind the counter, a large green apron covering his burly frame. His gloves and wrists were covered with flour.

"Morning, Farley," she greeted him, getting a grunt in return. "Some storm last night, huh? Nuttingwood lost power."

"Whaddya expect, up there in the middle of nowhere."

Alone, where no one could find him. "That's what Mr. Markoff likes about the place. It's private."

"Private like a hermit," Farley muttered back.

The Hermit of Nuttingwood. The moniker fit. It was sad and enigmatic. Now that she knew his story, or part of it, she couldn't blame him for wanting a little privacy, although retiring to the side of a mountain for five years still seemed a bit extreme. After all, she knew as well as anyone that life was seldom fair. The letter tucked in her satchel proved that. People used other people all the time. You learned to adapt.

Not to mention keep your distance. Mind your own business. Don't get too attached and think too far into the future. For people who didn't have the luxury of hiding on a mountainside, those rules were the key to survival. She knew because she'd been following them since she was four years old.

Except for this week. What was it about Alex Markoff that made her forget the rules?

"Better get your coffee while you can," Farley said, coming around to pour himself a cup as well. "Once the tourists wake up, they'll clean the place out."

She took it as a supreme compliment that he didn't lump her in with that group. "Isn't business a good thing?"

"Pain in the neck is what it is," Farley replied. "Always looking for some fancy flavor or asking if my beans are 'fair trade'. Says right there on the sign clear as day. Can't they read?"

Kelsey smiled over the rim of her coffee. "Guess not."

The older man was about to add more when the doorbell jingled. A group of two men and three women, clearly tourists, entered. The men wore pastel island shirts and khaki shorts—an outfit that was nearly uniform among visitors—while the women wore various forms of linen. All of them wore some kind of hat—either straw or baseball—perched on their heads.

"Do you have cappuccinos?" one of the women asked as they approached the counter.

"Everything we've got is on the counter," Farley replied, shooting Kelsey a look as if to say "see what I mean?"

"Who needs lattes, just give me a straight shot of joe," one of the men said. He was tall and athletic looking with sandy brown hair. Smiling at Kelsey, he added, "Too bad you can't hook up an intravenous line."

"Then how would you add sugar?" Kelsey asked.

"Who cares as long as it's going straight into my veins." The stranger grinned, then after a pause, pointed a finger at her.

"Nels Bïrdgarten's gallery showing, right? I was trying to think where we met. You look familiar."

If she had a nickel for every time a stranger tried that come-on, she wouldn't have to worry about paying off her debt. "Maybe our paths crossed somewhere in the city," she suggested.

"Could be. Or it was a cheap excuse to introduce myself. Tom Forbes."

At least he admitted the line was cheesy. Kelsey shook the hand he offered and introduced herself.

"So you're from New York," he continued. "Come to the Berkshires often?"

"First time. I'm here for the summer for a work assignment. You?"

"Every summer since I was eight. My parents have a place on the lake. Not a bad locale if you don't mind quiet."

You don't know quiet, Kelsey thought to herself. "I don't. Besides, you can't beat the coffee."

"Not New York standards, but it'll do, I suppose." Over at the register, Farley coughed. Oblivious, Tom raised the cup to his lips.

"Tom!" the female ringleader called over. "We're heading to the arts and crafts store."

"You go ahead, Moira. I'm going to finish my coffee, unless—" he flashed a bright smile "—I can talk you into breakfast at the Inn."

Kelsey chewed her lower lip. She should head back to Nuttingwood. On the other hand, it felt good to have someone want her company for a change. What she wouldn't give to have Alex toss even a hint of a smile in her direction.

She reached for a plastic to-go lid. "Why not?" she said, smiling back. "Breakfast sounds nice."

She got back to Nuttingwood far later than planned. Tom turned out to be pleasant company: charming, talkative, entertaining. A tad pompous but nice enough. He described himself as a social gadfly, doing a little bit of everything. "You know," he'd said when she asked, "a freelance project here, a blog article there."

In other words, he was rich enough that he didn't need to work.

When they parted company, he insisted on taking her cell phone number and made no bones about wanting to see her again. Had she been in New York, maybe she'd consider the offer, but here, under the circumstances, she wasn't so sure.

And her reluctance had nothing to do with her antisocial boss, she insisted to herself. Even if she did spend a good portion of the meal wondering what sharing breakfast with Alex would be like.

True to form, Alex was nowhere to be found when she returned, but Puddin' was. Someone had left the garden door unlatched and the cat had ensconced himself quite comfortably on her desk chair.

"And I thought I was pushing my luck," she said. "You know that nine lives thing is a myth, right?"

Puddin' rolled onto his back, exposing his belly.

"Easy for you to say. You're not the one with a negative checking balance." She'd made an extra large payment this month. It drained her account, leaving her barely enough to cover expenses. And Grandma Rosie's debt still loomed as mountainous as ever.

So while Puddin' might be willing to risk Alex's wrath, Kelsey wasn't. She needed this job.

"Sorry, pal, but I used up my defiance last night." Since Puddin' didn't care to cooperate by moving on his own, she gathered him in her arms. "Now," she said, walking outside and setting him gently on the stone terrace, "why don't you go find a nice bush to sleep under before the boss sees you."

"Too late." Alex appeared out of nowhere, brandishing a walking stick.

How on earth did he manage to sneak up on her like that? It was like he really was some kind of ghost. He glowered at Puddin', who appeared unimpressed.

"That thing's still here, I see."

"Good morning to you too," she replied. In addition to his specter-like approach, he managed to look uncommonly good this morning. Those khaki shorts and hiking shirt suited him way more than Tom. Probably, she stole a glance at his toned calves, because he actually hiked. "And this 'thing' has a name. Puddin'."

"You named a stray cat?"

"Even strays deserve an identity." She knelt

down to scratch Puddin's head. "Everyone wants to know they matter a little bit."

"As long as you don't mislead them or make them think they mean more than they do."

"Because they might get too comfortable."

"Or burned."

Were they still talking about the cat? No longer sure, Kelsey fell silent, letting the sound of Puddin's purring fill the void.

"Where did you go this morning?"

"Are you keeping tabs on me?"

"I saw you drive away."

Kelsey wasn't sure if she should resent or be flattered by the close attention. "I had some errands to run in town," she replied.

"Errands."

"Yes." She did know she resented the skeptical way he repeated the word. "You know, post office, grocery store... Farley had fresh baked apricot turnovers. I brought back some if you're interested."

Alex appeared to be only half listening, too busy was he rubbing the back of his neck. His eyes were half-closed, and he twisted his head back and forth like it needed loosening.

"Stiff neck?" Kelsey asked.

Naturally he gave her a suspicious look. "Why do you ask?"

"You're rubbing your neck same as you were last night. I made the assumption."

"You shouldn't make assumptions."

"And you shouldn't rub your neck so hard if you don't want people to make them."

Her comment earned a grimace. "I have a headache. Nothing I can't manage."

"Are you sure?" Upon closer inspection, she could see dark circles under his eyes and that his normally ruddy skin had a slight pallor. The sight kicked her maternal instincts into gear. Without realizing, she reached out to feel his forehead. His skin was cool and smooth. Touching it made the pads of her fingers tingle. "Did you take anything?"

"I'm fine." His expression remained guarded, but a note of tightness managed to creep into his voice. It was that note that drew her closer.

And closer. Until she'd practically eliminated the space between them. Her hand was still brushing his forehead. "You look pale," she murmured.

"You don't need to be concerned."

"I know I don't *have* to. Maybe I—"

The low sound of jazz music interrupted. Her phone. As expected, the moment the song rang out, Alex backed away leaving her hand hovering in the air. Balling her still tingling fingers into a fist, she reached into her skirt pocket with the other and fished out the phone.

"Frutti de Mar."

Between the static and the non sequitur, it took her a moment before she recognized the voice. "Tom?"

"Looks like I made as good an impression as I thought."

"We parted company less than an hour ago. Kind of hard not to remember."

She turned her back. Feeling Alex's probing stare burning holes in her spine, she tried her best to sound casual. "What can I do for you?"

"I told you. Frutti de Mar. Best gourmet seafood around, at least for this area. I find myself with a table for two and only one chair filled. I was hoping you could fill the other."

"You want to have dinner? Tonight?"

From the corner of her eye, she saw Alex walk away, their moment from before a distant memory.

If there had even been a moment. She could have imagined the whole thing. Just like last night's spark in the dark.

Or the way she was imagining the air cooling with his departure.

"Seven o'clock okay?"

"What?" Her attention had been on the man disappearing into the trees.

"For dinner. Does seven o'clock work for you?"

"I, uh…" It's not like she had any other plans. Tom was a nice guy. A pleasant guy who wanted to take her out to a fancy restaurant for dinner. But for some reason, she couldn't work up the interest.

Her eyes drifted back to the tree line. "Can I take a rain check?"

She'd give him credit. The rejection barely fazed him. "Sure. But so you know, I have every intention of holding you to it. We will have dinner one of these nights."

"If you say so." But she already knew she'd turn down the next invitation as well.

They talked for a few more minutes, basically polite chatter so her refusal didn't feel too unfriendly, before Kelsey went to work. For the next few hours she immersed herself in transcription until her brain couldn't take the dark subject matter any longer and screamed for a break. Then, unable to look at the screen another second, she saved her document, grabbed her coffee cup and headed into the great room.

What she saw stopped her in her tracks.

CHAPTER FOUR

ALEX sat by the French doors.

Actually slumped was a better description. Kelsey rushed towards him.

"Are you all right?" she asked, already knowing the answer. Eyes closed, face paler than before, he was leaning forward with a hand cradling his forehead. His walking stick lay discarded by his feet. "It's your head, isn't it?"

"Go away," he groaned through motionless lips. "I'm fine."

"Liar. You look like you're ready to pass out." He looked up at her with glazed eyes, proving her point. "I'm calling your doctor. What's his name?"

"No doctor."

"Are you crazy? This could be a complication from your injury." Like a blood clot or something. Her insides froze at the thought he could be seriously hurt and she hadn't realized.

"It's not a complication, it's a migraine." His eyes closed again. "I just need to sit for a while. Regain my equilibrium."

From the looks of him, that might take a while. Kelsey didn't think a person could look more miserable if they tried. She remembered when Rochelle, her second foster mother, would get migraines. She'd kick all the kids outside for the day, no matter the weather. "And no making noise either," she'd order.

At her worst, Rochelle had never looked as miserable as Alex.

Remembering Rochelle made her think of something else. "Do you take anything? Some kind of prescription?"

Alex made a rumble deep in his throat. "Upstairs. In the bathroom." He continued speaking that stiff-jawed manner, as if the mere act of talking hurt.

"Do you want me to help you upstairs," she asked, reaching for his elbow, "so you can take—"

"No!" He said the word forcefully, so much so he winced immediately, and dropped to a whisper. "I just need to sit. Alone. Please leave."

"And let you suffer? I don't think so. Where upstairs do you keep your prescription?"

"My bathroom medicine cabinet."

"Don't move. I'll be right back."

She dashed upstairs, making her way to the bedroom next to hers. Alex's room was exactly as she expected, chic and dark and very masculine. Rust, beige and brown, like a fall landscape. Magazines and books covered what looked like an expensive, king-size bed.

She walked into the bathroom, momentarily envious of the airy modern style. The scent of wood and clove hung in the air telling her Alex had been there recently. A plastic sleeve, presumably worn to keep his cast dry, hung from the shower rod and the mat in front of the shower stall was still damp. Suddenly she was assaulted by the image of Alex standing under the stream, water cascading down his body…

Blushing from the inappropriateness, she shoved the image away. Now was not the time to start some kind of weird, useless fantasy. She found the prescription bottle in the medicine cabinet. Grabbing it and a glass of water, she headed back downstairs.

Alex hadn't moved. If he hadn't shifted uncomfortably when she walked back into the room, she'd have thought him asleep. "Probably a little late for this to kill the pain completely, but it might help a little. Hold out your hand."

He grumbled, but did what she asked.

Kelsey smiled at her victory. "Now, how about

you lie down? Do you think you can make it to the sofa?"

"I've got a headache—I'm not paralyzed."

Good to see the headache didn't spoil his charming demeanor. She watched as he eased himself into an upright position. Body bent, shoulders and head stiff, he shuffled across the floor like an arthritic old man. It was all she could do not to wrap her arm around his waist and help him. In fact, if she wasn't certain he'd bite her head off, she would have.

Instead, she followed quietly while he made his way across the room and eased himself onto the sofa.

"Are you sure you don't want to go to your room? You'd be more comfortable in a bed."

"Too many stairs," he mumbled. "I'll be fine here."

The couch was too small and too pillow-laden to accommodate his lanky frame, so he'd ended up with one leg propped on the floor. His cast rested on his chest, while his good arm lay slung across his eyes. The helplessness of his position tugged at her heartstrings.

"You can leave now," he said.

She could. But she didn't. Drawing closer, Kelsey noticed his skin was covered with gooseflesh. In spite of the fact the afternoon sun poured through the windows heating the room, he was shivering.

"You're still here," he said in a low voice.

"And you're cold," she replied back. "Would you like a blanket?"

"No."

God, he was stubborn. What was he going to do, lie there and shiver? Did he know how pathetic that looked? She looked around for something she could use as a blanket. A dozen pillows and no throw. Remembering the extra blanket in her room, she ran up and got that, tucking it gently around his torso, being careful not to jar him too much.

"Why are you doing this?" he asked.

"Because you're shivering."

"I mean, why are you sticking around?"

"Oh, that." Why indeed? Truth be told, she couldn't explain, other than it hurt her to see him suffering. "What can I say? I have a rescue complex."

"In other words, I'm another cat."

The medicine was starting to kick in. Still, even thick with sleep, there was no mistaking the resignation in his voice as if he didn't believe someone could sincerely care. It made Kelsey think of the other night, when he was watching the rain.

Her heart ached a little more.

"Do you need anything else?" she asked. "Water? A phone?"

"I'll be fine. You can leave with a clear conscience."

"Thanks for the permission."

He didn't respond. Sleep had claimed him. Kelsey watched as his breathing slowly evened out.

Two hours later, she was still sitting in the living room, watching. She'd told herself she was only going to stay a few extra minutes. To make sure he was truly asleep before heading up to her room. But the longer she sat, the more she couldn't tear herself away. Couldn't stop studying his face. The way his brow smoothed in sleep or how his lips parted ever so slightly. Nestled among the pillows, he had a gentle serenity about him that, when awake, he hid from the world.

Unable to help herself, she tucked the blanket around him a little tighter. He smelled of clove and woods and sleep, and she had the overwhelming urge to lean closer and bury herself in the scent. Her fingers longed to stroke his cheek. Dear Lord, he was beautiful. She couldn't deny her attraction if she tried. But beneath the attraction, she sensed something else. Something she couldn't quite put her finger on. The sensation stirred inside her, faintly, tentatively, afraid to make itself fully known. She was afraid too. Because she wasn't sure if she wanted the sensation to go away.

Alex slept through the rest of the afternoon and into the evening. At some point, Kelsey considered waking him so he could go to his room, but she didn't. He looked too exhausted to disturb. Plus downstairs she could keep an eye on him.

At least that's what she told herself.

She'd been joking about the rescue complex. Truth was, she didn't know where this maternal streak of hers was coming from. As a kid, she sometimes helped the younger children with homework and stuff, but that was expected in a large household. But since moving out on her own, she'd focused solely on taking care of herself. Clearly something about Nuttingwood brought out her nesting instinct.

Something or *someone*?

After dinner, which she was pretty sure didn't come close to Frutti de Mar standards, she returned to the great room to find Alex beginning to stir. "Hey," she said softly, as his eyelids fluttered open, "you're awake." And feeling better, judging by the clarity in his gaze.

"You're still here," he greeted back, his voice still a little thick. "I thought you had dinner plans."

That's right, he walked away before the end

of her and Tom's conversation. "I took a rain check."

"Oh."

His response had a queer-sounding note she couldn't pinpoint. "Good thing too," she told him.

"Why's that?"

Slowly, he shifted himself into a sitting position. With his hair matted on one side and a crease on his cheek, he looked perfectly and adorably tussled. Kelsey's stomach twittered. "Well, for one thing, you'd have woken to a dark and empty house."

"News flash—I've done that for years. Goes hand in hand with the hermit thing."

The medicine still had a hold; his words were slurred and punchier than normal. Try as she might, Kelsey couldn't help a smile. "Funny, that's what Farley called you."

Sleepy cuteness turned sullen. "I'm sure they call me lots of things."

"What makes you think they talk about you much at all?"

"Try four hundred thousand, ninety-four search engine hits," he replied. "Or have you forgotten already?"

"No, I haven't forgotten," she snapped. When Alex sat up, the blanket she'd tucked over him slid toward the floor. Instinctively she picked it up. "But not everyone is as—"

"Nosy?"

"Curious," she shot back, "as I am." Her cheeks warmed remembering the whole exchange. Was he right? That once a victim of gossip, always a victim of gossip? She draped the blanket back over his legs. "Though if you ask me, moving up to a castle in the middle of nowhere, you're kind of inviting speculation."

"I'm here because I like my privacy," he replied in a clipped tone that said the conversation was over.

Kelsey noticed him rubbing his eyes. "Head still hurt?" She remembered Rochelle's migraines sometimes lasted for days, once getting so bad she ended up in the hospital on a morphine drip.

Alex grabbed the change of topic. "Some, but it's definitely better. The medicine helped. Along with the sleep. A few more hours and I should be fine."

Meaning she should take her cue and leave? "Are you heading upstairs?"

He shook his head, while at the same time closing his eyes and burrowing into the throw pillow. "Not yet. I'm comfortable right where I am."

"Very well then, I'll see you in the morning."

"Kelsey?"

He reached out and caught her wrist, an unnecessary gesture since she stopped as soon as he called out. "Yes?" she asked.

"Thank you."

That was it. Two words and nothing more, but Alex's expression was soft and sincere, and his eyes turned from metal to dove-gray, making the sentence sound like volumes. His grip stayed on her arm, simultaneously gentle yet firm. Kelsey could feel the pulse of each individual finger beating against her skin. Their cadence echoed the heart in her chest. A slow honey-coated sensation began twisting deep inside her, and she smiled.

"You're welcome." Reluctantly, she slipped her wrist free and headed upstairs.

"Did I really expect anything to change?" she asked Puddin' the next morning. "I mean, so I helped him with a headache. Big deal." One second of gratitude hardly changed anything.

"It was just for that one moment—" her skin tingled, remembering how his fingers encircled her wrist "—I felt like we understood each other, you know? That we connected.

"I should have realized it was my imagination." For starters, she didn't make connections. Not that kind anyway. And second, this morning Alex was still the dark, aloof man he'd been since her arrival. Worse, if that was possible.

"The guy's been through the wringer, that's for sure," she said, hitting the save button. "I'd probably do the same thing if I'd been ripped apart like that. Makes you wonder what he'll do when this book comes out."

If the book comes out. Her gaze traveled back to the dwindling stack of yellow pads. This morning Mr. Lefkowitz sent an e-mail requesting a progress report which she was avoiding answering. With all the cross-outs and redirection, she'd transcribed maybe a third of the book. Certainly not a complete novel by any means. The editor wouldn't be happy.

"If Alex doesn't start producing soon, I'll be stuck here till Christmas," she said to Puddin'.

Did Alex even celebrate Christmas anymore? The image of a somber, undecorated Nuttingwood popped into her head, breaking her heart. Didn't seem right he should spend the holidays isolated and lonely.

"Will you listen to yourself?" she said aloud. "What do you care how Alex Markoff spends his holidays?" This was a perfect example of why she didn't do connections. Connections started you down the road toward foolish, elusive concepts like home and family and holidays...

And kindred spirits with stormy gray eyes.

"That's it. Time for a break." Her thoughts were getting way too out of control.

On the terrace, Puddin' stretched and started to get up. Grabbing her empty mug, Kelsey sent a mock glare at the feline through the open French doors. "Don't even think about coming inside while I'm getting coffee," she told him, knowing full well he wouldn't listen.

Coffee was the one area where she and Alex had an automatic accord. Apparently they were both caffeine addicts so by unspoken agreement the pot remained full and fresh all day. Usually Alex made the first pot, then midmorning it was her turn.

There was only one problem. Alex had put the coffee grinder on the top shelf. He had been leaving the machine on the counter, but today he must have forgotten. Too much on his mind, perhaps?

She set her mug on the counter, then dragged a chair from the table, making a mental note to remind him he promised to keep the machine within her arm's reach. Not everyone loomed over six feet.

"You're standing on my counter," Alex said from behind her.

"What the—"

She nearly dropped the grinder. Worse, she nearly knocked her cup off the edge.

"One of these days I'm going to buy you a bell," she grumbled.

"I didn't realize my comings and goings were so important to you."

"They are when you insist on scaring the bejesus out of me every time you show up."

Coffee grinder in hand, she hopped off the chair, bringing Alex closer than she expected. Cloves and wood and awkwardness packed the kitchen. For what felt like minutes, neither of them moved, their bodies and gazes stuck in place. Kelsey found herself suddenly painstakingly aware of the stubble on Alex's cheeks and the way his lips were dry but soft-looking. Eyes traveling upwards, she realized he was studying her too. Or so it appeared. His eyes had an expression she'd never seen before.

"I'm—I'm making fresh coffee," she finally managed to stammer. What was it about his proximity that made her brain short-circuit? "How's your head?"

His hand touched his temple as if remembering what she meant. She had the crazy urge to do the same. "Better. Nothing left but a dull ache."

"Have you had anything to eat? An empty stomach doesn't help."

He broke the moment, moving away. "Are you always this concerned about other people's welfare?" he asked, opening the fridge, "or just mine?"

"Are you always this suspicious of people's motives? Never mind. Pretend I didn't ask," she added as he glanced over his shoulder.

With the atmosphere less charged, she returned to the task at hand, carefully measuring the beans into the grinder. A flick of a button filled the kitchen with a loud whir.

"Clearly you have no idea how awful you looked yesterday," she continued over the noise.

"I've been having migraines my whole life. Last time I checked, I survived them all. Besides, I didn't ask you to stay."

"Silly me, putting your health first." She turned off the grinder. "Next time I'll leave you to suffer all by your lonesome."

"Thank you."

"You're wel—watch out!"

Everything happened in slow motion. Alex had moved to her section of the kitchen and was reaching up to retrieve a cup from the cabinet. As he turned toward her, the outer edge of his cast smacked her coffee mug. The faded floral cup wobbled back and forth, then tumbled over the edge. Kelsey reached out to catch it, but moved too late. With a crack, the mug hit the floor and separated into three large pieces.

"No!" Her stomach churning, Kelsey dropped to her knees. Not her mother's cup. She blinked, hoping when her eyes opened, the cup would somehow reassemble.

No such luck.

Alex's legs appeared at her side. "I didn't realize the cup was so close to the edge."

"It's ruined." She looked up. His face was too blurry for her to read his reaction.

But she could read his voice. "It's just a coffee cup."

Just a coffee cup? Of course, that's how he saw it. As just another old piece of kitchenware.

"I'm sure you can find a replacement—"

"How? Go back in time?" If she paused a second to think rationally, she'd realize Alex had no idea what the cup represented. How could he know that the last tangible piece of her childhood—her real childhood with her real mother—lay in pieces on his kitchen floor? Moisture burned her eyes. She was going to cry, and she didn't care.

"Don't you understand?" she snapped, swiping at her cheeks. Of course he didn't understand. Living up here as a hermit, not caring if anyone cared about him or not. Why would he understand losing something precious? "It can't be replaced. It's gone. Ruined." A tear escaped down her cheek.

Angrily, she wiped it away. Dropping the pieces on the floor, she stormed from the room before she crashed completely.

"Kelsey!"

She ignored him. Nothing Alex could say would make a difference. All she could hear in her head were his words from before. "Just a cup, just a cup." They echoed with each step on the stairway.

Once inside the sanctuary of the guest room, she slammed shut the door, pressing her back against it. *Just a coffee cup.* Alex was right. What was a faded, chipped-up piece of stoneware anyway? So what if she'd carried the stupid thing from foster home to foster home? So what if…

The floodgates opened as everything hit her at once—her solitude, her past, her grandmother's crimes. Why didn't anyone want her? Was she that unlovable?

Out of answers, she sank to the ground and gave in to self-pity.

How long she stayed there crying, she wasn't sure. Thirty minutes. An hour. Eventually she stopped sniffling. What was done was done, she told herself. No amount of wallowing would change anything. There was nothing else to do but pick up the pieces and move on. She done so her entire life; she would do so again.

Swiping the moisture from her cheeks, she sniffed back the last tear and pushed herself to her feet.

The house was unusually quiet when she came down the next morning which, given its usual silence, said a lot. Perhaps yesterday's outburst scared Alex out of hibernation, and he was, at that moment, in town looking for men in white coats to carry her off. A fresh night's sleep made her realize how disproportionate her reaction must have looked to him. Of all her missteps, this might be the one that finally helped him get rid of her.

Puddin' was in his regular spot when she entered the office. She gave the napping cat a quick glance, sat at her desk, and while she waited for the computer to boot, drank coffee from a substitute mug, telling herself the change in flavor was all in her head. As usual, Alex's writing sucked her in, chasing away other thoughts. She welcomed the distraction, losing herself in today's words. It wasn't long before her absorption made her oblivious to anything but the story.

She didn't hear the door push open or the footsteps approach the desk. In fact, she didn't notice a thing until she heard a thump on the wood in front of her. Pulling herself out of her typist's trance, she looked toward the desk and blinked. There, in the middle of her papers, sat her coffee mug. Chipped and cracked, but whole again nonetheless.

"I doubt it'll hold liquid," Alex said. "But you can put it on a shelf or something."

She ran her finger along the rim, feeling the gaps where the pieces were unevenly glued together. If the thing looked like a battered piece of junk before, it looked like a pre-schooler's craft project now. A lump stuck in Kelsey's throat. Unable to trust herself with words, she settled for raising her gaze.

Alex's face was soft, reminding her of the day before. In the entranceway. "The cup means a lot to you."

Throat constricted, she nodded.

"I thought so. Consider it payback for the migraine."

"It was my mother's," Kelsey called out. She found her voice as he reached the door. Though he hadn't asked for an explanation, she wanted to give one. Wanted to explain why she'd reacted so poorly. "She died when I was four. This mug is the only thing I have that belonged to her."

Kelsey imagined him wondering what kind of family left a child nothing but a battered coffee cup, but he said nothing. He simply nodded in a way that told her he understood. At least the gratitude filling her insides made her feel like he understood. "Then good thing I had glue."

"Yes," she said, smiling up at him. "A very good thing."

CHAPTER FIVE

Stop being a coward.

Kelsey stood outside Alex's bedroom door for five minutes with her hand poised to knock. Much as she didn't want to, she couldn't put off this conversation any longer. Mr. Lefkowitz wanted a status report. After days of dodging his e-mail requests, she got a phone call. A very testy phone call. "I hope the reason I haven't heard from you is because you're too busy typing," he said as soon as she answered. That had been the high point of the conversation.

She knocked.

Alex's answer came back deep and distracted. "Yeah?"

Pushing open the door, she poked her head into the room and saw him seated at his desk near the window. Dozens of crumpled yellow balls littered the floor around his feet. He was working. A good sign. "Sorry to bother you."

"But you're going to anyway. What is it?"

"Mr. Lefkowitz called. He wants to know how the book was coming."

Alex didn't look up. "I'm sure you filled him in on all the details."

"Actually I told him you were making great progress and were almost finished."

That got his attention. He turned sideways to look at her. "Did you now? And why would you say something like that?"

Kelsey shrugged. Why indeed? She wasn't quite sure except as soon as she heard Mr. Lefkowitz's irritated voice, she felt the overwhelming urge to take Alex's side. True or not.

"Are you making progress?"

"Depends on how you define progress."

"Moving forward." Having pages to type. The last notebook was nearly transcribed and still no new ones had appeared. Which wouldn't be so terrible, if he was busy editing what had already been written, but as far as she could tell that wasn't happening either.

"Interesting definition." Tearing the top sheet from the pad, he added it to the collection of yellow wads on the floor.

Kelsey watched it arc and drop. "So I lied to Stuart."

"If you say so. Why would you tell him something you didn't know for certain?"

"I thought I was doing you a favor."

"A favor?"

"By keeping your editor off your back." His suspicious tone made her bristle. "You sound like I have some ulterior motive."

He shrugged. "Maybe you do."

Jeez. And she thought relations between them had thawed over the last couple days. Ever since he'd repaired her coffee mug, albeit poorly, she'd felt closer. So much for that illusion. "What could I possibly be after?"

"You tell me."

"Oh, brother." Shooting him a dramatic eye roll, she leaned against the door frame. "You caught me. Getting your medicine, lying to Stuart—they're part of a grand ploy to soften you up. Really, you should hear yourself sometimes."

"Do you blame me?"

The truth? Not really. But they needed to get past this issue. "You're not the first person to get burned by the people around him," she replied in a gentler voice.

"What's that mean?"

"Nothing." She wasn't about to get into a contest over who had suffered a bigger betrayal. "Look,

I thought I was helping. Next time I'll tell Mr. Lefkowitz the truth. That better?"

"Better would be not telling Stuart anything at all."

"I have to tell him something."

"Why?"

"Because it's my job, and he needs to know." She let out a long, calming breath. "Not everyone is out to get you, Alex, or get something from you."

"Could have fooled me."

"Wow." She understood his bitterness; she really did. But why couldn't he see she wasn't the enemy? Hadn't they made any headway over the past few weeks? "I'm beginning to see why he's paying me extra to work here."

Not wanting to wait to hear his response, which wasn't going to be something she wanted to hear anyway, she went to her room. Sometimes she wanted to kick Alex Markoff for his obstinacy. All she wanted was to be his friend.

Really, that's what you want? His friendship?

Yes, that was all. Sure, she was attracted to Alex. Incredibly attracted. But hit and run affairs weren't really her style. Affairs weren't her style, period. And neither was acting on her attraction—assuming Alex was remotely interested. Which, seeing as how he trusted no one, wasn't likely.

Screw it. She peeled off her cotton tank top and

threw it on the bed. If he didn't care about his manuscript getting done, why should she?

A knock sounded on her door. "Kelsey?"

What now? Grabbing her tank, she thrust it back on and opened the door. "What?"

A pair of very contrite eyes met hers, killing every ounce of her earlier acrimony. "Is Stuart really paying you extra to work here?"

"If I say yes, will you use it against me?"

His mouth had come dangerously close to curving into a smile. "I'll try not to." He looked around at the bare bones bedroom, checking out the setting like it was the first time he'd been there. "You're very neat," he said all of a sudden.

"Makes packing easier." As well as moving on.

Alex nodded, and in her mind she wondered if he wasn't agreeing with both points.

The coffee mug he had repaired sat crookedly on top of the bureau. He walked over and picked it up. "Not my best repair job in the world, that's for sure. I notice you don't use it, so I was right—it doesn't hold liquid."

"I didn't try." She'd been afraid to find out lest it fall apart again. After seeing it smashed to bits, she wasn't about to take any chances. Even now she was fighting the urge to slip the mug from Alex's grasp. "Why are you here? Did you knock on my door merely to confirm my pay rate?"

"Ah, so he is paying extra." Setting down the mug, he continued his tour, stopping at the window. His broad shoulders filled the frame. "How much?"

The appropriate answer would be "none of your business," but the truth came out without second thought. "Triple."

"Triple." He took a moment to let the answer sink in. "Says it all, doesn't it. That why you took the job? For the money?"

"Yes."

The look crossing his face as he turned was a mixture of surprise and admiration. "I appreciate the honesty. Though I have to say, you don't strike me as the mercenary type." He cocked his head to study her better. "What's your story, Kelsey Albertelli?"

Now was the time to tell him to bug off, same as he did whenever she asked a personal question. "It's complicated."

"How so?"

"Now who's prying into whose private business?"

"Point taken," he replied with a nod. Sincerity marked every feature and Kelsey realized, with more than a little admiration, that he wouldn't press her for more. He was respecting her privacy.

Her chest swelled. She wasn't used to respect. The notion that someone would honor her privacy made her feel...well, special, she supposed. She stared into Alex's eyes, feeling herself being drawn in.

The two of them were a lot alike, weren't they? Both keeping the world at arm's length, rather than offering or asking more than necessary. Her chest went from being tight to feeling warm and full. The feeling grew bigger and started inching its way outward, down her limbs and to her toes. A nebulous longing to be closer gripped her. Suddenly sharing her story didn't sound all that horrible.

"My grandmother, she—"

"No need to explain." He held up a palm. "You're right. I was prying."

Kelsey smiled. Again she appreciated the respect, despite the fact it restored their distance to arm's length.

"And thank you," he continued, "for covering with Stuart. I'm not used to—well, it's been a long time since someone did me a favor for no reason."

"I understand."

"I know." His long assessing look reached

deep inside her, stirring emotions she couldn't identify.

And wasn't really sure she wanted to.

A week later, Alex had a doctor's appointment to check out his arm. Since he couldn't drive his stick shift, Kelsey drew chauffeur duties. Normally she wouldn't mind, but she'd failed to factor in what it would be like sharing an enclosed space with Alex. His long frame mere inches from hers. His body heat mingling with hers the entire trip, filling the air with his scent. His hand rested on the armrest, close enough to her that when she touched the gearshift, the underside of her forearm would brush across his knuckles. Thank goodness, she chose to take her car rather than Alex's sports car. Driving a standard, with the distraction of continually touching him—no matter how lightly—would result in them ending up in a ditch somewhere.

Since silence only exacerbated the situation, she forced conversation. Fortunately, Alex was in a talkative mood. At least, talkative for him. After exhausting the weather and road conditions, she decided to take a risk and ask something she'd been dying to know since her arrival. "May I ask you a personal question?"

Of course, the moment she said *personal*, wariness crept into his expression. "What do you want to know?"

"How did you break your arm?"

"Oh, that." Relief returned to his face. "Stuart didn't tell you?"

She shook her head. "He only said you broke it."

"Well, score one for discretion." He sounded surprised. "I tripped over a root and fell while walking in the woods."

"You were by yourself?" Obviously. "How did you get help?"

"I broke my arm, not my leg. I made my way back to the house and called an ambulance."

Somehow Kelsey doubted the scenario went quite as smoothly as he described it. Navigating a wooded path with a broken arm… Poor man must have been in tremendous pain. "And you had no one to help you."

"You're assuming I wanted help."

She thought of the other day. "No, I'm assuming you could have used help."

"Didn't we cover the problems with assumption the other afternoon?"

"Was this before or after you were lying incapacitated on the sofa?"

"I would debate your use of the word *incapaci-*

tated, but in this case I got myself to the hospital just fine."

And came home by himself to an empty house. She knew Alex chose to live that way, but the idea of Alex alone and in pain made her sad. "What about painkillers and medication and all that?"

"I managed."

"I'm sure you did." Managed. It sounded so... lacking. Like he was getting by with the bare minimum.

You should know, Kelsey. Manage had been the story of her life. Manage and adapt.

Why then, did *manage* suddenly feel inadequate?

"So is that when you started writing longhand?" she asked, pulling herself back to the conversation.

"No, I've always written by pencil. Started when I was teaching and would scribble notes between—"

"You were a teacher?" She nearly hit the brakes.

"High school English."

"Unbelievable." She shook her head.

"What, you can't picture me as a teacher?"

"In a word, no." She couldn't picture him interacting with people, let alone teaching teenagers.

"It didn't last long. I was far more interested in

my own work than *A Tale of Two Cities*. But writing longhand stuck. You never know when some detail or passage will spring to mind." His mouth came dangerously close to curving into a smile. At least Kelsey thought she caught a glimmer before it disappeared. "I once wrote an entire short story during a dinner party."

"Really?" Now that was an Alex she could picture, hiding out from the crowd, lost in his work. "I finished your last notebook yesterday," she told him.

"Is that a not so subtle way of reminding me Stuart wants his book?"

"Yup." She smiled.

"Spoken like a true babysitter."

"Speaking of not-so-subtle reminders," she murmured.

"Hey." A hand touched her forearm. A rush ran up her arm and she had to squeeze the steering wheel to keep it from traveling further. "As babysitters go, you aren't that bad. Stuart could have foisted far worse on me."

"Wow." A sideways glance showed Alex's expression was sincere. "A girl could get a big head from that kind of sweet talk."

"I'll keep that in mind."

Meanwhile the memory of his touch remained

on her skin, a warm, firm pressure far more reassuring than it should be.

She cleared her throat, hoping to clear away the sensation too. "Since we've established that I'm the official whip cracker, will I be seeing more pages soon?"

Alex turned his face to the scenery. "Eventually."

There was little enthusiasm to his answer. In fact, if she didn't know better she'd say he actually sounded sad. Now she wanted to give him the reassuring touch.

Something inside made her refrain, settling instead for a smile and a change of subject. "Just planning my schedule. If I don't have anything to type, the more time Puddin' and I have to work on our tans."

"Puddin', huh?" There was a satisfying note of relief in his voice. "That mangy cat of yours still around?"

"Whoa, he's not my cat. Puddin' is strictly a free agent."

"Says the woman who named him."

"I told you, everyone deserves an identity. The world has enough faceless orphans."

"Orphan?"

"Stray, orphan. Same thing, right?" Kelsey brushed her hair behind her ear. She could feel

Alex studying her, wondering about the slip. He wouldn't ask though. He'd leave it up to her to explain or not, respecting her right to privacy. It was one of the traits she loved—

Check that. Admired. It was one of the traits she admired about him.

Love was nowhere in the picture.

Kelsey thought forty-five minutes flipping through gossip and consumer magazines would clear the queer thoughts from her head, but no such luck. The second Alex appeared in the doctor's reception area doorway, her pulse quickened. He was gorgeous no matter the setting, but the contrast between the institutional décor and his dark virility was awe-inspiring. She wasn't the only one to notice either. The nurses and receptionist all perked up upon his appearance too. Kelsey wasn't sure, but she swore one woman actually licked her lower lip.

Oblivious, Alex's eyes sought her out. "Dr. Cohen got tied up with another patient so I had to wait," he said in the flat, semi-annoyed voice she'd come to expect.

"No harm, no foul," she replied. "Gave me time to catch upon the latest gossip. Oh, and how to evaluate flat-screen TVs," she added quickly when she saw the disdain crop into his expression. "Are you ready to go?"

"Don't forget your appointment card," the receptionist called out.

Kelsey bit back her smile at Alex's rolled eyes. The receptionist was painstakingly scheduling his appointment, leaning forward a little more than necessary in her opinion. The woman shot her a jealous glare when she joined Alex at the check-in desk. Again, she controlled her urge to grin. Did her hermit have any idea how many heads he was turning?

Whoa. Her hermit? Where did that come from?

"Did Dr. Cohen say when the cast would come off?" she asked, shaking off the thought.

"End of summer. Same answer he gave me last time. I'm beginning to think he's incapable of giving an exact date."

"Probably because you'd hold him to it."

"That's a bad thing?"

"It is if your arm hasn't healed by then. Or maybe Dr. Cohen simply wants to string you along because he enjoys your company."

Alex made a noise deep in his throat and took the appointment card. This time Kelsey not only smiled, she giggled. Lately she'd been finding Alex's grumpy demeanor more amusing. Guess because he'd slipped enough times for her to know he actually had a heart underneath.

"While we're out, are there any other errands you need to run?" she asked while they made their way through the parking lot. "Bank? Library? Groceries? We were low on coffee this morning."

We? Again with the possessiveness. What was with her today?

Thankfully Alex either didn't notice or care about the slip. "Coffee would be good. Milk too. And maybe," he paused, as if unsure about his next words, "maybe some of those apricot turnovers."

Was that pink coloring his cheeks? Kelsey couldn't believe it. Dear Lord, he couldn't look cuter if he tried. Insides fluttering, Kelsey grinned. "All right then, we'll stop at Farley's."

CHAPTER SIX

She hadn't given it much thought but being lunch-time, the Leafy Bean was filled with customers. To a person, heads turned the second the doorbell announced their arrival. Turning not, she was certain, because they recognized the famous author, but because Alex commanded attention.

"Would you rather come back another time?" she asked.

"I thought you said we needed coffee."

"We do, but I forgot about the noontime crowd."

"I like privacy, Kelsey, I'm not sociophobic."

"I only meant…"

"I know what you meant, and," the corner of his mouth quirked ever so slightly, "I appreciate the gesture."

It felt like he'd verbally squeezed her hand. A blush warmed her cheeks. She gave him a half smile of her own. "You must really want those apricot turnovers."

"Hey, never underestimate the lure of coffee and pastry. Where does Farley stock the beans?"

"There's an entire display at the back of the store. You grab a couple bags and I'll get your baked goods."

He gave her a nod and headed off while she made her way to the crowded bakery counter, trying to shake off the weird domestic sensation surrounding the task.

"It's only coffee and turnovers," she reminded herself.

Farley was running around behind the counter, grumpy as ever as he accommodated orders and questions. When he saw Kelsey, he gave her a quick wave followed by a dramatic roll of his eyes when a customer asked if he used organic flour. Kelsey waved back. "Popular today," she commented.

"Big fund-raiser's kicking off at the Music Center this weekend. Everyone and his second cousin's in for it. And every one of 'em's got special orders," he added, slapping the cutting board with a loud, overly enthusiastic whack of his knife.

Kelsey shared a smile with the young girl at the counter. "I'll take a half-dozen turnovers," she said.

"Kelsey, is that you?"

She was taking her bag from the clerk when she spotted Tom Forbes coming towards her, charming

smile firmly in place. "What a pleasant coinci-
dence. I was going to call you this afternoon."

"You were?"

"I'm here for the concert this weekend. I thought
maybe you'd like to join me." The smile got a little
wider. "You still owe me that rain check."

"Right, rain check." She thought that had been
a way to save face, she didn't really think he would
follow up.

"So what do you say? Think you can get away?"

"Well, I…"

"Please don't say no." He flashed her an exag-
gerated pout. "My poor heart won't take a second
rejection."

Kelsey laughed. Somehow she doubted that
was the case. "Are you trying to make me feel
guilty?"

"Whatever it takes," he replied. "Do we have a
date?"

One dinner wouldn't hurt, right?

She was about to say yes when suddenly she
caught sight of Alex at the other end of store. Dark
and serious, he was studying a bag of coffee beans
like it contained the secret to life incarnate. A small
piece of her insides tumbled.

Dragging her attention back to Tom, she gave
him a polite smile. "Flattering as the guilt trip is,
I'm going to have to pass."

"Even if it means breaking my heart?"

"'Fraid so."

Tom shook his head, and shook off the rejection like she expected he would. "Guess I'll simply have to drown my sorrows alone."

"Somehow I don't think that's going to happen," she replied with a smile.

A shiver of awareness passed over her. Looking up, she saw that Alex was looking in their direction. "My boss looks ready to go," she said. "I better catch up."

Tom glanced over his shoulder. "Alex Markoff? That's your boss?"

"Yes." His instant recognition took her aback.

"You said you worked for a writer, but I had no idea…." Tom drifted off in thought for a second, before adding, "I thought he was holed up somewhere like a hermit."

"Never underestimate the lure of coffee and turnovers."

"He doesn't look happy that we're talking. In fact," Tom said, pursing his lips, "if I didn't know better, I'd say he looked jealous."

As if. More likely it was his suspicious nature coming home to roost. "Impatient," Kelsey answered. "I told you, he's ready to go."

"Is he the reason you can't have dinner?"

Although asked with a smile, the question had

a pointedness to it that she didn't like. "I have to go," she said. "Enjoy your concert."

Alex was lost in thought on the drive back to Nuttingwood. So lost, Kelsey wanted to squirm from the uncomfortable silence. If it weren't so Alex-like, she'd think Tom was right and he was jealous.

The silence was deafening. A hundred and eighty degrees from the rest of their day. Do not chatter, she chided. Just go with the silence.

"Turnovers smell good. The clerk said they were fresh out of the oven and still warm. Maybe I should have gotten more than a half-dozen."

So much for going with the silence.

"That guy from the store a friend of yours?" Alex asked.

"Acquaintance." She could hear the suspicion in his voice.

"Your rain check from the other night."

"Yes. He wanted to know if I would attend the concert at the Music Center with him."

They reached the large pine tree. Kelsey turned to the right, pleased she was finally recognizing landmarks.

Too bad she didn't feel as confident regarding the man beside her. "Would that be a problem?" she asked.

"What you do on your spare time is your business," he replied with a shrug.

Her insides tumbled again, only this time the fall was heavy and hard. Of course he didn't care. Why would he? Tom's comment simply put thoughts in her head. "Thank you for respecting my privacy."

"No problem."

They drove the rest of the way home in silence.

Kelsey assumed Alex would disappear as soon as she put the car into Park. To her surprise, he didn't. He stayed in the passenger seat, his long fingers tracing the hem on his hiking shorts. "You going straight to work?" he asked suddenly.

What work? She still hadn't gotten any new notebooks. "Why? You need me to do something?"

"No." Some kind of conflict seemed to play across his profile, as if he were having an internal war. She figured he was debating asking a favor. Never in a million years did she expect his next question. "Do you want to go for a walk?"

"A walk?" she repeated. With him?

"It's a hot day. The woods are cooler and you're right about the turnovers smelling good and since it is lunchtime…"

"Wait." She had to make sure she wasn't hearing

things. "You want me to go on a picnic with you?"

"I thought I might eat the turnovers in a cooler location and figured, since you did all the driving today, I'd ask you to join me. But," he shrugged, "if you've got other things to do, or get ready for…" He reached across his body for the door handle.

"No, I'll go," Kelsey said, stopping him. "Give me a minute to change first though." She flicked the edge of her peasant skirt. "This isn't the best outfit for walking in the woods."

As he looked her up and down, she told herself the flutter of excitement in her stomach was unnecessary. "Fine. I'll meet you at the edge of the garden in five minutes."

With more enthusiasm than she should have, Kelsey raced upstairs to her room. Since she preferred skirts and sundresses, she didn't have a lot of clothes suitable for walking in the woods. She settled for a pair of royal blue track shorts and a bright pink tank top. Her hair, she fished in a ponytail through an old baseball cap she wore when running. Hardly the most stylish of outfits.

Then again, like Alex said, it was simply turnovers in a cooler location. He wouldn't even notice. That is, if he was still waiting. She'd taken longer than five minutes. Snagging two bottles of water on her way through the kitchen, she headed toward the garden.

Alex was leaning against the garden shed when she arrived, looking like a slinged sentry. He looked so comfortable standing there she had to, yet again, quell her insides. Especially when she imagined his eyes scanning her appearance.

"Lead the way," she said with a smile. "I'm starving."

While she'd known there was a path leading up the mountain, she didn't anticipate how picturesque or how well traveled the path would be. Pine tree branches formed a canopy that shielded them from the sun while brown needles formed a soft carpet beneath their feet. Occasionally light would break through a gap and a white shaft would beam down on the ferns and underbrush that littered the ground. It was an otherworld of coolness, lush and green.

Kelsey had never seen anything like it, not Central Park, not even the view from her window, though that came close. No wonder Alex disappeared into here every morning.

"Is this where you fell?" She was afraid to speak too loud lest she disturb the tranquility.

Alex pointed to a bend in the path. "Up there.

I was watching a red squirrel jumping around the branches and caught the toe of my shoe."

The idea of somber Alex Markoff distracted by a squirrel made Kelsey giggle, earning her a questioning look. "Do you think the squirrel realized he nearly derailed the year's biggest literary comeback?"

"Is that what Stuart's calling it?"

"Among other things. A lot of people have been waiting for a follow-up to *Chase the Moon*."

"Good old *Chase the Moon*." Reaching up with his good arm, he pulled back a pine branch blocking their path. "My prize-winning albatross."

Kelsey ducked beneath the needles. "I'm sure there are a lot of writers in the world who wouldn't mind bearing that kind of burden."

"They can be my guest." Alex let go of the branch. It whipped into place with a loud thwap. "Sometimes I wish I'd never written the book. Life would be a lot easier, that's for sure."

The last sentence wasn't directed at her, but to the trees. Kelsey thought of the notepads that weren't appearing on her desk and of the dark, pain-riddled pages that had. "You don't want to write this book, do you?"

"Writing isn't the problem. It's publishing I hate. Publishing and everything that goes with it."

Remembering those articles, she understood

his reluctance. "Surely this time will be different though."

"Why? Because this time I'm not married?"

The bitterness in his voice didn't escape her. "I mean this time you'll know what to expect."

"Forgive me if I don't take comfort in the thought."

They resumed walking in silence, albeit more weighted than before. Every so often Kelsey stole a glance in Alex's direction. She wished she could read his thoughts but like always, they were shrouded.

Then, suddenly, as if reading hers, he spoke. "It's funny how life works. You start writing because you have stories you want to share with the world. Once you get your wish though, everything changes, especially if your story becomes The Next Big Thing." He announced the words to the air with his hand. "Suddenly, life stops being about the words and more about you. What you did, where you went, who you were with. What you can do for them. It's easy to get lost."

"I can see why a person can become jaded," Kelsey replied carefully.

"Jaded is the tip of the iceberg." He stopped suddenly, and setting the paper bag on a nearby rock, turned to face her. "I know full well I'm a nightmare to share a house with."

The admission, a blip compare to his other admissions, went straight to her heart. "Really?" she joked. "I hadn't noticed."

He met her attempt at deflection with serious eyes. "Most people would have told me where to go by now."

"Don't think I haven't been tempted."

Alex reached out and plucked a pine needle from her hair, his touch soft as a whisper against her cheek and setting off a freefall inside her. "Then I guess I should be grateful you're so patient."

Unsure what else to do, she tucked her hair behind her ear while Alex retrieved the turnovers and led on. Compliments? Openness? This couldn't be the same Alex Markoff. Suddenly, in this magical forest, he was different. They were different. Something was pulling them together. Connecting them.

But she didn't do connections.

What was going on?

The question dogged her for another quarter mile. Until Alex paused and held up his hand. "Hear that?" There was a soft rumble in the distance, like wind gathering speed through the trees. "We're here."

He led them up and around one final bend, to where the path opened. Kelsey's eyes widened and all her questions vanished in a fog of wonderment. "Oh my," she whispered.

They were at a side of a mountain river. The rumble she'd heard was the water racing down the slope, splashing over rocks in a rush to reach the end.

"Pretty amazing, isn't it?"

"Amazing doesn't begin to cover it," she replied, awestruck.

To her right, a pair of large flat boulders formed a natural ledge on which a person could perch overlooking the current. She watched, impressed, as Alex made his way across to the edge and sat down, his long legs dangling above the water. For a one-armed man, he was amazingly agile. Then again, he spent all day in these woods; he probably knew every rock and crevice by heart.

Suddenly she realized where they were. This was his sanctuary. She picked her way toward him, each step feeling like she was traveling sacred ground. That he would share this place with her of all people… Why, she wanted to ask.

Instead she sat down beside him. "Is this where you write?"

"Sometimes. Other times I head a little further upstream. The sound of the water drowns out my thoughts."

"Funny, I would think you'd need your thoughts to write."

"Not all of them."

Kelsey could buy that. Lord knows she had thoughts and feelings she'd like to drown out herself.

Alex dug into the bag and handed her a turnover, and she handed Alex a water bottle. They sat and ate, swinging their feet in the air, the cadence instinctively in sync. There was something very childlike to the moment, and Kelsey suddenly felt more carefree than she had in years. Maybe ever. She studied the pattern made by the water swirling beneath their feet, imagining Grandma Rosie and her debt being swept away in the whitecaps. "Is the water cold?"

"Stick your feet in and see for yourself."

"Is that a dare?"

"I don't do dares."

"Right. That's why you won't answer my question."

"I'm not answering because you might have a different assessment."

In other words, see for herself. Which meant yes, the water was cold. Different assessment her foot. It was a dare.

Feeling him watching her out of the corner of his eye, she slipped off her sneakers and socks. Then, scooting as close to the edge as she could without falling, she carefully, slowly dipped her toes in the water.

"Holy cow, that's freezing!" Felt like she stuck her foot in a bucket of ice.

"I take it back, we did have the same assessment," Alex remarked.

Damn if his eyes weren't sparkling. If she hadn't a good grip on the rock, their impact might have knocked her into the water. "You could have simply told me."

"You would have stuck your foot in anyway."

"No, I wouldn't."

"Yes, you would. Because I would have."

"That your way of suggesting we're alike?"

"Aren't we?"

She'd recognized that fact days ago. Seemed unlikely. After all, they were from completely different ends of the spectrum. Rich and successful versus poor and rootless. Hermit versus nomad. And yet, here they were, sitting on a rock in a world that, to Kelsey, felt suddenly very small and right.

She drew her knees tight. "Sure don't get to see sights like this in Throg's Neck."

"That where you grew up?"

"Among other places." She waited, grateful he didn't ask for a list. "How 'bout you? Did you always live in L.A? The clippings, remember," she added when she shot her a sideways look.

He shook his head. "I grew up in New York. We moved to L.A. a few months before…"

Kelsey didn't need for him to finish. She knew what he meant. "Do you miss it?"

"L.A.? Hardly."

"Sorry, dumb question, right?"

"No. There were parts of California I loved. Like driving along the coastline and watching the ocean." Looking at the cascades swirling below them, Kelsey could easily see him doing just that. "But I guess I'll always be a New Yorker at heart."

"Have you been back? I mean, since your marriage…"

"No."

"What about your family?" She was probably pushing her luck asking such personal questions, but the intimacy created by their surroundings made her press anyway.

"My father was in the Twin Towers. My mother followed a year later."

Leaving him alone. "They weren't there to see your success."

"No," he answered, his voice wistful and heavy.

"I'm sorry."

He shrugged. "Life happens."

"To some more than others."

"Ain't that the truth." Kelsey watched as Alex took a long drink, withdrawing into his thoughts. What goes on in that head of yours? she wondered. It felt like such a lonely place.

So much silence gathered between them that for a moment, she thought he forgot her. That is, until he spoke again. His voice was low, barely audible above the rushing water.

"She thought it would make her a star."

The comment wasn't what Kelsey expected. He had to be talking about Alyssa.

"I'd sold the movie rights to *Chase the Moon*. She figured my wife would have the inside track for the lead. I was foolish enough to think there was affection behind the ambition. But then I had a lot of misconceptions about people. Like I said, it's easy to get lost."

His confession broke her heart. He was, in her mind, being hard on himself. A man alone, without family or anchor to celebrate his fame, pursued by a sexy desirable woman. No wonder he got caught in her web. She wanted to reach out, cover his hand with hers and tell him he wasn't alone, but she refrained lest she scare away this rare show of vulnerability. "What made you realize—"

"That Alyssa was just using me?" He paused, chewing the inside of his cheek for a second. "I think I always suspected, I simply didn't want to see it. Alyssa was always about going out and being seen. At first it was novel, and of course, I wanted to make her happy, but I never enjoyed it."

Thinking back to the photos on the Web, Kelsey could see it. The discomfort behind his sober expression. "Guess she didn't think much of you writing a short story during a dinner party."

"Oh good Lord, no," he said with a laugh. "That, I think, might have been the final straw. That and the fact *Chase the Moon* got stalled in preproduction. Hard to piggyback on your husband's fame if there's no part."

So she left and used the divorce to piggyback instead. Her and his so-called friends. Leaving Alex alone again.

Her heart broke a little more. Yet at the same time it somehow managed to swell. She didn't know why he chose her to hear his story, but she was honored and humbled that he did. A sense of something deeper than companionship wrapped itself around them. At this moment, in this place, she felt closer to Alex Markoff than she'd ever been with a person. It was like they belonged together, sitting here on this rock.

"Do you have any idea what you'll do when you go back? Once this job is over?"

And like that, the illusion fell away.

"I don't believe in thinking too far ahead," she said, chasing away the dullness in her stomach. "Plans have a way of changing." Or getting yanked out from beneath you. "There are always temp jobs available. I'll find something that interests me."

"Another difficult boss that pays extra?"

"Hopefully I won't need to." When he cocked his head, she added, "I have a debt I need to pay."

"May I ask why?"

Maybe the tranquil setting lowered her defenses, or maybe she was feeling the remnants of closeness from before, but like the other night, Kelsey found herself wanting to share her own story. "My grandmother forged my signature on a loan application that she never paid back. And before you ask, no, she didn't have a good reason." Unless lack of a moral compass counted.

"Don't," she said cutting off what she knew was coming. She recognized the emotion in Alex's eyes. She hated that look, hated being seen as some pathetic orphan. Especially by him. "She'd never been much of a grandmother to begin with. The loan thing wasn't a big surprise when I found out."

"You know that legally, you don't have—"

"To pay? I know, but then I'd have to turn her in to the authorities for fraud."

"And you don't want to."

She gave him a weak smile. "Lousy grandmother

or not, she's the only family I've got. Besides," she looked away so he wouldn't see the shame in her eyes, "she's already a guest of the state. Check kiting."

A fish jumped in the stream, splashing water across her bare toes. Chin resting on her knee-cap, she ran a hand up and down her chilled leg. "Punishing her more felt petty."

Alex didn't respond. Kelsey didn't really expect him to. After all, how do you react when your assistant unloads that kind of information, other than be sorry you asked? From the way he folded into himself at her last comment, he definitely regretted asking. She never should have shared in the first place. Now every time he looked at her, he'd see poor little Kelsey whose grandmother ripped her off.

Instead of what? Kelsey the employee? Or Kelsey the woman?

"Just goes to show you really can't trust anyone, doesn't it?" she forced herself to say lightly.

"No, I guess you can't." His words, flat and far-away, made her sad.

"Anyway, thanks to you and Mr. Lefkowitz's increased pay rate, I'll have most of the debt paid by the fall and I can put the whole debacle behind me."

Unsure what else to do, she reached for her shoes

and socks. The movement pulled him back to the present and he looked up. "So my...temperamental behavior serves some purpose after all."

"Looks that way."

She tied her sneaker and together, they scrambled to their feet. Once again, Kelsey marveled at how effortlessly Alex maneuvered. He must be a sight to behold when he had two working arms.

"I don't know why you're complaining about waiting a month," she said, nodding at his cast. "You move pretty well."

"Move, perhaps. But I'd give my other arm to be able to scratch again. Do you have any idea how much my arm itches? And don't get me started on having to shower with my arm wrapped in plastic."

She held her hands up in surrender. "I take back my words. Your suffering knows no bounds."

"Thank you."

A crumb from a turnover clung to the hem of his sling. "Looks like we should have brought you a napkin." She reached out to brush it away.

The charge started as soon as her fingers touched the heavy canvas. The pull of a connection completed. Without thinking, she traced along the hem, running her fingers downward until they touched the hard plaster. From beneath her lashes, she saw

Alex watching her, his eyes bright like silver as they scanned her face. Looking for something.

The surface beneath her hand went from hard to soft. A couple brushes of her index finger and she realized she was touching Alex's skin. Color flooding every inch of her, she yanked her hand away.

"We—we should probably head back." She balled her fingers into a fist, blasting herself for the slip.

But Alex simply continued to study her, a new layer marking his inspection. Some new facet in his silver-gray eyes Kelsey couldn't describe. "There's a hogback another half a mile upstream with an amazing view," he said, tucking a stray tendril behind her ear. "Interested?"

"Sure." She had no idea what a hogback was, but at that moment, with him watching her like that, she'd follow him anywhere.

It was dusk by the time they returned. Impossibly, the second location was more idyllic than the first. A space among the trees where the rock formed natural stairs and you could sit and see the green valley below. Together they'd sat and watched the raptors catch thermals while finishing the last of the turnovers. The birds were, of course, captivating, but she'd found herself more captivated by the man whose knees provided her backrest. He was a presence that was impossible to ignore. A brush of his elbow, the whiff of his scent. Dear Lord, if he ever were to smile—really smile—in her direction, she'd be a goner. As it was, her pulse quickened every time he so much as looked in her direction.

"Thank you," she said as they climbed up the stairs to their rooms that night. "Today was…" She didn't have the words.

Turns out she didn't need them. "Yeah, it was." Alex leaned against the balustrade, his perpetually intense eyes dark and smoky in the dimly lit hall.

Kelsey's pulse skipped a beat. Her first instinct was to break his gaze and focus on something else. The energy in the air reminded her of a first date, although though they were a million miles from such a scenario. But still, a note of expectancy hung in the air. Like those nervous last minutes, right before the good-night kiss, when your mouth runs dry.

She bet Alex kissed wonderfully.

Alex pushed himself away from the rail and moved slowly toward her. Kelsey's insides started to spin. Her mouth went dry.

Seeking ballast, she reached for the doorknob behind her. "Good night."

He didn't miss a beat. In fact, he'd been reaching

for his own door. But his eyes were still smoky and dark when he looked in her direction. "Good night, Kelsey. I'll see you tomorrow."

The heat that night was oppressive. Or so it felt to Kelsey. Long after she said good-night to Alex, she lay on top of the covers, heat pressing down on the thin cotton T-shirt she wore as a nightshirt. That her sleeplessness was related to anything other than the heat, she didn't want to consider, even if images of Alex appeared every time she closed her eyes. *Alex sitting by the river. Alex's eyes as he said good-night.*

Speak of the devil. In the next room she could hear his bed creak and the sound of footsteps on the floor. Apparently she wasn't the only one having trouble sleeping in this heat as well. Interestingly, the humidity didn't feel nearly as strong earlier. A weather front must have moved in.

Maybe if she opened the window wider the air flow would improve.

With a sigh, she eased herself off the bed and padded to the window. At first, she was surprised to see a soft light spilling out onto the pine trees, till she realized the moon was directly overhead, lighting the yard like a spotlight. She heard the scrape of a window opening to her left. Then a second. Alex? Curious, she raised her window screen and looked out, coming face to face with her neighbor.

"Shhh," he admonished when she opened her mouth to speak. He pointed toward the trees. Kelsey followed his finger, wondering what he was doing.

Then she heard it. A soft, distinct hoot-hoot coming from the tree. A second later, a giant owl swooped down past her window, gliding low over the ground and disappearing into the shadows.

"Wow." In the night air, her stunned whisper sounded loud.

"Beautiful creature, isn't she? Usually she hangs out deeper in the woods, but she must have decided to do a little exploring tonight."

Kelsey looked down at the shadows, to where the bird vanished. She'd never seen anything like that before. "Think she'll be back?"

"Not tonight anyway."

"Isn't there some kind of rule about owls outside your window being bad?"

"Only if she shows up three nights in a row. I think you're safe."

"Good. I'd hate to have more bad luck."

"You and me both."

His comment only fueled her unsettled insides. What was it about his sadness that touched her so deeply?

"Still," she said, keeping the subject light, "she was beautiful." She turned her head to look at him. "I'm glad I got to see her."

"Me too."

And then, to her surprise, he smiled. A real, honest-to-God, full smile that put the owl's beauty to shame. It lit up his face and melted her insides. *Breathtaking.*

Fifteen minutes later, Kelsey was back on her bed counting sheep. This time she didn't even try to blame her sleeplessness on the heat.

CHAPTER SEVEN

SINCE she was awake early anyway, Kelsey decided to head into town for more pastry. She and Alex had eaten the entire batch on their hike. A thrill passed through her remembering the feel of his body shielding hers on the trail, another still as she recalled his smile last night. Then she firmly pulled herself together. It was just a hike and a bird-watching moment. Don't read too much into it. After all, who said the smile was directed at her? Maybe he was simply happy to see the owl up close.

Like it had been the day before, the Bean was jammed with customers, most in line for gourmet takeout. Here and there she caught snatches of conversation, all excited commentary about the gala concert that night. Farley, meanwhile, held court at the register, grumbling and grousing with each sale he rang up. Kelsey chuckled.

"If I didn't know any better, I'd say you were stalking me," a voice said in her ear.

Startled, Kelsey jerked her cup away from the coffee she was pouring, splashing it on the counter. She turned around to find Tom standing behind her wearing another of his ubiquitous tropical shirts. "Sorry," he said handing her a napkin. "I didn't mean to startle you."

"Since you're the one who's always walking up on me, shouldn't I be the one worried about stalking?" she asked, mopping up her spill.

He smiled. "Good point. Why don't we chalk it up to a mutual love of caffeine."

"Sounds good to me."

He reached past her to grab a cup. As he did, Kelsey got a whiff of flowery aftershave. Pleasant, but nothing like Alex's earthy scent. That, of course, conjured up another memory from yesterday. Without meaning to, she sighed.

"That was a pretty contented sound," Tom remarked. "What's got you in a such a good mood?"

"Who says I'm in a good mood?"

"For one, the sparkle in your eyes. Along with that smile."

"Just enjoying the beautiful weather."

"And here I thought it was my charming company."

Kelsey kept quiet while he prepared his coffee.

She didn't mean to be coy, but Tom's comments left her unsettled. Despite his jovial tone, she sensed an edge. Probably wasn't used to women turning him down, she imagined. Reaching for the half-and-half she shot him a smile, silently letting him know her lack of interest wasn't personal. He just wasn't her type.

"Do you have any potato salad with fat-free mayonnaise?" a woman at the counter was asking Farley.

"We got two types of potato salad. With and without egg. You want nonfat, you have to make it yourself."

Both Tom and Kelsey snickered. "Will you listen to him?" Tom chuckled. "You'd think he doesn't like making money."

"Nah, it's all show for the customers. I bet he'd miss them if they left."

"Unlike your boss."

Kelsey's smile faltered. "What's that supposed to mean?"

"Nothing. I only meant Farley pretends to not like crowds, while Markoff really doesn't."

"Al—I mean, Mr. Markoff, likes his privacy." And she wasn't about to betray it now with Tom. She turned to leave.

"Hey," he said, catching her shoulder. "I didn't

mean anything. I can appreciate the quirks of creative genius, and God knows, Markoff is a creative genius. I hope I didn't tick you off."

Some of her annoyance faded. "No, you didn't. I simply—well, my job requires discretion."

"Of course. I understand." He started to sip his coffee, then stopped suddenly with a thought. "Hey, you still not interested in the music festival?"

Kelsey had to hand it to him; he had perseverance. "Thanks, Tom, but I think I'll pass."

"Oh, no, I didn't mean come with me. I, uh—" he blushed "—already found another date."

"Good." It was Kelsey's turn to blush.

"Some friends of mine from New York bailed at the last minute and I have a couple extra tickets. If you're interested, you can have them."

"Really?"

"Sure. I'm not one to hold a little thing like rejection against a fellow coffee lover. You can take a friend. You interested?"

Despite knowing better, an image of Alex and her sipping wine in the moonlight flashed into her mind. She imagined him smiling again, only this time maybe standing a little closer.

It was a fantasy.

On the other hand, what would it hurt to take the tickets? She could always go alone.

"Sure," she answered. "I'm interested."

* * *

The local radio station talked of nothing but the up-coming event as she drove back to Nuttingwood. A gala like none the Berkshires had ever seen. Kelsey got a thrill listening to the buildup. Moonlight and music. Sounded like a wonderful evening.

Alex was already out on his walk when Kelsey got to the house. Leaving the turnovers she bought on a plate next to the coffeemaker, she filled her new green coffee mug and took it, along with her other surprise, into the office.

"Hey, Puddin', look what I brought home for you."

The cat meowed hello and trotted out to greet her. Or more accurately to greet the plate of fresh tuna she brought with her. "Everyone gets a treat this morning," she said, scratching his head. "You can have the rest before we go out tonight."

Her hand reached into her pocket and felt the tickets Tom had given her. What did one wear to a gala like none had ever seen? All she had was a pink cocktail dress left over from New Year's Eve. It had cost too much to donate away or stick in storage, so she'd brought the garment along. She loved the dress, but was it glamorous enough? Alex would know; he had far more experience with society events than she did.

With that one thought, reality regained control. All this thinking about Alex and his smile. And the concert. Why would Alex go to an event like that in the first place, let alone go with her? It wasn't like they had some kind of relationship.

But you'd like to, wouldn't you?

No, she wouldn't. She didn't want a relationship with Alex other than the one they had. They weren't even relationship material. He was too busy being angry with the whole darn world and she… she was temporary in every sense of the word. In a few more weeks, she'd be out of here, and they'd never see each other again.

Besides, she knew better than anyone that any feeling this good could never last.

"Tell me that cat isn't eating tuna fish from a plate."

She looked up in time to see Alex step onto the terrace. Their gazes locked, and he stopped in his tracks. Kelsey's insides, on the other hand, went into free fall. All of a sudden she felt very shy.

"Morning," he said, his voice dropping to a honey-eyed baritone that sent the free fall into overdrive. "You were up and out early."

"So were you."

"I couldn't sleep. The heat."

"I know. I mean, about the heat." In the early morning light, his eyes glinted like polished silver.

Unable to hold his stare, Kelsey looked to

Puddin'. "I couldn't sleep either so I went to Farley's for coffee. Brought back some turnovers."

"Pastry and tuna. That's quite a combination."

"Well, Puddin' didn't think humans should have all the fun."

"Interesting. I didn't realize you and he were on such intimate terms." Hearing the word *intimate* slip off his tongue so easily, Kelsey's breath hitched. It caught again when Alex grinned. Not as wide or bright a smile as the night before, but every bit as breathtaking.

"He's a very good listener," she replied, unable to stop herself from nervously tucking hair behind her ear.

"I bet. Any topics I'd be interested in?"

"I'll never tell."

"Ahh," he said, grinning wider. "You might not, but I know your partner's weakness." He leaned down to look at the cat licking his whiskers. "From the looks and smell, I'd say albacore white packed in water."

"You wouldn't sell me out for a serving of tuna, would you, Puddin'?"

The glint that had been shining in the sun grew hard. "People will always sell you out, Kelsey."

Ouch. The lightheartedness began to fade.

She was struggling with how to rescue the atmosphere when Alex turned to head inside. "I have two tickets to tonight's fund-raiser," she said in a rush, stopping him in his tracks. "Would you like to go?"

Alex didn't answer. He simply stared, looking as surprised as she felt.

"Never mind." Please say her face did not look as shocked yesterday as his did now. Why didn't she keep her mouth shut as she planned? "It was a silly thing to suggest. I don't know why I even suggested the idea." *Other than the fact you were getting that forlorn look and were walking away and I wanted to keep you with me.*

"What happened to your 'friend' from the store? I thought he invited you."

Who? "Oh, you mean Tom." She'd completely forgotten about both the invitation and the fact she'd told Alex about it.

"Won't he mind?"

"He and I aren't going together." She left out that he was the source of the tickets.

"Really?" She had to be imagining the interest in his voice.

"No." Although he wasn't asking for an explanation, the gleam in his eye, the one she was imagining along with the interest in his voice, compelled her to offer one. Or at least a partial one. "He's a nice guy, but not really my type."

"You have a type?"

Yes, you. She chased that thought away as fast as it formed. "Doesn't everyone?"

Alex nodded. "Sometimes. Other times a person catches you off guard."

She knew what he meant. "Anyway, never mind my suggestion. I can go alone."

"I'll go."

"You will?" Her voice traveled up at the end of her question, betraying all her surprise and excitement. Never in a million years did she expect him to accept. "Why?"

He went back to staring, this time actively searching her face as if the answer were contained there. "A woman like you shouldn't have to be alone."

For the rest of the day, Kelsey tried to keep her enthusiasm at bay. *Go alone,* she would remind herself whenever she started to get too excited. He meant a woman like her shouldn't have to *go* alone. A small slip of semantics, but important nonetheless. One version referred to escort status; the other implied...well, it implied arrangements she already knew weren't realistic.

Of course, neither version explained why he was suddenly shedding his hermit mode. She decided not to go there. Thinking about that only brought her back to the illusions she knew weren't possible.

And yet, despite all her self-lecturing, she was a bundle of nerves by nightfall. Sometime during the day, she realized tonight would be the first time Alex had ever seen her truly dressed up. As a result she spent what felt like hours getting ready, lying to herself that the effort was so she wouldn't embarrass her boss and not because she wanted to impress him.

Surveying her reflection, she offered herself a nervous smile. "Not bad." Her dress swirled about her calves; the shimmering pink made her look like a bright flower, and her makeup was more dramatic than normal. Nothing excessive, but enough that it played up her blue eyes. Deciding casual was best when it came to her hair, she clipped the front of her curls in a rhinestone clasp and let the rest tumble down her back.

A lot of work for a non-date, she thought with a sigh. And this wasn't a date.

Another point she spent the day reminding herself.

She headed downstairs to the great room where she found Alex staring out at the garden. That he looked great didn't surprise her. She'd long ago concluded he would always look great. Tonight, he wore a black suit. Long, lean and simple, the ensemble fit him both literally and figuratively. Even with his sling, the jacket somehow managed to drape seamlessly over his shoulders and down his back, with just enough snugness to hint at the muscles beneath. He looked a million miles away. Regretting his decision?

Softly, she cleared her throat, alerting him of her presence. "Hi."

He turned and his expression went from thoughtful to something darker but far from somber. His eyes swept the length of her, the appreciative glint leaving shivers in its wake. "Hi back."

"Are you ready to go?"

"Almost."

At first, Kelsey couldn't decide if his immobility was from reluctance or something else. He stood there studying her in that distracted way of his. Behind his eyes, wheels were turning, but about what he was thinking, she had no idea.

Then she noticed the tie in his left hand. Of course. "Need help?" Without waiting for the answer, she moved toward him. "Thank goodness it's not a bowtie. I'm only good with Windsors."

It wasn't the first time she'd tied a tie. But it was the first time the action felt so intimate. Worse, it felt natural. They stood mere inches apart, wood and spice drifting off Alex's skin. Kelsey struggled not to close her eyes and inhale, same way she struggled not to stare at his tanned skin or the hint of dark curls at the vee of his white shirt. "Can you button the top button?"

Part of her was hoping he'd say no so she could continue seeing his skin as well as touch him further. But, unfortunately, or fortunately, he did as she asked, and a moment later, she was looping the silk around his neck.

"Where did you learn to tie a tie?" he asked.

"School uniforms. In junior high one year, I was in charge of making sure all the kids in the house didn't look sloppy. Our foster mother—"

"Foster mother?"

Kelsey blushed, feeling the color all the way down her neck. "Grandma Rosie wasn't much of a guardian, I'm afraid."

"That's too bad."

Too bad indeed. She returned to somewhat lighter subjects. "Like I was saying, my foster mother was a stickler about appearance. She wouldn't let us leave the house unless we were all knotted and groomed. There was this one kid, Tyrrell, who couldn't stay neat if he tried. I used to tie his tie for him every morning."

"We had to wear ties with our school uniforms, too. Wretched things made it hard to do any kind of activity. I hated them."

Kelsey wasn't surprised. Men like Alex weren't

made for suits and ties inside. "I imagine Tyrell would agree. That's probably why his tie never managed to stay put for more than an hour."

She fished an end up and through. "I always wondered who took over fixing his tie when I left."

"How long were you there?"

"At that house? Eighteen months or so, I guess. I never really kept track." Knot complete, she drew it tight against his collar. "There you go. Not my best, I'm afraid. I'm a little out of practice."

"Good enough for me. Was it difficult?"

"Was what difficult? Tying your tie?"

Surveying her handiwork, she reached up and made a minuscule adjustment. It wasn't really needed; she wanted an excuse to keep her hands close to him.

"Moving so much," he replied quietly.

Her fingers paused in midaction. When did the conversation turn personal? "You get used to it," she answered with a shrug. "After a while, picking up and moving on becomes a lifestyle." Out of necessity, she added silently.

"Like temp work?"

Slowly, she looked up to find him looking down, his face serious and sincere. "Yeah, like temp work."

Time stopped for a second. Or so it felt by the

way the air grew thick around them. A dull thud vibrated against her fingertips. She realized it was Alex's heart, that her hands were pressed against his chest. The slow steady beat was nothing like the one racing inside her body.

"You're good to go." Needing distance, she backed away.

The radio station wasn't exaggerating when it said New Englanders were turning out in droves for tonight's fund-raiser. Celebrities, local leaders and every arts patron with access to the highway was in attendance. For Kelsey, entering the administration building was like entering a summer wonderland. The decorated room wasn't as colorful as Alex's garden or as tranquil as the cascades, but it was beautiful and elegant with its tea lights and floral topiaries. She felt like Cinderella on the arm of her handsome prince.

A handsome, silent prince. Alex barely said a word after they left Nuttingwood. He spent the drive staring out the window, his long fingers tapping the armrest. He was still a million miles away now. Although his face didn't show any expression, Kelsey knew he had to be tense. After all, there was a huge difference between stopping into the local store and attending a crowded gala full of New England's social elite. The night had to be bringing back memories of the world he thought he'd left behind.

"We don't have to stay long," she said to him.

The comment brought him back to attention. "What are you talking about?"

"The concert. I know you'd rather be somewhere else."

"Then you underestimate me."

"Are you telling me you'd rather not be hiking in the woods right now?"

His delayed shrug gave her his answer. "We're a little overdressed for rock hopping in the cascade, wouldn't you think?"

"Very funny," she said, rolling her eyes. "What I meant was that I appreciate you coming with me."

"Well, like I said, a woman like you shouldn't be alone."

There it was, that slip, again. Through she tried, the tremors of expectation running down her back made the remark hard to brush off. Perhaps he didn't know his word choice could be misconstrued. On the other hand, he was a writer so maybe he did.

"I—" Before she could say anything, a waiter approached bearing a tray of fluted glasses.

"Champagne?"

Kelsey shook her head. "Designated driver," she

lied, hoping Alex would follow his usual pattern and not press.

Unfortunately tonight seemed to be his night for behaving out of character. At least he waited until the server moved on before asking, "What's the real reason?"

"What makes you think there's a different reason?" She fiddled with the fringe on her shawl. *How did he know?*

"Your face. The corners of your mouth tighten when you're being falsely cheerful."

"They do?"

He nodded. "I noticed your first day, when you kept throwing me those fake smiles."

Feeling her skin getting hot, Kelsey suddenly regretted wearing a dress that revealed so much skin. The entire fund-raiser had to know she was embarrassed. "You noticed my smiles were fake?"

"I noticed a lot of things about you."

If the rest of the people in the room didn't see her blush before, they certainly did now. Alex's comment shot straight to her toes, its journey assisted by his tone of voice. A rough, gravelly tone that spoke of pleasure and more. Kelsey's insides turned to warm honey, and her knees threatened to buckle. Through lowered lashes, she watched as Alex raised his glass to his lips. "Wonder if

Stuart knew what he'd done when he hired you," he murmured over the rim.

"Done?" Distracted by how the champagne left Alex's upper lip shining, she'd missed his meaning. What did Stuart do other than hire a qualified typist? "He simply wanted the manuscript done on time."

"I wonder," was all Alex replied, and he took another sip. "Back to my original question, do you feel like explaining the designated driver excuse?"

"Who says it's an excuse? Oh, right." At his knowing smile, her fingers came up to touch her mouth. Very well, she might as well tell the truth. "Alcohol was the source of too many bad situations growing up." Hopefully her shrug looked nonchalant.

"With your grandmother?"

"Rosie had her share of drunken mishaps." So did one particular foster father, but she wouldn't go there. Not tonight. "Made me decide that when it came to drinking, avoidance was the best policy. For me anyway."

Those gray eyes softened. "I'm sorry."

"For what? You weren't there." She didn't want to talk about her past right now. The night was too beautiful to think about things she couldn't change.

Or things she couldn't have.

She drowned out the warning with a change in topic. "Did you see all these flower arrangements? I think there might be more flowers in here than in your garden."

"Hmm," was Alex's reply.

"You don't think so?"

"What I think," he said, leaning in a little closer, "is that you're an incredibly strong woman for having survived so much and coming out the other side so full of life."

"No stronger than anybody else."

"You sell yourself short. And as for the flowers…" He leaned in even closer. "You're far more colorful."

The air in the room shifted abruptly, becoming close and intense. Looking at Alex's expression, Kelsey saw that he felt it too. A bond of silent understanding formed between them. It felt like coming together at a center of a bridge from separate directions. Setting his glass down, Alex nodded toward a nearby exit. "Come with me," he whispered.

CHAPTER EIGHT

THEY managed to get as far as the exit before a large, blue-jacketed torso stepped in their path.

Tom Forbes smiled like he was greeting an old friend. "Kelsey! I thought that was you in the crowd." His eyes flickered from her to Alex and back. "And you brought a friend after all."

Not knowing what else to do, Kelsey smiled back. It was like being stuck in one of those movie moments where the heroine finds herself caught between two romantic rivals. Only she was caught between a guy with a bruised ego and… And she didn't know how to define Alex anymore. Didn't matter; the situation was still awkward.

"Aren't you going to introduce me?" Tom asked. He was still smiling, but the grin had a sharper edge.

"Of course." She tucked some hair behind her ears and found her manners. "Tom Forbes, this is—"

She didn't get any further before Tom stuck his hand out, completely ignoring the cast on Alex's right arm. "Alex Markoff. Big fan. I've followed your career for a long time."

Kelsey half thought Alex would ignore the handshake offer, but he didn't. He held out his left hand and allowed Tom to awkwardly pump it up and down. "Kelsey mentioned she was typing your manuscript," he continued.

"Did she now?" Alex slid his gaze toward her. She shrugged, knowing that wasn't what he wanted to hear.

"I mentioned I worked for a writer, and then he saw you the other day at Farley's."

"Can't wait to read it. Any idea when the book'll be out?"

"When it's finished."

Tom laughed, a little too affectedly for Kelsey's taste. The guy was trying too hard. "Hopefully that'll be soon. Been a long time since *Chase the Moon*. A lot of readers have wondered where you've been."

"Well, you can't rush the creative process," Kelsey piped up. Next to her, she could feel Alex's tension. The night was going well. She didn't want it spoiled because of Tom's overeager questions.

Meanwhile, Tom continued smiling that sharp smile. "No, I suppose you can't. Of course—" this time it was his gaze sliding in her direction "—having the right inspiration helps."

Okay, now he was definitely pushing his luck. Kelsey waited for Alex to refute him or cut him down with one of his cold stares. To her surprise, he did neither.

Instead, he took her hand. "Certainly does. If you'll excuse us, Kelsey and I want to get some air before the concert begins."

He pulled her toward the exit, not forcefully, but decidedly enough that anyone watching would know not to deter them.

"So, that's your 'friend'," he remarked, once they stepped outside.

"That's Tom." She knew he had an ego, but she hadn't expected him to act quite so…aggressive? She didn't expect Alex's behavior either. "Sorry about his questions. He really didn't know I worked for you until he saw you in the store. On the plus side," she added, "at least you know he wants to read your book."

"You're right," Alex replied.

She was confused. "About what? Him wanting to read your book?"

"Nope." Giving her fingers a squeeze, Alex

leaned in toward the crook of her neck and whispered, "That he's not your type."

Kelsey's pulse skipped a beat.

Outside the concert, on the grounds, organizers had forgone the standard spotlights in favor of lanterns strung from the trees, giving the grounds a romantic, amber glow. The early evening air still held the day's warmth, and the sky promised a clear, star-filled romantic evening. They walked the grass in comfortable silence. Every so often they would come across another couple who would nod hello as they passed.

Another couple. Kelsey knew she needed to correct her thinking, but with every step found it harder and harder to do. No sooner did she form the thoughts than they would slip away, lost in a haze of romance.

She stole a look at Alex. So tonight wasn't a date. They weren't a couple. But would it be so bad to pretend, if only for a little while? No one need know. She took a deep breath, savoring the scent of evening blossoms, and allowed herself a silent fantasy.

"Would you look at the view?" Kelsey said. They were toward the rear of the property, where the grounds overlooked Stockbridge Bowl. "Doesn't the water look beautiful?" Black and fathomless, with dapples of white, reflections of the lanterns dotting the surface.

She let out a soft sigh. "There's something very mysterious about dark water, don't you think? There's so much that you can't see. You have to look deep to really know what's there." She glanced over her shoulder at the man behind her. "Like people."

"That so?" His expression was gentle and tender. "And what do you think lies beneath?"

"More than meets the eye, that's for sure. Light. Beauty. Sensitivity."

"You sure? It could simply be more darkness."

"No," she said shaking her head. "The dark surface is simply camouflage. To protect what's underneath."

They both knew she wasn't talking about the water.

Alex reached over her shoulder to cup her cheek. Instinctively she nestled into his touch. His body drew closer, so close she could feel the straps of his sling through her thin silk wrap. Feeling them brush against her shoulder blades, she trembled.

"Cold?" Alex asked, his lips dangerously close to her earlobe.

Kelsey shook her head. "Not cold at all." In fact, she'd never felt warmer.

"Good." His hand slid downward slightly,

allowing his thumb leeway to trace her lower lip. "You know," he murmured, "the same thing can be said about flowers."

"Flowers?" Her body was too busy reacting to his touch to follow his comment clearly.

"Mmm. At first, all you see is an explosion of color and petals that won't last. But then they fool you, and you realize the blossoms are far sturdier and do a lot more than distract you with their beauty."

Gently, he urged her to turn and face him. "You, Kelsey, are a very sturdy flower."

That slow melting sensation grabbed hold of her spine, turning her insides soft. She could feel herself hovering on the edge of something. A shift between fantasy and reality that, if allowed to happen, might not be reversible. "Sure I'm not more a flowering weed?" she asked, seeking solid ground.

"Oh, but some of the sturdiest, prettiest, sweetest-smelling blossoms start out as weeds. They're also the ones you can't shake, no matter how hard you try."

"So I am a weed." Why didn't that sound bad to her?

"No, you're a completely original flower. One that's impossible to ignore. God knows, I've tried and failed all summer." He brushed the hair from her cheek.

Kelsey's mouth ran dry. Alex's words were touching a place deep inside her, a place she kept locked away from the world. The precipice loomed closer. Another step and she'd be lost to illusion and fantasy forever.

The fingers tracing her jaw reached her chin and tilted her face upward. She looked up and saw Alex's heavy-lidded eyes, as glazed and lost in the moment as she felt. "What would you do if I kissed you right now?" he asked.

"I—"

She didn't get the chance to finish.

Alex slanted his lips across hers. His kiss was like him: strong, confident with a hint of arrogant possession. As if he knew she'd readily submit. Doing just that, Kelsey wrapped her arms around his neck, and when she felt his tongue demanding entrance, she gave a soft sigh and complied. He tasted of mint and something more, something she suspected was uniquely Alex. It was heavenly.

The kiss ended far too soon. Alex was the one to break away, resting his forehead against hers. The air filled with the sound of their labored breathing.

"Well," he said once they'd regained their composure. "That—I—"

He was at a loss for words. Satisfaction filled Kelsey, that she could have that effect on him. "I know," she managed to whisper. She'd say more if he hadn't had the same effect on her. Although it was hardly her first kiss, it might as well have been. Her toes were still curling with pleasure.

There was an inevitability to the moment as well. Like they were simply coming to the end of a path they started back in June.

Alex's fingers were combing lazy lines through the loose hair on the back of her neck. Surrendering to the sensation, Kelsey closed her eyes. *I could stay here forever,* she thought, resting her cheek on his shoulder. "I hear music. Do you think the concert's started?"

"Don't know," he replied. "Possibly."

"Should we head back?"

He leaned back and looked her in the eye. "Do you want to?"

Something lurked behind his question—something important—but Kelsey was too lost in the moment to give it much thought. "Maybe in a few minutes."

"Just a few?" Alex teased.

"Maybe a little longer."

Alex cupped the back of her head. "Good answer," he whispered as he lowered his mouth to hers. "Good answer."

They never made it to their seats in the amphitheater. They listened from beneath a spreading oak tree at the edge of the lawn. Alex lay stretched on his side beside her. He'd shed his jacket, gallantly spreading it on the ground so her dress wouldn't grass stain. Every so often, she would look over and find him studying her with a contemplative expression. More often than not, he seemed to be studying her mouth which kept the memory of their kisses alive. Did he know her lips still tingled from the contact?

"What?" she asked finally, when his scrutiny became too much.

"Nothing," he replied. "Admiring the view is all."

He was lying. There was more to his gaze than admiration. She could see it pooling behind his eyes.

But, she didn't press. Couldn't press the issue, actually, because he leaned in and kissed her. A quick, chaste kiss, but enough to erase all thoughts.

The soloist, a pianist who really was quite good, switched from an overture to a ballad. Like the sultry music drifting into the night, Kelsey's insides slowed too. The whole experience was too dream-like to be real. It had to be a dream. Surely reality wouldn't feel this natural or this good. Would it?

Common sense told her to stop. That what she was feeling was nothing more than two people giving in to their attraction. But she didn't listen. As the music built to a crescendo, Kelsey drowned out the warning voice and let her feelings take charge. For the first time in her life she allowed herself to think that maybe, just maybe, she'd found where she belonged.

"What?" Alex asked.

It was her turn to stare at his mouth. How had she gone all summer without kissing them?

"Nothing," she said, bringing her lips towards his. "Enjoying the view is all."

Later that night, when Alex walked her upstairs, Kelsey couldn't feel her feet touching the ground. Come to think of it, she didn't remember feeling the ground since Alex kissed her. Had it dissolved away?

They stopped at her door. Pulse quickening, she leaned back against the wood and waited. Expectancy clung to the air. Only unlike the other night, she wasn't wondering about a good-night kiss, she was wondering if he would want more.

"Tonight was amazing," she said, looking up at him. "I can't remember when I had such a good time."

"Me neither. Hard to see it end, but—" he caressed her cheek with the back of his hand "—I think maybe it should. This time anyway."

Pressing her lips to the knuckles grazing them, Kelsey nodded. Even though her body was willing, taking things slowly was the right move. For now. And that Alex recognized that too only pulled her deeper under his spell. "Then I guess it's good-night," she said.

"Guess so."

Neither of them moved, making her giggle. "Good night, Alex."

He grinned, looking so boyish and adorable she nearly had trouble breathing. "Good night, Kelsey."

His mouth found hers. What started out sweet and gentle soon became heated, until the only sound Kelsey could hear was her blood pounding in her ears. Her bedroom door opened and they both stumbled across the threshold locked in the kiss. But instead of moving toward the bed as she expected, Alex lifted his head. "You make a man forget his resolve," he whispered, lips grazing her skin. "I better say good-night while I still can act like a gentleman."

Gently he pried her arms from his neck, ignoring her soft whimper. His kisses were far too addictive; she missed them already.

Reading her thoughts, he pressed one more to her lips. "Sweet dreams, Kelsey."

Sweet dreams? Wasn't she already dreaming? How else could she explain this evening?

She closed the door with a happy sigh. Was it possible for a woman to float away? Why not? She'd been floating all night, hadn't she?

Pressing her fingers to her lips, she smiled. They still tingled from Alex's kisses. His taste still lingered. She ran her tongue across her lower lip savoring his flavor. Remembering the possessive feel of his mouth as it covered hers.

Listen to yourself, she chided with a giggle. When did you get so fanciful?

She already knew. The moment Alex took her into his arms. His embrace felt secure. Right. She'd never felt anything so perfect.

Through the walls, she heard the scraping of a chair, followed by the sound of Alex's footsteps. What was he thinking right now? Was he thinking of her? Did he regret saying good-night? Was he, like her, counting minutes until they'd see each other again?

Dear Lord, she sounded like a smitten teenager. More proof tonight had to be a dream, because she'd never acted like that. Not even when she was a teenager. Surely, she'd wake up in the morning and reality would come crashing down. It always did.

Except for this time. Come breakfast, Kelsey

was still floating. In fact, she swore her feet didn't touch the stairs as she headed downstairs.

As it was normally her routine—although this morning felt anything but routine—she headed toward the office to check her e-mail. With all the activity yesterday, she hadn't touched base with Stuart. The editor hated radio silence. Weekend, weekday, it didn't make a difference. He no doubt flooded her inbox with requests for an update. Though she hadn't looked, she bet her cell phone inbox was full too.

Reaching the office, however, she paused. A soft, low voice drifted from the terrace. Looking out, she saw Alex, his back to her, his head focused on his lap.

"You're a mangy son-of-a-gun, you know that don't you?" He spoke in a singsong voice, like what you'd use to address a child. The rhythm washed over her, making her smile. "A big fat mangy thing."

A flick of orange flashed by his elbow revealing his conversation partner. Where she'd been floating, she now tumbled, her insides turning in a weightless free fall. That he could be so sweet with a cat he supposedly didn't like…

"Careful," she said, "he might get insulted."

Alex turned and flashed a brilliant smile. So brilliant Kelsey had to grab the door frame. To wake up to that smile every day. The thought popped into her head so quickly that for a second, her heart stilled. Surely she didn't really think this could be something permanent, did she? She wasn't a permanent person. Alex wasn't either. Was he?

"I don't think he cares what I say as long as I rub his belly," Alex said, still smiling. He looked back to his lap. "Unfortunately, pal, our moment is over."

He rose, the motion causing the cat to slide unceremoniously from his lap. "How about you?"

"Are you asking if I want my belly rubbed?"

"Mmm, interesting idea." A sultry sparkle appeared in his eyes. The free fall inside her gathered momentum. Doubly so when he crossed the space and slipped his good arm around her waist. "However, I'll settle for a good-morning kiss."

Their bodies molded together as if they'd never said good-night. "Now that," Alex said when they finally broke for air, "is how a morning should start. Who needs coffee?"

"Unfortunately I do," she said with a smile. His kisses were as wonderful as she remembered. So wonderful she still couldn't believe this—they—were real. "Once a caffeine addict, always a caffeine addict, I'm afraid."

"Cast aside for a cup of Italian roast. I should be insulted. Though I guess I can forgive you. This time." He punctuated his answer with a kiss to her nose.

"You're so generous."

"Plus, I already had a cup."

"Cheater!" Kelsey gave his arm a playful slap, which he laughed off.

"Tell you what. Why don't we go get you a travel mug, refill mine, and have breakfast on the rocks? I feel like playing hooky today."

"You do, do you?"

"Uh-huh. Think your boss will let you come play with me?"

"I don't know. He's pretty tough."

"Don't worry. I'll persuade him. I can be very persuasive when I try."

She'd been expecting him to release her so they could head to the kitchen, but he didn't. Instead, he nuzzled the crook of her neck.

"So I see," she replied. He was nibbling a path across her skin, his nose nudging the strap of her yellow tank top. Kelsey arched her neck allowing him better access. Her fingers slipped up to tangle his dark curls. A soft moan left her lips.

Alex swirled his tongue across the hollow above her collarbone. "That a yes?"

Yes, yes, yes. Right now she'd say yes to everything.

He gave her one more deep, toe-curling kiss before letting her go. "Good. Hold that thought. I'll grab some breakfast and we'll be on our way."

"Can I help?"

"Nope. I've got everything under control. You can think of other things you might need persuading about. And you, pal—" he turned to Puddin', who had reclaimed his spot on the abandoned chair and was waiting expectantly "—will have to find someone else to rub your belly. Kelsey and I have petting of our own to do."

Though outwardly she giggled, inside Kelsey shivered with excitement. Glancing up through her lashes, she whispered, "Can't wait."

"Me neither." He kissed her again and disappeared into the office.

Too full of anticipation to simply wait, she headed into the office herself and fired up her laptop. Might as well do what she started and check in with Stuart before he started sending telegrams or something.

Sure enough, there were close to a dozen messages from the man dating back over the past couple days. "Human grain of sand," she murmured to herself. He could wear down the President of the

United States. But it was his last message that caught her eye first. Marked urgent, the subject line read HAVE YOU SEEN THIS?!! Intrigued, Kelsey clicked open the link.

In a flash, her dream became a nightmare.

CHAPTER NINE

"But the biggest surprise of the evening was the reappearance of prize-winning novelist Alex Markoff, who let slip he's working on his long-awaited comeback novel. From the looks of things, the novel isn't his only comeback."

Alex slapped the blog printout on his desk, his palm landing on the photo of them kissing during the concert. "How did they—?"

"Camera phone most likely," Kelsey replied. Unfortunately paparazzi technology had become more advanced during his hermitage.

Upsetting as the photo was, however, it wasn't nearly as disturbing as the blogger's byline. Tom Forbes. Kelsey felt sick. "When I asked him what he did for a living, he said a little bit of everything. I swear, if I had known…"

Alex wasn't listening. He'd moved away from the deck over to the garden windows. Staring out at the tree line, he looked so worn down it hurt to look at him. "I should have known. What made me think the world—people—had changed."

The defeat in his voice killed her. She didn't have to see his expression to know it was shrouded in darkness. He was folding into himself. Retreating.

Kelsey's stomach churned. She might as well have really crashed to earth, the change was so sudden and sharp. Only ten minutes ago they were in each other's arms.

Damn Tom Forbes for using them like that.

You mean using you. God, what an idiot she'd been. The one thing Alex feared more than anything, and she led it straight to his doorstep.

She made her way to the window and placed a hand on his shoulder. A pang stabbed her heart when he flinched. "I swear, Alex, I didn't know. When he offered me the tickets, I thought—"

"He gave you the tickets?"

It was her turn to flinch, from both the harshness of his voice and the memory. It was supposed to show there were no hard feelings. A friendly gesture. "He set me up. He saw us at Farley's and he set us up. I had no idea he would misuse our friendship for a story."

"People use people all the time."

"Including me?"

He didn't answer, which hurt more than if he had. "I don't know what made me think the world would change. People are as miserable as they always were. Concerned only with their personal agendas, ready to sell you out at the first opportunity. You can't trust anyone."

"You can trust me."

Again, no reply. He was slipping away with each passing moment, letting the betrayals of the past take over. She could feel the gulf widening and her words couldn't reach across the chasm. Reaching out, she tried one more time. "It's one blog, Alex. One of a million. He's probably got no more than a dozen readers." But even as she offered her reassurance, she knew audience size wasn't the point. This was about the betrayal. A return to the world he left five years ago where his wife used his fame, and his friends sold him out to the highest bidder. "I know you're angry..."

"Angry?" He shook his head. "I'm not angry. How can you be angry at reality?"

"But it's not reality. Not everyone has an agenda, Alex, or is out to use you."

"Really? Name one."

"Me."

He looked at the hand she placed on his shoulder, then to her eyes. "Then you're the lone swimmer in a very cold ocean," he replied. "Not to mention naïve. You, of all people, should know I'm right."

Because of her grandmother. But this was

different. Surely he had to realize she wouldn't hurt him. *Except you already did.* "Face it, Kelsey, the world is never going to change." He shrugged off her touch. "I should never have thought otherwise. It was a mistake."

He was calling last night a mistake. Did that mean he considered her a mistake too?

Alex had pulled away and was heading toward the door. "Where are you going?" she asked.

"For a walk. I need to get out of here and get some fresh air."

"Good idea. Let's go to the rocks and you can clear your head."

"No."

Kelsey stopped. He'd said the one word she feared he would say. "But you just said—"

"I'm going alone. I need to be alone. The way I should have stayed in the first place."

Watching him disappear in the garden, Kelsey wondered if she'd ever feel this morning's joy again.

She should have realized a dream as good as this morning's couldn't last. By suppertime, she wondered if it ever existed. Alex still hadn't returned from his "walk." He was avoiding her. Kelsey sat in the great room, studying the garden. It was like the early summer all over again. Only this time

Nuttingwood felt colder and more empty than ever. Not even the insistent presence of Puddin' could dull the ache inside her.

Curse Tom Forbes and his blog. Did he have any idea of the damage he caused? She wanted to grab him by his tacky tropical print shirt and choke him until he apologized. Not that an apology would make any difference. Alex was gone. At the first sign of his precious privacy being invaded, he'd retreated into his woods. Into himself. Away from her.

Vision blurring, she blinked to keep the tears at bay. You'd think she'd be used to rejection by this point in her life.

That's what you get for growing complacent. Rolling to her side, she drew her knees to her chest. She should have stuck to her rules. Don't get involved. Don't form connections. But no, she had to let her guard down. Let herself fall for a man with stormy eyes and walls around his heart as thick as Jericho.

Fool. Thinking she was worth Alex dropping his defenses. Like the man said, she was a mistake.

She squeezed her eyes shut, blocking the tears. If only life came with do-overs. If it did, she'd push reset and never step foot on Alex Markoff's doorstep. Sadly, however, life didn't, and once again, she wasn't wanted.

* * *

When she opened her eyes again, morning was streaming through the windows. Still half-asleep she sniffed for the familiar smell of coffee, her insides dropping when she didn't find it. The great room was empty. A quick check of the kitchen and office revealed they were too. An empty glass in the sink told her Alex had come and gone. Still avoiding. Still retreating.

Well, no sense waiting for the inevitable. If Alex didn't want her around, she wasn't going to stay. Not where she wasn't wanted. Not anymore. Wiping a tear from her cheek, she headed upstairs to her room to pack.

Like moving in, moving out also came with a ritual. First the clothes from the closet were folded and sorted. When she got to the pink cocktail dress, she clutched the garment to her cheek. A faint trace of Alex's aftershave clung to the silk. Holding it close was like holding him. She inhaled deeply and wished she could hold on to the scent forever.

But nothing stayed forever.

Bureau contents came next. Underwear, T-shirts. The blue running shorts she wore their afternoon in the woods. She ran a hand across the cloth. She'd never felt more at home, more like she belonged than when she sat on those rocks with Alex.

"No crying," she told herself, swiping another errant tear. Tears were not part of the ritual. It was a rule. You left a place with your head held high, not looking back.

Lastly came the personal belongings. Gently she picked up her ceramic mug, cracked and crooked, never to hold liquid again.

Good thing I had glue.

Yes. A very good thing.

How could she ever look at the cup again without thinking of Alex? Her vision blurred. That was the problem with the rules. They didn't apply when your heart was being ripped from your body. A sob rose in her chest, choking off her breath. She tried to fight its release, but couldn't. Gasping for air, she finally let the tears break free. They ran down her cheeks in hot streaks.

Why couldn't Alex want her?

CHAPTER TEN

Iт took a while, but eventually Kelsey regained her composure. Placing the last of her belongings in her satchel, she took one last look at the room she'd come to call home. Outside the open window, a breeze rustled the trees. She thought of the owl and said a mental goodbye. The bird would be forever linked in her mind with the image of Alex's smile. Both had looked so breathtaking that night.

Like so many other things, that night was part of the past now. She was moving on, like she'd done so many times before in her life, and as she swore a long time ago, under her own terms. Eventually the ache in her chest would fade. She'd grown attached to places before and recovered.

Except this time it wasn't just a place, and she was far more than attached to Alex. She was in love.

She left her mother's coffee mug behind. In its new form, it reminded her too much of Alex.

Looking at it no longer gave her comfort. Better to leave the cup behind and make a clean break.

"Goodbye," she whispered, tracing the faded flowers one last time. Her summer at Nuttingwood was over.

Wonder how long it would take for Alex to notice she was gone?

Turned out Alex learned her plans immediately. He was walking up the stairs when she opened the door. Dust and sweat streaked his clothes, and there were mosquito bites dotting his skin. He moved with slow, deliberate movements, clearly trying to keep his head still. It didn't take a genius to recognize what was going on. "Headache?" she asked.

He looked up, the pale skin and dark circles providing her answer. "Nothing I'm not used to."

Except he hadn't had one in weeks. Not since that one afternoon. "Did you take your medicine?"

He shook his head. "I was on the rocks all night."

Avoiding her. Part of her, the angry, hurt part, decided he deserved his misery. Unfortunately, the other part of her, the bigger part, couldn't leave him when he was in pain.

Setting down her suitcases, she took his elbow. Despite the circumstances, heat rose up her arm.

"Come on, let's get you lying down, and I'll get your pills."

His eyes dropped to her suitcases as they headed to his room. "You're leaving."

"If I'm not around, Tom can't blog about our so-called relationship, can he?"

"No, I suppose he can't."

"That way you can get your privacy back."

"Yes, I suppose I can."

She led him to his room and to the side of his king-size bed. His bed was still unmade from the other morning. He'd kissed her in this doorway. She bit her lip before the memory made her sigh. Instead she focused on the business at hand and said, "Pills are still in the medicine cabinet, I assume."

Alex had slid beneath the covers when she returned. Seeing him lying against the sheets, his skin pale, his breathing ragged, Kelsey's heart ached. Even miserable, he was still the most breathtaking man she'd ever seen. *Don't let me go,* Kelsey wanted to plead. *Ask me to stay.*

She held out the pills and a glass of water. "You should have something to eat. You'll keep your medicine down better."

"I'll be fine. I just need to rest. What are you going to tell Stuart? About leaving?"

"I'll call him from the road and explain. He saw

the blog. I'm sure he'll get it. He'll send another secretary."

"At four times the pay instead of three," Alex slurred. Suddenly his sleepy eyes widened. "Your debt. You were counting on the money."

"I'll figure something out. I'm very good at adapting."

"Still, it's not fair that you should suffer." His eyes grew heavy again. The medicine and his exhaustion were too strong to fight.

Kelsey's fingers itched to touch his cheek.

"Like I said, I'll figure something out."

"I could pay it off for you."

Charity. Kelsey bit the inside of her mouth. She wanted his heart; he offered charity. Story of her life. "No, I don't want your money."

"But—"

"You're not responsible for my problems, Alex."

"Aren't I?"

No. He couldn't help not wanting her. "You're exhausted, Alex. Stop fighting and go to sleep."

"In a minute. What about Puddin'? What will you do with him?"

"He's a survivor too," she replied. "Put out a bowl of food in the morning and he'll forget all about me."

"You assume you're easy to forget."

Wasn't she? *Easy to forget, and easy to let go.* "Go to sleep, Alex."

"Kelsey, I don't..." The sentence drifted off unfinished. Guess she'd never know what he was going to say.

Unable to help herself, she pressed one last kiss to his parted lips and headed to the door.

One thing about emotional goodbyes, they left you drained. Kelsey barely got to the bottom of the hill when her own head began aching. Not having had her coffee this morning wasn't helping. Along with feeling guilty that she left while Alex was sleeping.

She didn't have a choice. He would be asleep for hours, she rationalized. If she stayed, she wouldn't get to New York until late, and she still had to find a place to sleep. Or worse, she would have to postpone leaving until tomorrow.

That's really why you left. You didn't want to spend another night and relive the rejection again in the morning.

Would someone *ever* want her?

Her caffeine-deprivation too loud to ignore, she turned onto Main Street. She could stop at the Leafy Bean and grab a cup for the road, before leaving the town—and the stubborn, guarded man she'd fallen so disastrously in love with—far behind.

Farley was in between rushes and stocking shelves when she arrived. Spotting him by the canned fruit, she gave a quick wave before heading toward the coffee station, grateful he wouldn't ask about her red-rimmed eyes. "How's the hazelnut this morning?"

"Same as every morning," he grumbled. "Popular. You tourists and your fancy coffee flavors. Hazelnut, French vanilla caramel nut. Italian roast. Every time I turn around I gotta brew more."

It was his way of saying the coffee was fresh. "Is this the largest size cup you have?"

"Do you see anything larger?"

"Thanks." Hollowed out with grief as she felt, Kelsey still smiled. The old man might be a cranky curmudgeon, short on patience, but he was an original. "I'm going to miss you, Farley."

He looked up from the canned peaches he was stocking and gave her a curious look. For a split second, she swore it was gratitude and—dare she say—affection sparkling behind his glasses. "Can't miss me unless you leave," he replied in typical Farley fashion.

The doorbell sounded and a female voice called out, "Good morning, Farley."

"What's so good about it," he snapped back

before adding under his breath, "Stupid customers. How's a man supposed to get any work done with everyone yapping away at me."

Yup, definitely she would miss Farley. She turned back to the coffee station, thinking there was a lot about the town she'd miss. She'd felt comfortable here. Which was part of the problem, she reminded herself. She'd let herself grow attached to her location. *Another connection.* She'd really broken her rules left and right this summer, hadn't she?

Sighing to herself, she added a healthy dollop of cream to her coffee. Farley believed in strong coffee, stronger than what Alex made. Alex made coffee exactly the way she liked.

Stop thinking about him. He was in the past now. He had to be. For self-preservation's sake, she had to stop dwelling on memories. Before leaving, she would ask Farley to look in on Alex, and then she wouldn't let his name cross her mind again.

Behind her, the new customers debated about groceries. Kelsey was reaching for a travel lid when suddenly a familiar female voice rang out across the store. "Tom, do you think two pounds of potato salad will be enough?"

Tom. Her hand stilled. The son-of-a… Anger replaced grief, welling up inside her like a summer storm.

"You!" She stormed toward the group of tourists, straight to the blond man in his tropical print shirt. Oh, it would be so easy to grab that flowered collar and twist. Or better yet, slap that smug-looking face. Especially when he smiled like nothing had ever happened.

"Hello, Kelsey. You saw the blog, I take it."

"How could you?"

"How could I what? Report news?"

Like he was a reporter. He was nothing more than a sleazy bottom-feeder. "Alex and I are *not* news!"

"Then what are you?"

"We're—"

From the corner of her eye, she saw Tom's companions watching the exchange with interest. Behind her, Farley was no doubt doing the same. Whatever she said would clearly be gossip fodder for them all.

Well, to hell with them and their gossip. He'd already destroyed whatever it was she had with Alex. What did she care if they talked more? "We're none of your business, that's what we are."

As expected, he waved off the remark. "Come on, of course you're my business. Alex Markoff's one of this century's most influential writers. People are interested in his life."

"That doesn't give you the right to splash our private moments all over the Internet!"

"Hey, if you wanted privacy, you shouldn't have made out in public for all the world to see." He smirked. "Or maybe attention's what you were looking for. After all, you did take those tickets."

Thawp! Thirty-six hours of hurt and anger erupted in her palm connecting with his cheek. The force of the blow could be heard throughout the store. It left a bright red print on the side of Tom's face. "Never come near me again," she spat.

She left the store without another word. From the road, she'd call Farley to check on Alex. Right now she wanted as much distance between her and Tom Forbes as possible.

Her foot didn't touch the brakes until the Bean, the town center and most of the buildings were gone from her rearview mirror. Five miles after that, the shakes began. Pulling over, she tried to calm herself by taking a deep breath. It didn't work.

Her hand still stung from the contact. Way to make a bad situation worse, Kelsey. She'd just given Tom the perfect headline for tomorrow's blog. Writer's Gal Pal Goes Ballistic. She balled her hand into a fist.

And wished she'd thrown a punch instead.

CHAPTER ELEVEN

NEW York City was noisy. In only a couple months Kelsey had forgotten exactly how noisy. She hadn't had a good night's sleep since she returned a week ago.

Who are you kidding? It's not the noise keeping you awake. She missed Nuttingwood.

She missed Alex.

At least financially, she was close to solvency. Last night she wrote out her last loan payment. Grandma Rosie's debt was gone. As she addressed the envelope, she realized she didn't get the same pang in her chest she used to get when thinking of her grandmother. Guess she was finally letting go of the old woman.

Too bad she couldn't let go of other things. A lump stuck in her throat. Two weeks and Alex was as lodged in her heart as strongly as ever. Curse him. The lump grew a little bigger. Why wouldn't he get out of her head? Why did he have to go and lower her defenses in the first place, worming his way inside and making her dream stupid, unrealistic dreams?

Making her fall in love.

Worst of all, she had become stuck. With her debt paid, she should be focusing on where to restart her life. The future was a clean slate. She could do anything she wanted. Problem was, nothing felt right. Not any of the jobs her temp agency found her. Not with any of the apartments she looked at. For goodness' sake, she was still in extended-stay lodging. She needed to make some decisions.

She needed to let Alex go.

Well, to start, she could mail Grandma Rosie's check and cross that item off her to-do list. Grabbing the envelope and her sunglasses, she headed out.

The minute she stepped outside, the heat and noise wrapped around her like a loud oppressive blanket. The ache in her chest increased tenfold. Oh, to feel the soft Berkshire breezes again, and smell the sweet smell of trees.

Stop it! Stop dwelling on things you can't have. Why couldn't she let go?

"Excuse me." A young woman wearing a plaid mini jumper and designer sunglasses approached her at the bottom of the front steps. "Kelsey Albertelli, right?"

The hair on the back of her neck prickling, Kelsey dodged the question. "Do you need something?"

"Is it true Alex Markoff stopped work on his book after you dumped him?"

"Excuse me?" The question caught her off guard. Enough that she foolishly stopped walking, giving the woman time for another question.

"His comeback novel. Is it true his publisher's suing him?"

Suing? Dear Lord, no. That couldn't be true, could it? "I—I—"

"Why don't you mind your own business."

Her insides stilled hearing the baritone. It couldn't be. The timbre was merely similar. They were talking about Alex so her mind conjured up his voice. That's what it had to be, right?

The reporter meanwhile was smirking to land such an exclusive scoop. "Maybe you'd like to address the rumors yourself, Mr. Markoff."

Kelsey turned to find a pair of storm-cloud-colored eyes. Her heart stilled. "Alex?" This had to be a dream.

Though if it was, then her dream was taking her wrist and pulling her away. "Print whatever you want," he tossed over his shoulder. "We have no comment."

Fortunately traffic, not to mention Alex's expert car dodging, kept the reporter from following them across the street. He pulled her through the crowds of pedestrians and down a block before releasing her. "Sorry about that," he said.

Not as sorry as she was that he'd let go of her hand. He was as handsome as ever. Instinctively, her body swayed toward him, seeking contact again.

"What are you doing here?" she heard herself ask.

He smiled that familiar sad smile that was but wasn't. "You got time for a cup of coffee?"

They found seats in a nearby coffee house. Settling in by the window, Kelsey couldn't but think if the reporter walked by, she'd have a perfect view. It was, perhaps, the only coherent thought permeating her brain, everything else drowned in a fog of disbelief. Alex. Here.

"Stuart put me in touch with your temp agency. They told me where to find you," Alex explained, sliding into the seat next to her.

He tracked her down? Don't get your hopes up, Kelsey. Just don't. "So you talked to Stuart."

"Oh, he and I have had several conversations. Some more colorful than others."

She could imagine. The editor had been furious when she called to resign. "He still issuing threats?"

"Nothing I won't work out."

Silence settled between them. Kelsey used the moment to study Alex. He certainly looked better than when she left. He'd gotten a haircut. The curls didn't brush his collar anymore. And he was wearing a striped shirt she'd never seen before, the sleeves rolled to the elbow.

That's when she realized. "You got your cast off."

He wriggled the fingers on his right hand. "Yesterday. Dr. Cohen finally got tired of listening to me complain."

"Must be nice to have two working hands again."

"Feels a little weird actually. Driving here was an adventure. I'm not used to shifting gears again."

"You should have waited till you had more practice."

"But then I would have had to wait longer to see you."

Kelsey grabbed her latte with both hands, steadying herself against the skip in her heart.

Unfortunately she couldn't steady her voice. "You wanted to see me?"

"You left this behind." For the first time, she realized there was a plastic shopping bag by his feet. He must have carried it in with them, but she had been too stunned to notice. Reaching into it, he pulled out a bulky tissue-wrapped package.

Without unwrapping, she knew what the object was. Her mug. "Why'd you leave it?"

"I decided it was time to let some things go."

"I see. What else did you let go of?"

Him. Fantasies. Kelsey kept the answers to herself, settling for running an index finger along the tissue and tape. "You didn't have to drive all the way down here to return a coffee cup."

"Ah, but this isn't an ordinary cup is it? And I didn't. I drove down here to see you."

She closed her eyes. "Alex—"

"You left without saying goodbye."

Is that what his trip was about? Closure? "You were asleep." *And didn't want her.*

"I wish you had."

"Why?" To drag out the inevitable? So he could reject her face to face? "Didn't Farley come check on you? I called and asked him."

"He did."

"Good."

"I would have preferred it had been you."

"I don't know why. You made where you stood pretty clear the second you took off for the woods." Leaving her.

Alex nodded, his Adam's apple bobbing in his throat as he swallowed her words. "I was angry," he said.

"No kidding."

"When I saw that blog article, it was like being thrust back in time. Alyssa and all those articles— it all came rushing back and it hurt. It hurt so much I could barely breathe. I just wanted to be numb again. To find someplace to hide again."

"I get that. Believe me, if anyone gets self-protection, it's me."

"I know. I told you before, we're a lot alike. Defensive and stubborn, among other things. It's why I had to wait and see you in person, because I knew you wouldn't take my calls."

No, thought Kelsey. She wouldn't have, however much she would have longed to.

He reached across the table and covered her hand with his. The warmth ran up her arm, igniting the familiar and painful heat. "When I woke up and you weren't there… The house felt so big and empty. For the first time since I moved to Nuttingwood, I truly felt alone."

Kelsey watched the fingers playing with hers. Her heart was afraid to believe what she was hearing. Surely she was misreading the situation. Again.

"I miss you." With his free hand, he caught her chin, forcing her to meet his eyes. "I don't want to be alone anymore."

Before she could respond, he leaned in and kissed her. A slow, tender, toe-curling kiss right there in the window for all the world to see. When he finished, he pressed his forehead to hers. "God, I missed you."

Me too. More than she thought possible. But as beautiful and perfect as the moment felt, could she trust it? "What about Alyssa? The past?" How did she know he wouldn't decide to hide again, leaving her even more broken?

"You're not Alyssa," he replied. "What we have is completely different. Though if I had any doubts—" chuckling, he pulled a folded piece of paper from his breast pocket "—this would have convinced me."

It was a printout of Tom's blog, written the day after their encounter at Farley's. She'd been too afraid to search for the article herself. As predicted, the story portrayed her as an out-of-control madwoman, an image helped along by a camera-phone shot of her just after she slapped Tom's face. The wild look in her eyes made her cheeks burn.

"Do you have any idea what I thought when I saw this?"

"I lost my temper. I'm sorry."

"Clearly. And don't apologize," Alex said, slipping the paper from her fingers. "No one has ever fought for me when it came to the press. Used me, sold me out, but defend me? Never. Seeing the photo made me realize how lucky I was to have you by my side, and that only a fool would push you away."

"Of course—" he tweaked the tip of her nose "—if someone had stuck around, I would have told her I'd figured that out while in the woods that night. Seems I'm not the only one with a habit of retreating."

She had retreated. She'd hidden behind her temporary status the same way he used Nuttingwood. And what happened? She got hurt anyway. Alex got into her heart, and no amount of running would lodge him loose.

Now with his declaration, he was offering her a chance to stop hiding. If only she could find the strength to accept.

Please don't let this be a dream. "Are you saying…"

"I'm saying I want you to come back."

He wanted her. The words were more beautiful than any novel he could ever write. Still, she hesitated. It all sounded too good to be true. "You mean as your assistant."

"I mean as a lot more than that. I want you. I need you." He cradled her cheek with the palm of his hand, his eyes bright and moist. "That's what I realized sitting out on those rocks all night long. I've needed you since the first time you knocked on my door."

"Could have fooled me," she said, lip trembling. Was this really happening? "If I recall you turned your back and walked away."

"Because I was a jackass," he said with a smile. Kelsey's insides melted at the sight. "You scared the life out of me. You made me feel so much. I liked it. More than I wanted to admit."

The smile grew serious. "But I'm not walking away anymore. Not from you or the feelings. I love you, Kelsey Albertelli."

With those three words, the last of the fear in her heart faded away. No one had ever told her they loved her, and hearing the words come from Alex felt like a dream come true.

Covering his hand with hers, she gazed into his eyes. Eyes no longer stormy but shining like silver. Shining with love. For her.

"I love you too," she whispered. She pulled him toward her for a soul-searing kiss, one that con-

veyed every ounce of emotion she felt and never
dreamed she'd be able to share.

When the kiss finally ended, she opened her
eyes and saw the same emotion pouring off of
Alex's expression. "What do you say, sweetheart?
Ready to go home?"

"So what do you think?"

Kelsey wiped a stray tear from her cheek. "I
think you're brilliant," she replied with a sniff.

"Thanks, but what about the story? Do you think
it's too schmaltzy?"

Alex paced around the bedroom where Kelsey
had camped out to read his finished manuscript.
Puddin' lay sprawled by her side, holding down
the pile of pages with his paw. Shortly after they
returned to Nuttingwood, Alex had been gripped
with a creative flash, spending hours scribbling
away on his yellow pads. Kelsey didn't mind. Alex
in the throes of a creative frenzy was a sight to
behold, all brilliance and distraction. The story
poured out of him and within a week he had a completed first draft. A beautiful, poignant tale of lost
and rediscovered love. "I know Stuart's expecting
the other book, but my writing reflects how I feel,
and I just can't write dark right now."

"I'm flattered."

"You should be." He flopped down on the bed

beside her and planted a kiss on her nose. "My very beautiful muse."

She kissed him back. "The story's perfect," she told him. "People are going to fall in love with your writing all over again."

"I don't care if readers love me, as long as you do."

More than she ever thought possible. "I think you're safe there." Sometimes she thought she would burst, she loved him so much.

"Good, because I plan on loving you forever."

Manuscript forgotten, they reached for each other. Later, as Kelsey lay sated and sleepy in Alex's arms, she felt him nuzzle her forehead. "I was thinking," he murmured. "Now that I've met my obligations to Stuart, why don't we slip away?"

She smiled. "You mean like hide?"

"Kinda, though I was thinking more like a honeymoon hideaway." He fingered the wedding band on her finger. They'd gotten married in the local town hall, during a break in Alex's writing. "What do you say? We could do Europe? Or is that too far from home for you?"

"I say—" she rolled over, and wrapped her arms around his neck "—that as long as I'm with you, I'm already home."

NINE-TO-FIVE BRIDE

JENNIE ADAMS

For Fiona Harper and Melissa McClone.
How much fun was this?

For Joanne Carr and Kimberley Young, with
thanks for making the www.blinddatebrides.com
trilogy a reality.

And to the special man in my life—I won't tell
we agreed on marriage on our first date if
you don't!

CHAPTER ONE

'YOU want us to turn this smaller bridge into a clone of the historic Pyrmont Bridge. I'm sorry, but we can't do that for you. The sites simply don't compare.' The boss of the Sydney-based Morgan Construction, Building and Architecture braced his feet on the uninspiring bridge in question, drew a deep breath and blew it out as he addressed the middle-aged man at his side.

Rick Morgan's rich voice held an edge of command and control that shivered over Marissa Warren's senses. The three of them stood atop the small Sydney bridge while the Morgan's boss explained the company's stance on the refurbishment plans. Rick could bring about virtually any architectural feat, be it in refurbishment or new construction. What he wasn't prepared to do was break his own code of working standards.

A pity Marissa couldn't push away her equally unfeasible reactions to the man. She hadn't expected an attack of awareness of the company's big boss. The girls in the office swooned about Rick, but Marissa was no longer interested in hot corporate types. Been there, so over that.

It must be the sway factor of the bridge getting to her. Or the sea wind pressing hard against her back trying to disrupt her balance. Those must be responsible for the odd feelings coursing through her.

Anything other than genuine attraction to this corporate high-flyer who owned the large company that employed her. Since she'd started at Morgan's six months ago she hadn't said more than 'good morning' to the boss in passing and, frankly, close proximity to a man with power on his mind made her want to run in the other direction, as fast as her pink glow-in-the-dark joggers could take her.

It hadn't exactly worked out well for her the last time, had it? Tricked, taken advantage of and publicly dumped, all in the name of career advancement. Michael Unsworth's, to be precise.

Marissa tugged her gold blouse into place over the chocolate skirt and noted Rick's words on her steno pad. *Not noticing him.* Not the charisma, nor the stunning grey eyes fringed with thick black lashes. Certainly not the leashed sensuality that seemed an integral part of him. So totally not noticing any of that.

Anyway, she'd just recently finished telling her Blinddatebrides.com friends Grace and Dani, aka Englishcrumpet and Sanfrandani, about her utter commitment to finding her Mr Ordinary. Though she'd only known Dani and Grace over the Internet a matter of weeks, they were wonderful women and understood and encouraged Marissa's dating goals. She meant to find that Mr Ordinary, to prove to the world... Well, simply to prove she could control her own destiny, thanks very much.

'This bridge isn't a key thoroughfare, Cartwright. It doesn't impact on port access for large seafaring craft.' Rick's strong tanned hand gestured to emphasise his words. 'It isn't a Heritage listed structure and its refurbishment won't make it look like one. The work needs to be about strength, durability and safety in keeping with the established design. The company's initial assessment explained this.'

The bridge spanned two small juts of Sydney's coastline. It rested within the city's sprawling confines but was far from core harbour material. Here there were no stunning views. No Sydney Harbour Bridge. No shell-shaped Opera House rising as though directly from the water.

Unlike Pyrmont, with its massive central swing span, this bridge was just a smallish, nondescript one tucked away on a commercial section of shore.

'You're not listening to what I want.' Cartwright's mouth tightened.

'I've listened. As did the Project Manager who liaised with you initially. The advice in his report was sound.' Overhead, a seagull offered a cry to the pale blue sky as it searched the ocean below for food.

Rick had a strong face to match his strong tone. Wide cheekbones and a firm square jaw that, even at nine-thirty in the morning, revealed a dark beard shadow beneath the skin. A tall vital man with thick shoulders and defined musculature beneath the perfectly cut charcoal suit and pale green shirt.

Marissa didn't want to be aware of him, but she couldn't seem to help it.

'We can make something truly stupendous of this area.' Cartwright repeated his mantra.

Again.

For about the tenth time, paying apparently no attention at all to Rick's explanation.

The company boss growled softly beneath his breath.

It was not a sexy growl!

Marissa inhaled the tang of sea air and Rick's citrusy after-shave cologne and stopped herself from closing her eyes in what would have been a completely inappropriate appreciative sigh.

Instead, she forced her attention to Cartwright's rounded face. Maybe she could help... 'Since you're limited with what you can do in terms of refurbishing this bridge, perhaps you could implement some onshore improvements to empha-sise the dock area and make the most of that aspect of things?'

'My thoughts exactly, Marissa. Something more commercially viable.' Rick cast a quick glance her way, offering a small nod of approval. The quirk of his lips that went with that approval made her tummy flutter.

Okay, so the company boss could show appreciation as well as look good. He still fell under the *Tall, Dark and Aggressive about Success* category.

She reminded herself rather desperately that that definition was one hundred per cent not right for her. Despite what her headed-for-thirty-years-of-age and back in the dating pool hormones might suggest otherwise. What did they know, anyway?

Enough to make her join a dating site, and to recognise an appealing man when she saw one?

The first had been a sensible, well-considered decision, nothing more, and, as for the second...

'Not going there,' Marissa muttered towards the foaming sea and tossed her head of curly hair before she remembered the hard hat squashed over the top of it.

Fine, so the impact was lost a little. And she hadn't actually been thinking about emotions. She'd made her choices clinically. That was all she needed to remember. Marissa grimaced and shoved the hat out of her eyes.

'Are you all right?' Rick leaned his head close to hers. The grey of his eyes deepened with a combination of amusement and interest as his gaze roved over the hard hat, her face, the hair sticking out about her cheeks and neck.

'I'm fine, thank you.' He probably wondered why she'd tossed her head like that. 'It was nothing, really. I had a twitch.'

In the brain. It started when I looked into your eyes this morning as you said, 'Good, you're here,' in that deep, toe-curling voice and it hiccups back every time I look at you or listen to you.

'Er…a twitch that made my head nod and the hat fall forward.'

Toe-curling, *authoritative* voice, Marissa. Get it right if you're going to think it at all.

'I see.' Though his lips didn't move, Rick's eyes smiled.

Marissa stared at that charming expression and thought, *deadly*. The man was deadly to her senses.

'A central steel swing span—' Cartwright began again.

'Would require a whole new bridge, one far larger than this one and located in deeper water.' Rick raised a hand as though to push it through his hair—also covered by a hard hat, except in his case he looked good in it—and dropped it to his side again. 'As Hedley told you in his assessment.'

'Hedley isn't management level,' the man spluttered. 'He doesn't understand some of the committee members' vision for the project. We could have the bridge swing open and closed at certain times of the day—a ceremonial thing even if only smaller craft passed through. It could create a major tourist attraction.'

'But you don't have the funds or planning permission to make that kind of change,' Rick pointed out gently, 'nor the conditions or traffic to demand it.'

'I have influence where the approval is concerned.' Cartwright suddenly turned to glare in Marissa's direction. 'Are you getting all this, girly? I don't see that pen moving.'

'It's a stenographer's pencil,' Marissa corrected kindly while Rick's big body stiffened at her side. 'I've written down every new piece of information you've provided and, actually, I'm almost thirty. Not quite a "girly" any more.'

'*Miss Warren* is part of the Morgan's team. She is not—'

'Not at all perturbed,' Marissa inserted while a flow of gratified warmth filled her.

Rick drew a breath. His gaze locked with hers and the starch left him. His voice dipped about an octave as he murmured, 'Well, you really don't look…'

'That old?' She meant her response to sound cheerful, unconcerned. Instead, it came out with a breathless edge, the result of that considering gaze on her. Of the way he had championed her, despite never having worked directly with her until today.

And perhaps a little because of her need not to feel quite as ancient as she did in the face of her looming birthday. 'Thank you for thinking so.'

Thank you very, very much and you look appealing yourself. Very appealing.

Did hormones have voices? Whispery ones that piped up right when they were least welcome?

First chance we get, Marissa thought, those hormones and I are having a Come To Mama meeting and I'm telling them who's in charge of this show. Namely, me.

Stupid birthdays, anyway. They should be cancelled after twenty-five and never referred to again.

You'll have found Mr Right by your birthday and won't have time to notice that over a third of your estimated life span has passed you by while you wasted some of it on Michael Unsworth, the cheating, lying, using—

'Well. What was it we were saying?' Marissa forced a smile. She mustn't think of Michael, *or* of Rick Morgan's charismatic presence.

'We were discussing this bridge...' Prosaic words but Rick's gaze moved over her with a delicious consciousness before it was quickly masked.

He was attracted to her!

Her hormones cheered.

Marissa frowned.

He couldn't be attracted. At all. Why would he be?

A moment later he blinked that consciousness away and turned to stare at the other man. 'Unless you have something new to add to the discussion, Cartwright, perhaps we could wind this up.'

Focusing on work was a great idea, really. If her heart had already done a little flip-flop dance, well, that didn't matter. She would simply force all systems back into submission because control was the thing.

Control her destiny and it couldn't hurt—*control*—her, and that was exactly how she wanted things to be.

Rick cleared his throat. 'Mr Cartwright, your committee members will have my report before your eleven o'clock meeting this morning.'

'There's no need to send it to everyone. I'll deliver it at the meeting.' The man actually seemed to believe that Rick would agree to this.

'I assure you, it will be no trouble to see the report into the hands of the whole committee.' Deep voice. Steel-edged politeness.

Marissa had arrived at work this morning expecting to be stultifyingly bored with office filing for at least the next several days. Instead, Rick's secretary had propped himself up in her doorway and croaked out his request that she meet his boss on site so he could take himself off to the doctor.

Next minute Marissa had been whipping along in a taxi, and then she'd found Rick waiting for her at the bridge site like a knight in shining hard hat.

Well, not really a knight. No horse. But he'd listened patiently as she'd given a flurried explanation to go with her sudden appearance, then he'd said, 'Yes, I know. Shall we?' and had cupped her elbow to escort her onto the bridge.

That constituted contact, which was why she could blame this entire blip in her reaction to him on her senses, not her intellect.

Rick went on, 'The report will explain why your ideas won't work, and will agree with my assessor's initial report and recommend the committee works directly with him from now on. Had there not been a temp from downstairs manning my office the day you made your appointment, you'd have been informed that you should meet with the Project Manager today, not me.'

Having a temp make an inappropriate appointment for him explained how Rick had ended up wasting his time on this meeting. Marissa had wondered. Her attraction to him didn't explain anything, except her hormones apparently hadn't read her Blinddatebrides profile or her list of requirements in a prospective mate.

Date. Prospective date. And this man wasn't one. She expected all of her to take note.

'You'll be billed for this discussion. I hope your interactions with our company will remain amicable and be a little more focused in the future.' Having made it plain that the man's efforts to bypass the proper channels hadn't come free of charge, Rick nodded. 'Now, if you'll excuse us.'

Good. It was over. They could get back to the office and Marissa could forget this weird awareness of the boss and return to her real work. In this instance, taking care of the backlog of filing Gordon had left behind before he'd gone on holiday and, once that was done, a long list of non-urgent hack work he'd left for her.

Rick's firm fingers wrapped around her elbow.

Instant overload.

Nerve-endings. Senses. Her gaze flew to his. He was already watching her. His fingers tightened.

For a frozen heartbeat his gaze became very intent indeed. Then he shook his head and swept her away along the bridge and she started to breathe again and reminded herself of her focus.

Nice. Ordinary. Guy.

Someone to have babies with. If they wanted to. At some point when they decided they'd like that. No rush at all. Again, Marissa was the leader of this particular outfit, not her clock or her hormones or anything else.

She frowned. What did she mean, *clock*? As in ticking biological clock? How silly. She simply wanted someone steady and dependable and completely invested in building a solid relationship of trust, friendship and affection with her.

Sure, that might mean a family one day, but she didn't feel driven to have children. Just because she found herself noticing mothers with babies in supermarkets and shops and on the street…

No. The Big 3-0 didn't stand for B. A. B. Y.

Not at all.

It only stood for birthday-she-didn't-want-to-think-about.

Hmph.

And just because she'd noticed the Morgan's boss…

'Tom explained he was unwell before he sent you out here to meet me?' Rick spoke the words as he steered her along. 'Did he give you his travel pack?'

'I met with Tom briefly at the office before his wife whisked him away to go to the doctor.' Marissa tapped the bag that slapped against her hip with each step.

Rick must be around six foot two inches tall. Much of it appeared to be strong, ground-eating legs, not that she wanted to think about his legs, or even his anatomy in general. 'And, yes, I have Tom's travel pack.'

The shoes that went so nicely with her chocolate-brown knee-length skirt were also shoved in the tote.

'You'll need it for dictation on the trip back to the office.' He hit the base of the bridge without slowing his pace, though he took care to make sure she could keep up.

As he walked forward he dropped his hold on her and drew out his mobile phone. The conversation when the number picked up brought an edge of concern to his face and deepened the grooves on either side of his firm, moulded lips.

Would those grooves crease appealingly when he smiled?

Not interested in the answer to that. Not interested in the lips that would form the smile, or the abandoned feeling in one particular elbow either.

'You'll recover, though?… What's the treatment?… Can Linda get some time off work? If she can't, I'll arrange nursing care for you.' He listened for a moment and some of the tension in his face eased. 'Okay. You've got it covered then, but if you think of anything you need, you let me know, and don't worry about work. I'll cope.'

He paused. His grey gaze examined her, frankly assessing her before he spoke again. 'It wasn't your fault I ended up at this meeting this morning, Tom. We agreed to put a temp in the chair that day and she apparently didn't know any better than to book me for this appointment instead of the Project Manager. Cartwright took advantage of that fact.'

The second pause lasted longer, or maybe it felt that way because his gaze stayed on her the whole time. 'Yes, I know and I suppose you're right. I'd had the same thought.' His tone softened. 'Now let Linda put you to bed, man. I'll check in with her later.'

Before Marissa could get all mushy over that obvious concern for his employee, or feel uneasy as a result of his focus on her, he closed the phone.

'Is Tom—?' She got that far with the question before he brought them to a halt beside a large slate-coloured four-wheel-drive car.

People called them *cars*. Marissa told herself this was a muscular extension of its owner. All strong lines and height and breadth and power. It was twice as tall as an ordinary car, and it should stand as a warning to her. There was no softness to be found here, no gentler side, just sheer strength.

Really? Because Rick had *seemed* quite considerate, as well as all those other things.

'Tom is ill with what appears to be a hard-hitting virus.

Ross River fever, the doctor thinks.' Rick removed his hard hat and ran his hand through his hair for real. Thick dark hair with a glint or two of silver at the temples. He was thirty-seven years old, her boss Gordon had told her, with degrees in both civil engineering and architecture.

Rick had used those and other skills to forge his way to massive success consulting on structural refurbishment and undertaking new construction work. Bridges, buildings, roads, he'd covered all of it and now had a team of several hundred people working under him, just in the office side of his business alone.

That was what Marissa needed to remember. The word 'driven' probably didn't begin to describe him.

Driven. Willing to do anything to get what he wanted, no matter how that impacted on others? Like Michael Unsworth?

'Ross River fever can be quite debilitating while it lasts, can't it? Tom did look very unwell this morning.' Marissa had worried for the man until he'd assured her that his wife would soon be there to collect him. She didn't want her thoughts on Rick, and she pursued the conversation with that in mind. 'I hope Tom recovers quickly and fully.'

'Linda will make sure he rests, and I'll be keeping an eye on his progress…' He used the remote on his keyring to unlock his car. Even the movement of those strong, long-fingered hands appealed.

'I'm glad I could fill in for Tom this morning, though the meeting turned out to be a bit of a waste of time for you.' Marissa wrestled with the strap of her hard hat and finally got the thing off. Wrestled to get her thoughts into submission at the same time. A quick shake of her head took care of any hat hair possibility, though she knew that nothing would keep her curls down for long.

'I appreciated that you got yourself here quickly when Tom couldn't. Make sure you hand your taxi receipt in for reimbursement.' He had his hand out, reaching to open the passenger door. It paused mid-stretch as his gaze locked onto her head and stark male awareness flared in the backs of his eyes. 'Your hair—'

'Is it a mess? I'm afraid I can't do a whole lot with it, though I do occasionally tie it back or put it up.' She uttered the words while she tried to come to terms with the expression in his eyes, with the reciprocal burst of interest it raised in her. Goosebumps tingled over her nape and down her arm. 'It's just that it takes ages and I was busy this morning,' she finished rather lamely while she fought not to notice those reactions.

'"Mess" wasn't really what I was thinking.' He murmured the admission as though against his will, and then, 'Let me have the hat.' His fingers brushed hers as he took it from her.

Warmth flowed back up her arm again from the brief contact. *Totally immune to him, are we? Doesn't look like it, and he definitely* did *notice you just now. You saw it for yourself.*

Oh, shut up!

He tossed the hats onto the back seat and ushered her towards the front one. 'Hop in. This was my third stop this morning. I have quite a bit of dictation for the trip back to the office. It's up to you whether you speak your notes into a recorder or write them down, but there are deals in progress, so we need to get moving.'

'I'm quite willing to be occupied.' *And you see?* The Morgan's boss *was* highly focused on his work, his success. All those things Michael had cared the most about, had used her to achieve. Marissa hopped, or rather, he boosted her up into the high cab of the car and she landed in the seat with a bit of a plop. It was a soft, comfortable, welcoming seat, contrasting with the strength of the vehicle itself.

Not that she thought Rick Morgan had a soft side to match

his car. She couldn't let herself think that. He was off-limits to her in any case and she needed her hormones to accept that fact without any further pointless comparisons.

The manoeuvre had also left rather a lot of leg exposed and she quickly tugged the skirt back into place.

Rick's gaze locked onto that expanse of leg and he caught his breath. Blinked twice. And then he strode around the front of the vehicle with his shoulders thrown back and a shuttered expression on his face that made her more conscious of him than ever.

He couldn't want her. In fact he was probably wondering why on earth he had noticed her at all. She would seem like part of the furniture to him. Like a coffee table with sturdy blocks keeping it low to the ground. Well, women her height didn't have slender legs that went on for ever, did they? Not that she was comparing herself to a coffee table.

'I'll take written notes.' She didn't want to speak aloud in front of him for who knew how long, repeating everything he said. That would feel far too intim—*uncomfortable*. 'It'll be more efficient.'

'Then let's see what we can do about cementing the positive outcomes that are riding on this morning's earlier visits.' He set the car in motion while she prepared herself—a man with power and achievement on his mind.

Michael Unsworth had been all about those things too, in the most arrogant of ways, though it had taken her way too long to see that, to see beyond his surface charm. He'd led her on, taken credit for all her hard work for him as though he'd done it all himself and, when she'd called him on that, he'd dumped her, had claimed their secret engagement had never existed. She was more than over all that, of course. It had happened months ago and she'd told him what a snake he was at the time.

Yes. Totally moved on. Her ongoing tendency to occasionally blare raging *I don't need a man* style music in her apartment at night notwithstanding.

She happened to like the musical accompaniments to some of those particular songs, and if she truly felt that way she wouldn't be trying to find a man she liked on a dating site, would she?

And you don't think you're so keen to find a man because Michael dumped you and your birthday will be the anniversary of the day you believed you and he became 'secretly' engaged as well as making you officially 'old'? You're not out to prove something? Several somethings, in fact?

She was simply out to do something positive and proactive about her future. She didn't even care if she found a man before she turned thirty. The dating site was a way to look around. If nothing eventuated, no big deal.

And this awareness of her boss… Well, it would go away. He might be *somewhat* nice, but that didn't change his corporate status. She would ignore her consciousness of him until it disappeared.

'Yes.' She was ready, under control and safe from the temptation of a corporate boss with power on her mind. Marissa clutched her pencil and hoped that was true!

CHAPTER TWO

RICK turned his car into the traffic and started to dictate. First came the report for Cartwright's committee meeting. Then a bunch of short memos to be emailed to various department heads regarding the other projects he had visited this morning. Marissa's pencil flew across the pages while she remained utterly conscious of his presence at her side.

In the confines of the big car she registered each breath and movement as he managed the congested traffic conditions with ease. Maybe joining a dating site had raised her overall awareness of men in a general sense?

That might explain this sudden inconvenient fixation on Rick.

He paused, glanced at her. 'All right? Are you keeping up?'

'Yes.' She waved the hand with the pencil in it and didn't let on for a moment that it ached somewhat from the thorough workout. 'Gordon always dictates when we're out on site work.'

Which had been all of three or four times since she'd started with her middle-aged boss six months ago, and Gordon always paused to ponder between each sentence.

'Take this list down then, please.' Rick went on to give a prioritised outline of workaday items—phone calls to be made, documentation to be lifted from files and information to be gathered from other departments within the company.

He had crow's feet at the corners of his eyes. They crinkled when he scrunched his face in thought or gave that slight smile, and made him look even better. Gorgeous, with character.

Whereas Marissa had spent over a hundred dollars on a miracle fine line facial cream last week, an action that had puzzled the younger of her Blinddatebrides friends Dani, and made Grace laugh, albeit rather wryly.

When Rick wound up his dictation, she gestured at the steno pad now crammed with instructions. 'Someone's going to be busy. There's also a BlackBerry in the pack Tom gave me. Do you want me to read you the day's list?'

In case he'd missed something in the estimated ten hours of straight work he'd just hammered out for whoever got the job of replacing Tom in his absence? She pitied those girls in the general pool on the first floor. Maybe he'd take two of them. Not her problem, in any case.

After this trip, Marissa would take her fine line wrinkles and go back to Gordon's office.

Rick probably wouldn't be in a good mood about the first floor help, though, given his last temp from there had booked an appointment for him to go out on a matter someone else should have handled.

'Yes, check through and see what I've missed, would you?' He signalled, slowed and turned and she realised with a start that they were back at their North Sydney office building. The city pulsed with busyness around them before he took the car underground, but she could only focus on *his* busyness.

Note to self about go-getter busyness, Marissa: it is not an endearing or invigorating trait.

She quickly pulled the electronic organiser from Tom's travel pack in her tote. Scanned. Read. Tried not to acknowledge the burst of irrational disappointment that swept through her.

'There's a notation of "Julia" for twelve-thirty.' He

wouldn't hear the slight uneven edge in her tone, would he? How silly to care that he was seeing someone. She should have realised that would be the case. It shouldn't matter to her that he was! 'That's the only thing listed that you haven't brought up.'

Of course the listing *could* be for any reason. Hairdresser appointment. An hour with his gym trainer. Or a pet schnauzer he walked faithfully once a day.

Dream on, Marissa.

'Ah, yes.' His face softened for a moment before he turned into his parking space and opened his door.

A go-getting corporate shark who had no business noticing the help if he was already involved. Probably with some sophisticated woman, maybe the daughter of a fellow businessman, or a corporate high-flyer herself. She'd be stunningly beautiful and *her* face cream would work like a charm, if she needed it at all.

You're being ridiculous. He barely noticed you in passing and he certainly didn't seem thrilled once he realised he *had. Nor do you want to be thrilled or notice him.*

Marissa released her seat belt, shoved the PDA back into her tote bag and drew out her work shoes.

With her head bent removing the joggers, she said in what she felt was a perfectly neutral tone, 'Feel free to go on ahead. I can either stop by the first floor general pool for you and ask them to send someone up, or bring the PDA and my notes to whoever you've chosen to replace Tom. You can pre-lock this monster so I just have to shut the door, I assume?'

'Thanks for the kind offer.' Rick watched as Marissa Warren pushed a second trim foot into a shapely shoe. She had beautiful ankles. And legs. And a sweetness in her face that had tugged unexpectedly at something deep inside him from the moment he'd seen her up close for the first time this morning.

He'd noticed her in the office, of course. He noticed all the staff. As owner and manager, it was part of his job to remain aware about who worked for him, though the company was so big nowadays and employed so many people that he didn't always have anything specific to do with some of the workers.

In any case Marissa was completely unsuitable as a woman he should notice, legs or not. He wasn't prepared to risk commitment and the failure that could go with it, and he didn't tangle with the kind of women who might want it. Marissa struck him as a woman who would want all sorts of pieces of a man that Rick might not have the ability to give. Not that he'd ever wanted to.

'I'll wait for you.'

She didn't realise yet there would be no parting. But this didn't have to be about anything beyond work requirements. And, ultimately, he didn't have a whole lot of better options.

'If you insist,' she muttered, and pushed her joggers into her tote bag.

Why he couldn't seem to take his gaze from her, he simply couldn't explain. Yet she'd drawn his attention from the moment she'd arrived at the bridge, that hard hat rammed down on her head like armour plating.

Most of the women in the office were either in their forties or fifties, married and/or otherwise committed, or giggling twenty-year-olds. Marissa didn't fit either of those groups. She didn't seem the type to giggle.

Maybe that explained this odd attraction to Gordon Slaymore's secretary.

Rick got out, closed his door, moved to her side and pulled hers open. 'Ready?'

'Yes. It was kind of you to wait, though unnecessary.' She stood at about five foot five inches in height with a compact body that curved in all the right places. Brown eyes sparkled one moment and seemed to guard secrets the next and that wealth of hair caressed her face and nape in all its curly wildness. Her nose was strong and straight, her mouth soft and inviting in a girl-next-door kind of way.

He shouldn't want to know about the guardedness or cheerfulness. Definitely needed to steer clear of the girl-next-door part. 'Let's go, then.'

'Right.' She would have got down without touching him. The intention to do so flared in her eyes.

Given the way he reacted the few times they'd touched, he should have allowed exactly that but some bizarre sense of perversity made him clasp her hand and help her. Then, because he didn't want to release his hold on her, wanted to stroke that hand with his fingertips, he dropped it altogether, closed the door and locked the vehicle.

He wanted to kiss her until they were both breathless from it, and when she joined him in the lift the urge to do that came very close to overwhelming him.

While he fought urges he usually had no difficulty controlling, Marissa reached out a small, capable-looking hand towards the panel. No doubt to press for the first floor and the help she thought he wanted.

Instead, he pushed the button that would take them directly to his floor, and thought how he would like to taste those softly pouting lips.

This wasn't happening. It *didn't* happen to him. He was no green youngster who reacted this way to a woman. He'd found her easy enough not to notice until now and he planned to go on not noticing her.

'Gordon's on holiday.' The abrupt announcement wasn't exactly his usual smooth delivery, but at least it got them back onto a business footing. 'You probably only had maintenance and catch-up work planned, you have some experience behind you and can keep up with my pace of dictation. I've decided it will be best if you assist me during Tom's sick leave.'

'You want *me*?' An expression rather close to horror flashed across her face before she quickly concealed it.

'I don't imagine I'll find anyone any better qualified and as easily available as you are.' He'd meant to state the words in a calm, if decided way. Instead they almost sounded bewildered. And perhaps a little insulted. He had to admit that her reaction had been refreshingly honest and appeared to come straight from her heart. Emotional honesty hadn't exactly been abundant from some of the people in his life.

And just where had that unhelpful thought come from? A very old place!

After a moment she murmured, 'Well, I'm sure it won't be for long.'

The grudging acceptance wasn't exactly effusive and it left him wanting to…impress her with how amenable he could be as a boss.

'Gordon has four weeks off, doesn't he?' Rick pushed away his odd reaction and forced his attention to matters close to hand. 'I seem to recall that from a brief talk I had with him before he left. I'm sure that will allow more than enough time for Tom to recuperate and return. If not, we'll simply deal with it. You can make whatever arrangements are needed to replace yourself in Gordon's office. Put a temp in there and have the first floor supervisor monitor the temp's progress.'

'Yes, of course. I didn't meant to sound… Well, I was just surprised, that's all.'

Oh, she'd meant it, but he pushed that aside too.

'Then, if you have no other questions…?' He paused and she shook her head. 'Good. We'll just get on with it, then.'

With his unwelcome awareness of her firmly set aside and filed, he whisked her out of the lift and into the hub of his work.

He would simply rein in his odd response to her and they would get along just fine.

Expediency. It was all about what was best for the company.

CHAPTER THREE

To: Sanfrandani, Englishcrumpet
From: Kangagirl
I had to cancel the after-hours second drink with the bank clerk guy. Work issues. I've been roped in to work for the big boss for the next while. Totally out of my control and since I don't know how long things will be busy and the bank clerk might want to see other women in the meantime, I didn't ask him to reschedule. Still, it looks like there will be one or two perks with this temporary job. I peeked ahead in the BlackBerry and we have a special meeting scheduled for tomorrow, a group of Asian businessmen. We're taking them to an animal petting zoo.

From: Sanfrandani
Ooh. What sort of animals?

From: Englishcrumpet
Kangaroos? I've always wanted to see one of those. I hope the different work goes well for you, Marissa.

'What did his last servant die of? I wonder.' Marissa muttered as her fingers flew at lightning speed to produce yet another memo that needed to be rushed urgently to one of their departments.

She absolutely did *not* enjoy the pace and challenge of working in Rick's sumptuous office suite with its thick beige carpet and burnished gold walls and stunning view over Sydney Harbour. And its frenetic pace. Maybe this workload was why Tom had gone down with a virus.

Except Ross River virus wasn't something one contracted due to stress. And the company boss did *not* fascinate Marissa more and more with each breath she took. He wasn't tremendously adept at his work, and appealingly sexy as he went about it. He was…obsessed by it. Yes, that was it.

He'd probably prove to be a terrible boss, never giving the poor overworked secretary a second thought after that initial consideration. And *she'd* refused to look his way for at least the last five minutes, anyway, so there.

Rick dropped another pile of papers and three tapes into her tray. 'You're coping all right? Not feeling too pressured? I know there's a lot of work, but we can take things steadily.' His gaze caught and held hers with quiet sincerity.

Which rather shot holes in her thoughts about him. She was far better off viewing him as a workaholic quite prepared to take her down with him! 'I'm managing. Thank you.'

He lingered in front of her desk for a moment and his gaze moved from her hands to her face and hair before coming back to her eyes. For one still moment she couldn't seem to look away and he…didn't seem to be able to either. Then he cleared his throat. 'That report hit the right places before eleven a.m.?'

'Report…' Oh, yes. Right. Well, he'd proofed the thing just minutes ago and she'd sent it. Except…Marissa forced her gaze from him to the square-framed clock on the far wall of the office space and realised it was now twelve twenty-five.

'I faxed the report on time to each committee member. You

must be due for your lunch appointment.' *She* must be due to remember he had that appointment, and what that meant. The man was not available. There was Julia in his life, not that Marissa imagined *herself* in Rick Morgan's life. Not in that way.

He doesn't have a photo of a woman on his desk.

Maybe he carries it in his wallet, or has it tattooed on his right biceps.

Oh, for crying out loud!

'We'll start again at one-thirty. Your meals can go on my account at the cafeteria while you're working for me, unless you prefer to eat elsewhere.' He simply announced this, in the same way any generous, thoughtful employer taking care of his employee would. 'If you need anything from your desk in Gordon's office get it as quickly as you can when you come back from your break.'

Right, and she was finished with fantasising about tattooed biceps too. *Julia. Remember Julia?*

'We're in for overtime, aren't we?' She asked it with an edge of desperation as she popped up out of her seat. The movement had nothing to do with feeling needed and energised and as though Rick wouldn't be able to function as well without her help. She wanted a lunch break, that was all.

She'd travelled the 'feeling needed' road already, hadn't she? The indispensable-secret-fiancée road until Michael Unsworth had no longer needed her slaving away on his behalf.

The smile on her face dissolved at the thought. She snagged her tote bag and headed for the office door. 'I will eat at the cafeteria. I often do, anyway. Have a lovely time with Julia.'

'Thank you.' He let her walk to the door before he spoke again. 'Could you bring me back two beef and salad rolls and a bottle of orange juice after your meal? I won't actually be eating lunch while I'm gone.'

Again, there could be a hundred reasons for that. Only one

flashed through her mind, though, and to her mortification her face became red-hot as a barrage of uninvited images paraded through her clearly incorrectly functioning brain.

'Certainly.' She bolted through the door and promised herself she would dedicate her entire lunch break to locating and lassoing her common sense and control, and tying them down where they belonged. 'I'll see that the meal is waiting when you return.'

She did exactly that after eating a sensible salad lunch that wouldn't get her hips into trouble and she didn't think about her boss. Not once. Not at all. She was a professional and she didn't give a hoot what Rick did with his time.

Marissa followed up this thought by rushing from the building to the convenience store situated at the end of the block. It was perfectly normal to buy an entire six-pack of raspberry lemonade and just because that was her comfort drink of choice didn't mean anything. Bulk was cheaper.

With a huff Marissa turned from placing the drinks in the fridge in the suite's kitchenette beside the boss's lunch and OJ and made her way to Gordon's office.

There'd be a temp tomorrow. For today the general pool was a little short-staffed so the office was silent as she collected the framed photo of her Mum and Dad taken last year just after they'd downsized into their two-bedroom home in Milberry, and a small tray full of bits and pieces—nail files, amazing hand cream to go with the amazing face cream, breath mints.

She also picked up the laminate of cartoon cuttings she'd collated a few months ago—cheery ones, joky ones, sarcasm about pets and life and getting up in the mornings. It made an entertaining desktop addition and there was no significance to the fact that she had avoided any cartoons to do with ageing.

Everyone got a day older each time they rolled out of bed

in the morning. That was life. It was certainly no big deal to her. And she'd left off cartoons about babies, children and families because…this was a laminate she'd wanted for work, and those things didn't fit into that world.

And the fact that you purchased a pair of baby-gauge knitting needles recently and two balls of baby-soft wool?

It had been an impulse buy. One of those things you did and then wondered why you had. Besides, she hadn't bought any knitting patterns to go with the wool and, if she did decide to use it, she'd knit herself a pair of socks or something.

She would!

Back in her new office, Marissa shoved the laminate onto the left half of the desk and quickly buried it beneath her in-tray and various piles of folders, typed letters and other work.

When her boss walked in and fell on the lunch she'd brought as though starved to death, Marissa kept on with her work and didn't spare him a glance. If she had a 'spare' anything, she would invest it thinking about which man she might date next off the Blinddatebrides website.

Silly name, really, because she wasn't desperate for marriage or anything like that. They'd had a special on and there were lots of nice everyday men out there, and her thirtieth birthday *wasn't looming*.

It was still weeks away, even if Mum had fallen eerily silent about it, the way she did when she got the idea to spring a surprise on her daughter. Marissa didn't want a surprise party—or any kind of party—and she hoped her Mum had understood that from her hints on the topic.

There was no big deal about wanting to find a man before she turned thirty anyway, and nor was Marissa's pride in a mess because she'd been duped and dumped.

She had her whole world in complete control, and she liked it just fine that way!

* * *

'Good afternoon, Rick Morgan's office, this is Marissa.'

Rick sat at his desk and listened as Marissa answered yet another phone call and took a message. He'd told her he didn't want to be disturbed while he worked his way through the report that had been delivered.

Yet he hadn't managed to tune out his awareness of her as she beavered away at her desk.

Maybe it was the way her hands flew across the computer keys that had him glancing her way over and over. Or the fact that when she thought herself unobserved her interest in the materials she processed showed all over her expressive face.

Frowns and nods of approval came into play until she finally printed out each piece of work with an expression of satisfaction. Would she be as open and responsive—?

That wasn't something he needed to know, yet the thought was there, along with others. Rick finished reading the report and scooped up the signed letters that needed to be mailed.

'You like hard work, don't you.' It wasn't really a question but he set the signed letters down on the corner of her desk and waited for her to answer anyway. That was another problem he appeared to have developed. He couldn't seem to stop himself from getting up from his desk and finding a reason to visit hers.

Once there, his gaze seemed to have a will of its own, roving constantly over her face and hair, the nape of her neck, the hands that moved with such speed and efficiency over the computer keyboard. He wanted those hands on him.

No. He did *not* want Marissa Warren's hands on him. Yet there was something between them. It had been there from the moment they'd met at the bridge this morning and he'd let her come to the most predictable conclusion about Julia because of that.

Now he wanted to explain, wanted her to know he was free—but he wasn't, was he? Not to get involved with his temporary secretary, or any other woman who wanted more than a casual physical interlude with him. He'd made his choice about that.

'Do I like hard work?' Her gaze flipped up to his. Almost immediately she veiled the sparkle in her eyes. A shrug of one shoulder followed. 'I guess I like to think I'm as efficient as the next person and there seems a lot to be done in this office at the moment. Or perhaps it's always this busy?'

'Tom and I work hard, but there's more to contend with right now than is usual, even for us.' To move his gaze from her, he shifted it to a photo of an older couple that she'd added to her desk. The woman had curly hair, cut shorter. Her parents...

Was she an only child or did she, like him, have siblings? An intriguing-looking laminated sheet covered the left half of the desk. Much of it had work strewn on top but the bits he could see appeared to be cartoon cuttings.

Her foibles and family history shouldn't interest him. Another sign of trouble, and yet still he stood here, courting time with her when both their interests would be better served if he didn't.

'Will it be a problem for you to work longer hours for the next few days?' That was what he really needed to know. 'Is there someone at home who'll mind?'

Marissa's answer was only relevant to him in terms of how it impacted here.

Except his body stilled as he waited for her response, and that stillness had little to do with concerns about his working life.

'Tom has welcomed the longer hours because he and Linda are saving to buy a house.' The words left his mouth in an explanation he hadn't intended to give. 'He's used to my ways and knows his way around this office. He copes.'

'I can manage any work Tom would have done.' She spoke the words with her chin in the air. An answer, but not all the information he had wanted.

'I don't doubt that.' He wanted her to know he thought well

of her. Wanted her to…think well of him. The last time he'd experienced this particular care about another's opinion of him, he'd been twenty years old and convinced he was in love, until the girl had started talking about the future—theirs—and he'd wanted to run a mile.

Just like his father, except Stephen Morgan was *in a family* and he did his running a little differently. Rick hadn't even tried for a less than overt approach. He'd got out of that relationship so fast he'd probably left the girl spinning and he'd avoided commitment ever since.

'I'm not…tied to any home responsibilities.' Marissa offered this information cautiously, as though she'd prefer not to have given it.

'Then I won't worry too much if I do have to ask you to work extra hours.' Rick stared into the warm brown eyes fixed unerringly on him and the moment stretched out, expanded to encompass not only the words they had exchanged but also what they weren't saying. The sparkle in the air between them. His awareness of her, hers of him, the denial of both of them.

Sexual attraction. That was all it was, but even so it wasn't wise and he *had* to realise that and move them past it. He drew a deep breath. 'It's clear you can cope with the workload. You've handled yourself very well so far today. I appreciate your efforts.'

'Th-thank you.' A pleased expression lifted the corners of her mouth and softened her eyes. 'I've simply done my job.'

Something about that softening brought back the urge he'd had earlier in the lift to kiss her senseless, and he lowered his tone of voice to a low rumble. 'So I've observed.'

'I can work whatever hours are needed. I'd just appreciate knowing so I can gear my social life accordingly.' She cleared her throat and couldn't quite seem to meet his gaze. 'I cancelled a drink after work today because I figured I wouldn't be out by five.'

Rick wanted to say there'd be no time whatsoever for her to spend on 'drinks'. Presumably with some man. He noted at the same time that she must be looking. Looking, but not seriously involved right now.

But women who looked and carried photos of their parents with them did want depth and permanency, and that kind of relationship was not on his agenda.

'I should get on, if that was all.' She reached for the pile of letters to be mailed, began to calmly fold them into the window envelopes she had waiting on her desk.

Dismissed by his temporary assistant. Rick gave a snort of amusement and reluctant admiration before he swung away. 'I'll be in my office and…er…I promise there won't be any more correspondence brought out for you to type today. I know your tray is still loaded.'

'No.' She didn't look up. 'You'll just hold it over for tomorrow so I won't get stressed out. I won't anyway, but that's okay. I understand the tactic. Gordon does the same thing.'

Now he'd been compared to a fifty-year-old.

Rick disappeared into his office, pushed the door closed so he wouldn't be tempted to listen to Marissa taking phone calls or watch her as she worked, and decided that it was very different working with her rather than Tom.

That explained his ongoing interest in her. He half convinced himself he believed this. Well, maybe a quarter. He immersed himself in his work.

At twenty minutes to six that evening Marissa stuck her head around his door. 'Your presence is requested at an emergency conference.'

He'd started to believe they might have nearly caught up on their workload. So much for that idea. 'Which department heads? What's the problem?'

She pushed the door open fully and read a spiel of information from her steno pad.

Rick gave a mild curse. 'Where? Have they assembled already?'

'Conference Room Two, and yes.' She had her tote bag on her shoulder and a determined glint in her eyes. Her computer was shut down and her desk cleared. Whatever work she had remaining she had tidied away. 'I assume you'll want us to join them immediately. If it ends quickly, we can come back.'

He got to his feet. 'I'll secure my office.'

She swept in beside him while he sorted files and locked them away. 'Anything on screen that needs to be saved before I shut this down?'

'No. Nothing, but I can do that.' He locked the final cabinet and swung round.

She'd clicked out of applications as he spoke and she stood there now, bent at the waist, leaning in to press the button on the back of the computer.

Rick's senses kicked him hard. She would have to possess the most appealing bottom to go with those equally devastating legs, wouldn't she? And he would have to notice it instead of being completely unaware of her, as he needed to be. He didn't want to notice her, or be impressed or intrigued by her or find her different or interesting or highly attractive!

If he'd thought it would help, he'd replace her with someone from another department but no other personal secretary had a boss on holiday. He certainly wasn't about to subject himself to some child from the general pool again. And, for goodness' sake, he could control this.

He always controlled the way he reacted to women. There was no reason why this situation should be any different. In fact, because she worked for him and he never, ever, mixed work with his social interactions that way, it should be easier still.

Yes, and it's been dead easy so far, hasn't it?

'Let's move.' He hid a grimace in his chin. 'Here's hoping the meeting doesn't go on too long.'

CHAPTER FOUR

MARISSA followed Rick along the corridor and tried not to look at the breadth of his shoulders, the shape of the back of his head or…other parts of him.

Not to mention the man was seriously compelling as a go-getter businessman…but what was she thinking? The terms 'go-getter', 'businessman' and 'compelling' were mutually exclusive in her vocabulary!

And just because he'd been kind to his secretary and had phoned in again to check on the man and declared he wanted to be told if anything—*anything*—needed to be done for Tom while he was recuperating, just because he'd treated Marissa herself with the utmost consideration he could manage within the demands of his work…

She still wanted a *nice ordinary guy*—hello? Fine, so maybe Rick did have a degree of niceness. His career outlook made him totally out of bounds for her.

Maybe he's a total playboy, she thought with a hint of desperation, remembering the Julia lunch date that hadn't involved lunch. A cad, a womaniser, a toad on a lily pad on a pond full of scum.

You don't think you're judging him ever so slightly on Michael Unsworth's record without getting to know the man first? Without even knowing just who this Julia is to him?

No. She didn't think that, and she wasn't grasping at mental straws to keep her hormones under control either. Rick Morgan wasn't for her. She'd road-tested one corporate man and decided that brand didn't suit her, and that was all there was to it.

'Sit here beside me.' He held the chair for her while the six men in the room glanced their way. 'You know what to do with the notes.'

She nodded to acknowledge the others' presence and Rick's words, and tried not to notice the brush of his hand against her back as he pushed her chair in for her.

The boss simply had nice manners, and so did a lot of accountants and shop assistants.

Butchers and bakers and candlestick-makers.

Marissa jabbed her pencil onto the page and locked her gaze onto its tip. 'I'm ready.'

To get the meeting over with. To go home for the day and log onto Blinddatebrides.com and read at least ten new profiles, answer any invitations she'd received and be really positive about them. And she had been positive to this point. It wasn't her fault if no spark of true interest had happened when she'd met any of her dates so far.

Unlike the spark that immediately happened when she'd met Rick Morgan.

Not a helpful thought!

The meeting went beyond long.

'So we find a way to meet the changes to the fire safety code without compromising on design integrity.' Rick referred to a skyscraper monstrosity the company was building on the city's shoreline. 'We'll simply present our clients with choices that surpass what they wanted initially.'

He raised several possibilities. While general discussion ensued, Marissa snatched at the momentary respite in note-taking. She should have eaten something more substantial than a salad for her lunch. Instead, she drew one of two bottles of raspberry lemonade from her tote bag and consumed half of it in a series of swallows. She'd planned to take both bottles in her bag home but at least it gave her an energy burst.

The conference moved on. Marissa consumed the rest of the drink, continued her work. Wished she could get up and walk around. Her right foot wanted to go to sleep. Another sign of impending old age?

There is no old age occurring here!

'It seems to me Phil's presented you with a workable resolution to the issue with the reservoir, Fred.' Rick caught the stare of the man at the other end of the oval table.

Marissa vaguely noted that Rick's beard shadow had really grown in now. Did he shave twice a day? Would he have a mat of dark hair on his chest as well? Her skin tingled in response to the thought.

What was wrong with her? She needed to focus *away* from the man, not so solidly on him that she noticed almost everything about him and wondered about the rest!

Rick's face showed no sign of fatigue, though the grooves on either side of his mouth did seem a little deeper.

It wasn't fair that men just developed character while women fought gravity. Women wrinkled sooner, got older faster. And people had coined entire sayings around the thirtieth birthday. *It's all downhill after thirty…*

'If you don't want to accept the plans,' Rick went on, 'I need to hear a good reason for that. Otherwise, I think we can move onto the next issue.'

Marissa nodded in silent agreement.

Just then Rick glanced her way and their gazes locked before his dropped to her mouth. He stilled and a single swift blast of awareness swept over his face and, very, very briefly, he lost his concentration and stopped speaking.

It was only for a second and probably no one else would

have thought anything of it, but in that single moment she had all of his attention—an overwhelming degree of attention, as though he could *only* focus on her. And, right down to her marrow, she responded with a depth of warmth and interest, curiosity and compulsion that…stunned her.

A moment later his face smoothed of all expression and he carried on with the meeting, and Marissa did her best to pull herself together.

Her lungs chose to function again after all, and she sucked in a deep breath and couldn't—simply couldn't—think about the strength of the response he'd drawn from her just then.

A burst of note-taking followed and when it ended she gulped down the second bottle of lemonade and tapped her foot incessantly. It was almost a relief to focus on her exhaustion and discomfort.

'Anything else?' Rick sent the words down the length of the table. He wanted the conference over with. It was eight p.m. and his secretary was wilting, her fluffy hair sticking out in odd places and the pink lip-gloss, that made him think of snatching kisses, all but chewed off.

Her shoulders were curved, her left elbow propped on the table while she pushed the pencil across the page with grim determination with her other hand.

He had the oddest desire to protect her from the workload he had inflicted on her—even while he'd noted her pleasure in it. He had the oddest desire for her, period. It had stopped his concentration earlier, had simply shut down all channels until he'd pulled his attention forcibly away from her. No person had had the power to disrupt his thoughts so thoroughly before.

It was more than simply a blast of lust, Morgan. Maybe you should admit that to yourself.

Yet what else could it have been? He didn't experience any other feelings. Just look at the way he'd run the one and only time he'd linked up with a woman who wanted more from him. More than his father could give, more than Rick knew if he could give. At least he chose to go forward honestly, not let anyone down…

Around the table, people scooped up folders and files.

Rick nodded. 'Then that's a wrap. Anything else, get it to me in writing tomorrow.'

The room cleared while Marissa continued to write. In the end, he reached out and stilled her hand by placing his over it. Gently, because for some reason she drew that response from him whether he wanted it to be so or not.

Touching her was a mistake. Her skin was warm, soft, and the urge inside him to caress more of it was unexpectedly potent.

Wouldn't his youngest sister gloat about this fixation of his? Faith had tried to convince him to fall for the 'right kind' of woman for years, to take the leap into emotional oblivion and surrender and believe he'd like it.

What was he thinking, anyway? This was all completely irrelevant. He'd done the not-getting-involved-life-alone mental adjustment years before and he hadn't changed his mind.

He never would. He'd seen too much, thanks to his father.

There were no *emotions* involved in desiring Marissa Warren. Just some unexplained stupidity. 'We're done here. Let's put you into a taxi so you can get home. Unless you drove to work?' He removed the steno pad and pencil from her grip, pushed them into his briefcase on the table and took her elbow to help her up. A simple courtesy, nothing more.

'I should type the notes while they're fresh. No, I didn't drive. I hire a Mini from a neighbour when I go to Milberry to see Mum and Dad. It's heaps cheaper than owning my own car and I don't often need to drive.' The words stopped abruptly as she came fully to her feet and swayed.

'Marissa? Are you okay?' He pushed her chair out of the

way with his thigh and caught her beneath both elbows even as he registered the personal snippets about her. Registered and wanted to know more, and cursed himself for his curiosity.

'Sorry.' She caught her breath. 'I feel a bit light-headed.' Her body sagged into his hold. For a moment her forehead rested against his chest and all that curly hair was there beneath his chin.

It came naturally to curve his body around hers. He simply did it without thinking. She felt good in his arms, smelled sweetly of gardenias and some other floral scent. He wanted to press his face into her hair and against her skin and inhale until he held the scent of her inside him.

Total insanity, and he had no idea where it had come from. It must be too long since he'd taken a woman to his bed. He had focused more and more on work over recent months.

'Take some deep breaths.' The instruction was to Marissa, though he could do with it himself. 'You won't faint on me, will you?'

'No, I just need a minute.' Her breasts brushed his chest as she drew a series of breaths.

His whole body was sensitised, his vaunted self-control rocked. He wanted to take her there and then, but he also wanted to cup her head in his hand, tenderly brush her hair from her brow.

Why was she faint, anyway? Lack of food? Was she ill?

'I stood up too fast and I shouldn't have had two bottles of drink in a row like that on an empty stomach. I think I gave myself a sugar overload.' Her fingers curled around his forearms.

'You should take better care of yourself.' The admonition skated far too close to a proprietorial concern. 'I shouldn't have had you work so late without food either.'

'It's my responsibility to eat enough.' She muttered something about thighs and coffee tables.

Rick gave in and raised his hand, stroking his fingers over the soft skin of her jaw. Simply to lift her face, he told himself, to search her eyes, see if she had recovered sufficiently.

Long lashes lifted to reveal brown eyes that slowly came into focus and filled with belated acknowledgement of their nearness.

Perhaps it was the late hour, the silence of the room or the many hours of work that had gone before that momentarily shorted out his brain, because he lowered his head, his lips intent on reaching hers, something inside him determined to make a connection.

She took a deep steadying breath and straightened away from him and the welcome he had glimpsed in her eyes was replaced with the rejection he should have instigated within himself.

The sense of loss startled him and his hands dropped away from her more slowly than they should have. None of this made sense. None of his reactions to her. They shouldn't even exist because he'd told himself to shut down any awareness.

'I'm sorry. I'm fine now.' She held out her hand for her notes and pencil. So she could keep working and truly faint?

'I'll keep these for you for tomorrow.' He closed the briefcase and guided her towards the door. He simply wanted to ensure his employee was okay. This had only truly been geared towards that.

Aggravatingly off-kilter, Rick took Marissa straight to street level and left the building at her side.

'Hand this taxi receipt to accounting so they can reimburse you as well,' he instructed as he flagged a taxi forward from the rank. 'Are you able to start at eight tomorrow? I realise that's early and today has exhausted you but, as well as our regular workload, there's a visit scheduled to a petting zoo. An early lunch for business discussions, and then the zoo itself…'

'I saw that in the BlackBerry.' Her chin hiked into the air and her brown eyes flashed. 'I'll be here at a quarter to eight so I can meet with the supervisor and brief one of the early shift temps on the work required in Gordon's office before we do whatever work we can and then leave. You don't need to make any allowances for me.'

Rather than making him feel bad for asking for another long day out of her, her expression of determination went straight to his groin—a reaction he needed as little as all the others. Perhaps he should have remained in the building and done some laps in the top floor swimming pool before he went home. Like a few hundred or so.

'Then thank you for your willingness to put in the hours.' Rick helped her into the taxi. He would *not* respond to her in such a confusing way again. It was intolerable and unacceptable and he was locking it down right now.

Just like your father would?

And he could leave his family life out of it. That had nothing to do with anything.

'I'll see you tomorrow.' He turned his back and strode away, promising himself he would leave all thoughts of her behind him.

'That's great. Keep smiling. You all look wonderful. Your families will love these photos.' Marissa had two cameras dangling from her left arm by their straps and another one in her hands. At her side Rick held three more.

They were at the brand-new Sydney animal petting zoo and their group of Hong Kong businessmen guests were one hundred per cent enchanted. She and Rick snapped pictures as fast as they could.

She'd made a vow to herself last night when she'd stepped into her sensible apartment in an equally sensible building in a suburb not far from her work.

Actually she'd made it online to Grace and Dani, since they were her Blinddatebrides buddies and, as well as enjoying their long-distance friendship, Marissa felt accountable to them for her dating efforts. It was good to make herself accountable so she would do as she should—find a nice, ordinary, no-surprises man to fall in love with.

Which meant she needed to forget all about being ultra aware of the boss—okay, so she hadn't admitted that part to Dani and Grace.

Rick is interestingly older, though, a mature man with lots of layers. Intriguing, complex.

Someone a mature, well-rounded, thirty-year-old woman might find appealing? Not that she was about to become mature. That made her sound positively ancient and, really, she was just beginning her life.

'How are the photos coming?' Though Rick's question was calm and sensible, the expression in his eyes as he glanced at her still held remnants of yesterday evening's interest.

Marissa's pulse fluttered. 'I'm almost done. Every digital camera is different but I think the shots I'm getting will be fine.'

'Good. That's good.' Rick gestured to the businessmen. 'Perhaps a group shot of all of you?'

He made the suggestion in the deep, even tone he'd used when Marissa had stepped into his office suite this morning and found him already immersed in a deluge of paperwork at his desk. A tone that said they were all about business. But his gaze had contradicted that.

The man had probably invented the term 'confusion'. For anyone near him, that was. And she hadn't wanted him to kiss her last night. She'd simply lost her focus for a moment.

'Hold the pose, gentlemen.' She forced a wide smile as she changed cameras again. 'I need another two photos yet.'

Ozzie the koala didn't seem to mind being held and oohed and aahed over. He sat quietly, his keeper at the side looking on. Ozzie looked utterly adorable with his thick fur and blunt nose and fluffy ears, though his claws were sharp and strong, made for climbing the eucalyptus trees he fed from.

Fortunately the koala was tame and well-behaved. If Marissa could tame her hormones around her boss in the same way, that would be helpful. She took a moment and tried not to *think of* Rick's presence close beside her, or the fact that more than simply her chemical composition seemed interested in him.

She had to see him as her boss and nothing else, and with that in mind, she switched her attention to work. 'Here's hoping this visit ends in a successful outcome.'

'The team seemed pleased with our talks. They'll meet with at least two other major companies before they leave Sydney and then there'll be a period of time before they make a decision, but I'm hopeful.' Rick lowered the final camera and turned his gaze to their visitors.

He smiled towards the group. 'That's the last photo.'

Mr Qi spoke quietly to the keeper and then gestured them over. 'We'd like one of our hosts with Ozzie. Miss Warren will hold him, please.'

To refuse in such circumstances would be out of the question. Instead, Marissa pasted a smile on her face and came forward to hand over her share of the cameras. She drew one long uneasy breath as Rick approached her.

His head bent close to hers. 'Are you okay with this? All the animals here are trained to sit placidly.'

'That's not…' She refused to admit the thought that being close to the boss, not the furry animal's manners concerned her. 'I've never held a koala but I'm not worried he'll hurt me. I just hadn't expected them to ask for this.'

'Sometimes we overlook our own tourist attractions,' he murmured and his gaze roved over her. For all the world as though he felt *he'd* overlooked *her*?

Well, she wasn't much to notice today, in any case. She

wore a drab navy cardigan buttoned to the neck over a soft white blouse. A long, ordinary, unadorned navy skirt completed the outfit, so there wasn't a whole lot worth looking at.

Covered from neck to calves in the most unappealing outfit she had? And mostly as a deterrent to herself? To help her not to think about her boss? Who, her?

'Keep the cardigan on while you hold him.'

His comment didn't make a lot of sense, but she gave a small nod to indicate her acquiescence before she turned to face their guests.

They all waited expectantly with cameras poised.

'This will be a thrill for me. Thank you for the opportunity.' It cost nothing to be positive, right? At least Rick hadn't realised the real reason for her unease.

That depressing, confusing, annoying, irritating and wholly aggravating thought disappeared when the keeper put the koala into her arms and another feeling altogether swept through her.

Ozzie cuddled into her like a baby, a warm soft weight with one arm draped over hers and his head turned to the side beneath her chin. Her arms closed around his warmth and a wealth of completely unexpected emotions clogged her throat before her thought processes could catch up with her reaction.

For one long aching moment as Rick stepped behind her, put his arm about her shoulders and she looked up into those intense grey eyes, she longed for the completion of a child. A baby to love and nurture, care for and protect, and the feelings that she'd suppressed over recent months—even longer—all tore through her.

She hadn't impulse-bought that baby wool to make socks for herself. A part of her had reached from way deep down inside for something she wanted, had tried to ignore—how could she want such a thing? It was so foolish to long for something that might never happen for her.

It took two to produce a baby—two willing people and a whole lot of thought and commitment and other things. She should only allow herself hopes and dreams and goals that she knew she could achieve. She certainly did not want to have her boss's baby. It would be absolutely beyond the point of ridiculousness to imagine such a thing.

Even so, Rick's eyes locked with hers and something deep flickered in his expression, something more than curiosity or simply a man noticing a woman.

Maybe he'd read all those thoughts in her face before she'd been able to mask them? Panic threatened until she assured herself he couldn't possibly have done so. She hadn't realised they were even there until they'd hit her so unexpectedly. Why would he realise such things about her?

'All right?' His gaze was steady as he looked at her, and she managed a shaky breath before the tension fell back enough so that their surroundings came into focus again and she felt in control of herself once more.

'Yes, thanks.' She let her fingers stroke over the koala's soft fur, let herself come back together. 'He's unexpectedly light for his size.'

'A wombat would be far heavier to hold—the compact steamroller of Australian wildlife.' Rick's quip helped ease the moment, they both smiled at long last, and then they smiled for the cameras.

When the photo session ended Rick's arm seemed to linger a moment before he dropped it, but he strode purposefully forward and with due ceremony invited the men to enjoy another hour at the zoo. 'I asked the keepers to save a surprise, and we hope you'll enjoy the opportunity to feed some wombats and kangaroos and other animals while you think over our lunch discussion. There'll be coffee and cake waiting at the restaurant for you when you're finished.'

He left them with smiles and bows and swept Marissa

away, who had now pulled herself together. That reaction earlier... It was just some crazy thing that had happened.

She removed her cardigan, rolled it into a ball and wiped her hands on it and warily acknowledged that perhaps biological ticking and the Big 3-0 did appear to have somewhat of an association inside her after all. What to do about that was the question.

When they climbed into Rick's big car, she set the cardigan on the floor behind her seat.

'They smell a bit, don't they?' Rick watched Marissa dispose of her cardigan and tried not to think of that moment back there when she'd first taken the koala into her arms and seemed so surprised and devastated, and he'd wanted to hold *her*, just scoop her up and take her somewhere and cuddle and comfort her.

'Yes, Ozzie smelled of eucalyptus and warm furry animal.' She buckled her seat belt and sat very primly in the seat, her back stiff enough to suggest that she didn't want to delve too deeply into her reaction to holding the animal. 'His coat was a little oily. Thanks for the hint to keep my cardigan on.'

She'd seemed empty somehow, and he'd wanted to give her what was missing, but his response had been on an instinctive level he couldn't begin to fathom. Well, it didn't matter anyway because she was his secretary, nothing more, and since that was exactly how he wanted things to be... 'You're welcome.'

He glanced at her. She was dressed conservatively, but the prissy white blouse just made her hair look fluffier and made him think all the more about the curves hidden away beneath the shirt's modest exterior.

So much for his vow not to think about her as an attractive woman after having his arms around her for those brief moments last night.

'You seemed well prepared for the koala experience.' Her voice held a deliberate calm and good cheer. 'Have you—'

'Held one? Yes. Once.' It hadn't left any notable impact on him, unlike watching her experience today.

Perhaps his instincts towards Marissa weren't entirely dissimilar to those he felt towards his sisters and nieces—a certain protectiveness that rose up because his father had failed to be there for them.

Rick tried to stop the thoughts there. Stephen Morgan was a decent enough man.

Except to Darla, and unless any kind of genuine emotional commitment was required of him. Then Stephen simply dropped the ball as he always had.

Rick forced the thoughts aside. There was nothing he could do about any of that, no way to change a man who inherently wouldn't change. No way to know if Rick himself would be as bad or worse than his father in the same circumstances.

'We often take our overseas business contacts places like this.' It didn't matter what he'd felt for Marissa—or thought he'd felt. By choice he wouldn't act on any response to her, and that was as much for her good as anything else. 'They have a good time and happy businesspeople are more inclined to want to make deals. Those deals mean money and building the business.'

He relaxed into this assertion. It felt comfortable. Familiar. Safe.

When Marissa turned her head to face him, her gaze was curiously flat. 'You're a corporate high-flyer and success means everything to you. I understand.'

She made it sound abhorrent. Why? And success wasn't *everything* to him.

No? That's not what you've been telling yourself and the world for a very long time now.

He did not need to suggest she got to know him better to see other facets of him—all the facets of him. Instead, he agreed with her. 'Success *is* very important to me. You're quite right.'

CHAPTER FIVE

MARISSA hadn't meant to offend Rick. Surely she hadn't? And he *was* a great deal like Michael Unsworth, only more so. She didn't hold that against him, but she had the right to protect herself by remembering the fact.

She didn't want to think about Michael. It was best if she didn't think about *Rick* in any light other than as her employer. And she certainly didn't want to dwell on that hormonal whammy that had hit her back at the petting zoo.

If she wanted something to cuddle, she probably needed a kitten or something.

Do you hear me, hormones and non-existent clock? This is my destiny and I choose what I want and need and don't need.

She refused to be dictated to on the topic by any internal systems. With that thought in mind, she worked hard for the rest of the day, and cursed the stubborn part of her that insisted on admiring Rick's business acumen as she came to see more and more of it in play. Couldn't she ignore that at least?

Maybe she should simply admit it. She liked his drive and determination. With a frown, she shoved another file away in the room dedicated to that purpose just off their suite's reception room.

More files were slapped home. Not because she was fed up with herself. She was simply being efficient.

Yes. Sure. That was the truth of it. A pity she didn't seem capable of the same single-mindedness when it came to finding Mr Right through Blinddatebrides.com. She'd yet to initiate any kind of invitation to a man, had cancelled that second drink yesterday, and hadn't looked at those ten profiles as she'd told herself she would. She'd been bored by all the candidates she'd met so far.

Grace had dated a man straight up on joining the site, even if she had panicked about it at the time.

Dani remained tight-lipped so far about dates but she sure seemed to have her head together about the whole process, right down to the site's efficiency and how it all worked. Why couldn't Marissa follow *her* plan there, and stop fixating on the boss?

Marissa had logged on in her tea break, anyway. It wasn't her fault she'd run out of time before she could do more than read some of the contact messages.

Shove, shuffle, push.

'I'll be on the top level for the next hour.' Rick spoke from the doorway in a tone that didn't reveal even the smallest amount of any kind of sensual anticipation he surely should feel in the face of yet another 'meeting' with the mysterious Julia, who seemed to have a place reserved for her almost daily in his diary.

That was something Marissa had discovered today as she'd scanned ahead further in the BlackBerry to try to gauge the kind of workload they might have ahead of them.

Well, good on him for seeing this Julia. With such a knowledge foremost in her thoughts, Marissa simply wouldn't look at him as an available man, which was *all to the good*.

It was just as well the woman didn't mind being slotted in like a visit to the dentist or a board meeting or teleconference, though.

Marissa shoved two more files away and forced herself to face him. 'You won't mind if I take a short break myself? I'll just talk on the Internet with friends. There's nothing in the diary—'

Marissa broke off a little uneasily, but Rick wasn't to know those friends were on an Internet dating site with her. Not that she cared who knew she had a subscription to a dating website. She could do what she liked. It was her life and just because she hadn't even told her parents she'd joined Blinddatebrides.com didn't mean she felt uncomfortable about it or anything.

Grace and Dani knew she wanted to find a nice man. Marissa had been very open with them really.

Her online friends were signed up to the dating site, of course, so Marissa hadn't exactly been exposing deep secrets by admitting she wanted to meet some men. And she hadn't told Grace and Dani everything about herself by any means. She certainly hadn't told them her plan to clinically vet those men until she found one she was prepared to fall in love with.

Well, that was her business, and it mightn't even happen and her vetting ideas made a lot of sense.

'Please do take a break.' Rick turned. 'I sought you out to suggest that.'

A moment later, after delivering that piece of thoughtfulness, he was gone.

Marissa appreciated the reprieve from close contact with him. That was what made her feel all mushy and approving, not only his consideration for her. She told herself this as she logged onto Blinddatebrides.com and scrolled through the messages she'd skimmed earlier. This time she made herself read them and follow through to look at profiles.

And she set her fingers to the keyboard and replied that she would be delighted—*delighted*—to arrange something with Tony, 32, computer software. Perhaps lunch tomorrow?

Marissa got off the site without checking for instant messages from Grace or Dani. She wasn't avoiding them. She just felt guilty about giving herself the time when she should be working, even if Rick was on the top floor of the building with Julia doing she didn't want to think about what.

When the fax machine made its warming-up sound, Marissa left her desk with a rather desperate alacrity. She'd struggled to concentrate on her typing despite her determination to plough through as much work as possible before Rick got back.

She snatched up the first page of the fax and skimmed it, and then read it more carefully while two more pages emerged from the machine. If the large 'urgent' stamp on the top of the first page hadn't been clue enough, the contents were, drat it all to pieces. She'd hoped for something to distract her thoughts, but not this way.

'I'll ring his mobile phone and tell him he needs to get back here. It's not my problem there's an emergency and I'll be interrupting…whatever.' She walked to her desk and pressed the speed dial for his mobile number, only to return the phone to its cradle when the thing rang from on top of his desk in the next room.

What now? Try another department head? Which one? The contents of the fax covered material from all the departments.

'Right, so there's no choice. It's marked for his attention specifically, and it's urgent.' Marissa snatched the door key from her purse and pushed it into her pocket. If she could have thought of any other way to handle this, she'd have taken it.

The trip to the top level went by far too fast. She'd never been up here before. There seemed to be a large atrium surrounded by rooms behind closed doors.

Rick's workaday lair? A place to come when he wanted privacy without leaving the building?

She'd crossed half the cavernous expanse of tiled floor flanked with tall banks of potted ornamental trees, the fax clutched in a death grip in her hand, before she realised the sounds of splashing weren't from an indoor fountain.

Marissa's gaze lifted and the view in front of her cleared just in time for her to see strong arms lift a little girl out of the water and pass her to a dark-haired woman who stood beside…a swimming pool.

Rick was in the pool, his wide shoulders and thick arms exposed and water dripping from his face and down his chest.

Just the right amount of dark hair there.

What on earth is going on here?

Child. Woman. Rick in the pool and not a sensual indicator to be detected in the room.

And finally this thought:

That's what the swimming roster that circulates by email means, the slots for before work each day.

She'd only seen the email twice, and had thought the staff took turns booking some *other* swimming facilities.

Marissa's steps faltered to a stop.

'Thank you, Unca Rick.' The little girl waited impatiently while the woman removed her flotation devices, only to immediately lean fearlessly over the edge of the pool, arms extended, to the man who was Marissa's boss—in a very different guise right now.

He was a specimen of male beauty and Marissa couldn't take her gaze from him. The child would have tumbled back in if the woman hadn't held onto her arm. If Rick hadn't immediately caught her by the tiny waist. Big gentle hands keeping her from harm.

The little girl planted a kiss on Rick's cheek and his arms came around her, his hands gently patting her back before he set her on her feet again beside the pool.

'You're welcome.' Oh, the soft deepness of his voice.

Marissa's abdomen clenched in a reaction she wholly did not want to admit was happening. She hadn't joined Blinddatebrides.com to find Mr Virile and Able to Produce Strong Children, nor Mr Gentle and Sweet With Said

Children. She certainly wasn't looking for those traits in the man before her.

'The next time *you'll* put your head all the way under the water, okay, Julia?' His smile was gentle, encouraging and, to Marissa, quite devastating. 'Fishes do that all the time.'

Julia…

The woman smiled and turned her head and the likeness between all three of them clicked it all fully into place.

This child was Julia—a sweet little girl about four or five years old with a shock of dark hair flattened wet against the back of her head and still dry in the front. The woman beside the pool was Rick's sister. The entire scene was so far removed from what Marissa had expected, she couldn't seem to find her breath or get her legs to move.

Or perhaps that was simply the impact of so much raw sensual appeal concentrated in the man in front of her, and the crazy twisting of reactions inside her.

And Rick wasn't involved.

Now she thought about it, hadn't Gordon said when she'd first started here that Rick was a solitary man and seemed to keep his dating low-key and…transitory?

And hello, that wouldn't exactly make him a candidate for a relationship. Plus Marissa didn't want to have one with him. He might be in a swimming pool, but the term 'corporate shark' still meant more than a boss doing laps in chlorine-scented water.

Oh, but he hadn't looked like a boss or a shark when he'd held his niece so tenderly in his arms. Marissa clenched her teeth because she *was not going down this track and that was that!*

Maybe she made a sound because Rick's head turned and his expression closed as though she'd caught him at something he hadn't wanted her to see.

Why would he feel that way about giving a swimming

lesson to his niece? Not only that, but surely he'd guessed what Marissa thought about 'Julia' and yet he hadn't said a word.

'I'm sorry for barging in.' Sorry and quite annoyed by his hidden depths, whether that made her unreasonable or not. 'I have an urgent fax and I thought—' She'd thought he'd be behind one of those closed doors beyond the pool with a lover. 'Er…I didn't realise there was a swimming pool up here.'

'It's not a problem. We've taken enough of Rick's time away from his work anyway.' The woman smiled as she wrapped her daughter in a towel and gathered her into her arms. 'I'm Faith, by the way. Rick's youngest sister.'

'Marissa.' She sought the comfortable communication skills that should have flowed naturally. 'Marissa Warren. I'm filling in while Rick's secretary, Tom, is on sick leave.'

'Ah, I see. For a while?' The other woman glanced at Rick and her eyes seemed to gleam. 'That should make for an interesting change.'

'It's not for all that long.' Rick cleared his throat. 'Didn't you say you needed to be going, Faith?'

His sister's mouth softened. 'Yes. There's a chance we might get a call from Russell tonight if things with his unit go as planned. I don't want to miss that. I asked Mum and Dad if they'd like to come over, speak with him and then watch you-know-who while I finish the call. The deployments are hard and he doesn't have his parents around, but Mum and Dad were too busy.'

Something in Rick's face seemed to tighten with… sadness? Some kind of regret for his sister? A measure of long-standing anger? 'What time? Do you want me to phone conference in from the office?'

'No, that's okay.' Faith lifted her daughter higher into her arms. 'Julia and I will be fine on our own but I appreciate the offer.'

They left after that and Marissa faced the company's boss where he stood in the water. No tattoo on the right biceps. Just muscles that seemed to invite the stroke of questing fingers. Marissa wanted to stay annoyed at him for concealing the truth about Julia from her. Instead, she could only see his kindness to his sister and niece, meshed with the appeal of a great deal of male sensuality.

Somehow *this* Rick was even deeper and more difficult to try to ignore. 'Your niece and sister seem lovely. It's…er…it's kind of you to give the little girl swimming lessons.'

'I'm a skilled diver and for some reason Julia feels safer in the water with a man.' His closed expression warned her off the topic, yet families were all about being there for each other, right?

Why would he mind her knowing he'd been there for his sister and niece?

Before she could consider possible answers, he climbed from the pool. In the brief time it took him to walk to the nearby lounger, snatch up a towel and wrap it around his hips, her concentration fled completely.

'I always try to swim here every day anyway.' His gaze swept, heavy-lidded and resistantly aware, over her. 'For the exercise.'

'You look very fit. Exceptionally fit, really. Quite muscularly fit.' Heat washed over her from her toes to the top of her head as she acknowledged that saying so might not have been particularly prudent. And why was he looking at her that way? He was the half-naked one.

Board shorts and a towel. The man is perfectly adequately covered. This was quite true. The problem was that the board shorts had clung, hadn't they? And the towel still left a lot of skin on display. His waist was trim and his shoulders were stunning.

'Your hair wasn't wet yesterday.' The blurted words were an accusation, as though, if his hair had been wet and she'd worked out he'd been swimming, she would have felt more prepared for the sight of him this way. 'And you didn't smell like chlorine. I have a really good nose for that sort of thing.'

'Today's the first day Julia's allowed me to put my head under the water, and I shower afterwards.' His hair fell in a dripping mass over one side of his forehead and was pushed back from the other.

Spiked lashes blinked away the droplets of water that clung to them. 'I want her to like swimming so I have to accommodate her fears. With her father away, she needs someone…'

'I…er…it must be difficult for your sister, having a husband in the armed forces and unable to do the daddy things at times.' Did the words even make sense? How could she concentrate, with every ounce of her so aware of the sight of him this way?

Not only that, but her hormones insisted on pointing out that Rick had seemed quite appealing indeed in the daddy role. Well, uncle, but it was the same general kind of thing.

Not really.

Yes, really.

She had to get over this idea of wanting a baby!

She had *not* thought that in association with Rick, anyway. She'd merely had a brief moment of considering how, in a bygone time, as in at *the dawn of time*, women may have reacted to strong men by wanting to…um…mate with them.

Which Marissa did not want to do—at all, whatsoever— with her boss.

It seemed expedient to get out of here. But she couldn't quite recall how to bring that about. 'Um…well…'

'Yes?' Rick's gaze locked with Marissa's. He felt worked up and overwrought for no reason he could explain. Other than to name the reason 'Marissa' or, at the least, 'his reaction to Marissa'. That was something he didn't want to do.

Her fingers tightened around the papers in her hands. 'The fax.'

'Let me see what it says.' He took the pages from her,

careful not to touch her. Bent his head to read while she finally looked everywhere but at him.

The knowledge of that belated restraint absurdly made him want her all the more. 'I'll need the files on this from the Civil Engineering department. Go straight there, will you? See if you can catch someone before they close for the day but tell him or her they don't need to hang around. This is something I'll have to address myself.'

'I'll go right now.' With relief evident in every line of her body and expression on her face, Marissa took the fax, wheeled about and escaped with it.

Rick watched her go. She seemed more than glad to get away from him now. Which was, of course, exactly as he wanted things to be…

CHAPTER SIX

From: Englishcrumpet
Just let Tony down gently.

From: Sanfrandani
Better to tell the man so he knows where he stands.

From: Kangagirl
I know you're both right. I don't want to hurt his feelings, that's all. Tony is a really nice guy. Maybe I shouldn't have met with him twice so close together. We had lunch the day after I found my boss giving his niece a swimming lesson on the top floor of our work building, and then we had dinner tonight. If I'd given myself more time between…

From: Englishcrumpet
Do you really think seeing Tony this Saturday or next would have made any difference? What exactly did you say was wrong with him, anyway?

From: Sanfrandani
No spark, wasn't it?

From: Kangagirl

Yes, and that's enough about me and my evening. Tell me about your dating efforts.

'This is a very tall building.' The words passed through Marissa's lips despite herself as they travelled up the outside of the building-in-progress in a cage lift.

It was Monday morning. She'd survived the disappointment of yet again finding 'no spark' during that second date with Tony, had also survived an entire week of working for Rick Morgan.

Had survived by the skin of her self-control, actually, and, really scarily tall buildings should be the least of her concerns.

For the real challenge, try genuinely not noticing the boss who'd taken her to the scary tall building in the first place, rather than merely pretending not to notice him. He superimposed himself on the Blinddatebrides men's profile pictures when she viewed them, took over her brain space during her dating efforts. Marissa felt a spark all right—towards completely the wrong man!

Her fingers tightened their death grip on the handrail inside the cage. 'And the lift is very fast.'

Dizzyingly so now she'd made the mistake of watching things whizz past. She'd thought that might save her from looking at Rick.

'We're quite secure, despite the fact you can see everything around you.' He took her elbow to help her off as the lift stopped. Held on while she came to terms with the height. Held on and her skin tingled while his expression deepened because of their nearness. 'Don't worry.' His voice seemed to come from deep in his chest as he placed his body between hers and the outside of the construction so she only saw him. 'I've got you. I won't let anything happen to you.'

She'd been half okay until he said that. Now she had to add chivalry to his list of attributes.

'Thank you, but I'm sure I'll be quite fine now.' She forced herself to step away from him, did her best to ignore the ache that doing so left behind.

Rick's hand dropped slowly to his side as though he too hadn't been ready to lose that contact.

Had touching her jolted him the same way? The answer was in the lock of his muscles, the tightness of his jaw and the way his lids lowered as his gaze drifted from her eyes to her mouth.

Then suddenly he turned to greet the site manager and the construction boss led them over every inch of the building.

Marissa composed herself and gave the tour her determined attention. This was a genuine meeting, the kind that should happen, not the sort where a man went on about turning a bridge into something completely made-over when that simply wasn't possible.

She took pages of notes of specifications that Rick would expect her to incorporate when he worked on his department memos after the visit and decided she was okay with this. She had it all under control now. All she needed to do was keep her attention on her work, not look at her boss any more than she had to and not think about him at all.

Yes. And that worked really well when they were in constant communication at point blank range, didn't it?

'Overall, the project looks good at this stage.' Rick nodded his approval as they finished their discussion at ground level almost an hour later.

'I'm happy enough with things so far.' The site boss pushed his hard hat back off his head. 'But we have two more days of work, maximum, before we need that shipment of materials from the Melbourne supplier. If we don't get it by then, we're stalled and that's going to cost us in time and wages.'

'And you think the reason for the delay is related to under-lying union issues at their end?' Rick nodded. 'Let me look into this. I'll see if I can get things moving for you. Do you have a copy of the order?'

'Right here.' The site boss removed it from his clipboard.

Rick took it, glanced at it and passed it to Marissa. 'At least you won't have to note all this down.'

Their fingers brushed. His words brushed across her senses at the same time. Just words, but his gaze searched her face, took her in as though he didn't realise he was doing it. As though he couldn't stop himself from doing it.

'I hope we can get back to the office soon.' She needed the security of her desk and at least some semblance of routine. She needed Tom to get better fast and come back to work so she could hide in Gordon's office.

More than that, she needed to stamp the words 'dating website' on her forehead so she remembered what she was supposed to be doing.

Not *supposed* to. *Wanted* to. *Must do. Was doing!* 'So I can get to work on this transcribing.'

They made their way back to work with Rick dictating on the way. Once at the office, Marissa worked on his depart-ment memos and, because they were so pushed for time, they ate lunch at their desks. The busy afternoon that followed shouldn't have allowed time to feel anything but the strain of hours of hard work, and yet she felt a great deal of *other* strain.

Marissa wished that strain away as she made yet another phone call for her boss. 'This is Marissa Warren. I'm filling in as Rick Morgan's secretary and need you to supply me with a list of names of all the people who've worked on the Chartrel project.' She clasped the phone against her ear and smelled Rick's scent on it from when he'd taken a call at her desk minutes earlier.

Marissa closed her eyes and inhaled before she could stop

herself. When she lifted her lids again, Rick's gaze rested on her from the other room, deep grey eyes honed on her.

She forced her attention back to her work, buried herself in it. Maybe she should never emerge again. That might fix things. When Rick came to her desk an hour later, she knew it hadn't fixed anything at all.

'I need you to take these to the departments personally, Marissa.' He held out several signed memos. 'I know we're busy, but I want you to wait for their responses.'

'All right.' She agreed without hesitation. Eager to please him. No. She wasn't overly compliant or willing to go the extra mile. She certainly didn't think they were equals in this and would both be rewarded at the end. The roles were clear. Hers and his. This wasn't the same as the past.

Rick wasn't using her to try to make himself look bigger or better.

Maybe not, but he was still using her in his own way. He'd swept her into working for him without giving her a choice.

Your employment contract states: 'and other duties as required'. He didn't ask you to do anything you're not obliged to do.

Fine. The man had every right to commandeer her. He was still too similar to Michael—all business orientation and focused on his work goals. Marissa held the thought up like a shield, and added another. She wanted to find a safe man, an ordinary man, and yes, okay, maybe she did want to get married and fulfil the promise of the Blinddatebrides.com website.

She *was* almost thirty. Surely a desire for genuine commitment was acceptable at that age? Her mother had been married a decade by then, with a child—what if Marissa could only have one baby, like Mum had?

Didn't it make sense that Marissa might be thinking of getting started on that? That was nothing more than a logistics thing.

She wheeled about. 'When I get back, I'll do something about the explosion out here that was once my…that is…Tom's desk.'

Not her desk.

Tom's desk.

Tom's chair.

She was keeping it all warm for *Tom* and nothing more. On this fortifying reminder, she left. Graciously and calmly, as befitted someone totally in control of her life, her hopes, her dreams and herself.

By the middle of the afternoon it was raining—a drenching fall that obscured the skyline and turned the water in the harbour choppy. Marissa stared at the dismal view before she turned back to the photocopier.

'Deep breath,' she muttered. This was an irritation, after all, not a major problem. She eased open the three side doors on the machine, the one at the back, and pulled out both paper drawers and hit the spring catch on the feed cover so she could see in there as well.

Paper jams happened and, yes, there would now be pages missing from the report and she'd have to figure out what she'd lost, but that was *fine*.

The printer had needed a new ink cartridge an hour ago. One of the computer applications had quit mid-keystroke and she'd lost a few minutes of work. The phone continued to ring hot and there'd been more people from other departments through the door today than in the entirety of last week. She had enough typing sitting on her desk to take her the rest of the day by itself.

Rick was also busy. He was deep in phone talks about some crisis or another right now and it was clear from the content of the several tapes he'd asked her to work on 'urgently' that he was handling the equivalent of photocopier breakdown times about a thousand from *his* desk.

The corporate shark was doing his thing with a great deal of style today, controlling his world, working through problems, making it all come together despite the difficulties and…thriving on it and being cheerful about it as he went along. Marissa did not find this at all stimulating, and it did not show her a different side of her boss, making it exponentially more difficult for her to keep viewing him as a corporate danger zone.

'Let's go. We're finished with this for today.' The day had felt interminable to Rick. From that trip up the building construction, when he'd wanted to protect Marissa, keep her safe, never let anything happen to her, through the rainy afternoon and on into this evening, Rick had struggled with his attraction to her.

She was amazing, the way she got down to work without a word of complaint, no matter what was thrown at her. And he…found that too appealing about her.

Maybe that explained this current madness, because not only was he determined to take her out of the office and feed her, he had no intention of letting her refuse. He took her bag from the desk drawer and pressed it into her hands, and drew her out of her chair.

Well, it was no big deal. Marissa deserved a reward for working so hard. As her boss, he wanted to give her that reward. He'd done the same for Tom countless times.

But this wasn't Tom and, the moment Rick touched Marissa, desire buzzed through his system and threatened to overwhelm him. Well, he would control that desire by the force of his will—maybe he needed to show himself he could do that.

'Wait. What are you doing? I have work up on the computer and I'm nowhere near finished.' She dug her shoes into the carpet, her eyes wide and startled as surprise and uncertainty and the same fire he fought in his bloodstream all bloomed in her gaze.

'We're going to eat and then go to our respective homes to get some rest.' That sounded suitably businesslike. A pity he ruined it by adding, 'The office can wait until tomorrow.'

Not only had he not intended to downplay the importance of his work, but his voice had mellowed as his gaze roved over her, over the hair sticking out from the times she'd whipped the transcription headset on and off, and bent over the photocopier cursing.

She had trousers on today. Pale tan trousers and a black cashmere top that hugged her curves, and soft leather lace-up shoes she hadn't needed to change for their fieldwork.

Though the clothing screamed 'comfortable' and 'sensible' it also lovingly displayed every curve. He'd believed himself beyond reacting to those curves now.

Fooled yourself, you mean.

Well, it was too late to back out of this dinner now. Instead, he scooped everything on her desk into the tray and locked it away while she gasped. Then he shut down her computer and hustled her to the door.

'We're eating.' As colleagues. An hour in her company outside of working hours might take care of his inexplicable interest in her in any case. What did he know of her, after all, personally? She might bore him to tears. He might do the same to her. 'Don't argue. There are shadows under your eyes. And if there's too much work for you we'll farm some out to the general staff.'

This was not an option that had ever occurred to him before. That it did now shocked him into a silence that lasted the entire ride in the lift to the underground parking area.

As he helped her into his big car, she spoke.

'I'm not overwhelmed by the workload and it's kind of you to want to feed me but I assure you I'm not faint or anything.'

She turned her head to face him. 'I've taken care to eat snacks regularly since that incident the first day.'

'I know.' He'd been watching, had checked on her though she wouldn't have realised he was doing it. And, because that knowledge of himself made him feel exposed, he reiterated, 'This is not a kindness. It's a reward for efforts rendered, for both of us, that's all. And I'm pleased to hear it about the workload because, in truth, I don't really like the idea of handing work out of my office.'

They passed the rest of the trip in silence. He figured it was just as well since the words coming out of his mouth didn't seem to be much under his control.

When they arrived at the restaurant, Rick settled Marissa at the table in the same way he seemed to manage everything. With care and courtesy and without any hint of being the user and taker Michael Unsworth was.

'Thank you.' How could Marissa keep up her shield against her boss when he behaved this way? Right now she didn't want to, and that was a dangerous attitude. 'I've finally managed to take a breath for the first time today. I guess…I'm glad you thought of this, of us catching a quick meal on the way home.'

Marissa toyed with her water glass and tried not to think how nice it *was* to be seated opposite Rick in the tiny restaurant tucked away in a side street only about a ten minute drive from his offices.

Bilbie's @ Eighty-Eight sported just a handful of dining tables, spaced far apart and lit individually with a fat red candle on a chipped saucer in the centre of each.

Rain stung the darkened windows and the street lights and car headlights blurred out there, but inside all was quiet and calm.

Well, except for the tension she felt as she finally lifted her gaze and looked into Rick's eyes. Because it was a tension that had nothing to do with residual work stresses, that had an intimacy to it that just wouldn't seem to leave them.

Despite Rick's assertion this was nothing more than a reward for hard work. Despite her need to be attracted to someone other than him.

The latter wasn't working out very well right now.

So why hadn't she declined this meal with him?

Good manners. It might have seemed churlish if she'd refused.

Sure, Marissa. That's what it is.

Rick tore a piece of dense crusty bread from the loaf and dipped it in the herbed dressing and held it out to her. 'It would take as long for you to go home and prepare something for your dinner.'

'Thank you. I didn't realise what I was missing. Here. With this restaurant. It's…a nice setting. You know, for colleagues to visit briefly on a one-off basis. I don't find it romantic at all. I'm sure you don't either. Overall, I'd say the place is homely.' She popped the bread in her mouth before she could say anything else.

The taste and texture of the food enticed a soft sigh from her. The sight of his intent expression as he watched her did the same again. 'The bread…the…er…the bread is delicious.'

'The décor could do with a facelift.' In the candlelight the grey of his eyes darkened as his gaze focused on her. His lashes cast shadows over the strong slash of his cheeks. 'I don't particularly like the colour red either. I prefer autumn tones, like your—' He frowned. 'Like the season.'

Like her hair and the clothing she chose to wear most often? Marissa felt warmed despite herself.

Was she so foolish that she couldn't avoid falling for this kind of man again? For her ex-fiancé's kind of man? Because Rick *was* corporate to the core. He wouldn't care about building a family or doing any of the things she wanted…

'Feta on warm salad.' A waiter deposited the entrées and

whisked a bottle of white wine forward, poured and left the rest of the bottle on the table. Disappeared again.

Rick drew a deep breath. 'Eat.' He gestured to the food, lifted his fork and seemed determined to back the tension off. Back it right off and keep it backed off.

Marissa wanted that too. To assist in that endeavour, she said a little desperately, 'You said you're a skilled diver. Is that something you've done for long?'

Small talk. Surely if she smothered them in small talk it would have the desired effect?

'I started diving in my twenties after my sister Darla... For leisure.' He sipped his wine and something in his face seemed to close up. 'I've dived coastal reefs and other places but nowadays I mostly work locally on some endangered species projects.'

'Your niece really is in good hands with her swimming lessons, then.' A flash of that day, of him bare-chested and off-centre as he'd made up excuses for those swimming lessons, did something warm and tingly to her insides. It softened her emotions and made it difficult to remember him as the high-flying boss, a man very much out of her emotional league.

'Your family—'

'I'd rather hear about you.' He didn't bark the words, but the closed door was clear just the same. 'About your interests. We probably don't have a lot in common.'

No. They probably didn't, and she should appreciate that he wanted them both to accept that.

Rick let his gaze slide to his hands for a moment as he asked, 'So. What are your hobbies?'

What hadn't she tried might be easier to answer. But here was her chance to bore him rigid.

Marissa realised they'd eaten their way through the food and she hadn't even noticed. Well, she was focused now.

'I've tried motorcycle riding. I was eighteen and had a

boyfriend at the Milberry further education college that year. He had tattoos and really long hair.' Was that enough boredom factor? 'I also tried my hand as a jillaroo on an outback station for twelve months but I guess that's a career, not a hobby. Does it count as a hobby if you just tested it out to see how it fit?'

She'd missed her parents a lot during that twelve months. And she was fighting to try to be boring. This wasn't supposed to be a cheerful reminiscence session.

His eyes gleamed with interest that he probably didn't want to feel either. 'I can't imagine you roping calves or whatever girl station hands do.'

Maybe if she went on some more he'd reach that stage of boredom they both wanted.

'I *can* ride a horse, though I'd only had pony club lessons before I went outback.' Her parents had found the money to give her those childhood lessons. They'd been filled with pride the first time she'd taken her little borrowed pony once around the walking ring all by herself. 'The jillaroo thing didn't really work out. I found I didn't like dust and big open spaces all that much.'

Instead of questioning her lack of intrepidity or yawning, he laughed. A deep, rich sound that rippled over her skin and made her catch her breath, and made him look years younger even as his laugh faded abruptly.

Their main courses arrived. Fillet of sole for her on a bed of spiced lentil mash, salmon steak for him with green beans and wild rice.

Marissa though he might leave the discussion there, or change the topic. Or simply let the silence grow as its own demonstration of his complete lack of interest in the minutiae of her life.

Instead, he caught her glance again and said, almost desperately, 'What else have you done with your time?'

'I went through a craft phase that lasted several years.' Surely he would find that very ordinary. She sipped her wine and a part of her registered the wonderful fruity tartness against her tongue before she went on. 'I crocheted a throw rug, made one patchwork quilt—a very small one. Tried out bag beading and made a tissue box cover, created my own calendar out of photos.'

Bought baby wool and hid it in the bottom drawer of my dresser, even though I know it's there and there's a part of me that wants to get it out and buy a knitting pattern for tiny little booties and work out how to make them.

Why did she have to feel this way? Why did she suddenly want all these things with an ever-increasing fierceness? Was it just because she was soon to turn thirty? Well, whatever the reason, it was highly inconvenient and she wished she didn't feel this way, and it was really not conducive to her peace of mind to have such thoughts in Rick's presence!

'And you've made a laminated desk cover of cartoons. I glanced at some of them. You've gathered some good material.' Though his words were bland, the look in his eyes was anything but.

'I've tried out a lot of different things. I'm not like that about work, though,' she hastened to add. 'I'm perfectly happy at Morgan's and hope to stay with the company for a very long time.'

'You've worked with us about six months, haven't you?' As easily as the conversation had rambled through her hobbies, it shifted to ground she didn't want to visit. 'What about before that? There's a stretch of time between those early things and now.' And now he looked interested in quite a different way.

Marissa tried not to let her body stiffen but she so didn't want to answer his question. She shouldn't have let the conversation head in this direction at all. 'I worked as a secretary in marketing for a number of years before…before I moved into my lovely position working for Gordon. I also like my apartment here better than the old one.'

There were no memories of her stupidity within its walls. Michael had never lived with her, but he'd spent time in her home.

Well, a complete break had been in order, and why was she thinking about that when she'd deliberately pushed it out of her mind straight after it had happened? Had learned the lesson and moved right along.

Had she? Or was she defensive on more than one front and trying to patch over the problems by finding a special man she could hand-pick at her own discretion? That question rose up just to add something else to her broodiness and worries about ageing, as if they weren't big enough problems by themselves.

Her mouth tightened. 'And Morgan's is a great company to work for. Anyway, you don't want to hear that boring stuff about me.' She waved a hand.

'Maybe I do.' His intent gaze questioned her. 'What made you leave your previous position? Was it a career choice or something more personal?'

She tightened her lips and shook her head, forcing a soft laugh from between teeth inclined to clench together. 'It was time for a change of pace for me, that's all. Now it's your turn. Have you ever learned to crochet or knit, or maybe taken cooking lessons?' Maybe those questions would shut him down?

'Funny. No. None of those.' For a moment it seemed he would pursue the topic of her career choices but in the end he let it go and moved on. 'I'm not much of a cook, to be honest.' And then he said, 'My eldest niece is taking lessons. She's sixteen and a combination of teenage angst one minute and little girl vulnerability the next. Darla, my other sister, is a good mother to her. The best.'

And then he speared a piece of bean with his fork and chewed it and fell silent and stayed that way until the meal ended.

Eventually he lifted the wine bottle. 'Another glass?'

'No, thank you. I've had enough.' She wished she could blame the wine for the slow slide away of the barriers she needed to keep in place in his company.

Instead of controlling her attraction, she longed to ask more about his family, despite his tendency to guard any words about them.

'Coffee, then.' Rick signalled and a waiter magically appeared.

She drew a breath. 'Yes, coffee would be nice.' Maybe that would sober her thoughts, though she'd had very little to drink.

The beverages arrived. His gaze narrowed on her. 'You're lost in thought.'

Not thoughts he'd want to know. She forced a smile. 'I *should* be thinking. About work tomorrow.' About the fact that they were boss and employee and this evening had been a reward to her as his employee. Nothing more. 'The rain seems to have stopped.'

'Yes.' He turned his gaze to the windows, almost as though he knew she needed a reprieve from his attention.

They finished their drinks in silence.

'I'll take you home.' He placed some notes inside the leather account folder and got to his feet.

Outside the restaurant, he ushered her into his car and waited for her address. When she gave it, he put the car into motion. She wanted to make easy conversation and lighten the mood but no words would come. Then they were outside her apartment building and she turned to face him.

'Thank you for feeding me dinner.' *Will you kiss me good-night? Do I want you to?* 'It wasn't necessary.' And she mustn't want any such thing. Naturally *he* wouldn't want it!

'Your cheeks are flushed. Even in this poor light I can see.' He murmured the words as though he couldn't stop them. 'It's like watching roses bloom. I took you to dinner to prove we have nothing in common but work, and yet…' He threw his door open, climbed out of the vehicle.

He did want her still. Despite everything.

The warmth in Marissa's cheeks doubled and her heart rate kicked into overdrive, even as she sought some other explanation for her conclusion. It *had to be* the wine.

She mustn't be attracted to him, or to his layers. Yet she struggled to remember all the valid reasons why not.

His hand went to the small of her back to lead her inside. 'Ready?'

CHAPTER SEVEN

'WELL, here we are, right at my door,' Marissa babbled as she opened said door, and then appalled herself by adding, 'Would you care to—?'

'For a moment.' He stepped in after her, and then there they were, facing each other in her small living room.

Her fourth floor apartment was functional and neat. A lamp glowed from a corner table. She flicked a switch on the wall and the room came fully into focus—the lounge suite in a dark chocolate colour with a crushed velvet finish, her crocheted throw rug folded neatly at one end.

Prints on the walls and a kitchen cluttered full of gaily coloured canisters and racks of spices completed the picture. 'It's nothing special,' she said, 'but I've tried to make it a home.'

'You succeeded.' His gaze went to the lounge and returned to her face, and a desire he had fought—they had both fought—burned in his eyes.

'Well, thank you again.' She shifted beside him. Wanted him to stay. Forced herself not to offer coffee, late night TV, late night Marissa...

'Goodnight. I shouldn't have come in.' His gaze tracked through her home again.

'Yes. Goodnight. You should...go.'

The muscle of his upper arm brushed the curve of her

shoulder as he turned. He made a choked sound and his fingers grasped her wrist.

'We mustn't—' But she lifted her head as his lowered and then his mouth was on hers.

He tasted of coffee and wine and Rick—a wonderful, fulfilling taste that she lost herself in. So totally lost herself…

Rick's stomach muscles clenched as he fought the urge—almost the *need*—to crush Marissa close. He didn't *need*. He made choices.

Like this one? What was he doing?

Marissa made a soft sound in her throat and her hand lifted to his biceps, and then his shoulder, over his shirt. He wanted her hand on his skin. Somewhere. Anywhere. To warm him…

When she finally stroked her fingers over the cord of his neck and up to the edge of his jaw, he pressed in to her touch. As though he couldn't survive without it. The feeling was shocking, almost unmanning, and yet still he kissed her, pressed nearer, kept going.

Rick caught her hand as it dropped away from his face. Caught it between their bodies with his and held it to his chest. Felt eased somewhere deep inside as he did this.

He meant to control this. It was only desire. It had to be—he could still prove it. Somehow. If he merely kissed her again, tasted her again and then…

The *and then* part didn't happen. Not in the way he intended. Not *Goodbye* and *Glad you enjoyed the dinner* and *That was nothing out of the ordinary.*

Instead, he should ask what the hell he was doing kissing her in the first place.

Even that question couldn't get through. Not with his lips fused to hers, their bodies a breath apart. It should have—it needed to. A part of Rick acknowledged that. He kissed her again anyway. Kissed her and drew her against his chest and wondered if he was stark, staring crazy as his heart thundered and his arms ached to keep her within their clasp.

Marissa didn't know what to do. She'd let this get out of her control and she didn't know how to bring it back. Rick's kiss, his touch, his arms around her all combined not only to swamp her senses but also to overwhelm her in too many other ways.

His hold felt like a haven, his touch what she had needed and waited for. Her emotions were involved in this kiss, and she couldn't let them be. She had to protect herself. He didn't even want to desire her, and she was determined to have no feelings for him. She *didn't* have feelings for him. Right? *Right?*

She gasped and drew sharply back. Her hands dropped from him.

He released her in the same instant, and stared at her as though he couldn't believe what he'd done. As though his actions astounded him. As though he'd *felt* them in the same deep places she had?

Don't fool yourself, Marissa.

His jaw locked tight. 'I showed a weakness of character by doing that. I apologise.' He stepped back from her and the warmth of his eyes returned to a stark, flat grey.

Marissa wanted to take consolation in the fact that he looked as though he had run a marathon, looked as torn and stunned and taken aback as she felt, but he'd soon recovered his voice, hadn't he? And his self-control. She had to do the same.

'This mustn't be repeated. I'll never participate again—'

'I don't mix work with pleasure, or pleasure with emotional commitment. I don't *do* emotional commitment.' He spoke the words at the same time, and then looked at her sharply. 'What do you mean—?'

'Nothing.' She cut her hand through the air. Best to simply deal with this moment, and do so once and for all.

He *was* corporate. He *didn't* feel more than physical interest in her. She had somehow managed to embellish this encounter as if she believed his response to her ran deeper, and his words right now made that absolutely clear. *No commitment.*

She wanted to ask *Why not?* Instead, she forced out the words that had to be said.

'There was an attraction between us and we both gave in to it for a brief moment.' That should put it into perspective. 'It was a mistake and now it's over and done with. I'm sure we'll both very quickly forget it.'

'I'm sure you're right,' he agreed and left.

From: Kangagirl:
I was dumped very publicly by my fiancé in an office environment where we worked together. Now I'm up to my neck in one again. An office situation and lots of hard work, I mean, not anything else because I wouldn't be that silly. I feel pressured, that's all.

From: Englishcrumpet
What's your ex-fiancé's name and where can we find him in case we want to let him know what we think of him? The dirt bag!

From: Sanfrandani
Marissa. Do you still have feelings for the guy?

From: Kangagirl
No. I couldn't possibly have!

But Marissa hadn't been thinking of Michael Unsworth when she'd given her half desperate answer to her friends when they'd discussed last night's dinner. She'd been thinking of Rick. She placed several more loose letters and memos onto the pin inside the file on her desk and told herself not to think back to that kiss at all.

She needed to forget her boss in that way altogether and get back to her dating plans.

No distractions. Especially no Tall, Dark and Delicious distractions.

Tall, Out of Bounds and Emotionally Blockaded, she amended. All the things she could never accept. Except the tall part.

And *she* wasn't emotionally blockaded. She was cautious. A whole different matter.

Rick's mobile phone beeped out a message on his desk.

Marissa forced her attention to her work. What she really needed was for Tom to get better and come back so she could go back to working for Gordon, and stop thinking about Rick.

The fax machine whirred. Marissa got up at the same time that Rick left his desk. They met in front of the machine and hers was the hand that reached first for the sheet of paper that emerged.

'I'll take that. I think it'll be for me.' He reached out his hand.

'Certainly. Here you go.' She passed the fax to him, couldn't help but see the image of a head and shoulders that filled the space. A cheeky smile that belied the wounded expression in dark eyes. Arched brows and thick dark hair and a bit too much make-up on the face, if the black and white image was anything to go by. The girl looked about sixteen. His older niece?

Curiosity slid in sideways to assail her before she could stop it.

The office phone rang. With the fax clasped in his hand, Rick strode to her desk and answered it. 'Rick Morgan.' A pause. 'What's going on, Kirri?'

There was silence as he listened to whatever response he

got and Marissa realised she was in the middle of the room, a party to a private conversation—something Rick wouldn't want her to overhear, if his reaction when she'd seen him with his other niece was any indication.

Marissa scooped a pile of files from the corner of her desk and headed for the file room. Rick's words followed her, as did that faxed image with the wounded eyes.

'You're as beautiful as ever, Kirri. You have lovely blue eyes and a killer smile and you're sweet on the inside where it counts most of all. And so is your mother. You know that, Kirrilea.' His tone was both gentle and fierce. *Not* exactly emotionally blockaded right now!

He drew a breath and Marissa glanced out of the file room at him—just a really brief glimpse—but that one moment showed he was holding back some kind of deep inner anger, wanting to comfort his niece and not let her hear that anger in him, all at the same time. 'Next time don't ask Grandad something like that, okay? Ask me, instead.'

Another pause while Marissa started to push folders away and tried hard not to listen, not to wonder about this grand-father who wouldn't tell a teenager she looked lovely, about her boss's family altogether. Rick had said, 'Ask me.'

She bit her lip. He must have plenty of commitment capa-bility, because he seemed to have it for his nieces, his sisters…

There were other things that week. A call from his mother. Final swimming lessons with his niece and the tinge of colour on the tips of his ears as he'd asked if Marissa might manage to make a certificate, perhaps with an image of a fish on it. Something to state that Julia had passed her first unofficial swimming class.

Marissa navigated each glimpse into his layers with the promise to herself that she wouldn't let them intrigue her. That she didn't want to help him unlock his inner ability to commit—she didn't even know if he truly possessed such a

thing. *He* clearly believed he didn't. That she didn't think of
his kiss constantly and wake in the middle of the night wondering what it would be like if they *did* live at the dawn of
time, if she had chosen him.

Tick, tock, tick, tock.

No. No tick-tocking. No Big 3-0 depressive, subconscious
birthday countdown, no biological rumblings at all, and no
remembering kisses. No, no, no!

On Thursday, while Rick dictated straight over Marissa's
shoulder to finalise a memo he didn't have time to even place
first on a tape, a woman rushed through the door and zeroed
her gaze onto him.

'I'm sorry. I'm probably interrupting, but something's
happened and I don't have to take the chance because I know
I committed to hostess duties for you tonight, Rick, and I'd
never let you down, but I just wondered…'

The woman was thin, with a determined air about her, and
she sported a feminine version of Rick's nose and jaw. She
flipped straight brown hair over her shoulder and for a
moment Marissa saw eyes very like the ones in that faxed pho-
tograph.

Marissa's interest—curiosity—spiked.

Anyone would be curious, she justified, and hated her
weakness where her boss was concerned.

'What's happened, Darla?' Rick strode around the desk,
clasped the woman's elbows. 'Is Kirrilea all right? Did our
fath—'

'Kirri's fine, and Dad is his typical self. There's no point
wishing he'll change because he's made it clear he won't, but
I won't have him upsetting my daughter—' She broke off. 'I
told Kirri to send you the fax. I hope you didn't mind.'

'I didn't.' He chopped a hand through the air as though to
dismiss the very idea. 'Tell me what's brought you here.'

Marissa printed the memo Rick had dictated. 'If Rick can sign this I'll put the phone on answering service and hand-deliver the memo. That way you won't be disturbed while I'm gone.' She would get out of their way and try not to think about his complexities. Or her ever-growing conviction that he had emotional commitment aplenty for his sisters and nieces and therefore why wouldn't he have the capacity for that in any other relationship?

'I'm so sorry. I'm Darla.' The woman stuck out her hand, shook Marissa's firmly. 'Forgive my rudeness. I was a little excited.'

Marissa liked Darla's honesty and her determined smile, the strength she sensed in her and, most of all, her clear affection for her brother.

'I'm Marissa. The borrowed secretary. Very transitory. And it's no problem.' Nor were the callisthenics of her brainwaves. Marissa would get those under control as of now. 'Please, excuse me.'

She took the signed memo, dealt with the phone, left them and delivered the memo.

Should she dawdle back to give them more time? It probably wasn't necessary. Rick would have taken his sister into his office.

He hadn't. They stood exactly where Marissa had left them. Darla was talking fast while Rick nodded.

Marissa's steps slowed as both heads turned her way. 'Um…'

Darla spoke first. 'Would you truly not mind the overtime, Marissa? Rick says you might be prepared to help him out, but I don't want to ask if it will cause any problems.'

Rick leaned a hand against the edge of Marissa's desk. Tension showed in the line of his shoulders and yet, when he looked at his sister, all Marissa could see was affection and…pride?

'My sister has the chance to meet with the central management team in charge of her real estate brokerage.' Rick's gaze met Marissa's and held. 'There may be a promotion in the offing…if you'd be prepared to hostess a business dinner at my home tonight.'

CHAPTER EIGHT

'OF COURSE. I'll be happy to hostess the event.' Marissa spoke the words while panic did its best to get a grip on her.

The business dinner at Rick's home had been noted in the BlackBerry. Everything went in there and, indeed, Marissa had prepared Rick some information so he could be fully informed before the evening. She'd thought that would be the extent of her involvement. The idea of spending a night working at Rick's side, in his home, in a whole other setting to the office, where she would see even more parts of him…well, it unnerved her even while her hormones set up a cheering section about it.

Marissa spoke to the other woman. 'If Rick feels I could be of assistance, I…I'm sure I can cope with hostessing the event.'

Somehow. Maybe. If she managed to get a grip on herself and her thoughts about her boss between now and then. Marissa tried to keep the hope out of her tone as she added, 'That is, if there's no one else more suitable, maybe someone else in the family who could take your place?'

'There isn't,' Rick said, squashing that hope quite flat.

A smile broke over Darla's face. 'Oh, thank you!'

The woman impulsively threw her arms around Marissa and then turned to her brother and hugged him. He cupped her head so tenderly in his hand as he hugged her back. A fierce well of protectiveness crossed his face before they separated.

Layers. How many more could he possibly have? Now Marissa's hormones had given up the cheer squad routine and brought out the tissues, going all emotional on her right when she didn't need that to happen.

'It's settled then.' Rick drew his wallet from his pocket and pulled out some notes, frowned when his sister opened her mouth. 'I know you like good luck charms. Buy one to wear tonight.' He gestured to the silver bracelet on her wrist. 'You'll find room for it on there somewhere. And get something for Kirrilea—a trinket. And tell her my secretary very kindly laminated that faxed page and I have it on my desk where I can enjoy it.'

Darla's fingers closed over the money and his hand, and a sheen of moisture came to her eyes before she blinked and turned away. 'God, I wish our father had half… Well…' She smiled with a fierce determination that quickly became the real thing as she turned once again to Marissa. 'Thank you. I hope I'll have good news after tonight but, even if not, I appreciate the chance to attend the meeting.'

She rushed out of the office at the same frenetic pace she'd entered it.

'If her speed is anything to go by, she probably does the work of five people and very much deserves a promotion.' Marissa made the observation lightly when she didn't feel light at all. But she would be okay tonight. *She would.*

'I know she deserves it.' He murmured the words without appearing to think about them.

There'd been no wedding band on Darla's finger, no mention of a man in the proceedings and an impression that Darla was alone and turned to her brother for emotional support.

Alone with a sixteen-year-old daughter. Darla hardly looked old enough. And Marissa now wanted to clutch at straws, even though something told her that would be futile. 'Did you really need me to help you tonight, or did you just want Darla to feel free to chase this job promotion?'

Rick's eyelashes veiled his expression as he answered. 'There's no one else suitable at such short notice.'

'Right, then I guess that will be fine.' She would simply maintain her professionalism and make it fine. She could do that. All it would require was a little concentration, a lot of focus and maybe some tranquilliser for the hormone squad!

A phone call came in then. Marissa thought she recognised the voice, but couldn't place it. When she asked for a name, the caller paused for a heartbeat before saying, 'Just put me through. I'm returning his call.'

Marissa connected the call.

Rick rose from his desk and closed his door after he answered the call. Super-secret business, apparently.

Marissa got on with her work.

Whatever, anyway. She had more important things to think about. Like tonight!

'I think Carl Fritzer is deliberately goading you on the topic of environmental issues.' Marissa directed the comment to Rick and then nodded her thanks to the catering guru as she accepted a platter of artfully arranged biscotti and small handmade chocolates.

The evening was more over than started now, and the three of them stood in the kitchen of Rick's penthouse apartment. It was a large and lush place—four bedrooms at least and functional in all the nicest ways but, for tonight, Rick had taken everyone outside to the rooftop terrace.

Marissa had fought with herself every step since she'd arrived. She didn't want to be delighted by his home, nor constantly and utterly aware of him in it. Didn't want to note that his midnight-blue shirt and black trousers made him look even more Tall, Mysterious and Compelling. She still wanted Ordinary, darn it. She did!

'I truly don't understand why Mr Fritzer would do that.' *Focus on work, Marissa.* 'What difference does it make to any possible business dealings between our company and his?' The stamp of ownership she put on her statement was a whole new problem. Since when had it been the 'Marissa and Rick team'?

Remember what happened to the 'Michael and Marissa' so-called 'team'? Well, you should!

Marissa forced herself to go on. 'Morgan's follows all the codes to the letter and, in a lot of cases, goes a lot further than most companies in its efforts towards environmental friendliness.'

'The man seems to consider a bit of goading as good entertainment value, but I noticed his colleagues don't seem to share his enthusiasm for the topic.' When Rick shrugged, his shirt clung to his broad shoulders, outlined the strength of the muscles beneath the cloth.

There was something different in him tonight when he looked at her, too. She couldn't pin it down, but he seemed to be weighing her up, or searching for something. He was perhaps softer towards her? More attentive? Interested in a different way?

Some of his examination seemed—she didn't know— almost empathetic or something? But that made no sense.

What if he *was* beginning to think of her in a deeper way? Given her determination to steer utterly clear of even noticing him, the thought shouldn't please her, yet she felt a reciprocal softening towards him.

'There may be something Fritzer is hiding about his own dealings or standards.' Rick's gaze caressed her face and neck as he went on. Did he realise he was doing that? 'I'll have a team investigate that possibility before I commit us to any work with the company. I can find out anything I need to know before they get to the stage of an acceptance of our offer of services.'

He hesitated and a combination of unease and knowledge, awareness and that same empathy flared in his eyes again. For a moment Marissa thought he would reach for her, right there in front of the caterer...

'Is that coffee? Just what's needed.' One of the female business delegates strolled inside. 'Can I help with anything?'

'I think we have it under control.' A frown crossed Rick's face before he lifted the tray of coffees.

Disappointment surged through Marissa and she told herself not to be foolish, forced her attention to the drinks Rick held on the tray.

The lattes bore everything from starfish shapes to mini Harbour Bridges in the foam tops. He thanked the caterer. 'The rest we can manage for ourselves, if you're happy to let yourself out?'

The young man scooped up a backpack from the corner of the kitchen. 'Cheers. It was a pleasure to help you, as always.' He strode to the apartment's front door and left.

They returned to the West Australian business delegation of men and women where they sat in big squashy outdoor chairs grouped around low tables.

Rick's apartment and exclusive terrace took up the entire top level of the building. The formal outdoor dining area seated up to twenty people. They'd eaten there with city views all around them and the lush foliage of the rooftop garden behind them. The sight and scent of flowers and plants and shrubs filled the area. Roses and mint, hardy native shrubs mixed with hydrangeas and mat-rush and Easter cactus.

His home was truly gorgeous and Marissa couldn't help but appreciate the beauty. He wore his wealth very comfortably here. He'd seemed pleased when she'd first arrived and admired his apartment and surroundings.

It was also a large enough home, and secure enough, that a small family could thrive quite nicely here if necessary. A house with a full garden would be better, of course, but children could enjoy the terrace garden, or be taken to play in the large park right across the road from the building…

Oh, what was she thinking? She had to focus on the business of the evening, not fantasies that were becoming more and more difficult to quash.

'Well, it's a lovely evening for a business function and this is the perfect setting for it.' She caught Rick's eye and gestured with her hand, but all that did was draw their attention to the fact that darkness had now fallen and, beyond the well-lit terrace, the city lights, Lavender Bay, the Harbour Bridge, and buildings of all shapes and sizes glittered before them.

The setting was romantic. Her hormones had recognised this immediately, even if Marissa had been busy trying not to notice the fact.

Why couldn't she stop viewing her employer in this way? Stop herself from developing a deeper and deeper interest in him when she knew that doing so was utterly futile? Was it because she felt she knew Rick better now? Somehow, she'd started to trust him as she'd watched him care for his sisters and nieces and saw his business dealings, which were far more frank than Michael Unsworth's behaviour had been in the workplace, or out of it.

'Well, here's the coffee, everyone,' she called. 'Actually, it's coffee *art*, with thanks to our now departed caterer.' She pushed the memories of Michael away and tried not to think about her shifting feelings towards her boss. Rick was much more difficult to dismiss than thoughts of Michael, and that knowledge was not comforting.

Rick didn't want any kind of emotional commitment. He hadn't said why, but he'd made that fact clear. She suspected it had to do with his father, or his family life generally, but what did it matter in the end? Her boss didn't want *her*. Maybe she should simply be grateful he was being honest about that. She started to hand out the drinks.

Rick watched Marissa hostess the small group, chatting as she went, and he thought about her use of the term 'we,' as though she felt as invested in the company as he did. He couldn't forget kissing her, nor reconcile himself to the shift inside him that had somehow been different from anything he had experienced before.

She looked beautiful tonight, all soft curves beneath the golden dress, her hair up and her nape tantalisingly bare. He wanted to press his lips to that soft skin, to somehow pay homage to her.

Thoughts battered at him. She looked right here—in his home. He wanted to keep her here. And other thoughts—of taking her to his bedroom, closing the door on the world and staying there with her until he knew all of her, understood all of her and she'd given all of herself to him. How could he want that when he would never give her the same in return?

Maybe he didn't want it. Not really. Couldn't this all be about lust and the confusion of feeling this way towards a woman he was working with and coming to admire in a working environment?

The business talk moved on. Fritzer goaded a little more, and Rick ignored it. He sat at Marissa's side, his arm stretched across the back of her chair in a gesture he knew was possessive, but he couldn't make himself stop it. He needed to be near her, close enough to touch even if he didn't.

Yes. He was in trouble, but he could control it. He must be able to do at least that.

Over coffee, talk turned to what the city had to offer.

One of the women leaned forward. 'We have half of tomorrow before we leave. I'm wondering what to do with the time.'

'There's plenty on offer in terms of entertainment, shopping, whatever you like, really.' Rick stretched out his legs, stared at the neat crease in the dark trousers. Imagined the gold of Marissa's dress against the fabric.

All roads led back to it. The fact that he wanted Marissa—still wanted her.

'You might consider the new animal petting zoo.' Marissa spoke the words to the other woman. Her gaze met Rick's and a delicate flush rose in her cheeks as she seemed to wish she hadn't raised the topic.

She went on, waved her hand. 'Holding a koala is a unique experience.'

And then he remembered *that* moment, the trembling of her shoulders and the rush of protective instinct that had coursed through him, had tapped into instincts he'd been ignoring ever since that moment.

'The koalas smell of eucalyptus oil, don't they, Marissa?' *Keep it light. That's all it can be.* 'Did you manage to wash the scent out of that cardigan?'

'I did get the cardigan clean, and I imagine our overseas visitors probably made good use of a dry-cleaner's after that visit.' Marissa lowered her gaze to her coffee cup. 'We've had some interesting moments during my brief time filling in as your assistant.'

Maybe she wanted to remind them both that this wouldn't last. That soon she would go back to her regular job and he wouldn't see more of her than a glimpse in a corridor from time to time. Maybe he should be glad she wanted to remind him of that.

Instead, a kaleidoscope of images and moments spent with her bombarded his mind and his senses. Marissa with a hard hat squashed over her curly hair that day on the bridge. Presenting him with a laminated certificate for his niece for completing her swimming lessons. Cursing at the photocopier beneath her breath when she thought he couldn't hear her.

He wanted Tom back on his feet but the thought of Marissa easing back to the periphery of his working life didn't sit well with him.

'We should go.'

'Yes, it's been a productive evening.'

'We'll take a vote with the full group and you'll hear from us.'

One by one their guests stood. It took another few minutes for Rick to see them completely out and away.

When Rick closed the door finally on the guests, Marissa moved to the terrace to collect the empty cups and return them to the kitchen. She turned as he joined her.

'I'll get the biscotti tray.' And then she needed to leave, to forget this glimpse into yet another side to her boss.

'Leave it for now.' He poured two glasses of liqueur, passed one to her and led her to the edge of the terrace with his hand on her arm.

'I guess we deserve five minutes to celebrate this evening's hard work. To enjoy the view now it's quiet and there's time to focus on it.' She couldn't help the observation that followed. 'Somehow I'd expected your apartment to be all chrome and black and sharp lines with the view carefully shut outside through long planes of plate glass. The terrace entertainment area surprised me. It's lovely.'

'I'm pleased you like it.' His gaze darkened on her, again seemed to search inside her.

Would he be as pleased to know she'd imagined it being a home to a family? No. He wouldn't, would he? She lifted the glass and inhaled the aroma of the drink. 'I smell spices and tea and rum. And vanilla?'

'It's Voyant Chai Cream. I think you'll like it.' He watched her over the rim of his glass as they sipped.

'Very smooth.' She sipped again. Savoured. Tried hard not to think about the war going on inside her body that shouldn't be going on at all, and especially not where Rick was concerned.

For the first time in her life Marissa was subjected to forces of her own nature, her own hidden needs, which she had never even considered she might struggle to control. She couldn't seem to stop herself from associating some of those desires with her boss. She forced her attention back to the drink in her hand. 'It's delicious.'

'Yes.' The single word seemed to wrap around her, be meant for her. All he did was match her sip for sip before he finally set his glass down, tucked his hands in his pockets and looked out over the harbour, and yet she felt his desire for her as though he'd spoken it aloud.

'It was a good night, don't you think?' He glanced at her, the heat in his eyes partially concealed, but very much there. Talked business as they should be doing. 'Despite that bit of goading, I expect they'll sign with us for their project.'

'It was—yes. I believe it was a successful evening.' She set her glass down with trembling fingers.

The softness of the city night cast his face in clarity and shadows. Just like the man. She had to pull herself together, to play this out the safe way, to keep her focus on their working relationship and not these odd, nebulous things she wanted that she didn't even know if she could ever have.

She should put herself to sleep or something until she'd passed her birthday, get it behind her so she could realise it hadn't changed anything, that she was the same inside and she didn't have to pine for a family of her own.

'In part, that success is thanks to you.' He let his gaze roam over her face. 'I think you captured all of them.' His hands fell to his sides. She thought he murmured, 'You captivated me.'

A long beat of silence followed as she fought with herself. Finally she spoke. 'I should go. Tomorrow is another working day.' Maybe if she reminded herself of that she wouldn't respond to him quite so much.

Marissa moved away from the view, from the sparkle of city lights. They stepped inside and she collected her bag from the kitchen. 'I'll get the doorman to organise me a cab straight off the rank downstairs.'

'I'll take you down.'

'There's no need.' She drew a breath as they paused before his door. 'Goodnight, Rick. I'm glad I could help. I hope your sister gets the job promotion. I got the impression it would mean a lot if she did.'

'Darla deserves the break. She's worked hard for that company for many years, first as a part-timer and working up to full-time once Kirrilea started school.'

'You're proud of her. Of your niece, too.' She faced him before the closed door, searched his eyes.

'They're easy people to be proud of.' Rick reached past her to open the door. His fingers wrapped around the doorknob.

And the tension wrapped right around them, too.

'Back away from me, Marissa. Tell me not to mess with a perfectly good working relationship. Tell me not to mess with you.'

'You've been different tonight.' She whispered the words and he braced his feet and drew her into the V of his body.

Her hand lifted to his chest and he kissed her. Pressed his mouth to hers and his body to hers, and pleasure and a feeling rightness swept through her.

'More.' He whispered the word.

Marissa lost herself so thoroughly in Rick's kiss, lost senses and feelings and responses and, yes, emotions, in him. When his lips left hers to trail over her ear to the sensitive cord of her neck, she closed her eyes and let the feel of his body against hers, his hands cupping her head, her shoulders so sweetly, sweep through her.

Could a man's touch communicate straight to the heart of not only a woman's senses, but also her soul? It seemed so.

She clasped her hands on his shoulders, curled her fingers around his upper arms and held on. When he skirted his hands up from her waist, over her back, to where her shoulders were bared by the wide cowl neck of the dress, she shivered.

A strained, needy sound passed through his lips. It was the last thing she consciously registered for long moments as they stood by his door, their bodies tightly entwined, her resistance and grand plans in shambles. Her bag lay at her feet. She had no idea when it had landed there.

'Say my name.' The words were harsh and possessive, demanding and enervating. 'I want to hear it. I don't want you to be thinking of him—'

What did he mean? A chill rushed over her skin and all through her body. She wrenched away from him. 'What do you know? What have you heard? About that fake engagement I believed was real? About Michael—'

'Ah, I didn't mean to say that.' He pushed a hand through his hair. 'I had to know why you left your last job, Marissa.' His eyes were dark and turbulent. 'The information about your personal life—I didn't ask for it, I stopped the man when I realised where he was headed with the conversation but by then it was too late.'

'Right. I see. So you phoned my old company to investigate why I left, and you found out things about me at that time.' If his gaze softened into pity she would die right there, and now it all made sense. This. This was the empathy he'd displayed earlier.

'Without meaning to find those things out, yes.' He seemed to search for words.

Apology. Regret.

Yes, she heard them in his tone but, most of all, she heard that he knew of that embarrassment. He now probably thought she was desperate and on a manhunt. What if he thought she'd set out to hunt *him*? Mortification, shame and anger crashed through her. She clutched at the anger because the others were too awful to bear.

'That call. I knew I recognised the voice.' And Rick had closed his office door and talked about her. 'I don't care if you say it was business.' Her voice shook. 'I'd started to trust you. I can't believe I did. What did the man tell you? That Michael Unsworth made a fool of me? What does that have to do with my good record at Morgan's?'

'Nothing. I didn't want that information. I didn't ask for it.' He reached for her hand but she drew back.

He went on in a low voice, 'I'm sorry he hurt you, Marissa.'

'Well, don't be sorry because I am totally over the way Michael treated me. I learned from it and I moved on. Was that what this kiss was about? Pity? Tell me!'

He drew a harsh breath into his lungs. 'You know better than that. I want you in my bed and I have from the first day I had you up on that excuse for a bridge with me. Maybe you should pity *me*, because I can't seem to get that desire for you out of my system, no matter what I do.'

Rick's admission stunned Marissa into silence. More, perhaps, because of the flash of something deeper than desire that burned for a moment in his gaze before he masked it.

Oh, will you listen to yourself, Marissa? Do you want to fall for Mr Corporate a second time?

Rick had just *proved* his ruthlessness to her!

But he'd also apologised and seemed as though he meant it.

She scooped her bag from the floor. 'I just want us to work together and get along and I want to follow my well thought out plans for my life in peace. Is that so much to want?'

'It isn't. It isn't too much to want.' He took a step towards her as she wrenched open the door. 'Marissa—'

But she didn't wait to hear what he might have said.

She left.

CHAPTER NINE

To: Sanfrandani, Englishcrumpet
From: Kangagirl
One last thing to tell you both. I spoke to Mum on the phone early this morning. We had a good talk and I let her know I'd rather spend a weekend with her and Dad a bit down the track after my birthday, that I'm really busy at the moment and don't want a party of any kind.

From: Englishcrumpet
I'm sure your mum will understand.

From: Sanfrandani
You can throw a big party when you're ready.

From: Englishcrumpet
Or not.

From: Kangagirl
People make a big deal out of the thirtieth birthday, but really, it's just another day on the calendar. I probably won't even think much about it at all.

Grace had instant messaged a little after that, a message Marissa caught on her way out the door to go to work. She'd asked whether Marissa was in denial about her thirtieth birthday.

Marissa hadn't had time to respond. And right now she was focused on other things. Rick Morgan things, to be precise. Work things. Marissa barrelled along the corridor towards Rick's suite of offices.

Anyway, she had to come to terms with that looming birthday. It wasn't denial to say it wasn't significant, it was the power of positive statement. Say it enough times and she'd come to believe it.

If she could apply the same outlook to her relationship with Rick—her *working only* relationship—that would be a great help.

As a mature professional, she could work with Rick until his secretary returned. She only had to survive that long and then she could forget him, forget what he knew about her. All she needed to do was hold her head up and he'd soon realise he had no reason to pity her.

Dani and Grace had blamed last night's kiss on too much alcohol or maybe an overload of successful business-related feeling when Marissa had calmly and casually discussed the topic with them via two separate Instant Message sessions last night and this morning—before she'd sent that later message about Mum and avoiding a birthday party.

You mean when you buzzed them, desperate for some support because you were scared stiff you'd let yourself fall for the boss only to find out he'd invaded your privacy?

She had *not* fallen for the boss, nor did she intend to. And he *had* invaded her privacy.

He's head of a multi-million dollar company and you've been working directly for him, handling some very sensitive material. He exercised his right to enquire about your past employment and he said he only *wanted to know about that.*

You know the department head who spoke to him is a big gossip.

Marissa had worked out the identity of the caller, of course. It had only taken the jolt of discovering that Rick had gone after the information for her to remember the owner of that somehow familiar voice.

Okay, fine, there was that. But she still didn't have to like it or feel comfortable. Rick *did* know her secret.

Perhaps he hadn't acted inappropriately, and he had seemed to truly regret the outcome. And she knew one of his secrets. That he wanted to make love to her, had desired her from Day One.

That knowledge did not thrill or tempt her. She couldn't let it!

Her initial IM sessions with Dani and Grace hadn't been the result of a desperate buzzing, either. More of a, *Hello, if you're there a talk might be nice but no problem if you're not* kind of buzzing. An, *I don't need help or anything. Just felt like chatting* sort of buzzing.

They were all friends. Grace had already confessed that she was concerned about her daughter Daisy going off on her gap year backpacking around Europe and Dani had admitted she had financial pressures and was worried about paying off her student loans from college and graduate school.

Marissa had owed it to them to contribute her share to the confidence stakes, and so she had admitted that she might be having a teensy tiny issue with awareness of her boss. Nothing dramatic. Certainly nothing to worry about. She could put it to rights.

Grace had been the voice of reason, had encouraged Marissa not to blame Rick too much for his accidental knowledge of her past. Dani had been a little silent on the subject, but certainly sympathetic. They'd swapped mailing addresses and phone numbers after their chats, and Marissa had visited the early opening post shop this morning and sent them both some gifts.

Chocolate. Australian chocolate, to be exact, because chocolate lifted your spirits and gave you confidence.

Because her friends might enjoy it, and Marissa did not need courage to face Rick again, even if she had eaten a chocolate bar this morning while mailing the others. All in all, she was dealing very well with her life right now.

She hadn't even thought about that knitting idea for the past couple of days. Not really. Other than to look at the wool, wondering about the exact blend of lemon and pink and blue of the variegated strands...

Marissa shoved open the door to the office suite.

'Good morning, Rick.' She spoke his name in a firm, even, totally in control and not at all kissed senseless or embarrassed or overwrought tone as she crossed the office space at a fast clip.

Stride in. Purposefully get to work. Keep it impersonal and he would soon see she was not at all carrying any scars from the past.

No? So why did you let that past dictate the kind of man you want in your future?

Because she'd learned from her mistake!

'Thank you, Collins. I appreciate you bringing that to my attention.' Rick's voice was pitched in a businesslike tone that had absolutely nothing to do with Marissa's greeting or, indeed, with her at all.

Because he wasn't alone, was he? How unprofessional of her to just storm in and start yammering away without even looking. Well, she'd only said good morning, but even so...

Concentrate, Marissa. If professionalism at all times is going to be your motto, you might start with attention to detail. Such as—who might be with your boss when you enter the office.

She hurried to her desk as Rick and the other man headed out of Rick's room. Right. Marissa set about sorting her in-tray's contents into 'Get it done early', 'Can wait until later this morning' and 'Yeah, sure she'd really get to this today. Not!' piles on her desk. The laminate covered in cartoons quickly disappeared beneath the piles of work. She wasn't in the mood to be amused anyway.

Rick saw his visitor out. The man gave Marissa a nod in passing. And then Rick turned to her and yanked at his tie and a wealth of regret showed in his eyes as he seemed to search for words.

'About last night…' He cleared his throat. 'About my investigating why you'd left your last position, I mean…'

'I overreacted.'

Please accept that as the truth, and please don't bring up the kiss that led to that discussion.

'My reaction was silly because that piece of past history is exactly that. I've moved on. I'm dating, at least casually, again—looking for a nice, ordinary guy. Let's just forget all of it. That's what I'd like the most at this point.'

If her request rang hollow, she hoped he didn't note it. And if his gaze remained as dark and uncertain as before, she couldn't let herself think about that. Professionalism at all times. She couldn't let there be anything else.

Rick's gaze searched hers before he nodded and murmured, 'I'm pleased you're prepared to forget it.' He didn't *look* pleased, but really, what would she know?

The next couple of hours passed in a flurry of the usual busyness. Rick worked on, but he had a hard time concentrating. He wanted to go out to Marissa, tell her again that he was truly sorry, somehow make up for the way he'd invaded her privacy. He didn't want to think of her 'dating casually' and how possessive and inappropriate was that?

'I was wondering, after everything, if Darla got the promotion? I meant to ask earlier but I…got distracted.' Marissa asked the question from his office doorway, and he looked up into brown eyes that had melted for him last night, had filled with warmth and delightful response before he'd ruined it all with his thoughtless words.

Ruined what couldn't be allowed to happen anyway. Maybe he should just be grateful that something had put a stop to where that kiss had been headed. And forget about her 'dating' plans. 'Darla got the promotion. I'm taking her and Kirri out during Kirri's school lunch break today to celebrate.'

'I'm really happy for her. Please pass on my congratulations to your sister when you see her.' Marissa turned away and went back to her desk and her work.

That was as it should be, right?

So why did Rick feel so empty inside, as though he'd almost grasped something special in his hands, only to have it slip away after all?

What was the matter with him? He pushed himself back into his work and tried not to think beyond it.

Marissa observed her boss's concentration on his work and tried her best to emulate it. She didn't want to think. About his complex family. About him at all.

The hours came and went and, late in the afternoon, after a quiet lull of concentrating solely on her work uninterrupted, the phone rang. She took the call, put it through to Rick. 'You have a call on line one. It's Tom.'

Rick murmured his thanks and she went on with her work.

'Tom.' His voice softened. 'How are you?'

Another phone line rang. As she reached for it, Rick said, 'Just rest and do whatever the doctor tells you, Tom. If it's another two weeks, so be it. Marissa—Marissa's holding the fort well enough in your absence.'

Marissa tuned out Rick's voice and answered the second call. 'Marissa Warren.'

'Marissa, it's Dad.' His voice was strained as he went on.

'Mum's in the hospital, love, with quite bad abdominal pain. They're doing tests right now and they're going to send her for an ultrasound before they—' He cleared his throat. 'To see what's wrong.'

'I'll come straight away, Dad. Is Aunty Jean—?' Panic flooded through her and she couldn't remember what she'd been going to ask.

'Yes, Jean's on her way.' Her father drew a breath. 'She should be here in another hour.'

'Good. That's good.' Marissa had to get to Milberry. It was her only thought as she clutched the phone tighter in her hand. 'You can't use your cellphone inside the hospital, I know, but you'll phone my cell once Mum's back from the tests, let me know if there's anything—?'

Marissa was in trouble. Rick ended his call with Tom and reached her desk before he realised he'd moved. As she raised her eyes and locked onto his, something deep inside him clenched.

'If there needs to be an operation they might move her to a larger hospital in another town.' Marissa paused and listened again. 'Yes, I understand we don't know enough at this stage. I'll just set off, Dad. You're right. That's all I can do for now. I love you. When you see Mum again, tell her I love her and I'm on my way.'

The moment she replaced the phone, Rick spoke.

'What do you need?' Whatever it was, he would get it for her, do it for her. The decision was instinctive. He didn't want to examine the significance of it, could only worry for the woman in front of him. 'Where's your mother? Let me know the fastest way you can be at her side and I'll make it happen.'

Marissa was already on her feet, her hand in the drawer to retrieve her bag when she stopped, looked up at him. She blinked hard and her mouth worked. 'Mum was rushed to hospital in all this pain.'

'What happened to her, sweetheart?' The endearment slipped out, perhaps as unnoticed by its recipient as it was unplanned by him.

Her brown eyes darkened. 'I only know it was abdominal pain. The ambulance had to get her from the newsagent's while Dad came back in from his work on one of the roadworks crews outside of town. Dad only got to see her for a second before they took her away, and they wouldn't tell him much. I have to get to Milberry. I need the Mini.'

'The car you hire from your neighbour.' He remembered her muttering something about that, the day she'd felt faint after their crisis meeting.

It felt so long ago, and a Mini wasn't the vehicle to get her out of the city and to her family with any kind of speed or comfort.

Rick caught her wrist between his fingers, rubbed his thumb across the soft skin. Hoped the touch offered some comfort, and silently acknowledged that a part of him wanted the right to more, whether that meant his emotions were involved in her, or not.

He couldn't worry about any of that now. 'Do any flights go to the township? I only know of it vaguely. It's rather off the beaten path, isn't it? How far is it by road? I can charter a plane for you if there's an airstrip…'

'There are no flights, no airstrip. Milberry doesn't have an airport. It's a reasonable sized town but there's nothing much around it.' Marissa stared at the mess on her desk as though she didn't know what to do with it, and then she stared at him as though she wasn't quite sure what to do with his offer either. 'It'll take me almost three hours in the Mini. Mum's been at the hospital about an hour already, I think.'

'I'll take you myself—'

'I forgot. My neighbour left Sydney this morning with the Mini.' She broke off and said in confusion, 'You'll take me?'

'My car will be faster than a Mini, faster than you having to hire something.' He wanted to beg her to let him do this for her. Instead, he made it a statement and silently urged her to simply agree with it. 'We can leave straight away.'

Confusion clouded her worried brown eyes. 'You can't… I can't ask…'

'I can, and I'm not asking you to ask.' *He* needed permission. Needed to be allowed, wanted to draw her into his arms and promise her everything would be all right, that he would fix everything for her. 'Give me one minute and we're out of here.'

He used that minute to get on the phone and instruct one of the senior staff to come in and pack the office up for them and secure everything.

His borrowed secretary was in trouble. He could help her and he'd chosen to do so. That didn't have to be any big thing, and his relief as Marissa put herself in his hands and allowed him to usher her from the building was simply that of a man who had got his way.

He told himself all this, but the intensity he felt inside didn't lessen.

In moments he had Marissa out of the office building, into his ground-eating vehicle and away. A glance showed that her face hadn't regained any colour. She was also utterly silent. 'Tell me the route.'

She gave him the directions and fell silent again.

Rick clenched his hands around the wheel and got them clear of the city. Once he had, he murmured her name and reached for her hand. He curled his fingers around hers and she cast a glance his way.

'Move into the middle seat so we can talk while I drive.' He tugged on her hand. 'You're going to tell me everything your father said, the name of the hospital your mother is in and all you know about her situation.'

She obeyed him without question, and that told him,

more clearly than anything else, the extent of her concern for her mother.

Once he had her shoulder pressed against his arm, her body close enough to feel her warmth and know she could feel his warmth, Rick relaxed marginally.

'Talk, Marissa.' He stroked his fingers over hers, registered the tremble that spoke of her tension.

'Dad said they were sending her for an ultrasound of the abdominal area.' She drew a deep breath. 'There's a small imaging facility in Milberry that does that sort of thing and they were opening it up for her. I guess the place must close at five. That would have meant another ambulance trip, though a short one.

'Dad wanted to go with them but the nursing staff said no. I suppose they needed to focus on finding out what…what needed to be done after the tests.' Her breath hitched as she ended this speech.

Rick squeezed her hand, drew it onto his thigh and curled his fingers over hers. 'There are lots of things that can cause pain that are not life-threatening. If it was her appendix, for example, an operation should set it to rights.'

She nodded. 'Maybe that's what it is.'

'How old is your mother? Has she enjoyed good health until now?'

'She's fifty. She never gets sick. Not like this. Neither of them do.' Suddenly the fingers beneath his curled with tension. 'What if…'

'What if we ring the hospital and ask if there's any news?' He inserted the question gently.

Marissa tugged her bag from the floor by its strap. Her fingers were curled beneath Rick's, against his strong thigh. She couldn't seem to make herself let go or shift away. She didn't want to leave the comfort of that press of warmth against her shoulder and arm.

Rick *wasn't* Michael Unsworth. He wasn't anything like her ex-fiancé. That knowledge was probably even more cause for worry, but right now she only had room to worry about Mum.

She lifted her phone. A moment later she had the hospital on the line.

'It's Marissa Warren. My mother…' she cleared her throat '…my mother, Matilda Warren, arrived by ambulance with abdominal pain. I'd like to know how she is.'

'Your mother is still under examination,' the woman on the end of the line said briskly. 'She's had several tests done and Doctor is with her now. We'll know more in a little while. Are you on your way to see her, dear? There might be more news if you leave it another half hour or so…'

'We're only about another hour away now.' Rick murmured the words.

She glanced at him, realised she'd ended the call and simply sat there with the phone in her hand.

'I've taken it for granted that they're there, in good health…' She trailed off.

'Then keep believing in that good health. And if she needs anything that I can arrange or help with, to be airlifted to a different hospital in a private helicopter or anything…'

'I hope she won't need that, but I appreciate your words.' She swallowed hard and her fingers flexed beneath his as she registered just how much his concern meant to her.

She couldn't think about that now, couldn't see his actions as a sign of his ability to care, or commit. 'We'll lose phone reception for a while about half an hour out of Milberry. I may not get to hear the test results until we're close to town.' Her gaze tracked over him despite herself. 'There's an area that doesn't pick up very well.'

'You should make any other calls now before we lose reception.'

'Yes, I'd better do that.' How did Rick feel about holding

her hand? Had he simply wanted to offer comfort? It felt somehow deeper than that, and he was so determined to help her, anything she might need...

He glanced her way. 'Did you want to try your father again?'

'No. Dad won't have his phone on inside the hospital, but I'd like to send a message to one of my friends.' She toyed with her phone. 'Yes, I think Grace would be out of bed by now, or at least close to it.'

She'd also arranged a drink after work with a man from the dating site. Marissa looked up his number in her phone listings—just as well she'd put it in there—and sent a quick message explaining her situation. Doing that made her aware, finally, of how close she was pressed to Rick's side, how much she'd been leaning on him, physically and emotionally.

'I'm sorry. I'm not usually so...needy.' She moved away to the passenger seat.

'You weren't.' He cast a glance at her that revealed warmth and caring in the depths of his eyes. 'There's nothing wrong with leaning on someone else sometimes.'

Marissa's phone gave a number of beeps and she quickly glanced at it. 'Two messages.'

She checked the first message. 'This one's from my friend Grace in London, well, an Internet friend, actually. She says, "Be strong, sweetie, and hugs and prayers for your mum. Grace xx." Grace has a nineteen-year-old daughter and has lived a complete different life to me in so many ways, yet I feel a connection with her. Knowing her is kind of like having a fun older sister.'

'What about the other message?'

She didn't really want to tell him about the man she'd planned to meet for a drink. Why had she bothered anyway? The thought rolled over her, and she did her best to push it away. Right now wasn't the time to try to figure out whether she was wasting her time on the dating site, whether her reasons for joining were even right...

Marissa opened the message reluctantly, and then relaxed. 'This is from another of my Internet friends, Dani. Grace must have forwarded my message to her. I didn't want to wake Dani.' She read the second message out. '"Sending prayers. Call me if you need 2. Any time!!!"'

'Where does Dani live? Is she an older woman like Grace?'

'San Francisco, and no. She's younger than I am and more ambitious in certain ways. Well, perhaps not *more ambitious*, but highly focused in her working life particularly, I think. Dani is at the start of her career and she's studied hard and really wants to have a great job. At the moment she's working in some dead end position she doesn't like to talk about and hoping something better will come along.'

'Do you have sisters or brothers, Marissa?'

He'd probably asked to keep her mind occupied. Marissa wanted to open up to him anyway. As she recognised that, she stared out of the window at the scenery flashing by.

Grassy paddocks on either side of the road interspersed with native gum and paper-bark trees. Hills undulated as far as the eye could see and gave a sense of quiet and open space very different from the teeming life of the city.

They weren't too far from Milberry now. What would he think of her home town?

'No sisters or brothers. I'm an only child. Maybe that's why I want...' She broke off, cleared her throat. 'Mum and Dad only ever had me, but Mum made sure I had lots of chances to play with other children, to get the social interaction I needed. What about you? Just the two sisters?'

'Yes. I'm the eldest. Darla's in the middle, and Faith is the youngest.'

And his sisters had married, made families, but Rick hadn't.

Minutes passed. Marissa clutched her phone and willed it to ring.

'There's the ten kilometre sign.' She stiffened in her seat and, as though their nearness had brought it about, her phone finally complied with a ring tone. With a gasp, she fumbled for it and quickly answered.

'Yes. Yes. Okay. All right. I can't wait to see her.'

While Marissa paused to listen to her caller, Rick slowed at the outskirts of the township.

'We'll see you soon, Dad.' She ended the call and sat forward to give Rick directions.

CHAPTER TEN

'WE'RE to go straight to Mum and Dad's unit. I don't know what to think!' Marissa's words tumbled out in a rush, concern warring with threads of relief she couldn't truly believe. Not yet. 'They've let Mum go home with my Aunty Jean to watch over her. Aunty's a registered nurse.'

'How could they release her so quickly after such pain?' Rick put the question that was filling her thoughts into words. 'What was the diagnosis? Is this a decent hospital we're talking about? If not, we'll get her admitted somewhere else.'

'Apparently a cyst ruptured on one of Mum's ovaries. She is still in some discomfort but it's not severe now. They say she just needs to rest with the appropriate medication. Once they were certain of the diagnosis they let her go.'

Marissa drew a quick breath. 'It is a good hospital, the staff are reliable and Aunty Jean wouldn't let them release her unless she was confident Mum was up to that. Even so, I need to see her. If I look at her, I'll know—'

'How do we get to your parents' home?' He gestured ahead of them. 'Let's get you there so you can see for yourself.'

'If you follow this road it will take you straight through the main street of the town.' He understood what she needed and that...warmed her. 'After the Region's Own Bank building you turn left and Mum and Dad's unit is in the second street on the right.'

His gaze glanced left and right as he followed the directions she'd given him.

Many of the homes were red brick or weatherboard with corrugated iron roofs. Just about every front garden had rose bushes or camellias, a front fence with a wrought iron gate with an old-fashioned curlicue scroll design on top, and a mailbox on the right-hand gatepost.

There were vintage cars interspersed with sedans and utility trucks in the main street.

A rally weekend, Marissa realised vaguely, and sat forward in her seat again as they neared the turn to her parents' home.

'That's their place.' She pointed. 'The small pale brick one with the red sedan and green station wagon parked out front.'

Rick followed Marissa's directions and parked on the street behind the other two cars. He studied the workmanship of the square building design, with its regulation small porch, front window awnings and slightly curved pathway from the front fence to that porch, but his thoughts were focused on the woman at his side.

He'd expected Marissa to leap from the vehicle before he'd even parked it properly. Instead, at the last minute, she turned to face him.

Her eyes were wide, her expression a combination of concern and chagrin. 'I haven't thanked you for dropping everything to get me here the way you did and for your kindness during the trip. It…well… I hope Mum truly is a lot better, though I'm still concerned for her, and I appreciate—'

'I know you do, and there's no need to say anything.' Maybe she was hesitating at the last moment out of fear of what she would find. If so, the sooner she saw her Mum the better. He opened his door and came to her side to help her out.

With her hand clasped in his as he helped her down, he admitted, 'I wanted to bring you.' He'd needed to, in the same way he'd needed to fix things for Darla over the years, for Faith.

No. Not the same. This was different.

Yes. It's more than those urges have ever been.

He didn't want to think that. Their gazes met and held for a brief moment and something flared between them. She did fly up the path then, and rapped on the door even as it opened from inside.

Rick followed more slowly and watched as a man with thinning grey-streaked dark hair pulled Marissa into his arms and held her tight. The comfort given and exchanged in their hug caught at something inside Rick and his chest hurt as he acknowledged the deep closeness playing out in front of him.

'Dad, this is the boss of Morgan's, Rick Morgan. I told you and Mum I'm working for him while his secretary is on sick leave and Gordon is on holiday.' Marissa rushed the words out and then her voice softened. 'Rick, please meet my father, Abraham Warren, but he prefers Abe.'

Did Marissa's face soften on *his* name? It had seemed to and while something inside Rick took the thought in a stranglehold and refused to let it go, heat rode the back of his neck as he shook the older man's hand and murmured a greeting.

He was concerned. He needed Marissa to see her mother and feel assured that the woman would be okay. It wasn't anything else. Certainly not some misguided and misplaced hope that Marissa's father would approve—*like*—him.

'Thank you for bringing Marissa to us.' Abe stepped back. If he noticed anything odd in Rick's demeanour, he didn't show it.

Rick wished he had some of the same self-control.

Abe went on, 'Come inside, both of you. Marissa, Mum's fretting that you rushed to get here, but she's also bursting to see you. Maybe she'll settle down and rest once she has.'

The combination of protectiveness and residual worry in the man's tone said it all.

The small unit had a living area filled with a two-seater couch and several chairs. A kitchen backed onto the area and there were rooms packed tightly together off a hallway to the right.

Bedroom, bedroom, bathroom, Rick guessed. The laundry room would be at the back behind the kitchen. A woman emerged through an open door and smiled at Marissa. Hugged her briskly and stepped aside. 'Go on and see your mum. A rupture is nasty and it can be very dangerous but your mum's going to be just fine and I'm staying two nights to watch her in any case. It only took me two hours to get here from Tuckwell. I left quickly when your dad phoned.'

Marissa stepped through the door and disappeared. A moment later Rick heard a soft sob quickly stifled, followed by a rush of low words. Marissa's voice and another one— older, soothing and being soothed. He wanted to burst into the room, do something. *Hold Marissa and never let anything upset her again.*

Instead, he stood in the middle of the living room, fists clenched as he forgot all about the two people waiting there, watching him. Then he turned to Marissa's father. 'Your wife truly is well enough to leave the hospital? Marissa was worried.'

'Yes, and Jean will help me keep an eye on her.' Abe examined Rick with shrewd eyes that seemed to have realised something about his guest. Maybe that Rick had eyes only for his daughter.

Rick ran a hand through his hair. 'It's been an uneasy few hours. Far more so for you, I'm sure.'

Abe stared hard at him for a long moment before he spoke again. 'Very true. Now, how long have you and my daughter—'

'Well, it must be time for a cup of tea.' The nurse cleared her throat rather noisily. 'How about I put the kettle on, Abe?

I'm sure Tilda would enjoy a cup about now. We probably all could do with one.'

On her way past Rick, she gestured towards one of the squashy cloth-covered lounge chairs. 'Why don't you have a seat? And I'm Jean, Tilda's sister, though I'm sure you've worked that out.

'We can make our way through the introductions properly in a minute and you can tell us how the vintage car festival seems to be shaping up, how many of the cars you saw as you drove in.' She glanced at Abe and her gaze seemed to warn him off launching a more personal inquisition. 'It's one of Milberry's special weekends, you know.'

Rick had given away more of an interest in his borrowed secretary he should have. At the moment he couldn't raise much concern for the fact. Marissa had needed to get here. Rick had needed to smooth a path for her and he'd go on smoothing one for as long as he felt it was needed.

'I'm afraid I didn't take much notice of the traffic on the way in.' Rick took a seat as ordered and put his hands on his spread knees. He gave himself time to look around this room owned by the people who had raised Marissa. There were photos of her everywhere.

Marissa as a baby, toddler, child and teenager and more recent ones.

'Her hair was always curly.' He murmured the words, took the cup that Jean offered, nodded his thanks. Cleared his throat. 'It is rather noticeable. Her hair.'

'Yes.' Jean slipped into the other room to deliver the tea to Marissa's mum.

That left Rick and Marissa's father. 'There won't be any lingering effects from the illness, I hope?'

The older man rubbed a work-worn hand over his tanned jaw. 'She's exhausted now and they've given her some medication to deal with the after-effects but they say in a few days she won't even know it's happened. I'm just grateful…' He swallowed and took a deep breath. 'Now, if I can just get her to rest properly until she really is all better I'll be satisfied. We could both get a bit of leave from our work—'

'Rick, will you come in and meet Mum before she tries to have a nap?' Marissa asked from the doorway of her mother's room, and Rick rose immediately to his feet.

He caught her hand in his briefly at the door. Then he searched her face and noted the slight redness around her eyes. Asked in a low voice, 'Will she mind me seeing her when she's not a hundred per cent?'

'Probably.' Marissa's smile held relief and gratitude and a wealth of affection for the woman Rick had yet to meet. 'But her curiosity about my boss will overrule that.'

He didn't feel like a boss right now. The expression in Marissa's eyes as she looked at him, the way she'd curled her fingers around his hand—those hadn't seemed very business-like either.

They stepped into the bedroom together. There were no chairs. It wasn't a hospital room, but the room shared by two people who'd loved each other and lived together for many years. A framed wedding photo hung on the wall at the foot of the bed. Knick-knacks sat cheek by jowl on a dresser with a man's watch and a well-worn hat.

Rick imagined sharing such a room with Marissa. The idea was alien and stunning all at once. He turned to the woman in the bed. 'I'm very sorry to know you've been unwell, Mrs Warren.'

Marissa stepped past him, went to her mother and caught her hand in hers, pressed it to her face and kissed the back of it before she eased down gently to sit on the bed beside her mum. 'Yes, you're not allowed to pull a stunt like that again, Mum. You scared me silly.'

'I'll try not to.' Tilda Warren shifted slightly in the bed and, though her face bore the marks of the strain and discomfort she'd experienced, she looked enough like Marissa that Rick couldn't help but like her on sight.

She smiled at Rick. 'Thank you for bringing Marissa to us. I won't pretend I'm not glad to see her. The last few hours were a bit frightening and I'm glad to see my girl.'

'And now you're going to rest and hopefully go to sleep.' Marissa fussed a little and then, with obvious reluctance and an equal amount of determination, prepared to leave the room. 'I'll look in on you later, even if you've gone to sleep. Just to be sure…'

'Thank you, love.' Tilda sighed. 'I admit I feel rather wiped out and I think I probably will sleep, at least for a while. They gave me painkillers. You'll need some dinner, though, and—'

'And we can take care of that by ourselves,' Marissa interrupted with a loving smile, and they left the room together.

The depth of the relief Rick felt surprised him. That Marissa's mother would be okay; that nothing had happened that would cause Marissa a lot of long-term unhappiness.

When Marissa stared rather blankly at the contents of the fridge, he asked if there were any restaurants or take-away food places in the town. 'You've all had a stressful time. Let me at least pick up something for dinner.'

He did that, managing it without stepping on Abe's toes. Abe sat with his wife even after sleep claimed her before he finally emerged and spent some time talking quietly with his daughter while his sister-in-law got up and down at intervals to look in on Marissa's mum.

They spoke in hushed tones of nothing much. Abe asked a little about Rick's business. Jean asked about his roots, and Rick admitted he'd never lived outside the city, that his sisters and nieces were there. His gaze tracked Marissa's every movement. He had a plan for how he might do something for her mother as well…

* * *

Mum truly would be okay. Marissa looked in on her one last time and finally started to believe it. As she acknowledged this, some of the things she'd pushed aside in her haste to get here filtered through at last, and she frowned for a whole other set of reasons.

She stood and collected her bag from where she must have dumped it beside a lounge chair when she'd first come into the house. 'You'll be all right through the night, Aunty?'

'Absolutely, and Abe can handle me creeping in and out of the room a few times to see to meds and things tonight.' Jean rose to her feet as well. 'It means turning you out of the spare room, though. There's only a single in there with the sewing machine.'

Marissa glanced towards Rick. He'd also got to his feet and stood watching her. In truth his gaze had rarely left her since they'd arrived, and she felt ridiculously warmed and…comforted by that knowledge. 'If Rick doesn't mind, we'll find a couple of rooms in one of the motels for the night. I'd like to visit Mum again tomorrow morning and then I know we'll have to leave.'

Jean patted her arm. 'Your dad will look after her and she'll stay quieter if there aren't too many people here to distract her from that. You know what she's like. She was already saying she wanted to get out of bed and start organising things.'

They were all on their feet now, and Rick gestured towards the second bedroom in the house. 'Do you keep anything here, Marissa? Maybe you should gather a change of clothes and some nightwear and a toothbrush before we go.'

'You won't get any rooms.' The words came from Abe as he slapped a hand against his thigh. 'I forgot about the impact of the vintage car festival. All the motels are fully booked, or so it said in the paper this morning.'

'And Rick has no spare clothes, not even a toothbrush.'

Marissa turned his way. 'I'm sorry. I didn't give that a thought when we left Sydney. I do have a few things here, but you—'

Rick shrugged his broad shoulders. 'I'll make do, and maybe we can go to a motel in a nearby town?'

'The nearest town large enough is mine, and it's a two-hour drive away.' Jean pointed this out with a frown. 'You'd both be most welcome to stay at my place but it's a long way.'

At that moment a soft knock sounded on the front door. Her father opened it.

It was Mrs Brill from the end of the street, a busy woman with five children and a truck-driver husband. She had a casserole in one hand and a key in the other.

She held out the casserole. 'This is for dinner tomorrow night, and I saw the extra cars outside and wondered about accommodation. I've got the converted garage with a sofa bed that pulls out and a camp-bed I bought at a garage sale for the second room in there.'

'That would be really helpful. We were just wondering how best to work that out.' Jean spoke the words in her brisk, no-nonsense way. She took the casserole and handed it to Marissa, who carried it through to the kitchen.

By the time Marissa returned, matters were decided—Mrs Brill had left to start the short walk back to her home and Rick held the key to the converted garage.

CHAPTER ELEVEN

MARISSA gathered her things into a carryall. Her father bundled some more things in on top for Rick to use and, with a murmured word of thanks, Rick drove them the short distance to the end of the street.

He pulled to a stop before an unpretentious home with a large front garden and larger back garden. Mrs Brill had walked ahead of them and took them straight through to the back, where the garage sat surrounded by a swing set and a collection of children's toys and bikes and other things.

'Thank you. This is very kind.' Marissa managed to choke out the words without looking at Rick at all. Mrs Brill *was* kind, and Marissa appreciated the hospitality. She just couldn't imagine her multi-millionaire boss, with his city central penthouse apartment with all mod cons, here.

'You're welcome, love. You even have your own shower and loo.' Their hostess disappeared with a wave.

Rick unlocked the converted garage, flipped the light switch and they stepped inside.

The room had a square of someone's old carpet slung over a concrete floor, unlined walls covered in dartboards and fishing paraphernalia, and a sofa that converted. A pile of bedding and two bath towels sat waiting on it.

A door to the right opened into a second room.

Marissa bit her lip. 'It's probably not what you're used to, but it was very good of Mrs Brill.'

'It's fine, and it was very generous of her.' Rick set the bag down on the floor and tossed a can of deodorant in on top that he'd taken from the glove compartment of his car.

'I don't know what Dad's put in the bag for you.' For no clear reason, Marissa's face heated and she looked everywhere but into Rick's eyes.

She hadn't thought too much about their accommodation until now, and was realising that it could feel a little awkward for a whole other lot of reasons.

The moment the thought rose so did her consciousness of him.

'Toothbrush, disposable razor, a pair of boxer shorts still in their wrapping, T-shirt, and the ugliest pair of long john style pyjamas I've ever seen.' Rick's tone deepened as he spoke those last words, as his gaze met with hers and held.

'Dad usually wears a T-shirt and boxers to bed. Maybe he wasn't thinking straight.' She spoke the words with a hint of confusion, felt far more as her senses began to respond to Rick's nearness, to the intensity that had risen in his gaze.

'He's your father. He was thinking perfectly.' Rick turned abruptly towards the second room. 'I'd better set up the camp-bed so we can both get some sleep. Mrs Brill said it hasn't been used since she bought it.'

Marissa's face heated even more as she recalled some of Dad's questions to Rick, about his work, his prospects. Surely her father hadn't viewed Rick as a possible boyfriend or something?

You've kissed the man and you are *still attracted to him. Maybe Dad noticed that.*

'You don't have to… I wouldn't want you to think, or feel you need to…'

'You really are tempting when you blush like that.' He

spoke the words in a hungry tone of gravel and midnight. 'God knows I'm trying not to notice, Marissa, but I think you know what I am thinking, and for all that those thoughts appear to have me by the throat right now, they can't do either of us any good.'

'You…you're right. I'll take the camp-bed. It won't be very large and you'll probably only have a sleeping bag for it, and a pillow. No doubt Mrs Brill left a pillow.' The words babbled out of her as they stepped into the second room together. 'See, there's a pillow there.'

'I thought I'd driven you away, you know—lost your approval and good regard when I made the mistake of looking into your working history.' The softening of his tone seemed to sit uneasily with him, yet his gaze revealed how that thought had bothered him.

Rick's jaw clenched as he stared at the pile of canvas and wood and springs and hooks. 'I didn't need to do that, Marissa. I knew it but I went after the information anyway because I felt you were holding something back from me. It's too late to undo it but I want you to know I very much regret the incident.'

'I believe you.' She couldn't raise any anger. Not in the face of his regret, and all he had done for her since.

He's not Michael Unsworth. You can't continue to compare the two. Rick is a far better man in so many ways.

It was a dangerous conclusion, even as she admitted the truth of it. Rick's layers were beginning to make too much sense, appeal too much. She had to remember he still wanted nothing to do with the kind of relationship she hoped one day to find. He didn't want commitment.

Since that seemed to be all she wanted lately, with a side order of Family and Babies and Not Feeling Old When She Turned Thirty thrown in, it would be a very good thing if she could stop being so attracted to her boss.

He drew a breath. 'I'm glad you've forgiven me. Now, let's see about this camp-bed.'

'It looks rather old. So does the sleeping bag.' She eyed both dubiously and returned her gaze to the bed. 'I'm guessing there probably isn't an instruction manual for putting that together.'

Rick glanced at her. One brief, intent, aware glance as the walls of the room seemed to close in on them. He rubbed a hand over the back of his neck. 'I'm sure I can figure it out, and you won't be sleeping on it. I will.'

He tossed the pillow and sleeping bag aside, crouched down and started to assemble the bed. In fact, he had it put together minutes later.

Marissa smiled despite herself. 'I should have known you'd do that with the same precision you do everything.'

With a slight smile he picked up the sleeping bag, unzipped it and laid it flat over the surface of the bed, then leaned down to press the centre with his hand. 'See? It looks quite comfy. I'm sure it'll be fine.'

He turned to reach for the pillow. As he did, the bed snapped down in the middle and up at both ends. Wood crunched and splintered. Springs twanged and bits and pieces flew in all directions.

'What—?' Rick pulled her back, his shoulder turned to protect her from anything that might fly through the air.

Seconds later it was all over, and so was the bed. Marissa stared at the splintered old wood, bits of torn canvas, the sleeping bag tangled within it all, and springs that had irrevocably sprung. 'Oh, my. That was rather dramatic, wasn't it? It made matchsticks out of some of it.'

'Dramatic? The thing could have taken out your eye. And how I'll explain this to your Mrs Brill—' Rick broke off with a disgusted manly snort of outrage and offence. 'I'm *certain* I put the bed together correctly.'

'Oh, I'm sure you did. It just…cracked under the pressure.' A laugh burst from her. She just couldn't help it. 'Your face! This isn't a corporate implosion, you know.'

'I'll arrange for a new bed to replace it.' He growled the words and kicked one of the larger pieces of wood with his foot. 'Maybe we can get rid of the evidence before morning.'

'That—' Another laugh choked out of her. 'We could bury the evidence in the garden.' Her grin spread. 'Shovels at twenty paces. I won't tell if you don't.'

His brows snapped down and he glared at her and she laughed all the harder until she had to lean over with her arms wrapped around her tummy.

'I don't see anything the least bit amusing about this.' His lips twitched. He kicked another piece of wood out of the way.

A moment later he started to laugh as well. His deep chuckles filled the air.

Marissa grinned at him and sucked up lungfuls of air and then, to her mortification, tears welled in the backs of her eyes. She blinked them back, turned away so he wouldn't see while she fought for control.

'Hey. It's okay.' Gentle arms came around her, turned her into his chest. 'Your Mum's all right. Your aunt said she'll be almost as good as new tomorrow.'

'How did you know?' The moment he reached for her she'd wrapped her arms around him. Now she lifted her head, gave it a rueful shake even as her body wanted so very much to press to his and never move away. 'I don't know where that came from. I thought I'd settled down after I saw for myself she was okay. And *I'm* fine now, aside from feeling silly again.'

'You could never be silly.' He closed his eyes and kissed the tip of her nose and then he just…held onto her.

She could have stayed there for ever—in his arms, giving and receiving comfort and closeness.

But she wanted more. Her body wanted to meld to his, curves to angles, softness to strength.

'I mustn't…' He murmured the words and set her away from him.

He retrieved the sleeping bag then, and shook it. Splinters of wood rained onto the floor. Many more of them stuck like porcupine quills to the sleeping bag's thin, lumpy lining.

'I'll sleep on the floor.' His voice rumbled the words. 'Why don't you take a shower and I'll make up the other bed for you before I wash? You'll want to be up early in the morning to see your mum again.'

'Thanks.' Their prosaic words did nothing to cover the tension that had risen between them. 'I…I guess I will have a quick shower.' She'd raided the room at the unit for a pair of comfy pyjama bottoms she'd had about a hundred years, a spaghetti-strap stretchy top and loose jumper and old jeans and a shirt to wear for tomorrow, toiletries and spare panties.

Marissa bundled up what she needed and disappeared into the bathroom that had obviously been somebody's DIY project. She couldn't let Rick sleep on the floor with splinters sticking all through that sleeping bag, but she needed to pull herself together a little before they had that discussion.

Rick showered while she sent text messages to Dani and Grace and let them know that Mum was going to be okay, though she planned to keep a closer eye on her parents' health from now on!

When Rick came out of the bathroom, Marissa was already in the bed, the jumper discarded, and had brought the pillow from the other room and placed it beside hers. Action seemed the best way to address the issue.

Rick's gaze roved over her face and shoulders and snapped back to her eyes. 'Is this a good idea?'

She'd glanced at him, just once, before she too focused her attention solely on *his* face. That single moment had revealed his broad tanned chest, narrow hips and thighs encased in dark boxers, long bare legs. 'We have to be sensible.'

The comment referred to him sleeping in the bed, not on the floor, but could have referred equally to her runaway thoughts right now. She wanted Rick to climb into the bed, wrap his arms around her and make love to her. She wanted it with her senses, and with deeper emotions. She wanted it for herself, not only because her hormones were giving her trouble. She was afraid to look deeper into all the other reasons she wanted it.

'I'll use the sleeping bag. I shook it out.' He said the words even as his gaze devoured her and tenderness formed in that gaze. 'If not on the floor, then I'll sleep on top of the bedcovers.'

'The sleeping bag is prickled right through with splinters still. I checked.' That tenderness somehow helped her to regain some of her equilibrium. She gestured as calmly as she could to the space beside her. 'It's roomy enough. We'll stick to our sides. I just want to sleep and forget the stress of worrying about Mum during that trip.'

It was the right thing to say.

He relaxed a little at last, murmured, 'I guess if there's no choice, there's no choice.' He turned the light off, plunged the room into darkness and she heard him pad across the carpeted floor towards her.

One last bout of nerves got her then.

'You didn't wear Dad's pyjamas. Not that you should have. No doubt you thought they were quite hideous and it's not as though he should try to intimidate you or imply anything about the two of us or try to circumvent certain behaviour.' Each word tumbled after the other. 'Not that we intend to indulge in such behaviour.'

The bed dipped as he sat on the edge. 'I…er…I don't usually sleep in any… No, I didn't wear the pyjamas.' A rustling sound followed as he settled into the bed right beside her. All that naked skin on his upper torso and…

His weight rolled her into the middle. Their bodies brushed before she quickly pulled herself back to her side.

'Sorry.'

'My fault.' He inhaled. Stilled. Finally murmured into the darkness, 'You smell the same. Of flowers.'

They were facing each other in the darkness. She knew it from the direction of his words and she thrilled to that small knowledge even when she shouldn't have.

'I…er…yes. The perfume…I keep some of the perfume in my bag.' If she leaned forward a little, would they touch? Would he wrap his arms around her and kiss her?

Don't think about it, Marissa. You're being sensible now, remember?

'I hope the smell isn't bothering you.'

'No.' His voice dipped to a low, dark tone. 'It's not bothering me.'

For a moment, silence reigned and then he said painfully, 'I don't want to hurt you. What your parents have with each other, what you deserve to have, I can't go there. Relationships for me…don't go there. Because of my family, the example of my father. I'm not assuming, or suggesting anything…'

'It's fine. It's always best to say what you're thinking, make it all clear.' And he had, and it was hard to hear it—hard when they lay so close together and her body longed for the touch of his.

A part of her still wanted his touch now, and a part of her wondered if it would be so bad. If she gave in to her desire for him, even though there could be no future in it. Just one time, to make love with him—with due care and responsibility—so she could at least have that experience, that memory of him.

But that was all it would be, because he wasn't Mr Right For Her. All else aside, he didn't match her criteria. He was still Mr Corporate. 'Um…well…we should go to sleep.'

'Yes. We definitely should sleep.' Rick wanted Marissa so much he ached all over from it. The way she'd been with her parents this evening had caught at something inside him, had deepened his feelings towards her in ways he hadn't been able to fathom or control. It was why he'd pushed her away with his words.

'*You* should try to sleep, anyway.' He doubted he would do the same with her so close.

His leg brushed against hers as he repositioned himself in the bed and he registered a long length of flannelette.

The ugliest and most unromantic nightwear in the world for women. Wasn't that what they said? She had apparently covered herself from belly to ankle in the stuff. Her shoulders had been bare, with just a thin strap indicating some kind of fitted top.

Images of running his hands over her legs and thighs over that thick cloth invaded his brain anyway. He felt far from repelled right now.

He forced his attention to other things. To the reason they'd come here. Maybe, if he focused on that, he would find the control and distance he needed to endure this night without reaching for her, without reaching for all he wanted *from* her and *with* her that he must not take. 'Are you okay now, Marissa? About your mother?'

'Yes. I cross-questioned her about what had happened until she probably wanted me to shut up, but I needed to know she truly would be all right.' Marissa's breath caressed his face as she sighed into the darkness.

Did she realise exactly how close they were? That their heads were turned intimately towards each other?

'Mum said I didn't need to rush here, that she didn't expect that.'

'She wanted to see you, though. Your father told me he was glad you'd come so quickly.' *Her* family held a strong bond for each other.

He didn't have that with his parents. And he didn't know *how* to have it with a woman. Marissa was right to want someone who didn't come with a bunch of complications attached.

You could figure it out. You could risk it.

He stilled, and then he clamped down on the thoughts and an unexpected well of anger towards his father rose up instead.

No. Rick would never risk short-changing a family the way Dad had, and that meant not risking his own family, period.

'Mum was worried about missing shifts at the news-agent's. Silly thing.' Marissa fell silent and Rick thought she might finally try to go to sleep, or at least pretend to, as he would.

Then she spoke again in a low tone of admission. 'It scared me to see Mum vulnerable. My parents have always been strong and I've never thought about losing them. I should do more to show how much I appreciate them.'

'What would you do? They seem happy, and proud of you. I looked at the pictures of you in their living room.' Had looked—had wanted to touch each one. Had wondered if she had a child, would it have her hair? Those expressive brown eyes?

'Some of those pictures are awful.' Despite the words, a smile filled her tone.

He'd planned to bring this up in the morning, but, 'What about sending your parents on a holiday? I've done it for my sisters occasionally.' He drew a breath, wished he could see her face to know if she would allow him to do this for her, to give her this.

He'd been thinking of it since Abe had said he wished he

could ensure his wife rested properly. 'I have a holiday home on the Queensland coast that's vacant right now, just sitting there doing nothing. They could spend a week there. Your father mentioned he'd like to take her away, that they could both get holiday. He wants to make sure she spends proper time resting up. In truth, I'd appreciate having someone there to check the place is being looked after properly under the caretaking arrangements I've made for it.'

In the face of her silence, because he didn't know what she was thinking, he added, 'It's easy to reach. They could fly direct from the nearest airport.' He considered trying to sell her on the local attractions. Made himself stop speaking and wait for her answer.

'I'm sure they'd love it. I'll talk to Dad and I'll buy them plane tickets.' Her hand reached through the darkness, found his upper arm and tracked down it until she found his hand and gripped it. 'Thank you for thinking of it, Rick. That will be perfect for them, and it's very generous of you.'

He couldn't prevent himself from lifting their joined hands, kissing her fingers, pressing that hand against his chest and drawing a deep breath as he held it there. 'You're welcome. I'm happy to do it, and they'll be helping me at the same time.'

His heart had started to thump. Just because he had her hand pressed to his chest. Just because…he wanted her so very much.

'Try to sleep.' He rasped the words past an inexplicable ache in his throat, releasing his grip on her hand one finger at a time because he couldn't manage more. 'I traded cell-phone numbers with your father and obviously they have yours. If they need you they'll call, but I don't think that'll happen, and your mum will probably be happier if you seem well-rested when she sees you tomorrow.'

'Goodnight, Rick.' Marissa didn't expect to sleep. She lay there absorbing the slight musty smell of the room and Rick's far nicer scent of soap and deodorant and warm man beside her. Thought about her mum and dad and what Rick had done for her today, and about his family and his limitations…

How ironic that she now wanted Mr Tall, Dark and Aggressive About Success and he'd made it clear he could never be right for her.

Rick woke to the tenderest feeling deep inside, and realised he had Marissa clutched in his arms like the most precious of bundles. His face was pressed into her hair and her softness seemed to melt into him.

His arms locked and for a long, still moment he couldn't let go as his heart began to hammer and emotion swamped him. A cold sweat broke out on his brow.

'Rick,' she murmured. Her eyelids fluttered up to reveal sleepy eyes and something deep inside him shifted and parted and tried very hard to let her in.

Panic welled inside him and he eased his hold on her and moved away.

'Is it morning?' Her lips were soft, so kissable, her face flushed from sleep.

Heat flared in his body then, but even that couldn't fully wipe out his earlier feelings of…what?

He didn't know, only felt the ache still, that had seemed to insist that if he held her close enough he could somehow assuage that emptiness.

'It's early, but yes, it's morning.' He rolled to the side of the bed, swung his legs over and sat with his back to her. Tried for coherence—he who always had control of himself and now felt he had very little of any. 'We should take our showers. Maybe once we're both through it'll be a reasonable enough time to visit your mother. I'll leave a cheque for Mrs Brill to pay for the broken bed in the other room.'

Rick retrieved his clothes from the carryall and shut himself in the bathroom. Perhaps a blast of cold water would straighten out the confusion of his mind—and settle his senses!

CHAPTER TWELVE

'IT'S good that your mother seemed much better this morning, and I'm glad she and your father let us talk them into taking that holiday.' Rick's hands tightened slightly around the steering wheel as he spoke. 'You're happy with how long you stayed, the amount of time you had with her?'

He wore her father's T-shirt loose over his suit trousers and looked a little rumpled and delicious and appealing and, beneath that, tense. He'd been that way since they'd woken this morning with their arms around each other.

In that first moment, before she'd remembered his words of warning to her last night, Marissa had hoped he might kiss her. The desire had been there in his gaze, but with other emotions she hadn't fully understood. He'd seemed almost uncertain for a moment, somehow shocked and uneasy at the same time.

After that he'd withdrawn physically from holding her. She'd remembered why that was the only sensible course of action. He still seemed withdrawn.

Except when your eyes meet because, in the first instant when that happens, you have all his attention and there's warmth amongst that attention. Warmth and desire and...

No. There was no *and*—there couldn't be. She had to keep her imagination and all the hopes it wanted to raise under control.

'I hope you didn't mind hanging around for hours again. I would have liked to stay longer but it will be easier for Dad to get Mum to rest if I'm not there, and then, when she's recovered enough, he'll whip her away for that week at the beach. They'll probably go on Tuesday, if she continues to feel better.' Perhaps, if they discussed this kind of thing, he would eventually relax?

And you, Marissa?

She admitted she had formed a bond inside herself to him somehow in the past day and night, despite everything. To wake held in his arms had felt safe and right and wonderful. It had seemed to tell her in physical action of a great deal of his care and she had wanted—

She'd wanted to give that care back to him in the same way, and that knowledge terrified her because Rick had simply been holding her. If he'd felt something, perhaps it was empathy because she'd been afraid for her mum. And Marissa couldn't let herself feel a great deal more for him.

You're sure you don't already feel those things?

Uneasy, she shifted in her seat. These feelings surpassed even the confusing and disconcerting ones of longing for a baby, of feeling so broody and so resistant to the idea of turning thirty and being alone.

'I'm just pleased Mum seems so much better. And I really do appreciate what you did to take me to her.'

'I hope she doesn't go through anything like that again.' He drew out to overtake a slow-moving truck, and smoothly returned them to their lane.

They'd left Milberry after brunch at Mum and Dad's unit. Marissa had missed her computer access this morning. She'd come to rely on checking in for instant chat messages from Grace and Dani. How would she get on now with her plan to find Mr Right on the dating site when her thoughts centred so much on Mr Couldn't Be Right?

What would Dani and Grace think of this morning's events?

Nothing, because I'm not going to tell them. Marissa focused her stare out of the window without really looking at anything they passed. Grace and Dani were her friends. They meant a lot to her and she *liked* confiding in them but she had to sort these feelings out about Rick for herself.

Sort them and then leave them behind. Her chest hurt at the thought but she wasn't falling for him. She liked him, appreciated him.

He was not someone she could love.

And you, Marissa? You're completely straightforward? You're not carrying around any emotional complications?

She didn't have any family troubles. And she refused to consider any memories of fiancé troubles. She was over all that.

As he drew his car to a stop outside Marissa's apartment building, weariness tugged at Rick. He turned his head, noted the shadows beneath Marissa's eyes. 'Let's see you up to your place.'

'Come up with me.' Marissa made the request in a soft tone edged with concern. 'I want you to drink some coffee before you go any further. It's been a big weekend and…we woke very early this morning.'

Even this obscure reference to those moments in a borrowed garage tugged at him. At his senses, he assured himself. Only in that way. He wanted her still. Enough that he couldn't get the thought of making love with her out of his mind.

This was true, but he also couldn't get the thought of *holding* her out of his mind. Holding her and never letting go. He'd warned her off, but now *he* didn't want to be warned off, even though that was the only option for Stephen Morgan's son. Was this what Faith had meant and what he'd said he wouldn't do? Was he poised on the edge of that dive into emotional oblivion?

If so, he didn't like the feeling, and he could not allow himself to take that leap. Even the thought of that being a possibility terrified him.

Just as his father must have felt terrified, and had thus drawn back?

It wasn't the same.

Maybe it was exactly the same. Did that even matter? His instinct told him he mustn't—couldn't—want Marissa so deeply, so for her sake. Yes, for her sake he had to shut those feelings down.

'Coffee's ready. It's only instant, I'm afraid, but I didn't want you to have to wait too long for it.' Marissa carried the drinks into her small living room, only to find Rick sprawled out on her sofa, his chin on his chest. Spiky lashes formed crescents on strong male cheeks. He'd lain right back so his feet dangled off the end of the third cushion. He was fast asleep.

He looked younger, exhausted, and somehow vulnerable this way. Her heart ached as she stared at him. Feelings she hadn't meant to allow welled inside her, wanted to be set free.

How could this one man have found his way into such hidden parts of her so easily and so quickly? The mega-boss man. She had judged him by Michael's standards when she shouldn't have. Rick cared for his sisters and his nieces, was capable of acts of kindness.

He had also stepped outside her perception of acceptable boundaries when he'd investigated her; he wasn't right for Marissa.

Because he didn't have enough to give to a relationship. Because he would always have a ruthless edge—the part of him that had made him a success in business, even if he'd gone about achieving that success by more acceptable means than Michael. What if he turned that edge on her? Hurt her with it, as Michael had hurt her?

Marissa set aside the coffee, covered Rick with her one and only patchwork quilt from her handicraft phase and went into her bedroom with her laptop computer. It was time to sign onto Blinddatebrides.com and do something proactive about the *real* future she needed to seek.

To: Englishcrumpet, Sanfrandani
From Kangagirl
Did you know you can tell how old a woman is by what happens when she pinches the skin of the back of her hand between her fingers?

From: Englishcrumpet
Thanks a lot, Marissa. Now I feel really depressed.

From: Sanfrandani
I don't get it. Is that one of those English/Australian jokes?

From: Kangagirl
If the skin goes back quickly, you're not old.

From: Englishcrumpet
Sigh.

From: Sanfrandani
Oh. Well, my skin seems okay, and…er…duty calls. I have to say goodbye for now. TTYL.
Sanfrandani has signed out.

From: Englishcrumpet
What's going on, Marissa? I'm getting the same vibe I get when Daisy is holding something back from me.

From: Kangagirl
It's nothing. Actually, it's something. I thought I could sign

on to Blinddatebrides.com and find Mr Nice, Ordinary and Unthreatening. I thought I could vet candidates and find one to match my criteria and magically make us fall in love with each other or something. That I could keep myself safe from getting hurt that way. My thirtieth birthday is getting closer and I don't want to get old, I'm starting to wonder if I'm scared I'll never have a chance to have a baby, and I think—I think I might have sort of half slightly started to fall for my boss.

From: Englishcrumpet
Oh, Marissa.

From: Kangagirl
I don't know—maybe I should quit my Blinddatebrides subscription. I'm not sure I can keep looking for a man on the site any more.

From: Englishcrumpet
You must have had an exhausting time of it. Why don't you have a rest and worry about your Blinddatebrides plans and all the rest of this later? Maybe this will all look better when you're not so tired. One thing I know is Dani and I won't want to lose your friendship!

From: Kangagirl
I don't think I could cope with losing either of you. I am tired. I think I'll close my eyes for a little while. Over and out for now from Australia.

'I phoned Mum earlier. I thought she might have wanted to

hear how Russell was doing,' Faith said to Rick as she walked with him to his car.

It was mid-afternoon on Sunday. Julia was taking a nap inside Faith and Russell's house, and Rick had just eaten lunch with his sister.

'Marissa said it must be hard for you, having Russell away.' The comment simply came out of him, in the same way so many thoughts of Marissa got past his defences.

And yesterday Rick had fallen asleep on Marissa's couch, only to wake hours later and discover her asleep on her bed, her laptop in power saver mode beside her.

Rick had wanted to kiss her awake and make love to her. More than he'd wanted anything in a long time. He'd wavered, had reached for her, but then he'd touched the laptop control pad and a website had shown on the screen.

Blinddatebrides.com. We pride ourselves on our success stories.

There were pictures of brides and grooms smiling into each other's eyes as though they'd found the whole world there. Marissa had been logged in. There'd been an IM chat still sitting in the corner of the screen. He hadn't read it, but it was clear she was a member of the site. Quite possibly the friends she'd mentioned, Grace and Dani, were also on the site.

Rick had walked away and kept walking because that was the right thing to do. The only thing he was able to do. He wished he could stop thinking about her, but that didn't seem to be possible, no matter how much he wanted it.

'She seems really nice, Rick.' His sister touched his arm. 'Why don't you—?'

'That won't happen for me.' The words were harsher than he intended. 'I'm sorry, but you know that's not in my plans.'

'I know you like to tell people you're too old and set in your ways and that the company owns you and any other excuse that feels reasonable at the time.' Faith spoke the words in a low tone. 'I don't think it's the truth. You don't want to be like our father, so you hold yourself back.'

Rick chopped a hand through the air. 'I don't want this conversation with you.'

'Well, too bad, because maybe it's time we had it!' She drew a harsh breath. 'Do you think I don't see what he's like, Rick? Do you think it doesn't bother me every day to know our father treats you and me and my husband and my daughter better than he does Darla or Kirrilea simply because Darla had the bad luck to do something that made him uncomfortable, that put pressure on him which he refused to face up to?'

'He loves everyone in the family.' But their father only loved to a degree, didn't he? It might seem as though Stephen had perfectly normal feelings towards some of his children, his grandchildren, but the reality was that it seemed that way because they hadn't pushed him outside his emotional comfort zone. 'If it came down to it, he'd ignore all our needs…'

'Of course he would.' Faith swung to face him. 'If he knew Russell came home from active duty the last two times and cried in my arms for hours, he'd cringe away from it. When Julia gets older and starts to test her boundaries like Kirri's doing now he'll draw back from her too, and the thought of that kills me. If I decided to do something to totally shake him up—'

'That's enough.' For the first time in his life, Rick shut his sister up. 'This conversation is finished. Just leave it, all right?'

Faith's expression froze and then she reached past him to yank his car door open. 'Maybe I've been wrong to believe you're better. To think you could have something with a woman like Marissa. Maybe it's best if you don't.' She stepped back. 'You acted just like him right now.'

Rick drove half a kilometre down the road before he pulled over and used his mobile to phone Faith's house. 'I'm sorry. I didn't mean any of that.'

'I didn't either! I had the phone in my hand to ring you.' Her breath shook as she inhaled. 'You're not like him, Rick. I should never have said it. You've always been there for Darla and me, and our daughters. You're the complete opposite of Dad. Please don't ever believe otherwise.'

Rick reassured his sister and ended the call. But Faith's initial words had been right. He was *exactly* like Stephen Morgan. He'd already proved it once before and left a woman broken-hearted.

CHAPTER THIRTEEN

'I WOULD have taken you out, Darla.' Rick needed to pull his head together, to figure out why he'd lost control when he'd talked with Faith.

Well, Marissa didn't want him anyway, so why was he worrying about it?

Because Marissa is the reason you became so upset?

And, instead of working out anything, he was hosting a family gathering.

His sister toasted him with the gourmet sandwich in her hand and shook her head. 'I didn't want you to take me out. Not this time. This mightn't be anything amazing, but the celebration is on my tab and I want it that way.'

'It's all great.' He meant that. He just hoped she got what she needed from this.

Because Darla had invited them all, and Kirri was at her side and Stephen stood in the corner making polite noises and Rick was so tense he thought he might lose it if anything went wrong for his sister today.

'The sandwiches are fabulous, Darla. Do you mind if I ask which caterer you used?' Marissa asked from beside him.

From the moment Darla had phoned to ask if they could do this today, Marissa had got right behind his sister's plans.

Right now, she couldn't have said anything better if she'd known. Darla grinned and Kirrilea ducked her head with a pleased flush.

Marissa's eyes widened and she laid her hand on his niece's arm. 'It was you? I'm so impressed. Will you tell me what the combination is that has sun-dried tomatoes and cottage cheese and that delicious tangy flavour?'

She'd hit it off with his sisters beautifully—liked Darla on an instinctive level that showed in every word she spoke to her, made Kirri feel great and enjoyed Julia's childish chatter.

If the knowledge of that made Rick possessive about her, maybe he was. If each time he looked at her he wanted to drag her out of there and to the nearest bed and hold her and make love to her, that fact didn't seem any easier to change either.

Rick's mouth tightened and, since there was one thing he *could* do right now that would be utterly appropriate, he forced himself to leave Marissa's side and went round the room charging glasses, moving back to stand beside his sister.

He turned to face Darla and cleared his throat. 'I think a speech is in order. Particularly as you and Kirri have spoiled us all so nicely with food and drink.'

His free hand reached for Darla's. 'You've come a long way from the part-time real estate receptionist who took rental payments over the counter three days a week. You've worked your way up through the ranks and your promotion is well deserved.

'I'm even more proud of what a fabulous parent you are to a very special, wonderful daughter.' The words of pride and love poured out of him and somehow eased him. 'I love you, Darla. I couldn't be more proud of you in all the ways there are.'

'Thank you, Rick. Those words mean the world to me.' Darla smiled through suddenly bright eyes as a still silence descended over the room.

Marissa felt the thrum of heartache mixed with the deep emotion between sister and brother.

So much hurt, and now that she'd observed Stephen Morgan in action, she believed she understood. Rick's father was a pleasant man. He cared for his family. That was quite clear. But he wanted to care only on his terms. Any time things drifted to any kind of emotional ground, he closed himself off from it.

Even in the simple act of his youngest granddaughter running to him for a cuddle. He had patted her head but he hadn't picked her up. That meting out of a measured amount of affection was so sad, and how difficult he'd made it for his family.

She smiled at Darla with determined good cheer. 'Congratulations. I hope the job promotion is all you want it to be.'

Faith hugged her sister and got a bit tearful. Hugged Rick and got equally tearful.

Rick's mother gave her daughter a peck on the cheek and a smile, and their father cleared his throat and declared it must be time they all left. It was only a brief lunch, after all. He'd reached the door, his wife close behind him, when Darla's mouth firmed and she reclaimed Rick's hand.

'That lovely speech deserves one in return, and in fact I chose to do this here because I wanted to say a few words and I felt this was the right place for them.' She turned her gaze to Rick and her heart was in her eyes so clearly that Marissa caught her breath.

Their parents hesitated in the doorway, but Darla didn't seem to care whether they stayed or left.

Rick started to shake his head, but Darla simply set a jaw very like her brother's and went on.

'Without you, Rick, without your financial support and your encouragement and your unconditional love, I don't know if I could have done any of this.' She swallowed hard. 'You were there when my beautiful girl was born. You'd have come into the labour suite if I'd let you. Instead, they told me you paced non-stop outside until it was over.'

Her gaze skimmed her daughter's down-bent head and returned to her brother. 'Thanks to your financial support, I could be at home with my baby and eventually get my career and my finances on track.'

Rick's Adam's apple bobbed. 'I did very little—'

'You helped me get where I am today, and you helped me know I didn't have to be scared or feel alone or deserted.' Darla's voice cracked. 'You loved my daughter from the day she was born and you've loved me from the day I was born, and I love you and I just…need to say that today.'

She hugged her brother and Rick held her in a tight embrace. His shoulders were taut, his eyes closed as though against such pain. Love for his sister filled every plane and angle of his face.

Marissa took a step towards them before she could stop herself. She needed to hold Rick. To assure him he'd done enough for his sister, that he could…love?

But they drew apart then and after a moment Kirrilea stuck her arm through her mum's and glanced beyond her to the couple near the door.

Her eyes were far too mature for her face as she said, 'Grandad, you probably have golf or something, so don't feel you and Grandma have to stay. We're fine here.'

The older couple left with brief farewells, acting as though nothing were amiss and there'd been no outpouring of emotion in the room just moments before. As though they hadn't been dismissed, if politely. As though they weren't lacking—

'Darla—'

'Don't worry about it, Rick.' Darla squeezed her daughter's shoulders. 'Wise heads on young shoulders, huh? I think we're really okay here. This was a good thing. It was. And it's time for us to head out.'

It was time for Marissa to remember, too, that Rick being able to love his sisters didn't mean he could commit his heart elsewhere. Why was she even thinking this, anyway? *Her* heart was far from involved.

A few minutes later, everyone had left.

'It's time to get back to work.' Rick's preoccupation was clear as he murmured the words, later on, back at the office, but he settled behind his desk and drew a folder of reading material in front of him.

Marissa might even have managed to set aside her reactions and thoughts about him if she hadn't stepped into his office to leave some letters for signature and seen that he'd tacked the laminate of his niece to the wall by his window where it competed with the view of the harbour. Where he would look at it at least a hundred times a day.

And she admitted it. She wanted to ask a thousand questions and tell him she understood so much more about him now and she wanted him to see all he had inside to give. All he had already given.

Rick had dropped everything to rush her to her mother, but he'd also done all he could to allow Tom a comfortable and worry-free recovery. He had been *kind*. That wasn't the same as a romantic commitment.

Marissa got down to work. She wished she could shut her thoughts down altogether.

'Our Hong Kong businessmen called while you were in the filing room,' Rick said from the doorway of his office half an hour later. He looked rumpled and somehow determined and resigned and intense all at once. 'Tom phoned minutes before them.' His voice turned to a harsh, low rumble. 'He'll be back in the office on Wednesday.'

'That's two days away. I thought he was taking longer.' The whispered words fell from her lips as the shock of that knowledge passed through her. Just two more days and she would cease to see Rick all day every day, work closely with him. Would cease to feel a close part of his life, even if that closeness was only in her…heart?

In her thoughts, in the fact that they had drawn together out of necessity for a short time! Marissa stiffened her spine and tried hard to hide her shock and the dismay she didn't want to admit.

'Well, that's great. Tom must feel a lot better. I'll do my best to leave everything in good order for him, and Gordon is due back on Monday, anyway. I'd been wondering how that would work out.'

Rick ran his fingers through his hair. 'Yes. It will be convenient for…everyone.'

He would be rid of her, wouldn't have to fight his attraction to her any more. Wasn't that what he had wanted from the start? To *not* want her?

'We leave for Hong Kong tomorrow after lunch.' His jaw clenched. 'It will be a two-night stay. They'll tell us with due formality they've chosen to do business with us and, though they could have done that over the phone or with a contract in the mail, it's due process for them, and important we acknowledge the gesture and respond as they expect.'

'And, because I participated in the initial dealings here, they want me along?' Did *Rick* want her presence there, or did he wish he didn't have to take her with him? 'I've never visited Hong Kong and, though my passport is current, I can invent a reason not to attend if you don't want—'

'I want you to come.' His gaze touched over her hair, each facial feature, dwelt on her mouth and came back to her eyes. 'I'd like to show you some of the sights, take you shopping.'

He wanted to give her a last huzzah before it all ended?

The knowledge somehow hurt and wrapped around her heart, all at once.

Marissa tipped up her chin. 'I'd like the chance to visit Hong Kong, see a few of the sights and my presence is expected. I don't want to let the businessmen down.'

It seemed business was all they had left now.

Rick sent Marissa to bed straight off the plane the first night in Hong Kong. He knocked on her hotel room door the next morning and realised how much he wanted this time with her.

His plans, his way of showing her—what? A good time in a place she'd never visited before? So he could say goodbye this way and not look back afterwards? His body burned with the need to be near hers. His emotions burned for her in ways he had never expected or experienced.

Something had happened that day when Darla had brought their family's relationships to the fore and Kirri had dealt with her grandfather with a teenage combination of kindness and something close to pity. Rick had felt as though, finally, an issue that had hovered over all of them had been addressed.

Quietly and without any particular fanfare, but that exchange with his sister had loosened something tight way down inside him.

Rick hadn't realised how the situation had festered, even while he'd believed he had pushed it all aside.

But you're still like your father.

He didn't want to be like Stephen, but he'd already proved he was. Marissa didn't deserve that. She needed someone tender, gentle, and completely committed to her. Someone who would *know* his ability to meet all her needs.

'Good morning. These rooms are great. I have the most amazing view of Victoria Harbour and the city.' Marissa stood framed in the doorway of her room.

A fierce determination seized him. For today he planned

to spoil her and indulge her and enjoy her. He would have *that much*.

And then she could go back to Gordon's office and to her search for a man?

Her gaze rushed over him like a warm breath and ducked away again, and all his senses fired to life despite himself. No. He still didn't want her searching for a man, but he chose to push that thought away for now.

'All the colour and activity I glimpsed last night really is as stunning as I thought.' She touched her hair self-consciously, smoothed her hands over cream trousers, and skimmed the buttons of her brown long-sleeved blouse.

Nervous. She was nervous.

You could try speaking instead of standing here eating her up with your eyes.

She'd said the view was stunning.

'It is a great view.' But he meant the one in front of him right now. 'We have a spending budget for today,' he ventured, and wondered if she'd believe him if he said their business-men hosts had provided it.

'Work-related expenditure? Tax deductibles?' She raised a hand to her hair again and he wished he could pull the ribbon from it and let it loose.

Instead, he took her arm, led her away from the room. 'Not all of it, no, but I'll be very disappointed if you don't join me and enjoy the day. We're going to visit a temple, see an outdoor Chinese opera, shop, ride in a rickshaw.'

'It sounds magical.' Did her voice hold a touch of wistfulness?

Rick forced a smile. 'We don't meet our hosts until this evening. They've planned a pre-dinner cocktail cruise on a junk so we can see the light show. The pace here is frenetic and the volume of people can take you by surprise so stay close to me and tell me if you need a time-out if I don't create one for you soon enough, okay?'

* * *

Rick took Marissa through all the things he'd promised. A wiry man pedalled them along the street in a rickshaw with a gaily coloured top. When they'd taken in the awe of a Buddhist temple and the outdoor opera and so much bustling activity in the markets that Marissa felt dizzy with it, Rick hustled her into an opulent boutique hotel restaurant tucked away between towering buildings.

'This afternoon we'll shop.' He made the announcement as they ate food he'd chosen from a confusingly long list of Cantonese dishes—small servings of prawn and pork dumpling, steamed bean curd with salted fish sauce and other stunningly flavoured foods they interspersed with sips of tea.

'I've already bought some things.' She gestured to the goodies bundled at their feet. 'For Mum and Dad.'

'This afternoon I want you to buy for yourself. Pretty things. Whatever takes your fancy.' He lowered his eyes as though he couldn't quite meet hers as he admitted this.

The desire to burrow her fingers through the hair at his nape rushed through her. When their eyes locked she saw a sharp ache in him before he blinked it away.

'Rick…' She wanted him to open himself to her, to let her in totally. 'I can't let you buy me—'

'Yes. You can. If you don't, I'll only add the money to your pay.' His stare compelled her, almost implored her. 'Don't think too much, Marissa. Just agree. It would please me.'

Her hand tightened in her lap. How could she deny him when he asked her this way?

When he seemed to need this so much?

Just as he'd needed Darla to let him do something to help make her attempt at a business promotion successful. No. Not like that, because he *loved* Darla. This was *kindness*, nothing more.

'Then I guess we really are going shopping.'

They finished their meal and he ushered her to her feet. He

arranged for their packages to be returned to their hotel for them, and he took her shopping.

Patiently and with absolute pleasure as she delighted herself in the most sumptuous retail experience she would perhaps encounter in her life. She wouldn't spend much. Just one or two things to please them both.

'What about this shop?' Rick drew her attention to a store full of exquisite silk garments and she knew she wouldn't be able to walk out of the place empty-handed. She stopped short. 'Oh, no.'

'Yes. Pick something to wear tonight. There must an outfit here you'd like.' He turned her to the displays of clothing.

She found the dress almost straight away. A simple cream sheath with a lovely watermark effect in the fabric. It was sleeveless, with a high traditional collar and exquisitely fitted bodice covered in tiny hand-sewn pearls. Her fingers reached for it, stopped just shy of touching as she imagined how much it might cost.

'Try it on,' he growled before he spoke in Cantonese to the shop assistant nearest them.

Moments later, tucked into the privacy of a changing room, Marissa lifted her arms and allowed the dress to glide over her head and settle against her curves.

The rustle of the fabric was almost sinful—whisper-soft and sleek—and the dress fitted as though made for her. She had to have it, wanted to wear it. For him.

No. Because it was beautiful, lovely.

While Marissa tried the dress on, Rick bought a shawl to go with it and arranged for it to be delivered to the hotel. A cream and brown confection that reminded him of her skin and her hair and her deep, expressive eyes.

When she emerged from the changing room with her face flushed a delicate pink and the dress clutched carefully in her hands, a surge of possessive heat rose inside him. He wanted to lavish gifts on her for the rest of his days, dress her in beautiful things and then strip those things away from her body and make love to her slowly and thoroughly and never have to stop.

And afterwards he wanted to hold her, cradled in his arms. None of which could ever happen.

'Did it fit?' Even to his ears, his voice was low and rough, sensual and far too intense. He'd brought her here to say goodbye, but he'd intended to control that leave-taking, not have to fight himself all the way.

'Yes. Yes, it fitted.' She swallowed, looked as though she didn't know whether to run or come closer.

It was too much. His fingers reached for her wrist and the warmth of her soft skin. He circled the fragile bones and inhaled slowly. Her pulse fluttered beneath his thumb.

'The…er…the shoes I've packed will go nicely with the dress.' She lifted her other hand, dropped it before she touched him. 'And it really is—'

'Beautiful.' But not as beautiful as Marissa. He released her reluctantly, completed the transaction for her and then rubbed a hand over the back of his neck.

'There's a jewellery store beside this one. I'd like to pick up something for my sisters and nieces.' And he would like to buy Marissa all kinds of necklaces and bracelets.

'I might like a scarf or something from here before I go.' She glanced around her. 'Out of my own money. I'll meet you in the jewellery store in a few minutes.'

Dismissed again, very nicely, and despite himself he couldn't help the tug of a smile as he remembered other times she had dispatched him.

Rick left her to it.

His body tingled with awareness as he walked out of the store, and with an odd ache because he didn't like separating from her. He could say it was because he needed her close for her sake. She couldn't speak the language. But he practised his Cantonese to keep the skills. It often wasn't needed, and she was more than capable of keeping herself safe without him.

The jewellery store was top end, and had every conceivable gift item. Rick's gaze shifted to the display of engagement rings. What kind of ring had Michael Unsworth given Marissa, if any?

His brows drew down. At the same time his gaze landed on a ring that would be perfect for her. A rare amber stone set against rich brown tiger's eye and surrounded by diamonds. It would match her eyes and hair. He wanted to buy it for her. Dear God, he wanted to—

Rick turned away from the display with a stifled sound of shock and rejection and…disbelief.

And then she was there beside him, a small store bag clutched to her side with the top pinched tightly together so there was no chance he would glimpse inside it.

Her gaze went to the displays of jewellery, though not the engagement rings. 'I wonder if I could find something for Dani and Grace. I think it's just as well we'll need to leave here soon. This sort of retail therapy is rather addictive.' She glanced up at him then, and her face stilled. 'Are you—?'

'I'm fine. I'll…help you look.'

She cast one or two uncertain glances his way as they browsed, but eventually he must have pulled himself together enough that she stopped wondering what was wrong with him.

Rick didn't know the answer to that. He helped her choose gifts for her friends and, when he purchased items for his sisters and nieces and mother, added a jewelled headband for Marissa. He was under control again. He couldn't be anything else, could he?

'The "Symphony of Lights" is aptly named.' Marissa breathed the words and felt her senses come alive from all directions.

They were aboard an authentic junk on Victoria Harbour.

Mr Qi had explained the meaning behind the themes but she'd got stuck on 'awakening' for she feared she had awakened to Rick and she didn't know what to do about it.

Rick stood behind her on the deck of the junk. To their left, bright orange sails caught the sea breeze with startling efficiency as they moved through the water. Rick's legs were braced. His hands held her lightly under her elbows and, if she leaned back just a little, she could pretend he held her as a lover would.

The war of emotion and delight and wonder and sensation battered at her from without and within, snatched her breath. All because of a powerful man in a business city that provided the perfect backdrop for all the things about him she had sworn she would never like, and now found she…liked too much.

A fringed end of brown silk shawl brushed over her wrist and she stroked her fingers over the delicate fabric. 'You shouldn't have bought me this.' But she was glad he had. Her delight when she'd stepped into her room and found it on the bed had rippled through her.

She wore the jewelled band in her hair as well, felt rather like a princess in all her finery.

'The shawl matches the colour of your eyes. I couldn't resist it.' Maybe he didn't intend her to hear the low words, but she did, and she shivered in his hold.

After the light show they returned to land and ate in a traditional restaurant overlooking the harbour. Rick looked stunning in a dark suit and starched white shirt, the gold and onyx cuff-links at his wrists flashing occasionally when he gestured with the hands that had cupped her elbows with warmth and sweet tenderness during the light show.

His tie was burgundy silk. She'd bought it and had pushed it into his hands at the end of their shopping trip, and she liked to see it on him. Felt far too possessive about him.

Now, his gaze strayed to her continuously and his fingers

idly stroked that tie as he talked business with their hosts until Marissa struggled to breathe normally, her heart and body awash with longing for him.

She'd fallen in love. She finally let the truth of it rise from deep in her heart, as soft as the whisper of silk against her skin, as frightening and devastating as the meaning of life.

Mr Qi had talked about the themes behind the light show while blue and red and green and yellow and pink light reflected off the water. Marissa had taken in the show but it was Rick's nearness at her back that had made her feel awakened. Now she longed for partnership and celebration with Rick but he didn't want that. He didn't want any of that with her.

She swallowed back the emotion that clogged her throat and dropped her gaze lest Rick see what was in her eyes.

'Thank you for organising for us to see the light show and for this wonderful evening.' Marissa addressed her words to Mr Qi, to all their hosts, tried to smile and seem natural as she praised the city, its beauty, the temples and age-old religions and staggering strength of the Hong Kong business world.

'We are pleased you've enjoyed our city.' Mr Qi turned to Rick. 'And pleased to create a business bond with Morgan's for our Australian building investments.' In his flawless English Mr Qi went on to outline the group's decision.

Rick murmured words of appreciation.

Two more hours passed before they finally wrapped up the evening. By then every nerve in Marissa's body was stretched tight. She hadn't set out to love Rick—couldn't believe she'd allowed it to happen—but she did and she didn't know what to do about it. She wanted a family with him. Wanted *his* babies. Wanted him to tell her that thirty wasn't so old and that he thought she was beautiful and always would think that, even when she was very old indeed…

When they got back to Australia she'd return to Gordon's

office. Would Rick remember her? Think about her? Or quickly forget her and go back to a brief nod as he swept by, his thoughts centred on his work and not the woman who had helped him with it for a short time?

They left with handshakes and bows and the assurance of a deal large enough and lucrative enough to raise Rick's business profile more than ever. At the last moment Mr Qi presented Rick with an embossed envelope. 'Perhaps you might like these.'

Rick thanked him, tucked the envelope inside his inner jacket pocket and then they were away. He took her back across the harbour. It was like crossing a big river and, before she was ready for it, they were inside their Kowloon hotel once again.

Rick took Marissa to her room in silence, so attracted to her in the lovely dress and all the more to the softness in her eyes and the guarded vulnerability there. He held her shawl. It had slipped from her shoulders as they'd crossed the harbour and he'd taken it into his hands, the soft fabric warmed from her body.

She paused outside her room. Turned to face him. 'Thank you for a wonderful day, for the gifts.' Her hand rose to touch the jewelled band that held her curls off her face.

His hand lifted to her shoulder, captured a lock of her hair and pressed it between thumb and finger, because he couldn't stand not touching her, yet it only made him want her more. 'I'm glad you wore your hair down tonight. It's you. So vital and alive and free.'

If she knew how much he wanted to bury his face in that mass of curls, to inhale the essence of her and hold her and somehow wrap her around him and inside him…

'I don't ever look sleek and neat as a pin, no matter how hard I try.' Her lips tilted in a soft attempt at a smile.

'You look…' Holdable. Kissable. 'It's you. I hope you never change.'

'It won't matter. Soon you won't even notice me. You'll go back to passing me in the corridors with a nod—'

'No.' He didn't know if he could ever dismiss her from his thoughts. Rick tugged her into his arms before he knew his own intention, took the possibility of other words from her mouth with his lips.

As his arms closed about her and her mouth warmed beneath his, he fought his demons and didn't know any more whether he had lost or won, only that he needed her.

How could holding her be such torment? How could he let her go?

She drew back with a gasp. A pulse fluttered at the base of her throat. Her eyes were wide and uncertain, filled with desire and…anguish.

'Marissa—'

'Wh-what did Mr Qi give you before we left?' Her words were an attempt to draw back from the brink.

He blinked and struggled with harsh stark feelings that tore at him. Why had he thought he could bring her here and not want to make love with her? That he could give her the sights and sounds of Hong Kong and not want her for himself?

He tugged the envelope from his pocket and flipped it open. There were photos. Two of them, taken at the petting zoo. Mr Qi had had the digital images made into prints for them. In the first photo Marissa had the koala in her arms. She smiled and, behind her, Rick smiled for the cameras. He stared unblinkingly at that first photo for a moment before he tilted it forward.

The one behind it made him catch his breath because in this photo her heart was in her eyes. The wounds she'd sustained when her fiancé had dumped her, her need to know she could connect in a meaningful way again and have it work out for her. The ache in her as she'd held that bundle of fur in her arms. Her tender feelings for the man in the picture.

He was that man, and he wanted those feelings from her even as he recognised the expression in his eyes in the picture. Longing, hunger. He'd thought it wouldn't show. Hadn't realised the strength of those feelings, even then. The thought of making love to her, of giving her something she wanted and thus locking her irrevocably to him in the process, rushed him, shocked him. Even as he admitted he'd known all along that longing for a child had been part of her reaction that day.

'A couple of prints from the petting zoo.' He cleared his throat, turned the envelope so she could see the top print, and then tucked the small packet back into his pocket.

His desire to kiss her, possess her, tore at him and he backed away from it and from her because if he touched her at all he wouldn't stop. 'It's late and we have a long flight ahead of us to get home tomorrow.'

'To get back to work and our usual tasks. In my case, anyway. You'll just go on as before, but with Tom.' Marissa almost asked Rick to stay. The words trembled on the tip of her tongue but, before she could find the courage to say them, or the sanity to stop herself, he took the decision from her.

'Goodnight.' There was a bite in his voice that was self-derision and intensity and longing and refusal wrapped into one. His room was across from hers. He entered and closed the door with a soft click that seemed far too final.

She sagged for a harsh, struggling moment before she let herself into her own room, and with a sound wrenched from her, fell back against the door. Her spine welcomed the hard surface, the chill inanimateness of it, while her heart railed at her, told her to go to him—

She tugged the jewelled decoration from her hair, set is on the bedside table. Thought of Rick in that room across the hall, so close. Took a stumbling step towards the door.

The rap from the other side made her heart slam in her chest. She lunged for the doorknob and wrenched the door open and knew, *knew in her heart that if there was any way she could keep him with her, even just for the one night, she would.* All thoughts of self-preservation were gone, lost to her, because if she could only love him once then she wanted to.

He held her shawl crushed inside a white-knuckled fist. He didn't even pretend it was the reason. 'Tell me no, Marissa. Tell it to me right now.'

She drew a shaken breath. Her fingers wrapped around his strong hair-roughened wrist. 'I need you tonight, Rick. Here and now. I'm only prepared to tell you that.'

CHAPTER FOURTEEN

RICK crossed the threshold of Marissa's room without any awareness that he had moved. He only felt her body in his arms as the door clicked locked behind him and his mouth came down over hers.

It wasn't an easy kiss, or a soft one. He covered her lips with his and took every part of her that she would give. Possessed and suckled and stroked until his blood bubbled in his veins and his body shook and his emotions roiled and he didn't know how to quiet them, how to assuage them.

'I want this.' She sighed the words into the crook of his neck and pressed her lips to his skin there.

He buried his free hand in her hair, lodged it deep in the wild curliness as he tipped up her head to give him the access he wanted to her mouth. Her chin and face and neck.

The need for her turned molten, raged through him and made his knees quake and his heart stutter with—

Not longing. Not a need so deep it was unfathomable. He could not acknowledge that, be at the mercy of that. Yet his hand in her hair gentled to reverent pressure as he brought her head forward and let himself have the softness of her, the sweetness of her as their lips touched, brushed, in the gentle kiss he should have given her to start with.

He tossed the shawl onto the bed behind them, a splash of brown against the soft golden tone of the quilt.

Let him please her, wring everything from this time with her—for both of them. Let him at least have that, give her that. It was a supplication and a hope and a determination as Rick gave himself—all of him that he could—to the woman in his arms.

Stroking hands over her hair and the skin of her arms. Whisper-soft kisses to soothe the startled sensitivity of her lips where he had kissed her.

Where Marissa had ached from Rick's focused plundering of her senses, her heart melted in the face of his gentleness. The man, the layers, the complexities. Maybe no person would ever truly know all of him and, despite the ache in her heart for him and for the knowledge that he didn't share her feelings, he felt something.

He gave her something. Perhaps more of himself than Michael had ever given.

The thought surfaced and she pushed it away because Michael was a shadow. A piece of the past.

Rick was real and here in her arms and if her heart broke tomorrow and went on breaking she would have to find a way to survive it somehow because she couldn't end this. She would not deny herself this.

So she would give him her heart in her touch and the haven of her arms, just this one time. It was madness and insanity and the essence of a need so deep she couldn't fathom it. She faced it and chose it.

'I want to feel your warmth.' She needed that.

Her hands pushed his jacket off broad shoulders, down muscular arms, flung it across the chair behind him. With shaking fingertips she traced the hard heat of his chest, touched the silk tie.

'I'm glad you wore this.' The sight of it on him had raised proprietorial instincts she hadn't known she had.

The primitive emotions warned her how far she had fallen. She didn't want to know. Not now. Not yet.

'I'm glad you wore the dress and shawl.' His words were a low growl as her fingers worked the tie out from beneath his collar.

His hands roved restlessly up and down her arms. She sensed both urgency and his restraint, the war of the two inside him. The tie disappeared and the flat of his hand pressed into her back between her shoulders, pressed her forward until their bodies locked once more.

'You bought them for me.' Clothes he had wanted her to have. Clothes she had wanted to wear for him.

'And you put them on with those dainty high heeled shoes and all I could think about all night was touching you, your beautiful legs wrapping around me, welcoming me.' He made a harsh sound and stroked his thumbs over the points of her jaw. 'Since that day when I lifted you into my car I've thought about your legs—'

He kissed her and praised her and murmured all the ways he wanted to show her how beautiful he thought her, and Marissa forgot about coffee table analogies and fear and what would happen tomorrow, and lost herself in him.

Rick's hands shifted to the back of her dress and his gaze was intent on hers as he set her skin free inch by inch until cool air touched her back and warm fingers skimmed over her spine.

This was really happening and she made the choice to take everything, give everything that could be shared, to awaken and celebrate in this moment, with him.

'I need your hands on me.' He lifted her hand to his mouth, kissed her fingers and placed them against his chest over the fabric of his shirt. 'On my skin. Over my heart. Please, Marissa.'

The gravelly plea curled around her heart. He must feel

something for her. His rough plea suggested he did, his gaze echoed it. Need. He did need her somehow.

She stepped back and his arms dropped to his sides. Spiky lashes swept down as his gaze locked on her mouth, roved her body with possessive intent and with awe.

She released the buttons on his shirt one by one. Feasted with her fingertips upon the skin stretched tight across his muscled chest, let the abrasion of dark curly hair fill her senses. One cuff-link came away. The other. He shrugged the shirt off his shoulders and flung it away, wrapped her in arms that felt as though they could shelter her for ever.

Then Marissa's breath caught on a stifled sound of longing that came not only from her senses but also from deep in her soul and heart.

He tipped up her chin and searched her eyes and emotions warred in his gaze before he crushed her close, his hands flat against her back as he pushed clothing away. 'Say my name. I need to hear it.'

'Only you, Rick.' She had no room in her heart or her senses for any other. 'I only want to think of you, of this—this moment.'

His arms trembled as he laid her on the bed. He reached into the pocket of his trousers, laid a small foil packet on the night-stand beside her and bowed his head as though fighting with himself somehow.

Marissa let her gaze encompass that gesture and swallowed hard. 'I thought you might have to raid the supplies in the bathroom.'

She could tell him she was on the pill, that she'd stayed on it since Michael, but she didn't want to bring the other man's name into the room. It would feel like sacrilege.

Rick knelt on the floor at her side, stroked skin too tight and too hot and stripped away the layers until she was naked before him—and naked emotionally—and she shuddered with vulnerable need and would have covered herself.

'Don't.' He spoke that single hoarse word and his arms closed around her. He buried his face against her heart and shuddered, a strong man on his knees and emotionally vulnerable to her. Right now, that was who he was, as vulnerable as her.

She clasped his shoulders and tugged. 'Come to me. Please, Rick.'

Rick shed the rest of his clothes and joined Marissa, drew her into the hold of his arms and against his body, and they touched in so many places finally.

He was drowning in Marissa's arms, in an overload of wrenching feeling that welled up from somewhere deep inside. His hands shook as he ran them over her face, caressed her neck and shoulders and the dip of her waist.

A convulsive swallow made him aware of the tightness in his throat as he buried his gaze in soft brown eyes blurred with warmth and longing.

'This night.' He spoke the words, a benediction and a warning and a promise. 'For this night you're mine.'

'And you're mine.' Her arms bound him to her. 'For tonight *you're mine*.'

He hadn't known anything of pleasure. Not until now and it swamped his senses, poured over him and through him and her fierce words were right at the centre of it.

When she opened herself to him, his heart filled with aching wonder and stark desperation. He loved her with his body and his touch and his senses, with everything within him he still didn't fully understand and when it ended, he kissed her and, cradled her in his arms and didn't want to leave her.

Eventually he forced himself to release her. He padded to the bathroom, and returned to her side and climbed back into the bed. His arms tightened around her and he couldn't prevent the tight sigh of sound that escaped as he buried his face in her hair.

He didn't know how to handle the overload of feeling, the possessiveness that rose up, the wild thoughts of finding ways to make Marissa stay with him, to keep her at his side. The temptation to take her again without benefit of any package…

'You were all I needed,' she whispered as she drifted into sleep. 'In the end, you were all of it anyway. I hadn't realised…'

And she'd been all to him, despite those temptations. He held her until she slept and he stayed at her side, his arms around her, and felt the hours slide away one after another until there were too many gone and he felt panicky and lost and somehow shattered because she *had* been all, but she was wrong that he'd been enough for her.

He rose from the bed then, quietly retrieved and donned his clothes.

Brushed his fingers over the shawl abandoned at the foot of the bed and took the memory of her hair spread across the pillow, her soft mouth and the touch and taste of her with him as he left the room.

As he backed away emotionally, just as his father had done for as long as Rick could remember. Wasn't that what he was doing?

You don't want to hurt her. The way your father has hurt Kirri and your sisters and would have hurt your mother if she didn't choose to push it all away.

It was sound reasoning.

Why did it leave him so hollow inside?

To: Sanfrandani, Englishcrumpet
From Kangagirl
So much has happened in such a short space of time, I don't know where to start. Well, I guess it doesn't matter where I start. The ending is still the same. I fell in love with Rick and he doesn't feel the same way but I don't want you to worry about me because I'll get over it. Tomorrow when I go to work I'll be back in Gordon's office.

Rick's secretary will be back, you see, so he won't need me any more, and my boss will be back, so it all works out. I'm glad, really. And it's my birthday on Friday. I've entertained a lot of nonsense thoughts about turning thirty. As though the day means anything, really.

And I bought you both a little something in Hong Kong. You can expect a small package each in the mail in the next week or two, depending on the vagaries of the postal service at either end…

To: Englishcrumpet
From: Sanfrandani
I'm worried about Marissa. She's so generous, thinking about us when it's clear her heart is breaking. I don't know how to help her. I wish she hadn't fallen for this guy. That's twice in a row that she's loved and ended up devastated, and this time it seems even worse for her. It doesn't seem fair!

To: Sanfrandani
From: Englishcrumpet
All we can do is be there for her. I wonder if she could have avoided this? Love seems to survive even the greatest resistance sometimes, whether it's welcome or not.

CHAPTER FIFTEEN

'MARISSA. I didn't expect to see you here.'

The male voice was familiar. Marissa looked up into Michael Unsworth's bland, suave face and blinked her eyes. He had to be a mirage. Fate wouldn't be so cruel as to do this to her just days short of her birthday, when she already felt miserable and depressed and…heartbroken for a man who simply didn't want to love her or even keep her in his life. Not his personal life, not his close working life.

Rick Morgan was that man. Not this echo of the past.

But here Michael stood, right in the middle of the coffee shop she'd slipped away to for lunch. 'Michael. Excuse me. I'm late getting back to work.'

It was only the barest of white lies. She looked at the man and she felt nothing but a distanced dislike because of his shabby past behaviour. Rick had her heart. There was no room for any other. Not in any way.

'Er…look, Marissa, I didn't intend for you to find out this way.' Michael's voice oozed sympathy but the feeling didn't reach his eyes. 'Especially so close to your…er…well…to your birthday. I promise you if I'd known you'd be anywhere near this place—'

'I can't imagine why you would be concerned about seeing me near my birthday or any other time, and the last time I checked, people could eat where they liked.' Marissa didn't want to revisit his earlier birthday promise to her—that they would be secretly engaged and eventually get married and love each other for ever.

How could she have been so foolish as to even think she'd fallen for him anyway? He wasn't half the man Rick was.

And how could you be so foolish as to love Rick, who told you he would never commit to you?

'Who is this, Michael? A friend of yours?' A woman drew level with them.

Several things registered with Marissa in that moment. The woman was Jane McCullough, the daughter of Michael's company boss. The two of them were clearly together. And Jane was pregnant.

The feelings Marissa had thought she had under control about having a child made themselves known again then. 'You... You're expecting a baby.' Her voice wobbled. 'Congratulations.'

And Jane was much younger than thirty. Probably no more than twenty-five...

'Marissa, this is my fiancée, Jane McCullough.' Michael inserted the words with a hint of warning in his tone.

What did he think she would do? Tear out the other woman's eyes because she had him and Marissa didn't, because she was starting the family Marissa now knew she would never, ever have? If she couldn't have that with Rick, she would never want it with anyone.

'We've met in passing, though I don't know if Jane would remember her father introducing us.' Marissa offered a polite nod to the woman. A smile was beyond her right now. 'I hope you're keeping well.'

I hope Michael is true to you, truer than he ever was to me.

Jane frowned as she apparently considered the signifi-cance of Marissa's past involvement with Michael.

And Marissa excused herself a second time and walked away. The only good thing she could think of as she stepped back into the Morgan company building was that at least she'd eaten a wholesome sandwich and even a piece of fruit for her lunch. 'There'll be no fainting on the job today.'

Rick would be proud, but it wasn't about Rick any more. Hadn't been since they'd got off the plane days ago and he'd finally faced her fully.

'If the protection fails and there's a baby, I'll take care of you. I expect you to let me know.'

That was what he had said, the only words about the night they'd shared, the most wonderful experience of her life and she'd thought it had meant something special to him as well. In her heart she still believed it had, but just not enough. He'd looked at her then with such anguish in his eyes, but ultimately he'd turned away.

They'd spoken since. Awkward words when she'd bumped into him on her floor, when he'd dropped by Gordon's office to speak to him, and twice when Rick had visited the company's cafeteria at the same time she had.

She didn't remember seeing that much of him before she'd started working for him. Maybe he'd been there but she hadn't truly noticed. Now she noticed everything, longed for each glimpse of him. How could she go on day after day this way? Seeing him, speaking briefly with him while their gazes locked and she fought all her longing for him and needed him so much she kept thinking she saw the same longing in him?

It had to end. The torture had to end but she didn't know how to make that happen.

'Marissa.' Rick stepped into the lift behind the woman he couldn't get out of his mind. 'I thought I might see you at the cafeteria today.' He'd been looking, going places she might be…

'I went out instead.' Her low words were guarded.

He stood beside her and felt helpless. And then she raised her hand to press the button for her floor, as she had done that very first day, and all the moments they had shared since then washed through him and he realised…

He'd fallen in love with her. The ache in his chest couldn't be anything else. The need to be near her any way he could…

'You…er…where are you going? You haven't pressed for a floor.' Her mouth softened to a vulnerable line as she looked at him for one brief moment, seemed to take in every feature as though she needed to commit him to her memory as much as she needed to be with her.

I'm going to whatever floor keeps me with you in here the longest.

'Er…the top floor. Swimming.' In truth, he hadn't been up there for ages. He'd lost interest in most of the things he routinely did, had only kept going with his work because it made the time pass. *He loved her.* Where did he go with that? He, who hadn't believed he could…

Marissa pressed the button for the top floor and the floor she shared with Gordon, and her hand dropped to her side. He wanted to capture her fingers in his and never let go. He wanted a chance with her. His heart leaped into his throat and stayed there. Words pushed past anyway. 'Please, will you—'

Ding.

The lift stopped, the doors slid open. She glanced at him and a choked sound came from her throat. 'I have to go. I have to get back to work. I can't—' She stepped out of the lift and was gone.

But maybe not completely gone from him? As the lift doors closed and he felt as though his heart had stayed behind on that other floor with her, Rick pondered that emotional leap.

He wasn't like his father. How could he be when this love in his chest, this need for Marissa, filled all of him? He just hadn't known what love was—the real, strong, all-encompassing love of a man for only one woman.

Was it too late? He didn't know, but he understood now what he had to do...

Her birthday was almost over. Well, the working part of it was over at least. For the first time, Marissa had contemplated calling in and pretending she was sick so she wouldn't have to go to work today.

But she'd gone to work and she'd got through the day without even a glimpse of the company boss, and now all she had to do was manage the birthday dinner her parents had sprung on her after all.

Marissa left her apartment and climbed into the taxi her mother had arranged for her. She even managed a slight smile as she thought how much Mum must have enjoyed putting together this 'little surprise', complete with an 'undisclosed destination' for this taxi ride.

Hopefully the driver knew where he was taking her!

Well, Marissa would enjoy the night if it killed her. She owed her parents that much.

Eighty-eight storeys above ground level, Rick waited in a restaurant in Sydney's Centrepoint Tower building. The tables faced panels of glass that gave a moving panoramic view of the harbour and city.

Rick only had eyes for the woman who followed the waitress towards the table set for eight. Marissa wore the silk dress bought in Hong Kong, the shawl spread across her shoulders. Her face held determination and unhappiness she was working very hard to mask, and surprise. That last was the result of believing her parents had sprung a birthday event on her after all, no doubt, and of that 'surprise' leading her here.

He'd begged for her parents' co-operation to make tonight

happen, had laid himself bare to get it, and after a thorough grilling from Abe and a gentler one from Tilda, they'd come through for him. Tilda had admitted that Marissa had made it clear she didn't want to celebrate this birthday, that the date itself had unpleasant memories for her, thanks to her ex-fiancé, and, on top of that, her daughter didn't seem to be coping very well with the idea of turning thirty.

To Rick, Marissa's age was perfect. *She* was perfect. He'd chosen this restaurant because he wanted to lay all of the city at her feet. Maybe that was whimsical, but he'd gone with his heart. Now he had to convince Marissa of his love, and convince her to let him love her and prove those thoughts to her. If she would let him. If she could find something in her heart for him.

Would her smile fade and utter rejection replace it when she noticed him? Had he left it too late and lost her, if he ever truly had a chance with her in the first place? His fingers moved to the outline of the ring in his pocket and for a long moment his breath froze in his chest and he thought his lungs might give out and he'd end up on the floor.

He knew the precise moment she spotted him, noted his presence, instead of her parents.

In fact, Abe and Tilda were here, waiting beyond them tucked away near the bar with Rick's sisters and nieces. Close enough to know the significance of this meeting, far enough away not to overhear any softly spoken words and not to distract Marissa during these first moments.

Marissa's step hitched. Unease bloomed in her too-pale face. Her gaze shifted to the empty seats at the table and came back to him, and she started to turn away.

'Please don't leave without hearing me out. When you've done that, if need be, I'll be the one to go.' His heart hammered as he stepped forward.

'I don't understand. I was supposed to meet Mum and Dad. How… Why…?'

'I asked them to help me arrange this. I phoned your father and talked him into this because I realized…I had to do this…' There were no smooth words and his throat tightened and an inexplicable rush of emotion swamped him.

'You're so beautiful tonight.' So beautiful it squeezed his heart just to look at her. 'I'll always remember how you looked in that dress the first night you wore it.' And afterwards, as he'd stripped it away from her and they'd joined in the most intimate way possible.

Why hadn't he realised then that he loved her? That his *heart* needed her? Why hadn't he come home to her then?

'I want you to go. My parents must be on their way and I don't want them to know how I feel…' She stopped the words.

They stood beside the end of the table, and instinctively he caught her hands in his. There were diners all around them, people enjoying the wonder and pleasure of the night as though dining in the sky itself.

He could only see the woman before him and he spoke in a low tone filled with the emotion inside him because he couldn't hold back the words. He didn't want to. She had to have all of them, all of this, he'd finally realised. 'I thought if I stayed away from you that would be best for you.'

To tell her with her parents and his sisters waiting was the only way he could think of to let her know he meant this. That he would risk everything.

Rick took a deep breath. 'I told myself you would find someone better, someone who didn't have the issues behind him that I do. But I love you, Marissa, with all my heart and mind and soul. I didn't understand what it meant when I made love with you that night and didn't ever want to let you go, but I know now.'

A soft sound came from her throat and she swallowed hard. 'Don't do this to me, Rick. Don't say things like this to me when you can't mean them.'

'I mean them. I mean all of it.' He drew her forward. His arms ached to hold her and for a moment the ruthless side of his nature goaded him to simply pull her into his embrace and try to get what he wanted through a connection they had already proved, but he wouldn't do that.

Because she deserved all of it, even if at the end she turned him away.

'You made it clear you wouldn't love me, that you only wanted that one night. That you wanted to be single. Because of your family history.' Marissa didn't know what to do. She wanted to turn away, to rush out of this glittery setting that spread all of Sydney at her feet but, with Rick's hands on hers, she couldn't move at all.

She couldn't make herself break even this tenuous hold, and she couldn't stop the hope that rose in her heart. 'You don't have to feel sorry for me or think because I'm turning thirt—'

'I'm seven years older, Marissa. You might consider that too old, I don't know. I don't care about either of our ages because I only want you, and I swear I'll make you forget your ex-fiancé.' His words were tortured but determined. 'If you'll just give me the chance, say you'll stay with me, maybe one day you'll learn to love me, to want me.

'I know what I told you, that I couldn't commit. You understood why I believed that, but I was wrong. I know this because you have all my heart. Every part of it.'

It was the most humbling and loving of speeches and her hands squeezed his as she felt the eyes of people around on them, but she could only see Rick, only look into deep grey eyes that couldn't seem to shift their gaze from her.

'If you're worried I'll be pregnant, I'm sure I won't be. You took care of me.'

Could Rick truly love her? Oh, Marissa wanted to believe it, but how could it be true?

'It's not about a possible pregnancy, though I want my

baby growing inside you.' He uttered the words in a low tone filled with need. 'I want lots of babies with you, as many as will make you happy and I want them for myself too. I want you working at my side or at least close by every day and I want us to go home to the same bed at night. Most of all, I just want the chance to love you.'

'Oh, Rick. I want those things with you.' They would be a dream come true, better than any plan she could have conjured up and tried to set into motion through Blinddatebrides.com. He didn't know about that, about exactly how she'd gone about her dating efforts.

'I don't want to hold back any more. Not from you. Not ever from you.' His hand rose to cup her face, to skim over her hair, as he seemed to search for words. Finally he spoke them, his gaze never wavering from hers. 'I've spent a lifetime pushing down the fact that my family isn't perfect, that my father couldn't meet certain emotional needs. I thought I couldn't do any better.

'What I didn't realise is I *did* fill the gaps he left. Darla helped me see that, and I don't have to feel guilty for acknowledging how he is.'

Marissa's heart ached for him. 'No. You're not to blame for any of that.'

'I want to follow the example of *your* father, and love with all my heart. I want to love *you* that way, Marissa, if you'll let me.' His gaze seemed to worship every part of her as his hands rose to stroke her arms, to gently cup them in strong palms. 'Years ago I thought I was in love, but the feelings… weren't real. Not like what I feel for you. I backed away, and I thought I did it because I was like my father, but I know now that wasn't it. I didn't love her because she wasn't you, because I could only love you. I was waiting for you.'

His mouth softened and his eyes softened and all his love for her welled into the air between them until she had to believe it, couldn't deny it any longer.

'Oh, Rick.' Marissa's breath caught. She clasped his arms where he held her, wrapped her hands around thick muscle covered in the constraint of cloth and remembered those strong arms holding her as he'd gently led her to paradise. 'You truly love me?'

'Yes.' His voice dropped to a low whisper. 'Yes, if you'll let me, I will love you for the rest of my life and I swear I'll never let you down or leave you wondering or wishing I'd given you more, opened to you more. You'll have all of me, Marissa, the good and the bad, if you'll take me.'

The sounds around them seemed to fade to nothing as she stared into his eyes. Outside, the city lights winked and seemed to tell her the time had come. That this *was* the real thing and somehow, magically, it had come to her, despite her fears and her foolish worry about getting older and her joining a dating site so she could hand pick her fate, as though that were possible.

'I want to agree,' she whispered and his hands tightened and his muscles seemed to lock as he stood before her, waiting. 'But there are things you don't know about me. About what I've been doing, what I've wanted out of life and how I went about trying to get those things.'

'Like looking on a dating website?' He didn't seem the least surprised, or concerned. 'That day you fell asleep in your apartment and I fell asleep on your sofa, I came into your room and saw the site on your laptop. When I realised how much I love you I thought about joining up and trying to woo you from there, but I didn't want to wait that long to tell you how I felt. Once I realised how much I love you—'

'I was going to hand pick a man exactly right for me.' The words burst out of her—a confession, an admission of the ignorance of her plans. 'I thought if I made my choice clinically I'd be able to guard myself, not get hurt.'

His fingers stroked up and down her arms while his gaze

lingered on each feature of her face and finally came back to look deep into her eyes. 'I'm not perfect. I'm far from it, but I love you with all my heart and I'm hoping that will count for something. And I won't put my career before you. I want you to know that because I think your ex-fiancé did that.' He made it a vow as his hands lifted until his fingers were in her hair. 'I'll make whatever changes are needed so that can never happen because you will always be first with me. Over and above everything.'

How her heart soared then and, even as it did, she knew she had to be equally honest. 'It was foolish of me to believe I could find love the way I planned to.

'I looked at the pictures of happy couples and I wanted that too because I'd been used and humiliated. I thought my heart had been broken but I didn't love him. Not the way I love you. I could never love anyone the way I love you and I realise now that you can't choose love. It comes to you. It finds you.'

'It found me the day I looked at a woman with a hard hat squashed down over her curls and a sparkle in her eyes.' He drew her hand to his chest, pressed it over his heart where she could absorb the deep beat.

A beat that told her how much he meant this. 'It stuck around as she called the photocopier names and rushed to be at her mother's side and lay in my arms in a bed in a borrowed garage and a bed in a sumptuous hotel room on the other side of the world. I bought the clothes because I didn't want you to forget me, but I can't forget you.'

He clasped her hands in his and there, in front of the entire restaurant, he drew something bright and glittery from his pocket, held it between his fingertips and went down on one knee. 'Please say you'll marry me, Marissa. Give us a chance. Let me give you all the things you've been longing for.'

'I want to marry you, spend my life with you.' Her heart hitched as his fingers tightened over hers, and one final confession poured out of her. 'I bought baby wool. To knit booties. I really do want a baby and I don't think that's something that's going to go away. But I want a baby…with you, not with anyone else.'

His fingers wrapped so hard around hers, he almost crushed them. 'That's…I want that more than I can tell you.'

'Oh, Rick.' And she let go of the last foolish fear, the pride that had led her to try to find Mr Right in all the wrong ways when he had been there in front of her all the time. 'I love you with all my heart.' The words came *straight from* her heart.

His fingers trembled as he wrapped them around hers. The mouth that was usually firm and commanding wobbled a little too as he held the ring at the tip of her finger and looked into her eyes as though seeking her permission. She swallowed hard and, through a sheen of tears, looked at the exquisite ring.

'I asked Mr Qi to get it for me.' Rick cleared his throat. 'Actually, I talked him into flying it out here personally with a whole bunch of paperwork from the jeweller's and other stuff to make sure it could be delivered straight to me. I spotted it that day we were there…'

He'd gone to all this trouble for her. To make this special for her. A birthday to remember, so different from that other one. Her voice was a whisper of love and need as she said finally, 'Then I think I'd like to wear it now, if you truly do want this.'

'I do.' He slid the ring home, a perfect fit and the perfect symbol of all he felt for her.

And then, as she tugged on his hand, he got to his feet and crushed her into his arms and she felt his deep shudder of relief and longing as he pressed his face into her neck and murmured her name over and over.

'Thank you, my darling.' His fingers found their way through her hair to her nape. 'Thank you for putting your trust in me.'

'I love you, Rick.' Her hands touched his arms, his shoulders. 'I love you so much.'

He kissed her then, in front of the diners and the waiters and all of Sydney outside the sparkling windows.

When they finally broke apart, pleased laughter and murmurs of 'Hear, hear!' and 'How lovely!' broke out around them.

Rick drew Marissa around then, and she gasped.

Mum and Dad, Darla and Faith and Kirrilea and little Julia all stood there. They smiled, grinned. Her Mum and Darla and Faith had tears in their eyes.

Marissa's gaze flew to Rick's. 'You asked me in front of all of them. You went down on your knees in front of not only the strangers in this room, but in front of your family and mine. If I'd said no—'

'I wanted you to have your proposal in front of everyone so you'd know I meant it, that I would put my heart on the line for you.' A wealth of determination and love and understanding and hope shone in his eyes. 'Especially in front of the people that matter the most to both of us.'

His parents weren't among that number. Had he asked them to come, only to have them turn him down?

'It doesn't matter, Marissa.' He seemed to read her thoughts. *'You're here.'*

'And *most* of our family are here.' His and hers—and they would share that family.

Marissa promised herself there and then that she would weave Rick into *her* family, with Mum and Dad and Aunty Jean and the others, and she would work equally as hard to be part of his family, with his sisters and his nieces and, yes, his parents, who cared to a degree but also had their faults.

She wrapped her arms around his shoulders and drew his head down and kissed him fiercely, and when they broke apart and he told her she certainly knew how to pick her moments, she laughed and linked their arms together.

'I'm picking *every moment* for us, from now until forever.' And Marissa raised her voice and told the man she loved, 'Because you're my Mr Absolutely Right and you always will be, and I want the world to know I love you exactly as you are. I don't want *you* to change in any way.'

There were hugs all around and eventually they sat down to dine and celebrate a birthday that had turned out to be a milestone for a very different reason.

Marissa looked at Rick's ring on her finger and thought of being with him, of going home with him day after day. Old? One day she hoped to be. With Rick, and their children around them.

As their family spoke among themselves and the meals were brought out, Rick touched the shawl at her shoulders and bent his dark head to hers. 'I'm going to marry you with a big wedding and all the trimmings and all of Sydney looking on. I hope you're ready for that.'

'Maybe not *all* of Sydney. That would be rather a crowd.' But her smile broke through. 'I do want the world to know I'm yours, and you're mine, and I'd like to share our joy with as many people as we can.' She fell silent. 'A big wedding would take a lot of planning, though, and it would mean we'd have to wait months for it.'

'I'll put a team onto the matter. One of those wedding planner teams.' It was his turn to fall silent, but not for long. 'Everything has to be perfect for you but if I keep a close enough eye on it all…'

A glint of corporate determination filled his gaze.

She watched the plans click over and his expression become more and more focused and her heart melted for him all over again.

'You'll move in with me before then, won't you? Now that I have you, I don't want to let you go.' He hesitated. 'Or I can move in with you. Anywhere you want; I just want us to be together. I want to wake up every day with you at my side, make love to you until I've shown you how much I love you, how much you mean to me.'

A lifetime of togetherness. Her heart filled and she twined her fingers with his, simply because she could. 'Then I think maybe we should start on that plan as soon as possible and I would like to live in your apartment, at least at first. Later we might want a…different location.'

'For our children.' The possessive words wrapped her in desire and warmth and promise. 'For when *our* family of two becomes three or more.' He lowered his voice again. 'I want to make love to you quite desperately right now, Marissa Warren.'

The first opportunity they got, after the cake and the good wishes, they slipped away.

And later, as Marissa lay in Rick's arms and he told her again how much he loved her, she gasped.

He rose up on one elbow and looked into her eyes. 'What is it?'

'I've just realised I have a little explaining to do to my Blinddatebrides.com friends. At least my subscription has a few months left to run, so I can keep using the IM facility to chat with them, and I can check out profiles for them.'

Rick barely flinched before he relaxed again. 'I'll help you, if you like. Just so long as you take *your* profile off the "available" listings.'

'The only man I want to be available to is you.' She kissed him and they lost themselves again.

And, a very long time later, Marissa murmured, 'I wonder which of my online friends—Dani or Grace—will be next to find *her* Mr Right on Blinddatebrides.com?'

SWEPT INTO THE RICH MAN'S WORLD

KATRINA CUDMORE

This book is dedicated to my mum. I miss you
with all my heart.

CHAPTER ONE

'HELLO? IS ANYONE HOME?'

Her lungs on fire, Aideen Ryan desperately heaved in some air as she waited for someone to answer her knock and call. She had run in the dark through gale-force winds and rain to get to Ashbrooke House: the only place that could give her shelter from the storm currently pounding the entire Atlantic coastline of Ireland.

Ashbrooke House, stately home of billionaire Patrick Fitzsimon. A man who, given the impenetrable walls that surrounded his vast estate and his über-wealthy lifestyle, was unlikely to welcome her intrusion.

She straightened her rain jacket and ran a hand through her hair. *Oh, for crying out loud.* Her hair was a tangled mess. Soaked to the skull and resembling a frizz bomb... She really hoped it wouldn't be Patrick Fitzsimon who answered the door. Not the suave, gorgeous man she had seen in countless magazines. A man who stared at the camera with such serious intensity and intelligence that she had held her breath in alarm, worried for a few crazy seconds that he could see her spying on him.

The only sightings anyone ever made of him locally was when he was helicoptered in and out of the estate. Intrigued, she had looked him up. But just because she'd been unable to resist checking out her neighbour, one of the world's 'top ten most eligible billionaire bachelors', it didn't alter the fact that she was determined to keep her life a man-free zone.

A nearby tree branch creaked loudly as a ferocious gust of wind and rain swept up from the sea. How was her poor cottage faring in the storm without her? And how on earth was her business going to survive this?

Pushing down her spiralling panic, she took hold of the brass knocker and rapped it against the imposing door again, the metal vibrating against her skin.

'Hello? Please…I need help. Is anyone home?'

Please, please, let one of his staff answer.

But the vast house remained in silence, while beyond the columned entrance porch sheets of rain swept across the often written about formal gardens of Ashbrooke.

And then slow realisation dawned. Although outside lighting had showcased the perfect symmetry and beauty of the Palladian house as she had run up the driveway, not a single interior light had shone through the large sash windows.

In her panic, that simple fact had failed to register with her…until now.

What if nobody was at home?

But that didn't make sense. A house this size had to have an army of staff. The classically inspired villa had a three-storey central block, connected by colonnades to two vast wings. The house was enormous—even bigger than the pictures suggested.

Somebody simply *had* to be home. They probably just couldn't hear her above the storm. She needed to knock louder.

She grabbed hold of the knocker again, but just as

she raised it high to pound it down on the door the door swung open. As she flew forward with it all she could see was a tanned, muscular six-pack vanishing beneath a grey sweatshirt, its owner in the midst of quickly dressing. But not before she headbutted that glorious vision of masculine perfection.

It was like colliding against steel. As she ricocheted backwards she heard a loud grunt. Then hands gripped her upper arms and yanked her back from slamming bottom first on to the ground. The momentum pulled her back towards that hard body, and this time her forehead landed heavily on the person's chest with a thud.

For a moment neither of them moved, and her already spinning head became lost in a giddy sensation of warmth, the safe embrace of another human being, the deep, masculine scent of a man...

She couldn't tell who sprang away first, but as embarrassment barrelled through her, her eyes dropped down to bare feet and dark grey sweatpants before travelling back up over a long, lean, muscular body. Dark stubble lined a sculpted jawline. Taking a deep swallow, she looked up into eyes that were the light blue of an early-morning Irish spring sky. How often had she tried without success to replicate that colour in her designs?

Patrick Fitzsimon.

Those beautiful blue eyes narrowed. 'What the—?'

'I'm sorry I woke you, but my home's been flooded and everything I own is probably floating to America at this stage. I tried to drive into Mooncoyne but the road is flooded. My car got stuck. I was so glad your gates were open...I thought they would be locked, like they usually are. I honestly didn't know what I was going to do if they were locked.'

He held up a hand in the universal *stop* position. 'Okay. Slow down. Let's start again. Explain to me who you are.'

Oh, why did she jabber so much when she was nervous? And, for crying out loud, did she *have* to blush so brightly that she could light up a small house?

Pushing her hand out towards him, she said, 'I'm Aideen Ryan. I'm your neighbour. I live in Fuchsia Cottage…down by the edge of the lough.'

He gave a quick nod of recognition, but then he drew his arms across his impossibly wide chest and his gaze narrowed even more. 'What is it you need, exactly?'

Humiliation burnt in her chest at having to ask for help from a stranger, but she looked into his cool blue eyes and blurted out what had to be said. 'I need a place to stay tonight.'

His mouth twisted unhappily. For a moment she feared he was about to close the door on her.

But instead he took a backward step and said, 'Come inside.'

At best, it was a very reluctant invitation.

The door closed behind them with a solid clunk. Without uttering a word, he left her standing alone in the vast entrance hall. Her body started to shake as her wet clothes clung to her limbs. Her teeth chattered in the vast space and, to her ears, seemed to echo off the dome-shaped ceiling, from which hung the largest crystal chandelier she'd ever seen.

Why couldn't she have a normal neighbour? Why did hers have to be a billionaire who lived in a palace at the end of a mile-long driveway? She hated having to ask for help. From anyone. But having to ask for help from a megarich gorgeous man made her feel as though the universe was having a good laugh at her expense.

When he returned, he passed her a yellow and white striped towel without comment. Accepting it gratefully, she patted her hands and face. For a moment their eyes met.

Her heart stuttered as his gaze assessed her, his generous mouth flattened into a grimace, his long legs planted wide apart, his body rigid. Her breath caught. She felt intimidated by the intensity of his stare, his size, his silent unsmiling presence. She lowered her gaze and concentrated on twisting the towel through her hair, her eyes closing as an unaccountable nervousness overtook her.

'So where's your car?'

'I tried to drive into Mooncoyne but the river had burst its banks at Foley's Bridge. It's the same on your estate—the bridge on your drive is impassable, too.'

He shook his head in confusion. 'So how did you get here?'

'I climbed on to the bridge wall and crawled along it... My car is still on the other side.'

Just great. Not only had he been woken from a jet-lagged sleep, but now he realised he was dealing with a crazy woman. This was all he needed.

'Are you serious? Are you telling me you climbed over a flooded river in gale-force winds? Have you lost your mind?'

For a moment a wounded look flashed in her cocoa-brown eyes, but then she stared defiantly back at him.

'The sea was about to flood my cottage. I called the emergency services but they are swamped with the flooding throughout Mooncoyne. And anyway they can't reach here—Foley's Bridge is impassable even to them. You're my only neighbour. There was no other place I could come to for shelter.' Throwing her head back, she took a deep breath before she continued, a tremor in her voice. 'I did contemplate staying in my car overnight, but frankly I was more concerned about hypothermia than climbing along a bridge wall.'

Okay, so she had a point. But it had still been a crazy risk to take.

He inhaled a deep breath. For the first time ever he wished his staff resided in the house. If she'd been here, his housekeeper, Maureen, would happily have taken this dishevelled woman in hand. And he could have got some much-needed sleep.

He had awoken to her knocking jet-lagged and perplexed as to how anyone had got past his security. All of Ashbrooke's thousand-acre parkland was ring-fenced by a twenty-foot stone wall, built at the same time as the house in the eighteenth century. The impenetrable wall and the electronic front gates kept the outside world away.

Well, they were *supposed* to.

He would be having words with his estate manager in the morning. But right now he had a stranger dripping water down on to his polished limestone floor. He had an urgent teleconference in less than four hours with Hong Kong. To be followed up with a day of endless other teleconferences to wrap up his biggest acquisition ever. The acquisition, however, was still mired in legal and technical difficulties. Difficulties his teams should have sorted out weeks ago. The arrival of his neighbour at this time of night was the last thing he needed.

He glanced at her again. She gave him a brief uncertain smile. And he did a double take. Beneath that mass of wild, out-of-control hair she was beautiful.

Full Cupid's bow lips, clear rosy skin, thick arched

eyebrows and the most expressive eyes he had ever seen, framed by long dark eyelashes. Not the striking, almost hard supermodel beauty of some of his exes. She was… really pretty.

But then with a twinge of guilt he realised that she was shivering, and that she had noticeably paled in the past few minutes.

'You need to get out of those wet clothes and have a shower.'

A glimmer of heat showed on her cheeks and she shuffled uneasily. 'I don't have any spare clothes. I didn't pack any. I only had time to get some office equipment and files out…the things I had to save.'

Oh, great. Well, he didn't have any spare women's clothes hanging around here. He had never brought any of his dates to Ashbrooke. This was his sanctuary. And it had become even more so in the past few years as his ever-growing business demanded his absolute concentration.

Deep down he knew he should say some words of comfort to her. But he was no good in these situations, at saying the right thing. God knew his history with his own sister, Orla, proved that. His skill in life was making money. It clearly wasn't having effective personal relationships.

The thought of how he had failed not only Orla but also his mum and dad left a bitter taste in his mouth as his eyes moved up to meet his neighbour's. Two pools of wary brown met him. He could provide this woman with practical help. But nothing more.

'Pass me your jacket and I'll show you to a guest bedroom. I'll find you some clothes to wear while you shower.'

Her hands trembled as she shrugged off her pink and red floral rain jacket. Beneath it she wore a red and white striped cotton top, a short denim miniskirt, black wool tights and Converse trainers. Not exactly clothing suitable for being outdoors in the midst of an Atlantic storm.

The wet clothes clung to her skin. Despite himself he let his gaze trail down the soft curves of her body, gliding over the gentle slope of her breasts, narrow waist and along the long length of her legs.

When he looked up she gave a shrug. 'I didn't have time to get changed.'

She must have mistaken his stare of appreciation for incredulity. Good. He certainly didn't want her getting any other ideas.

He took her coat and in silence they walked up the stairs.

He glanced briefly at his watch. He would show her to her room and then go and get some sleep. He needed to be at the top of his game tomorrow, to unravel this mess his acquisition teams seemed incapable of sorting out.

She followed him up a cantilevered stone staircase. Despite her longing to get changed out of her rain-soaked clothes—not least her trainers, which squelched with every step—she couldn't help but stop and stare at the opulent rococo plasterwork that curved along the walls of the staircase. Exquisite delicate masks and scallop shells rendered in porcelain-like plaster had her longing to reach out and touch the silent angelic faces, which seemed to follow her steps with knowing smiles.

It was one of the most stunning rooms she had ever seen…if you could call a hallway a room. Good Lord, if the entrance hall was like this what was the rest of the house like? *Talk about making a girl feel inadequate...*

Ahead of her he continued to climb the stairs, his tall, broad frame causing an unwanted flip in her stomach. He was big, dark, and handsome beyond belief. And you didn't need to be Sherlock Holmes to figure out that he wasn't too keen on having her here.

Well, she wasn't too keen on being here herself. She'd much prefer to be at home, snuggled up in her own bed. Having to face the displeasure of a billionaire who, given his monumental success at such a young age, was probably hard-nosed and cold-hearted, was not exactly her idea of a fun night.

Upstairs, he led her down a never-ending corridor in silence. She had an insane urge to talk, to kill the tension that seemed to simmer silently between them.

'Your helicopter often passes over my cottage. Do you travel a lot?'

'When required.'

Okay, so it hadn't been the most interesting or insightful of questions, but he could have given a little more detail in the way of an answer. It wouldn't kill him to make a little small talk with her, would it?

He stopped and opened a door, and signalled for her to enter first. As she passed he studied her with a coolness that gave nothing away. She found herself giving him an involuntary smile. But when his face remained impassive, apart from the slight narrowing of his eyes, she felt rather silly.

His cool attitude pinged in her brain like a wake-up call. She was here out of necessity, not because she wanted to be, and he shouldn't be making her feel so uneasy. She straightened her back with resolve and pride and marched further into the room. First thing tomorrow morning she was out of here.

But she hadn't gone far when her steps faltered. 'Oh, wow, this bedroom is stunning…and it's *huge!* A family of six could easily sleep in that bed.'

An imposing oversized bed sat in the middle of the room, surrounded by sofas and occasional chairs covered in glazed cotton in varying tones of sage-green. An antique desk and a vanity table sat either side of the white marble fireplace.

He didn't acknowledge her words of admiration but instead made for the door. 'I'll go and get you some clothes to change into.'

When he was gone she pulled a face. Did she really have to sound so gushing? Right—from here on in she was playing it cool with Patrick Fitzsimon.

Two doors led to a bathroom and a dressing room. In the bathroom she eyed the shower longingly. She didn't suppose he would be too impressed to return to find her already in the locked bathroom, the shower running, making herself at home…

This was all so horribly awkward. Barging in on a very reluctant neighbour at this time of night…

But then a giggle escaped as she imagined his expression if he returned to a closed bathroom door and, beyond it, the sound of her voice belting out a show tune inside the running shower.

Her laughter died, though, when she walked back out into the bedroom to be confronted with the exact frown she had imagined. As she reddened he threw her a stark look.

'Is something the matter?'

'No…it's just that my wet shoes are making the sound of a sickly duck whenever I walk.'

Oh, for crying out loud. So much for playing it cool. Where had *that* come from?

He looked at her as though he was concerned about her sanity. With a quick shake of his head he placed the bundle in his hands on to one of the fireside chairs. 'Have a shower and get changed. You'll need to wash and dry your clothes for when you leave in the morning. There's a laundry room at the end of this corridor—please use that.'

With that, he turned away. His back was still turned to her when she heard him say goodnight.

'Is it okay if I get myself a drink after I shower?'

He slowed at her question and for a fraction too long he paused, a new tension radiating across his broad shoulders.

When he turned she shrugged and gave an apologetic smile. 'I could really do with something to warm me up. If you tell me how to get to the kitchen, I'll pop down there after.'

Cue a deepening of his grimace. Just for a moment she wondered how gorgeous he must be when he smiled, because he was pretty impressive even when grimacing. *If* he ever smiled, that was.

'Turn left outside the bedroom door and you will find another set of stairs a little further along that will take you down to the west wing. The kitchen is the fifth door on the left.'

He twisted away and was gone before she could voice her thanks.

She exhaled heavily. Was he this abrasive with everyone, or was it her in particular?

God knew she had met plenty of curt people in her

line of business, but there was something about Patrick Fitzsimon that completely threw her. In his company she felt as though an invisible wall separated them. She got on with most people—she was good at putting them at ease. But with him she got the distinct feeling that getting on with people was pretty low on his agenda.

On the bed, she unfurled his bundle: soft grey cotton pyjama bottoms and a pale blue shirt, wrapped around a toothbrush and toothpaste.

Her heart did a funny little shimmy at the thought of wearing his clothes, and before she knew what she was doing she brought them to her nose. Her eyes closed as she inhaled the intoxicating smell of fresh laundry, but there was no hint of the scent she had inhaled earlier when she'd fallen against him. Salt and grass…and a deep, hot, masculine scent that had her swallowing a sigh in remembrance. For a few crazy seconds earlier she had wanted to wrap her arms around his waist. Take shelter against his hardness for ever.

She threw her eyes upwards. What was she doing? The man was as cold as ice.

Anyway, it didn't matter. After tomorrow she would probably never see him again. And she was not interested in men right now anyway. Her hard-won independence was too precious. From here on in she wanted to live a life in which she was in charge of her own destiny. Where *she* called the shots.

One night and she was out of here. Back to her work and back to nights in, eating pizza and watching box sets on her own. Which she was perfectly happy with, thank you very much.

CHAPTER TWO

SIXTEEN BEDROOMS, EIGHT reception rooms. A ballroom that could cater to over three hundred guests. Two libraries and countless other rooms he rarely visited. And yet he resented the idea of having to share this vast house with someone. He knew it made no sense. It was almost midnight. She would be gone within hours. But, after spending the past few years immersed in the solitude of his work, having to share his home even for one night was an alien and uncomfortable prospect.

Two years ago, after yet another bewildering argument with his sister, he had come to the realisation that he should focus on what he was good at, what he could control: his work. He had been exhausted and frustrated by Orla's constant battle of wills with him, and it had been almost a relief to turn away from the fraught world of relationships to the uncomplicated black and white world of work.

He hadn't needed Orla to tell him he was inept at handling relationships, though she happily did so on a regular basis, because he'd seen it in the pain etched on her face when she didn't realise he was watching her.

He still didn't know what had gone wrong. Where *he* had gone wrong. They had once been so close. After his mum had died he had been so scared and lonely he had thought his heart would break. But the smiling, gurgling Orla had saved him.

And then his father had died when Orla was sixteen, and almost overnight she had changed. She had gone from being happy-go-lucky to sullen and non-communicative, and their once unbreakable bond had been broken.

The scrape of a tree branch against the kitchen window pane brought him back to the present with a jolt.

He put the tea canister next to the already boiled kettle. Then he wrote his house guest a quick note, telling her to help herself to anything she needed. All the while he was hearing his father's incredulous voice in his head, scolding him for his inhospitality. And once again he was reminded of how different he was from his father.

Note finished, he knew he should walk away before she came down. But the image of her standing in his entrance hall, a raindrop running down over the deep crevice of her full lips, held him. Lips he had had an insane urge to taste…

His instant attraction to her had to be down to the fact that he had been without a steady bedmate for quite some time. A lifetime for a guy who had once never been able to resist the lure of a beautiful woman. But two years ago his appetite for his usual short, frivolous affairs had disappeared. And a serious relationship was off the cards. Permanently.

And, anyway, she was his neighbour. If—and it was a big *if*—he ever was to start casually dating again, it certainly wouldn't be on his own doorstep.

He turned at a soft knock on the door.

Standing at the entrance to the vast kitchen, she gave him a wary smile.

He should have gone when he could. Now he would be forced to make small talk.

She had rolled up the cuffs of his pyjama bottoms and shirt and her feet were bare. He got the briefest glimpse of a delicate shin bone, which caused a tightening in his belly in a way it never should. Her hair, though still wet, was now tamed and fell like a heavy dark curtain down her back. For a moment his eyes caught on how she had left the top two buttons of the shirt undone, and although he could only see a small triangle of flesh his pulse quickened.

He didn't want to be feeling any of this. He crumpled the note he had left her into the palm of his hand. 'The kettle is boiled. Please help yourself to anything you need.'

'Thank you.' As he went to walk to the door she added, 'I didn't say it earlier, but thank you for giving me shelter for the night—and I'm sorry if I woke you up.'

She blushed when she'd finished, and wound her arms about her waist, eyeing him cautiously. There was something about her standing there in his clothes, waiting for his response, that got to him.

He felt compelled to hold out an olive branch. 'In the morning I will arrange for my estate manager to drive you home.'

She shook her head firmly. 'I'll walk. It's not far to the bridge.'

'Fine.'

It was time for him to go and get some sleep. But something was holding him back. Perhaps it was his thoughts of Orla, and how he would like someone to treat *her* if she was in a similar predicament.

With a heavy sigh he said, 'How about we start again?'

Her head tilted to the side and she bit her lip, unsure.

He walked over to her and held out his hand and said words that, in truth, he didn't entirely mean. 'Welcome to Ashbrooke.'

Her hand was ice-cold. Instinctively he coiled his own around the soft, delicate skin as gently as he could.

'You're cold.'

Her head popped up from where she had been staring at their enclosed hands and when she spoke there was a tremble in her voice that matched the one in her hand. 'I know. The shower helped a little, but I was wet to the bone. I've never seen a storm like it before.'

He crossed over to the cloakroom, situated just off the kitchen, and grabbed one of the heavy fleeces he used for horse riding.

Back in the kitchen, he handed her the fleece.

'Thank you. I…' Her voice trailed off and her gaze wandered behind him before her mouth broke into a wide glorious smile. 'Oh—hello, you two.'

He twisted around to find the source of her affection. His two golden Labs had left their beds in the cloakroom and now ambled towards her, tails wagging at the prospect of having someone else to love them.

Both immediately went to her and bumped their heads against her leg. She leant over and rubbed them vigorously. In the process of her doing so her shirt fell forward and he got a brief glimpse of the smooth swell of her breasts. She was not wearing a bra.

Blood pounded in his ears. It was definitely time for bed.

'They're gorgeous. What are their names?'

'Mustard and Mayo.'

Raising an eyebrow, she gave him a quick grin. 'Interesting choice of names.'

A sputter of pleasure fired through him at the teasing in her voice. And he experienced a crazy urge to keep this brief moment of ease between them going. But that didn't make sense, so instead he said curtly, 'Remind me of your name again?'

Her eyes grew wide and her cheeks reddened. With a low groan she threw her hands up in the air. 'I *knew* it. I woke you up, didn't I?'

He folded his arms. 'Maybe I'm just terrible at remembering people's names?'

Her eyes narrowed shrewdly. 'I doubt that very much.' And then she added, 'So, do you always go to bed so early?'

The moment she had the words out an even deeper blush bloomed on her cheeks and her lips twisted into a small wince.

Something fired in his blood. 'Only when I have good cause to.'

Her mouth fell open.

For a moment they just stared at one another, and the atmosphere immediately grew thick with awareness. Two strangers, alone in a house. She was wearing his clothes. The spark of something happening between them had his pulse firing for the first time in years. And warning bells rang in his ears. She was his neighbour. He was not into relationships. Period. He was no good at them. He had a long day ahead of him. He needed to walk away.

A coil of heat grew in Aideen's belly.

Propped against an antique wing-backed chair, in the low light of the kitchen, Patrick looked at her with an edgy darkness. She stood close by, her back to the island unit. She dropped her gaze to the small sprigs of flowers on the material covering the chair, instantly recognising the signature motif of a luxurious French textile manufacturer. Everything in this house was expensive, out of her league. Including its owner.

She should talk, but her pulse was beating way too quickly for her to formulate a sensible sentence. He went to stand up, and his movement prompted her to blurt out, 'Aideen Ryan… My name is Aideen Ryan.'

Rather reluctantly he held out his hand. 'And I'm Patrick Fitzsimon.'

Thrown by the way her heart fluttered once again at the touch of his hand, she said without thinking, 'Oh, I know that.'

'Really?'

For a moment she debated whether she could bluster her way out of the situation, but one look into his razor-sharp eyes told her she would be wasting her time. 'Every time I drove by I was intrigued as to who lived here, so I looked you up one day.'

His expression tightened.

She realised she must sound like some billionaire groupie or, worse, a gold digger, and blurted out, 'We *are* the only houses out here on the headland. I wanted to know who my only neighbour was. There was nothing else to it.'

After a torturous few seconds during which he considered her answer, he said, 'I'll ask my estate manager to drop down to you tomorrow. He can give you his contact details. That way if you ever need any help you can contact him directly.'

For a few seconds she smiled at him gratefully, but

then humiliation licked at her bones. He was putting a filter between them. But then what did she expect? Patrick Fitzsimon lived in the moneyed world of the super-rich. He wasn't interested in his neighbours.

'Thanks, but I'm able to cope on my own.'

He stood up straight and scowled at her. 'I didn't say you weren't.'

She gave a tight laugh, memories of her ex taunting her. 'Well, you're not like a lot of men, then…'

The scowl darkened even more. 'That's a bit of a sweeping statement, isn't it? I was only trying to be helpful.'

The last sentence had been practically growled. He looked really angry with her, and she couldn't help but think she had hit a raw nerve.

She inhaled a deep breath and said, 'I'm sorry…I'm a bit battle-scarred at the moment.'

He stared at her in surprise and, praying he wouldn't ask her what she meant, she said quickly, 'I don't know about you, but I could do with a cup of tea. Will you join me?'

He looked as taken aback by her invitation as she was. Did she *really* want to spend more time with this taciturn man? But after the night she'd had, and three months of living alone, the truth was she was starved for company.

He looked down at his watch and when he looked up again frowned at her in thought. 'I'll stay five minutes.'

Could he have said it with any *less* enthusiasm? He looked edgy. As though he wanted to escape.

He walked towards the countertop where the kettle stood. 'Take a seat at the table. If you prefer, I also have hot chocolate or brandy.'

'Thanks, but I'd love tea.'

Instead of going to the table she walked to the picture window in the glass extension at the side of the kitchen. The faint flashing light from the lighthouse out on the end of the headland was the only sight in the darkness of the stormy night.

'Do you think my cottage will be okay?'

He didn't answer immediately. Instead he walked over to her side and he, too, looked out of the window towards the lighthouse. In the reflection of the window she could see that he stood four, maybe five inches taller than her, his huge frame dwarfing hers.

'I called the emergency services when you were in the shower. I really don't know what will happen to your cottage. The timing of the storm surge was terrible—right at the same time as high tide. I thought the worst of the storms was over, but April can be an unpredictable month.' He turned slightly towards her. 'I know you must be worried—it's your home—but you're safe. That's all that matters.'

His words surprised her, and she had to swallow against the lump of emotion that formed in her throat. He didn't try to pretend everything would be okay, didn't lie to her, but he didn't dismiss how she was feeling either.

She gave him a grateful smile, but he looked away from her with a frown.

He moved away from the window, back towards the table, and said in a now tight voice, 'Your tea is ready.'

For a while she looked down at the mug tentatively, two forces battling within her. The need to be self-reliant was vying with her need to talk to someone—even someone as closed-off as Patrick Fitzsimon. To hear a little reassurance that things would be okay. And then she just blurted it out, the tension in her body easing fractionally as the words tumbled out.

'It's not just my cottage, though. My studio is there. I have some urgent work I have to complete. I missed a deadline today and I have another commissioned piece I need to deliver next week.'

His silence and his frown told her she had said too much, and her insides curled with embarrassment. The man was a billionaire. Her problems must seem trivial to him.

She twisted her mug on the table, knowing he was studying her but unable to meet his gaze.

'I'm sorry to hear that. I didn't realise. What is it that you do?'

'I'm a textile designer.'

He nodded, and his eyes held hers briefly before he looked away. 'Try not to think about work until tomorrow. You might be worrying for no reason… And even in the worst of situations there's always a solution.'

'Hopefully you're right.'

'Do you have anyone who can help you tomorrow?'

She shook her head. 'I haven't got to know people locally yet, and my family live in Dublin. Most of my friends are either there or in London.'

Realising she still hadn't touched her tea, she sipped it. In her nervousness she pulled the mug away too quickly and had to lick a falling drip of tea from her bottom lip.

Her heart somersaulted as she saw his eyes were trained on her mouth, something darkening in their intensity. Then very slowly his gaze moved up to capture hers. Awareness fluttered through her.

'I heard someone had bought Fuchsia Cottage late last year—why did you move here to Mooncoyne?'

He asked the question in an almost accusatory tone, as though he almost wished she hadn't.

'I saw the cottage and the studio online and I fell in love with them straight away. The cottage is adorable, and the studio space is incredible. It's perfect for my work.' Forcing herself to smile, she said, 'Unfortunately I hadn't bargained on the cottage and studio flooding. The auctioneer assured me it wouldn't.'

He gave a brief shrug of understanding. 'You weren't tempted to go back to your family in Dublin?'

'Have you seen the price of property in Dublin? I know it's not as bad as London, but it's still crazy.' Then, remembering who she was talking to, she felt her insides twist and a feeling of foolishness grip her. Clearing her throat, she asked, 'Has Ashbrooke always been in your family?'

He looked at her incredulously, as though her question was ridiculous. 'No…absolutely not. I grew up in a modest house. My family weren't wealthy.'

Taken aback by the defensive tone of his voice, she blurted out exactly what was on her mind. 'So how did all of this happen?'

He studied her with a blistering glance, his mouth a thin line of unhappiness. In the end he said curtly, 'I was lucky. I saw the opportunities available in mobile applications ahead of the curve. I developed some music streaming apps that were bought by some of the big internet providers. Afterwards I had the capital to invest in other applications and software start-ups.'

She couldn't help but shake her head and give him a mock sceptical look. 'Oh, come on—that wasn't luck.'

'Meaning…?'

'Look, I ran my own business for five years. I know

success is down to hard work, taking risks, and being constantly on the ball. Making smart business decisions…I reckon luck has very little to do with it.'

'All true. But sometimes you get a good roll of the dice—sometimes you don't. It's about getting back up when things go wrong, knowing there's always a solution to a problem.'

His words were said with such certainty they unlocked something inside her.

For a good few minutes she toyed with her mug. The need to speak, to *tell* him, was building up in her like a pressure cooker. Part of her felt ridiculous, thinking of telling a billionaire of her failings, but another part wanted to. Why, she wasn't sure. Maybe it was the freedom of confessing to a stranger? To a person she wouldn't see after tomorrow? Perhaps it was not being able to talk to her family and friends about it because she had got it all so wrong.

'I lost my business last year,' she said in a rush.

Non-judgemental eyes met hers, and he said in a tone she hadn't heard from him before, 'What happened?'

Taken aback by the softening in him, she hesitated. Her pulse began to pound. Suddenly her throat felt bone-dry. 'Oh, it's a long story, but I made some very poor business decisions.'

'But you're back? Trying again.'

He said it with such certainty, as though that was all that mattered, and she couldn't help but smile. Something lifted inside her at the knowledge he was right. Yes, she was trying again—trying hard. Just hearing him say it made her realise how true it was.

'Yes, I am.'

His serious, intelligent gaze remained locked on hers. 'What are your plans for the future?'

His question caused a flutter of anxiety and her hands clenched on the mug. She shuffled in her seat. For some reason she wanted to get this right. She wanted his approval.

She inhaled a deep breath and said, 'To build a new label, re-establish my reputation.' She cringed at the wobble in her voice; it was just that she was so desperate to rebuild the career she loved so much.

He leant across the table and fixed his gaze on her. It was unnerving to be captivated by those blue eyes. By the sheer size and strength of him as his arms rested on the table, his broad shoulders angled towards her.

'There's no shame in failing, Aideen.'

Heat barrelled through her and she leant back in her chair, away from him. 'Really?' She pushed her mug to the side. 'What would *you* know about failing?'

His jaw hardened, and when he spoke his low voice was harsh with something she couldn't identify.

'Trust me—I have failed many times in my life. I'm far from perfect.'

She looked at him sceptically. He looked pretty perfect to her. From his financial stability and security and his film-star looks to this beautiful house, everything *was* perfect...even his spotless kitchen.

He stood and grabbed both mugs. With his back to her he said, 'I think it's time we went to bed.'

Once again he was annoyed with her. She should leave it. Go to bed, as he had suggested. But curiosity got the better of her. 'Why are you here in Mooncoyne? Why not somewhere like New York or London?'

He turned and folded his arms, leant against the counter. 'I met the previous owner of Ashbrooke, Lord Balfe, at a dinner party in London and we became good friends. He invited me to stay here and I fell in love with the house and the estate. Lord Balfe couldn't afford the upkeep any longer, and he was looking to sell the estate to someone who felt as passionate as he did about conserving it. So I agreed to buy it.' His unwavering eyes held hers and he said matter-of-factly, 'My business was growing ever more demanding. I knew I needed to live somewhere quiet in order to focus on it. This estate seemed the perfect place. And also Mooncoyne reminded me of the small fishing village where I grew up in County Antrim.'

So *that* was why he had traces of a soft, melodic Northern Irish brogue. 'Do your family still live there?'

Another quick look at his watch. He flicked his gaze back up to her. He looked as though he wasn't going to answer, but then he took her by surprise and said, 'No, my mum died when I was a boy and my dad passed away a number of years ago.'

For a moment their eyes locked and incomprehensively she felt tears form at the back of hers. 'I'm sorry.'

Blue eyes held hers and her pulse quickened at the intimacy of looking into a stranger's eyes for more than a polite second or two. Not being able to look away…not wanting to look away.

Then his hands gripped the countertop and he dipped his head for a moment before he looked back up and spoke. 'It happens. I have a younger sister, Orla, who lives in Madrid.'

'Do you see her often?'

His mouth twisted unhappily. 'Occasionally.'

His tone told her to back off. Tension filled the room.

She hated an unhappy atmosphere. And she didn't want
to cause him any offence.

So, in a bid to make amends and lighten the tension,
she said what she had been thinking all night. 'You've a
spectacularly beautiful home.'

He gave a brief nod of acknowledgement. 'Thank you.
I'm very proud of the work we've done here over the past
few years.'

'How many staff do you employ?'

'I've cleaning and housekeeping staff who come in
every day. Out on the estate my estate manager, William, employs twenty-two staff between the stables and
the farm.'

'No housekeeper...even a butler?'

His mouth lifted ever so slightly. If she had blinked
she would have missed it.

'Sorry to disappoint you but I like my privacy. And I
can cook for myself, do up my own buttons, tie my own
shoelaces...'

She knew she was pushing it, but decided to push her
luck as curiosity got the better of her. 'A girlfriend?' She
tried to ignore the unexpected stab of jealousy that came
with the thought that there might be a special woman in
his life.

Something dark flashed in his eyes and he quietly answered. 'No—no girlfriend.'

She tried to fill the silence that followed. 'So nobody
but you lives in the house?'

'No. Now, I think it's time for bed.'

So they were all alone tonight. It shouldn't matter, but
for some reason heat grew in her belly at that thought.
This was a huge place for one man to live in alone.

Though she stood in preparation for leaving the

kitchen she didn't move away from the table. Instead she said, 'Wow. Don't you get lonely?'

'I prefer to live on my own. I don't have time for relationships.' He studied her sombrely. 'Why? Do *you* get lonely?'

Taken aback, she answered, 'I'm too busy. I can—'

A tightness in her chest stopped her mid-sentence. Maybe she *had* been lonely these past few months, and had been denying it all along in her determination to get her business back up and running again.

She shrugged and looked at him with a half smile. 'I must admit it's nice to talk to someone face to face for a change, rather than on the phone or over the internet. I seem to spend all my days on the phone at the moment, calling prospective clients.' With a sigh of exasperation she added, 'I really should go and visit them. It would save me a lot of time being put on hold.'

'Why don't you?'

She felt herself blush. 'Most of my clients are based in Paris, and it's on my list of priorities to visit them.' She couldn't admit that financially she wasn't in a position to travel there, so instead she said, 'But, to be honest, part of me is embarrassed. I haven't seen any of them since I lost my business. I suppose my pride has taken a dent.'

'Go back out there and be proud that you're back and fighting. *I'm* going to Paris next week…' He didn't finish the sentence and a look of annoyance flashed across his face. His tone now cooler, he said, 'You have a long day ahead of you tomorrow. I'll walk you back to your room.'

He called to the dogs and led them back to their beds in the cloakroom.

As they approached the bottom of the stairs she gave him a smile and offered him her hand. 'Thank you for tonight.' A surprising lump of something had formed in her throat, and her voice was croaky when she finally managed to continue to speak. 'Thank you for taking me in. I plan on leaving early tomorrow, so in case I don't see you then, it was nice to meet you.'

Tension seemed to bounce off the surrounding walls and she felt dizzy when his hand took hers. 'I wake before dawn, so the security alarm will be disabled after that.' With a quick nod he added, 'Take care of yourself.'

He walked away, back towards the main entrance hall.

She walked up the stairs slowly, her head spinning. What on earth had possessed her to tell him so much? And why on earth did the thought that she might never see him again make her feel sad? The man obviously didn't want her in his house.

As she lay in bed the memory of his incredible blue eyes and quiet but assured presence left her twisting and tumbling and wishing the hours away so she could leave for home. Where she could lose herself in her work again.

And when sleep finally started to pull her into oblivion her tired mind replayed on a loop his deep voice saying, 'You're safe. That's all that matters.' Words he would probably say to anyone. But when he had said them to her, he had looked at her with such intensity it had felt as though he was tattooing them on her heart.

CHAPTER THREE

PATRICK TORE ALONG the bridle path that cut through the woods, pushing his horse harder and harder. Soft ground underfoot, branches whizzing by, the flash of vivid, almost purple patches of bluebells, calm cool air beating against his skin...

When they reached the edge of the woods they raced through the parkland's glistening green grass. They leapt time and time again over the ditches separating the fields. Adrenaline pumped in both man and mare.

They followed the ancient pathway that hugged the coast and galloped in the steps of the medieval pilgrims who had come to Mooncoyne abbey.

The rising sun slatted its thick rays of sunlight through the window openings and he pulled the horse to a halt by the entrance. He dismounted and walked into the nave.

He hadn't managed to get back to sleep again last night. Instead he had lain awake, wondering how his conversation with Aideen Ryan had become so personal so quickly. It had unsettled him. That wasn't how he operated. He didn't open up to anyone.

For crying out loud, he had almost suggested to her that she travel with him to Paris. His guess was that it wasn't just pride standing in her way of going, but also financial difficulties. In the end he had ended the conversation, been glad when she'd made her own way to bed, because he hadn't been able to handle how good it was to talk to someone else, to actually *connect* with them.

And, despite himself, he was deeply attracted to her.

All of which was dangerous.

He threw his head back and stared up into the endless depths of the blue sky.

Hadn't he already proved he wasn't capable of having effective relationships? He had a string of exes who had been beautiful but superficial. A sister who wouldn't talk to him. And a nephew or niece he would never get to know.

The baby would be born in the next month. He should be there. Supporting Orla. At least she was willing to accept his financial support. If she had refused to do so then he really would have been out of his mind, worrying about how she was going to cope.

His call to Hong Kong earlier had gone well. If he kept up the pressure for the remainder of the day, with the rest of his acquisition teams, then the deal would go through later tonight. It would be strange for it all to be over. For months he had worked day and night to see it happen.

A strange emptiness sat in his chest. What would he do once the project was over?

The slow tendrils of an idea had formed in his mind but he kept pushing them away. But as he walked through the ruins of the abbey the idea came back, stronger and more insistent this time.

He should help Aideen. It was what any good neighbour would do. It was what his father would have done.

But would he be crazy to do it? Last night he had lowered his guard around her. He couldn't allow that again. If he was to help then it would have to be done on a strictly business basis. He could help her re-establish her business, mentor her if required. He knew what it was like to throw your heart and soul into a business. And he knew only too well the pain of failure.

He would help her. And it would all be professional and uncomplicated.

The memory of a deep voice snaked through Aideen's brain. She gave a small sigh, smiled to herself, and stretched out on the bed.

But then her eyes popped open and she looked around, disorientated. Small shafts of daylight sneaked under drawn curtains.

Slowly she remembered where she was. And what she had to face today.

Dreaming about Patrick Fitzsimon was the last thing she should be doing.

The cottage. Deadlines.

For a few seconds she pulled the duvet up over her head. Maybe she could just stay here in this warm and dark cocoon for a few days.

With a groan she pushed back the cover. Time to rise and shine. And face what the day had to bring.

Anyway, it couldn't be any worse than being forced out of the business she'd once created. She had survived the past year, so she would survive this.

She pulled the curtains apart and winced as daylight flooded the room.

The view out of her window was breathtaking. Below her, formal box gardens led down to a gigantic fountain that sprayed a sprout of water so vigorously upwards it was as though it was trying to defy gravity. Rose gardens lay beyond the fountain, and then a long rolling meadow, rich in rain-drenched emerald green grass, ran all the way down to the faraway sea.

Though the sun was still low in the sky the light was dazzling, thanks to a startlingly clear blue sky.

Had last night's storm been in her imagination? How could such furious weather be followed by such a beautiful day?

She could almost convince herself maybe her cottage hadn't flooded. That the weather was a good omen. But she had seen the ferocity of the sea. There was no way her cottage had got away with avoiding that angry swell.

When she had come to view the property she had fallen in love with the old cottage and its outbuildings, arranged around a courtyard garden. Fuchsia had dangled from the hedgerows and fading old roses had tumbled from its walls. It had seemed the perfect solution then.

But now her income was sparser and more sporadic than she had projected, and sometimes she wondered whether she could make this work. That was one of the worst consequences of losing her business: the vulnerability and constant questioning of whether she was doing the right thing, making the right decisions.

But a burning passion for her work along with a heavy dose of pride got her through most days. She would sacrifice everything to make this business a success.

Her heart was a different matter, though. It felt bruised. To think that once upon a time she had thought her ex had loved her...

Pressing the edges of her palms against her eyes, she drew in a deep breath.

A quick shower, an even quicker coffee, and she would

head home to start sorting out whatever was waiting for her.

She mightn't even see Patrick. Which would be a *good* thing, right?

Heading to the bathroom, she sighed. Just who was she trying to kid?

The truth was giddiness was fizzing through her veins at the prospect of seeing his tall, muscular body, the darkness of his hair, and his lightly tanned skin which emphasised the celestial blue of his eyes.

Showered and dressed, she was about to open the bedroom door when she spotted a note pushed under it. Picking it up, she read the brief words.

Aideen,
I will drive you back to your cottage. Help yourself
to breakfast in the kitchen. I will meet you in the
main entrance hall at nine.
Patrick

It was a generous offer, but she needed to face the cottage on her own. It was her responsibility. She had taken up enough of his time as it was.

And then she studied the note again as an uncomfortable truth dawned on her. Was he offering to take her as a way of ensuring that she left? Humiliation burnt on her cheeks.

She checked the time on her phone. It was not yet eight o'clock. She would get changed and then go reassure him that she was leaving and was perfectly capable of making her own way home.

Thirty minutes later she had searched for him throughout the house but there was no sign of him. Her search in this exquisite house, as she'd gasped at the beauty of the baroque ballroom, with its frescoed ceiling, mirrored walls, and golden chandeliers, had brought home how different their lives were.

She was writing a note for him in the kitchen when the cloakroom door swung open.

Over off-white jodhpurs and black riding boots he was wearing a loose pale green shirt, the top three buttons open to reveal a masculine smattering of dark hair. His skin glistened with a sheen of perspiration.

He came to a stop when he spotted her at the table.

'Good morning.' He moved across the kitchen in long strides while adding, 'Help yourself to breakfast. I'll have a quick shower and be ready by nine.'

His manner was brusque, and she was left with no doubt that he just wanted to get the business of taking her home over and done with. Embarrassment coiled its way around her insides and she wanted to curl up into a protective ball against his rejection.

But instead she gave him a sunny smile. 'Thank you for the offer, but there's really no need for you to drive me. I've taken up enough of your time.' He turned to her with a frown and she added, as way of explanation, 'I'll collect my car down by the bridge. I could do with a walk anyway.'

'I'm coming.'

Didn't he trust her? Was he always this insistent?

'No, honestly—you've done enough.'

He leant against the island unit at the centre of the kitchen. 'Aideen, there's no point in arguing. I've made up my mind.'

His cool composure set her teeth on edge. 'I want to go to the cottage by myself.'

'Why?'

Oh, for crying out loud. 'Because I can manage. The cottage is my responsibility. And I have no doubt that you are an extremely busy man. I can't take up any more of your time.'

'I'm taking you. End of story.'

She was leaving. Why wasn't that enough for him? She gave a small laugh and said jokingly, 'You don't have to personally escort me off the estate, you know.'

He obviously didn't enjoy her joke as annoyance flared on his face. 'Do you really think that is why I want to drive you to the cottage? That I want to make sure you leave?'

Thrown by his anger, she challenged him back. 'What other reason could you possibly have?'

His blue gaze held hers for a long time, and then, with a deep inhalation, he said in a quiet voice, 'Why can't you just accept that I want to help you?'

He moved beside the table and hunkered down beside her. Heat coursed through her veins at having his powerful body so close by, at seeing the movement of the hard muscles of his thighs beneath the thin fabric of the jodhpurs, the beauty of his lightly tanned hand and forearm which rested on the table beside her.

He didn't speak again until she met his determined gaze. 'Let me help you.'

Why wasn't he listening to her? She was able to look after herself—she didn't need any help.

'I appreciate the offer, but I can manage by myself.'

He stood, his jaw working, and eyed her unhappily. 'As you wish.'

With that, he strode out of the kitchen without a backward glance.

* * *

For the second time in less than twelve hours Aideen
knocked at Patrick's front door. If she'd hated to ask for
help the first time around then it was ten times worse
now. Talk about having to eat humble pie...

As she waited for her knock to be answered she looked
back towards her car. Thankfully it had started immediately, and although the floor was a little damp, the files
and office equipment piled on to the back seat and in the
boot had escaped the storm and flood waters.

Unlike her cottage.

She needed to think straight, but her mind was ping-
ponging all over the place. Work. Deadlines. Insurance
claims. Where would she even start in finding a reputable
builder to carry out the necessary repairs?

She turned to the sound of the door opening.

A middle-aged woman stood there, a puzzled look on
her face. As though she was surprised to find someone
standing at the door. 'Can I help you?'

'Can I speak to Patrick, please?'

The woman looked totally taken aback. To assure her
that she wasn't some random stranger, Aideen quickly
added, 'I'm Aideen Ryan. I live in Fuchsia Cottage, down
by the lough. Your estate manager was at the front gates,
repairing them after last night's storm. Patrick had told
him how my cottage flooded last night and he let me in
when I said I needed to talk to Patrick again.'

'Oh, you poor thing. Of course—come in. Sure, half
the village is flooded. I never saw anything like it in
my life.'

The woman led her to a large reception room off the
entrance hall, chatting all the way.

'You took me by surprise. We don't tend to get many

visitors. Make yourself comfortable and I'll let Patrick know you're here.'

It took Patrick so long to arrive that for a while she worried that he was refusing to see her. He marched into the room, his brow furrowed. He was wearing a light blue formal shirt, open at the neck, fine navy wool trousers and expensive tan-coloured shoes. It all screamed expensive Italian designer and he looked every inch the successful billionaire that he was.

She gave him a crooked smile. 'I'm back.'

His frown didn't budge an inch. 'So I see.'

She took a deep breath. She had to focus on work. A little bit of humility had never killed anyone. 'My cottage is uninhabitable. The insurance company is sending out an assessor tomorrow. I tried to go to Mooncoyne, but Foley's Bridge is still impassable.' Trying not to wince at his deepening frown, she said in a rush, 'I was wondering if it would be possible for me to work from here… until the flooding subsides.'

His head tilted forward and he pinned her with a look.

'It's just that I have a commission I need to complete by the end of today and I need access to the internet.'

'What condition is the cottage in?'

Her stomach lurched, but she clenched her fists and forced herself to speak. 'There's still floodwater in both the cottage and the studio. Most of my furniture and all the fitted furniture will probably need to be replaced. At a guess, and after speaking to the insurance company, I'll be out of the cottage for at least a month.'

She was feigning calmness about the whole situation but she wasn't fooling him. The storm damage was exactly as he had anticipated. He clenched his teeth in frustration.

Why had she been so stubborn in refusing his offer to go with her? He'd had some spare time then. Now he had back-to-back meetings scheduled for the rest of the day.

He would give her fifteen minutes. Get her to see the sense of his plan. And then he would get back to wrapping up this acquisition.

'How about all your personal belongings? Are they okay?'

'All of my clothes survived, but not my shoes—unfortunately.' A sad, crooked smile broke on her mouth before she added in bewilderment, with a catch in her voice, 'I mean, *shoes*! They are the least of my worries… but I loved them so much.'

'Where are you going to live?'

'I'm not sure… I called the Harbour View Hotel but they're completely booked out tonight, and apparently all the bed and breakfasts in a ten-mile radius are the same because of people having to evacuate. I'll probably have to stay in one of the hotels in Ballymore.'

There was no way she was going to manage the renovations from twenty miles away and work on her commissions at the same time.

'It's going to be difficult for you to manage the repairs from Ballymore. I'll get William, my estate manager, to project-manage the renovations for you.'

She stared at him in disbelief. 'Why on earth would you do that?'

'Because you need to concentrate on your business—not spend your days driving all over the countryside and chasing builders.'

'I appreciate the offer, but I need to manage the renovations by myself.'

'Why?'

Tiredly, she rubbed her palms over her face and looked at him imploringly. 'Let me ask you the same question. Why? Why are you doing this?'

Taking a step closer, he stared down at her. Boy, was she obstinate. 'Maybe I just want to help you. Nothing more.'

'I can't accept your help.'

'Why not?'

'Because…'

This woman was impossible. *Why* wouldn't she accept his help? She was as bad as Orla.

He gave an exasperated sigh. 'Aideen, will you stop being a pain and just agree to letting William sort out the renovations…? It's not a big deal. And I don't know about you, but I have better things to be doing than standing here arguing about my motives.'

Not a big deal to him, perhaps, but it was to her. She needed to rebuild her life by herself, on her own terms.

Bewildered, she said, 'You don't even know me.'

'So? You're my neighbour. That's a good enough reason for me to want to help.'

He made it all sound so simple. And for a moment she wanted to believe him. But then a siren of warning sounded in her brain. She needed to be in control of her own life. 'I don't want to sound ungrateful, and I do appreciate your offer, but I have to manage the renovations by myself.'

'And what if your business suffers as a result?'

She flinched at the truth of his words. Ballymore was twenty miles away, on twisting roads. Trying to manage the renovations and run her business from a hotel room was going to be a nightmare.

Frustration at the whole situation had her arguing back. 'I'll manage.'

His mouth tensed at the anger in her voice and he considered her through narrowed eyes. 'You *are* stubborn, aren't you?'

'So it has been said in the past,' she muttered.

On an exasperated exhalation he folded his arms. 'Your business has to be your number one priority. William will sort out the renovations. You will move in here until the cottage is ready, and on Sunday you will come to Paris with me.'

A bolt of pain radiated through his jawline as he clamped his teeth together. Hard. For a few seconds he wondered at the words he had so casually tossed out. Disquiet rumbled in his stomach. Was he about to walk into a minefield of complications by inviting this woman into his life? But in an instant he killed that doubt. This was the right thing to do. She needed his help. Even if the horror in her eyes told him that she wasn't ready to accept it yet.

Stupefied, Aideen stared at him for the longest while, waiting for him to give the tiniest indication that he was joking. But his mouth didn't twitch...his eyes didn't soften.

She gave a laugh of disbelief. 'Are you being serious?'

'Yes. I have meetings in Paris all of next week. You said yourself that you should be out meeting clients. Well, now is your opportunity. I have a chateau close to Paris we can use.'

'But I would be intruding.'

'Look, you've seen the size of Ashbrooke. My chateau outside Paris is large, too. You can set up a temporary studio there for the week. We can keep out of each other's way.'

Shaking her head, she folded her arms across her chest. 'You said last night you like living on your own... and so do I. It won't work.'

'We'll lead our own lives. I'm simply offering you a bed and a place to work—both here and in Paris. You come and go as you please. My chauffeur will be available to you whenever you need him. It doesn't have to be more complicated than that.'

'But *why*?'

'What is it with you and your questions? Why don't you believe that I'm just trying to be a good neighbour? That it's the right thing to do? I admire your tenacity and I want to support you in rebuilding your business. I think you need help even if you are too stubborn to admit it yourself.'

Taken aback by the powerful intensity of his words, she wavered a little. 'I'd pay you back.'

Taking a deep breath, he said with exasperation, 'I don't want your money. Can't you just accept it as a neighbourly gesture?'

'I'll be paying rent.'

He held up his hands. 'Fine. You can pay me once your insurance money comes through. Now I need to get back to work. I'll show you to the library, where you can work today. Use the same bedroom as last night to sleep in.' Out in the corridor, he added, 'You met my housekeeper, Maureen, earlier. Speak to her if you need anything. I'll get William to call in to see you and together you can discuss the renovation plans.'

She followed him to the library. Was she crazy to agree to this? But it was the only sensible option open to her. Wasn't it she who had said she would do anything to make her business a success? Just how hard would it be to move into his house for a month? She would have the space she needed and she would be close by the cottage to keep an eye on the renovations. And she did need to go to Paris.

It was a no-brainer, really. But could she really cope with living under the same roof as him? When there was this strange push-and-pull thing going on between them…attraction vying with wariness?

But it wasn't as if he was welcoming her with open arms anyway. He was a busy man who travelled the world. She mightn't see him for most of the time she was his guest.

A little while later, she was about to go about unpacking her car when she glanced around to see him watching her with a dark intensity.

How long would it take for him to regret asking her to stay? If he wasn't already doing so…?

CHAPTER FOUR

MONDAY MORNING. THEY HAD flown to Paris the day before, and today he had a number of client and in-house meetings before him. The acquisition had gone through on Friday evening.

He had set Aideen up with a temporary studio space in the library of the chateau, and she planned on spending the day organising meetings with clients.

He jogged past the walled garden in the grounds of the chateau and then broke into a sprint. He had dined out last night with his French management team. Glad to have an excuse to leave the chateau and her offer to cook them dinner.

They had both worked on the plane over yesterday afternoon, but he had found his gaze repeatedly wandering towards her, intrigued by how absorbed she had been in her work. With her hair swept up into a messy bun she had stared at her laptop screen, her long fingers tapping the delicate column of her neck in thought. And he had wondered what it would be like to have those fingers run against his skin.

After that, the thought of sharing dinner alone with her had set alarm bells off in his brain. He had to keep his distance.

Taking the steps of the garden two at a time, he ran across the stone terrace that traversed the entire length of the back of the sixteenth-century chateau. He entered the house and walked towards the kitchen. Was that *baking* he smelt?

An explosion of household goods were scattered across the surface of the island. The shells of juiced oranges, an upturned egg carton, an open milk bottle teetering precariously on the edge of the unit. Behind them, a trail of baking tins and bowls was scattered along the kitchen counter.

He turned to the sound of footsteps out in the corridor. Aideen walked towards him, a huge bunch of multi-coloured tulips in her arms, a carton of eggs in her hand, rosy-cheeked and bright-eyed, a wide smile on her face. Her hair, thick glossy waves of soft chestnut curls, fell down her back.

'Oh, you're back.' She flashed him a quick smile before her gaze darted guiltily to the chaos behind him. 'I thought you would be out for a while yet.'

'What's happened to the kitchen?'

'I'm making breakfast. I hope you don't mind.'

Actually, he did. He wanted his kitchen clean and tidy, as it usually was. Not this mess.

She sidestepped him and began to search through the kitchen cupboards.

He gritted his teeth and tried to resist the urge to start clearing up the mess himself. His stomach, however, had very different thoughts as it rumbled at the delicious sweet smells of baking.

She plopped the tulips in a vase she had found in a cupboard and placed it on the kitchen table. 'I met your gardener earlier, and he gave me the use of his bike to cycle down to the village so that I could go to the *boulangerie*. But then I ran out of eggs, so I had to go again. The cycle down is easy but, boy, the hill back up is tricky. The countryside here is beautiful, and the village is so pretty. When I came back he gave me these flowers from the garden—aren't they stunning?'

The tulips did look good, but something about their cheery presence in the kitchen niggled him…they were just too *homely*.

For a few seconds she looked at him expectantly. When he didn't respond she smiled at him uncertainly, before rolling up the sleeves of her pink and white striped shirt.

'I'll tidy up here and then put some breakfast on. In honour of being in France, I'm going to make us *oeufs en cocotte*.'

He looked at her, bewildered. And slowly it dawned on him that she was expecting them to have breakfast *together*.

For a few brief seconds he was tempted to give in to the tantalising aroma of fresh baking filling the room. But a glimpse of her white lace bra as she bent over to swoop up the errant milk cap from the floor had him coming back to reality with a bang.

This wasn't what her stay was supposed to be about. A bed and an office… Not seeing too much of her. *That* was what he had signed up for. Not this cosy domesticity. Not some breakfast routine that could quickly become a habit. Not feeling desire for a woman first thing in the morning.

'I don't eat breakfast.'

It was almost the truth. He usually just grabbed some toast and coffee and took it to his office, eager to start work.

She was going about gathering up all the empty packaging on the island unit and paused briefly to give him a quick look. 'But that's crazy. After exercising you should eat.'

His spine stiffened and his jaw muscles tightened. Irritated, he grabbed a mug from the cupboard and went about making himself a coffee. 'I'm not hungry.'

At the sink, she rinsed out a cloth before she turned and caught his gaze. 'Have *something*. I wanted to thank you for having me here. For the flight over…the accommodation. I have some croissants and a baguette I bought in the *boulangerie* earlier warming in the oven.' She stopped and grimaced before admitting, 'My first attempt at *oeufs en cocotte* didn't quite work out, so I had to pop out for more eggs, but I'll have them ready in ten minutes.'

For a moment he almost wavered. 'I appreciate the gesture, but I'll stick to my usual coffee.'

With a disappointed sigh she added, 'If you won't eat, at least let me make the coffee for you.'

He threw his hands up in surrender. 'If you insist— two shots of espresso.'

'I've set the table out in the courtyard. If you would like to go out and sit there I'll bring you out the coffee.'

His head darted to the outdoor dining table in the courtyard. His fine china and cut glass sat on top of a white linen tablecloth. A jug of freshly squeezed orange juice sat next to silver salt and pepper pots. The courtyard was filled with an abundance of springtime flowers and the whole setting looked like a magazine feature on the ultimate romantic breakfast.

'Thanks, but I'll stay in here. I have to leave for work soon.'

At the kitchen table he clicked on to his usual newsfeed, using his tablet. He tried to concentrate on the various market analysts' commentary on his acquisition but she'd switched on the kitchen music system to an upbeat radio breakfast show. The DJs spoke in rapid French, sounding like children who had overdosed on a breakfast of sugary cereal.

And as if that wasn't bad enough she then proceeded to chat away herself, over their manic laughter. 'What a beautiful morning! Going to the *boulangerie* this morning reminded me of the summer I spent here as a student. I had an internship in a design house and I was penniless. I ate baguettes for the entire summer. I used to stare longingly at the patisserie stands, wishing I could afford to buy an éclair or, my favourite, a millefeuille.'

She continued this monologue while fiddling with the coffee machine's controls.

'Do you want some help?'

'No, I'm fine. I'll work it out.'

As she fiddled and twisted Patrick stared at the financial reports, very little detail actually registering. What *was* registering was the round swell of her bottom, the long length of her legs in skinny faded denim. Which only added to his growing annoyance.

Was it because he hadn't been with a woman for more than two years that he sometimes caught himself thinking that she was the most beautiful woman he had ever met? It wasn't just her prettiness, the seductive curves of her long-limbed body. Something shone through in her personality—a happiness, a strength of will that was beguiling.

He almost sighed in relief when she eventually popped a mug of coffee before him.

'Milk or sugar?'

'Neither, thanks.'

Sweet Lord, it was the strongest coffee he had ever tasted.

'I've messed up the coffee, haven't I?'

A crestfallen expression on her face, she waited for his answer.

He leant back in his chair and raised an eyebrow. 'I could probably stand on it.'

She moved to take the mug. 'I'll try again.'

'No!' That poor machine couldn't take it.

She planted her hands firmly on her hips. 'I take it you're not a morning person?'

'Correct in one. I like good coffee, silence, and preferably a tidy kitchen—not Armageddon.'

For a brief second a mixture of hurt and anger sparked in her eyes before she turned away.

She switched off the radio and then quickly cleared the countertops. She wiped them down and then filled the sink with a gush of steaming water in readiness to wash the used pots and pans piled high next to it.

A small part of him wanted to relent, to give in to his hungry stomach and her chatter. To start off the day in something other than the usual silence. A silence he now realised was somewhat lonely.

But if this was to work he needed to stand firm. Start as they meant to go along. Better to upset her than to give her any unrealistic expectations of what their time together would be like.

'I'm going for a shower.'

She didn't turn around at his call, just nodded her head in acknowledgement. But when he reached the door she said, 'I was only trying to show my thanks, you know.'

She turned from the kitchen counter and stared at him defiantly.

When he didn't speak she reddened a little and crossed her arms. 'I went to a lot of effort.'

He retraced his steps back across the room to where she stood. Her gaze rose up to meet his. 'Firstly, I don't eat breakfast. Secondly, I think we need to have some clear boundaries if this is going to work.'

She gave a tight laugh. 'What on earth do you mean by "boundaries"?'

Her laugh rightly mocked his stuffiness, and although he knew he deserved it he was in no mood to defend himself. 'Aideen, I want to help you in re-establishing your business. Nothing else.'

Her blush deepened, but her hands clenched tight at her sides. 'I was making you breakfast. That's all. What's the big deal?'

'I don't want you getting any ideas.'

She drew herself up to her full height and plopped a hand on her hip. 'Trust me—I won't. A workaholic, taciturn, controlling man is the last thing I'm looking for in my life.'

Workaholic, he would admit. But taciturn and controlling? What on earth was she talking about?

'Right—explain to me how I'm taciturn and controlling?'

'You had the next month of my life all planned out before you even spoke to me the morning after the storm.'

'So? It was the most logical plan. Even you agreed with it.'

'Yes, I agreed with it. But not once did you stop to understand just how difficult it was for me to accept it.'

Baffled, he asked, 'What do you mean?'

'I mean I lost not only my business last year. I also lost my pride and self-respect. Having to accept help from you made me feel like I was failing again.'

'That wasn't my intention.'

'I know. But maybe if you'd stopped and thought about how I might possibly feel—if you'd asked me my opinion—then you might have understood.'

She had a point, but he wasn't going to admit it. So instead he challenged her. 'And taciturn?'

'Do you really need to ask? You have barely spoken to me in the past two days.' Biting her lip, she studied him before she added, 'If you don't want me around why did you invite me to stay with you?'

Her bluntness left him for the first time in his life slightly speechless. But then anger rose up in him. 'I don't *do* breakfast...or small talk. I'm not going to be your friend. Now, if you will excuse me, I have to get ready for work.'

He marched away, down the long corridor and up the stairs to the master bedroom, yanking off his tee shirt as he went. Irritation ate into his bones.

As he stood in the shower he scrubbed his hair and defended himself against what she'd said. He wasn't controlling...or taciturn. She was exaggerating. She was saying he was wrong for being decisive. Well, 'decisive' had got him where he was today.

But as the water pounded down on his scalp the uncomfortable realisation that her words might have some truth began to creep into his consciousness.

Had focusing solely on work for so long numbed him to others' feelings? Yes, he was decisive and logical... but did he sometimes steamroller over others?

And as he dressed he began to grasp why he had been

so disturbed by her attempts to make him breakfast. Why it had irked him so much.

It had unsettled him just how good it was to arrive home to activity, to the comfort of having another person in the house. Of course the fact that it was Aideen, looking so happy and gorgeous, added to that uncomfortable realisation. Because it would be so easy to fall into the trap of enjoying her company, of wanting more with this woman.

Aideen emitted a low groan and dropped her head down on to the smooth mahogany wood of the library desk.

Could this day get any worse? First she had messed up with Patrick at breakfast. What was supposed to have been a small gesture of thanks had blown up in her face. Why hadn't she just let him walk away? Did it really matter that he hadn't wanted to accept her gesture of thanks?

He had left for meetings soon after, with a curt goodbye, and she had spent the day alone in this breathtakingly beautiful chateau, on a hill overlooking the Seine, annoyed about their argument but having to be cheery as she made phone calls to organise her own meetings for the coming days.

Several times with prospective new clients she hadn't even got past the receptionist. But she had eventually managed to organise enough meetings to make the trip worthwhile—some with colleagues she hadn't seen since she'd lost her old business.

Just now she had ended another call to an ex-client. The entire call had been a tense mixture of arduous questioning and awkward silences that had left her feeling completely flustered.

'Tough call?'

Her head jerked up and her stomach lurched as she saw Patrick standing in the doorway.

'The usual.'

She was cross with him—and hurt, and embarrassed. And she couldn't bring herself to look at him. But when he came and sat on the table she was working at she couldn't help but glance in his direction.

'I'm sorry for not being tidy…for taking over the kitchen. I just wanted to say thank you for everything you have done by making breakfast… I guess it backfired.'

'You don't need to thank me. I suppose I'm finding it a little strange to be sharing my home with someone else.'

She'd only been here a day and he was regretting it already. She shuffled some books and placed fistfuls of marker pens and pencils into canisters, glad that her hair had fallen forward and blocked his view of her face. Which was burning in embarrassment.

'I can move out, if this isn't working for you.'

The touch of his hand on her arm had her jerking back in surprise. Her stomach flipped and her throat tightened when she looked at him, her eyes transfixed by the perfection of his thick dark eyebrows, now drawn into a frown, and by the length of his fingers when he drew a hand over his cheek in a gesture of exasperation.

'No. That's not what I mean. I think we need to give each other space, but also adapt to the other person's way of doing things. I've been under time pressure recently, with the demands of my work. I might have rushed to make decisions without taking how you would feel into consideration.'

She felt stupidly relieved by his words, and without

much thought said teasingly, 'Are you apologising to me in a very roundabout way?'

His lips quirked a fraction. 'I suppose I am.'

'So, basically, I need to stop making a mess of your kitchen and you'll try not to be so grumpy?'

His gaze challenged hers playfully. 'And I'll try to eat some breakfast.'

'You have a deal.'

He pushed himself back a little further along the table, creating more distance between them. 'Now, do you want to talk about that call? Who's Ed?'

Her stomach flipped over. The designer had asked her bluntly why she should use her consultancy over Ed's—her ex. She had put forward her track record in designing, her competitive price points, but she knew the designer was still unconvinced.

As she knew to her cost, Ed could be very persuasive and economical with the truth. There had been little point in protesting that a lot of the designs Ed claimed as his own were in fact hers. The designer wasn't likely to believe her. Of course she could take Ed to the courts as a way to claim her rightful ownership, but she didn't have the financial resources to do so.

And Patrick had heard her conversation.

Embarrassment flamed on her cheeks. She had only told her friends and family some of the details, too hurt and humiliated to tell them everything. So how on earth could she be expected to tell a billionaire that she had been so naïve and trusting? This stunning chateau alone told the story of his incredible success and obvious business acumen.

Also, as stupid as she knew it was, it still hurt that he hadn't wanted her breakfast. And every time she saw him she fancied him even more, which was starting to drive her a little crazy.

She lifted a box on to the table. She couldn't speak. Hurt, attraction, embarrassment all swirled away inside her, turning her brain to mush and catching hold of her tongue.

She worked with her back to him, but Patrick could still see how her fingers trembled as she scattered folders and loose cuts of material on to the desk. It was clear that she was going to pretend not to have heard his question. The surface of the desk was quickly disappearing under a mountain of her belongings.

Who was Ed and what hold did he have over her to cause this unease? Something that felt suspiciously like jealousy twisted in his stomach. He breathed it out. He wasn't going there. This was about helping her professionally. Nothing more. And although he was curious about this he would hold off asking her about him again… for now.

As she fought with the now empty cardboard box a low sigh of exasperation sang from her lips. Strangely compelled to ease her upset, to see her smile again, he stepped towards her and took the box, twisting it flat. A quick glance at the messy desk had him saying, 'This won't do. This room is all wrong. Come with me.'

He grasped her hand in his and almost at a run led her down the corridors of the vast chateau.

'Where are we going?'

'You'll see.'

What on earth was he doing? She should be protesting, should be working. But it felt so good to be chasing down corridors with him, to have his hand holding hers.

He brought her to a vast empty room, bathed in evening sunshine, with the warmth of the sun bouncing off the parquet flooring. White wooden doors and windows formed the entire length of the garden-facing walls.

'This is the orangery, but while you're here you can use it as your studio. The library is too dark and small—especially for someone like you, who likes to...' His mouth lifted ever so slightly and after some thought he said, 'Who likes to spread their work around. This is a better space for you to work in. There are some trestle tables stored in an outside storage room. There's other pieces of furniture stored there, too, that you can use. I can get my staff to move them in here tomorrow morning, when they start work, or if you want we could go and get them now ourselves.'

She was completely thrown, and moved by his suggestion. The room would be perfect to work in. She had two options: thank him and run the risk of the emotion in her chest leaking out in gushing thanks, or brazen it out and tease him back.

It was an easy decision. 'Are you saying I'm messy?'

'Based on the evidence of the papers scattered around the library just now...and the kitchen this morning... then, yes, I'd say pretty confidently that you're messy.'

She gave him a mock withering look. Once again she felt completely disarmed by his thoughtfulness. 'This would be perfect. The light and space in here is incredible. Thank you.'

'Good. Now, how about we go and get those tables?'

A little while later, as he helped to unpack a box, he gestured towards her company's logo.

'Where did you get the idea for your business name? Little Fire?'

'It's what Aideen means in Gaelic.'

'I didn't know that.'

'It also felt like a very apt name for the type of business I want. I want to create a small bespoke design consultancy—to be an innovator in the industry. A consultancy that is respected for its passion.'

'It suits your personality, too.' He said it in a deadpan voice, but once again there was a faint hint of humour sparking in his eyes.

Taken aback, she looked away. When she eventually glanced back the humour was gone.

'Are you going to tell me who Ed is?'

She didn't want to. She wanted to bury him in the past. But she needed to answer his question in some form.

'He was my business partner. I set up the company by myself and he joined me a few years later. I was having cash flow problems and he was able to inject capital into the business. We had been to university together and it felt like a good fit for him to come on board.'

'I'm hearing a big *but* here.'

'A very big "but", unfortunately. He insisted on taking a majority share in the business. After that we expanded too rapidly—spent capital on projects we shouldn't have. I shouldn't have agreed to him having a majority share— it led to an inequality in our partnership and gave him the leeway to overrule me. We started arguing. Eventually it became clear that he wanted me out of the business and he made life difficult for me. I tried hanging in there, but in the end I knew I had to go.'

Perched on a trestle table opposite her, he looked at her sombrely. 'What did he do?'

She pulled a wooden bistro chair to the trestle table she'd been working at and sat. She needed to do something while she spoke to avoid having to look at him. To pretend this was an inconsequential conversation. So she started to order by colour the pile of swatches she would take to her meetings in the coming days.

'He overruled all my decisions. He belittled me in front of clients. He dropped heavy rumours that I was difficult to work with.'

'Is that why you're so hesitant about visiting clients?'

'Yes. It's embarrassing. I don't really know how much he said to our clients and whether they believed him. I'm hoping not… But I'm going to do everything I can to make this a success. I love my job. Adore the creativity involved and all the opportunities I get to work with different designers. No two days are the same. I just have to make sure I build up my client base quickly to meet my overheads.'

She glanced up and caught his eye.

'And you know what? I want to prove Ed wrong, too. He said I would never make it on my own.'

'That's understandable, but be careful that proving him wrong doesn't distract from your energy, from your focus.'

She wasn't quite certain what his point was…and she wasn't sure she wanted to fully understand…so she shrugged it off. 'It won't.'

And he knew she had, because without missing a beat he said, 'Okay, tell me what you're going to do differently with this business.'

It was a good question. She knew instinctively a lot of things she would do differently, but hadn't consciously addressed them. She had been in too much of a rush to start again.

For a few minutes she thought about it, her fingers

flicking against the edges of a blue cotton swatch. What *would* she do differently?

'I need to manage my cash flow better—not expand too quickly. Meet with my clients on a more regular basis…communicate with them.'

He nodded at her answer, but fired another question at her immediately. 'Fine, but at a strategic level what are you going to do differently?'

For a while she was lost as to how to answer him. And then she thought about her client base. 'I need to think through what my target market is… Perhaps I'm too diversified at the moment.'

'Spend time thinking about those issues—those are what matter. Not Ed. Don't waste any more time on him. He's not worth it. You lost that business, which was tough. But it's in the past now. Your focus must be on the future.'

Her pulse raced at his words but she forced herself to smile. 'I know. You're right. I need to go and get some more files from the library.'

She practically ran from the room. She heard him call her name but she didn't turn back. Of course he was right. But the hurt of losing the business lingered stubbornly inside her and it was hard to move on from it. To just push it aside. Everything he said was true and right, but she wasn't ready to hear it yet…especially from a billionaire.

His assistants in Dublin and Berlin had long gone home, but after finishing a conference call with his development team in Shanghai later that evening Patrick checked in with his assistant in Palo Alto. He updated his calendar with her for the coming days and ended the call.

He spent the next hour reading the daily reports he

expected each of the managing directors of his subsidiaries to file.

The projected revenue for a new construction industry project management database was not performing as expected. He emailed the management team responsible and listed the new sales strategy he wanted them to follow.

When that was done he checked the time on his monitor. It was not yet nine. In recent months he had frequently worked until twelve. It felt a little strange to have all this spare time. He switched off the bank of monitors on his desk and walked over to the windows overlooking a dense copse of trees. In the dusk, flocks of birds swirled above the treetops, a pink-tinged sky behind them.

How was Orla doing? Should he call her? One of them would have to end this impasse between them. But it was she who had caused it. It was up to her to call.

From the corner of the window he caught a glimpse of Aideen working in the orangery. She was sitting at a trestle table, staring out towards the garden, lost in thought.

Anger bubbled in his stomach at the treachery of her former business partner. He could understand her desire to prove him wrong. If it was him he would exact revenge. But the guy wasn't worth it. She needed to focus on the future and not on the past.

He was tempted to go and speak to her. What was it about her that drew him to her? He certainly admired her tenacity and her determination to start again. And the moment he was in the same room as her, he was sidetracked by her radiance and beauty. By her positive outlook on life. By her smile. By the thick curtain of hair that seemed to change colour according to the light—chocolate-brown at times, filled with highlights of cinnamon and caramel at other times. By her body, which called to the most elemental parts of him...

Yes, she talked too much, and was way too messy... but after two years of silence part of him yearned for her chatter, for her warmth, for her positive outlook on life.

Another part of him wanted to shut it all out. At least that way he wouldn't be able to mess up a relationship again.

And at times her honesty and openness left him floundering. This morning and this evening she had spoken with an emotional honesty that had made him stop and think. And he wasn't sure if he liked that. She spoke about the past while he preferred to ignore it.

Knowing now, though, what she had gone through with her business collapse, made him want to protect and help her even more. He wanted her business to succeed and he would give her all the support that she required.

He just needed to ensure that he kept it strictly professional.

CHAPTER FIVE

WEARING FOUR-INCH HEELS on a day when she had to race
from meeting to meeting using the Paris Métro hadn't
been one of her best ideas.

At least her short-sleeved silk button-down dress,
which she had designed and created using one of her
new range of textiles, was comfortable. And thankfully
it had also proved to be a major hit with many of the designers she had met with today. They had commented on
the dress the moment she had walked into their studios,
and it had been the perfect icebreaker for her to introduce the rest of her range.

Her toes were pinched, though, in her never-before-
worn shoes, as she walked out of the headquarters of one
of Europe's leading online luxury fashion retailers. But
she still didn't regret her refusal to use Patrick's chauffeur for the day.

It was bad enough that they had travelled to Paris on
his private jet. That they were staying in his unbeliev-
ably beautiful chateau. She couldn't accept any further
help from him.

This morning they had travelled together into the
centre of Paris and he'd had his chauffeur, Bernard,
drop her at her first meeting. She had been too nervous

to chat, and for once had been grateful for Patrick's silence.

But as she had been about to leave the car he had looked at her with a gentle kindness that had almost floored her and said, 'Believe in yourself.'

She stepped through the automatic sliding doors out on to the street and paused. The building was at the corner of an intersection of five boulevards. Which way was the Métro again? And would it look odd if she walked barefoot?

And then, a little further down the street, she spotted him—leaning against a lamppost, watching her. She faltered at the intensity of his gaze. And then his mouth curled into a smile and she came to a complete stop. He'd smiled at her. He'd actually *smiled* at her.

She knew she was staring at him in shock but she couldn't help it. He was smiling at her! And it felt like the best thing ever.

She smiled back, beyond caring that she probably looked really goofy. And for a joyous few seconds they simply smiled at each other.

Her heart was beating crazily, and her stomach felt as though it was an express elevator on a busy day.

He was so gorgeous when he smiled. Dressed in a bespoke dark navy suit and a crisp white shirt open at the collar, he wore no tie. Other pedestrians did a double take as they passed him by. And if she'd been in their shoes she, too, would have walked by with her mouth open at the sight of the extraordinarily handsome man standing on the pavement, his eyes an astonishing translucent blue, a smile on his delicious mouth.

Heat rushed through her body, quickly followed by a sharp physical stab of attraction.

As she walked to him she tried to disguise the blush that burnt on her cheeks by fussing with the laptop and samples bags in her hands.

'Hi. What are you doing here?'

'You told me your last meeting of the day was here, so I thought I'd come and see how your day went.'

He said it with such sincerity the air whooshed out of her lungs and she could only stand there, looking at him with a big soppy grin.

This was all so crazy. How on earth had she ended up in the city of love with the most incredible and gorgeous guy in the world smiling down at her?

'You look very happy.'

'I'm working on not being taciturn.'

She had to swallow a laugh as she eyed him suspiciously. 'Are you mocking me?'

'Possibly. How does a martini sound?'

She should say no. Pretend to have some work she needed to do back in his chateau. Keep her distance.

But instead she said, 'That sounds like heaven.'

He signalled down the boulevard. Within seconds a dark saloon had pulled up beside them.

His chauffeur had dropped them at his favourite bar in Paris. It had been a while since he had been to the sleek hotel opposite the Jardin du Luxembourg, but it was still as fun and lively as he remembered. And it served the best martinis in the city.

They had spoken little during the journey. The minute she had sat in the car she had slipped off her shoes, leant her head back on the headrest with a sigh and looked out at the familiar Parisian sights as Bernard took them down the Champs-élysées, then Place de la Concorde, and crossed the river at Pont de la Concorde.

'Are your feet still hurting?'

She had looked at him warily. 'Kind of.' Then, with a rueful smile, she'd added, 'Okay—I admit they're killing me. Lord, I miss my old shoes. Stupid flood.'

When she had earlier refused to use his car for the day, at first he'd been irritated at her stubbornness, but then he'd had to admit to himself a grudging admiration for her determination to be independent. But it did still irk him a little. Using his car would have been no big deal.

The lighting in the bar was low, and light jazz music played in the background. Her eyes lit up when the waiter placed their drinks on the table with a flourish. A kick of awareness at just how beautiful, how sexy she was, caught him with a left hook again.

Earlier that left hook had caught him right in the solar plexus when she had walked out on to the street from her meeting. Her black dress with its splatters of blue-and-cream print stopped at mid-thigh. And long, long legs ended in the sexiest pair of red shoes he'd ever seen. Red shoes that matched the red gloss on her lips. Lips he wanted to kiss clean, jealous of the effect they would have on any other man.

Despite himself he hadn't been able to stop smiling at her. And when she'd smiled back, for the first time in a long time, life had felt good.

'So, how was *your* day?'

It had been so long since anyone had asked him that question he was taken aback for a few seconds. She leant further across the table and looked at him expectantly, with genuine interest. Tightness gripped his chest. He had pushed so many people away in the past two years. And now this warm, funny and vibrant woman made him re-alise two things: how alone he had been and how much he must have hurt those he had pushed away.

Would the same thing happen to her?

He felt as though he was being pulled by two oppos-ing forces: the need to connect with her versus the guilt of knowing that by doing so he was increasing the like-lihood of hurting her when it was time for her to return to her cottage.

But once again the need to connect won out.

'It went well. I finalised my negotiations to buy out a mobile software application for hospital consultants.'

'That's brilliant. Congratulations.'

She lifted her martini glass and together they toasted the negotiations. It felt good to celebrate an acquisition with someone after all this time.

Her head tilted in curiosity. 'What are you smiling about?'

He scratched his neck and looked at her doubtfully. *Oh, what the heck?* He would tell her. 'I was just think-ing that sitting in a bar with you, toasting an acquisition, sure beats my attempts to train the dogs to high-five my acquisitions.'

Her laughter was infectious, and they both sat and grinned at each other for a long while.

'You can always pop down to my cottage to celebrate in future.'

Instantly a bittersweet sadness reverberated in the air between them. Across the table her smile faded, and he could see her own doubt as to whether they could ever have such an easy relationship.

He needed to get this conversation back on neutral ground. 'Tell me about your day.'

She gave a groan. 'My first meeting was a disaster. It was with an ex-client who grilled me on the stability of my business and how I was going to deliver on projects now that I didn't have a team behind me.'

Her hand played with her glass and her chest rose heavily as she exhaled.

'To be honest, after that meeting I was ready to give up and head home.' A smile formed on her mouth. 'But on the Métro I thought about what you said to me this morning—to believe in myself.' She paused and ducked her head for a moment. When she looked up, there was a blush on her cheeks, but resolve fired in her eyes. 'I decided you were right. So I dusted myself down and got on with the next meeting.'

This morning she had been visibly nervous about her meetings, but he had deliberately not asked too many questions, nor overwhelmed her with his ideas on how she should approach things. He knew he needed to give her some space. Allow her to face this on her own.

Her comments about him being controlling had hit home and he was consciously trying to curtail his perhaps, at times, overzealous attempts to help her. He would help—but at the pace she needed. That hadn't stopped him from thinking about her all day. Or from leaving his meeting in the eighteenth arrondissement early to ensure he was there when she left her last meeting.

'The rest of the day went much better, thankfully. At lunchtime I met up with a designer friend, Nadine, who is over here from London on business, too. She has just received a major order from a chain of exclusive US boutiques—it will completely transform her business. And she wants me involved, which is really exciting.'

She smiled with such enthusiasm he was sorely tempted to lean across and kiss those full, happy lips.

She scanned the room and gave a nod of approval. 'Great choice of bar, by the way.'

He had to lean towards her to be heard properly above the chatter and music surrounding them. 'I used to live in St Germain before I moved to the chateau.'

'You *lived* in St Germain! I've always dreamt of living in the centre of Paris. Oh, you were so lucky. No offence—your chateau is lovely and everything—but why did you move?'

He wasn't sure he liked the direction this conversation was going in, so he gave a noncommittal answer. 'I like the space and peace of the chateau.'

A shake of her head told him she wasn't going to let it go. 'But you have that already, with Ashbrooke. Why would you want to live outside Paris when you have this incredible city to explore?'

He took a sip of his martini. 'I was tired of city life. And, like at Ashbrooke, I wanted peace and quietness in which to focus on my work.'

She shook her head in bewilderment before saying, 'Just for me, describe your apartment here.'

He was about to say no, but she looked at him so keenly, so hungry for detail, that despite his better judgement he gave her a brief outline. 'It was a two-storey penthouse in a Haussmann building overlooking Île de la Cité.'

'So you had views of Notre-Dame and Sainte-Chapelle? Remind me again why you gave *that* up.'

'For the peace of the countryside—for the space.'

'But why do you have all that space if you have no one to share it with?'

Taken aback by the bluntness of her question, and because it was too close to the bone, he speared her with a look. 'You really don't hold back, do you?'

Her head tilted for a moment and then she said in a more conciliatory voice, 'Not really… But why do you live in such isolated spots? What's the attraction?'

'I spent most of my twenties travelling the world to meet work demands. In recent years I've wanted more stability, a less chaotic and frantic pace. So I've opted to work out of Ashbrooke predominantly and travel only when necessary. And, anyway, I like the countryside. Who *wouldn't* want the ocean views that are at Ashbrooke?'

'I love the countryside, too… But you live behind tall walls, away from the rest of the surrounding communities. Do you never feel alone?'

Lord, she was like a dog with a bone. With someone else he would have cut them off a long time ago, but she asked these questions with such genuine curiosity he found himself reluctantly answering them.

'I don't have time to even *think* of being alone, never mind feel it. Trust me—it's not an issue in my life.'

'What about friends and family? Do you see them often?'

Right—he'd had enough of this. Time to change the subject. 'I see them occasionally.' He nodded at their now empty glasses and said, 'Would you like to walk in the Jardin du Luxembourg before we head back home?'

She nodded enthusiastically, and as they walked out of the bar together his attention was hijacked by the sensual sway of her hips in the high heels. Bewildered, he shook his head, trying to figure out just what was so hypnotic about her walk—and also how she'd managed to get him to talk about personal issues he had never discussed with a single other person before.

The martini and the relief of having survived the hurdle of visiting clients for the first time had combined to make her a little light-headed. So she had happily accepted his suggestion that they stroll through the park.

The paths were busy with joggers and families. A few times she caught Patrick smiling at the antics of careening toddlers and something pulled tight in her chest.

Did he ever want a family of his own? The question was on the tip of her tongue a number of times but she didn't dare ask.

They passed by a bandstand, where a brass band played happy, toe-tapping tunes to a smiling and swaying audience.

'I spoke to William today. The renovations are going well. You'll be glad to hear I will be out of your hair in less than a month after all. It might be three weeks, tops.'

He glanced across at her and then away. 'That's good news.'

A dart of disappointment had her asking, 'That I'll be gone soon?'

He came to a stop and folded his arms. He looked down with good-humoured sternness. 'No. That the renovations are going well.'

Emotion swirled in her chest. She shuffled her feet on the gravel path and she, too, crossed her arms. 'I'm really grateful for everything you have done.'

He looked beyond her, towards a group of children sailing model wooden sailboats on a pond. 'It's not a big deal.'

Of course it was a big deal. But he clearly didn't want to make out that it was.

Evening stubble lined his jaw, adding a rugged masculinity to his already breathtaking looks. How incredible it would be to feel free to run a hand against that razor-sharp jawline and to look into the eyes of this strong, honourable man. Her heart hammered at the thought that in the future some other woman might get close enough to him, might feel free to do exactly that. And he might welcome it.

She pushed away the jealousy that twisted in her stomach. Instead she nodded towards the children he was looking at and said, 'My dad's hobby is model boats. As a child I spent a lot of my Sundays standing in the freezing cold in Herbert Park in Dublin, wishing his boat would sink so that I could go home.'

He gave a bark of laughter and shook his head. 'You sound like you were a wicked child.'

'I used to get into a fair share of trouble, all right. I always blamed my two older brothers, though! Did Orla do that with you?'

He gave a heavy sigh. 'Don't get me started. She used to insist on coming everywhere with myself and my friends. Half the time she would cause mischief—running through people's gardens as a shortcut, helping herself to something from their fruit trees along the way. But when neighbours rang to complain it was always me they mentioned, never Orla. She was so small they couldn't see her.'

For the first time since they'd met he was speaking with genuine ease and affection about someone close to him. He was so animated and relaxed she longed for it to continue for a while.

'What was the village you grew up in like?'

'Everyone knew everyone. I went to the local school and spent my weekends with my friends—either on the beach or playing at our local Gaelic football club.'

Referring to the two traditional Gaelic sports played in most clubs, she asked, 'Hurling or football?'

'Both, of course.' For a while he paused, and then he said, 'I still remember my first day going to the club. My mum took me down and I was so excited to be wearing the club jersey. All the other boys on the street wore it all the time.'

Her chest tightened. 'Do you remember a lot about your mum?'

His voice was sad when he said, 'Just snapshots like that.'

And then he began to walk away.

She had lost him. To that silence he often fell into. She wanted to bring him back.

She followed him and after a while said, 'So, do you get your good looks from her or your dad?'

That elicited a smile. 'So you think I'm good-looking?'

'You know you are. I bet you were the heart-throb in school.'

He laughed at that. 'To answer your question—I take after my dad. Orla's more like my mum.'

'What was your dad like?'

'Hard-working, loving, supportive. A family man and a good neighbour. Orla and I were the centre of his world. He worked several part-time jobs to ensure he was at home when we were. Money was pretty scarce. It used to worry me, but he would just shrug and say that as long as we had one another that was all that mattered. When Mum died he was determined we wouldn't miss out. He even learned how to sew so that he could make us costumes for school plays.'

A lump formed in her throat at hearing the love for his father in his words. In a quiet voice she said, 'He sounds like he was a really good man.'

His eyes met hers for a moment. She felt her breath catch to see the soft gratitude there.

'He was. Each Christmas he would leave us both a memory chest under the tree, filled with little mementos he had collected for us during the year: our sporting medals, awful paintings and poems we'd created in school that only a parent could love, photos of our holidays.'

He paused as a catch formed in his throat. It was a while before he continued.

'In the chests he would also leave a handwritten list with all the reasons why he loved us.'

Her own throat felt pretty tight, but she forced herself to speak. 'What a lovely idea.'

He nodded to that.

They walked beside the urn-lined Medici Fountain and paused where Acis and Galatea, the lovers from Greek mythology, carved in white marble, lay reclined in a lovers' embrace. Their embrace was so intimate she had to look away.

'You said you used to worry about money when you were younger? Is that what motivates you now?' she asked.

'Partially. But it's also the challenge, and knowing that my products are making a difference in people's lives. Especially in the medical field, where they can have a huge impact on how services are delivered to patients. I also like to know that I can provide for others, too.'

She wondered if he meant Orla, but something in the look on his face kept her from asking.

They continued walking, and she said after a while, 'I'm sorry you lost your mum and dad…Patrick. It must have been very difficult.'

'You just get on with it, don't you? There's no other choice.'

'How old were you when you lost them?'

He inhaled deeply before he spoke. 'Seven with my mum…twenty-two with my dad.'

He'd been so young. To lose your mum at seven… She couldn't even begin to think about losing her parents, never mind at that age. 'What age was Orla?'

'She was just a baby with my mum—sixteen when my dad died.'

'Oh, the poor thing.'

He glanced towards her, and then away again quickly, but not before she saw the pain in his eyes. 'Orla found my dad when she came home from school one day. He had died from an abdominal aneurysm.'

For a while she was lost for words. What could she say about such a terrible loss? 'I'm so sorry. It must have been a terrible shock for you both.'

'It was.'

'I bet you were a great older brother, though, which must have helped her a lot.'

Instantly he stiffened and a coolness entered his voice. 'I tried to be.' He gave his watch a quick glance. 'We'd better get back. I have a conference call with Palo Alto in less than an hour.'

Thrown by the sudden change in conversation, and knowing instinctively that he deliberately wanted to end their chat, she looked at her mobile phone. It was almost eight.

'Do you have to take that call? You never seem to stop working.'

He gave a quick shrug. 'I have a problem with a system roll-out over there.'

'But you must have endless directors. Do you really need to have such a hands-on role?'

They exited the park and walked towards Bernard, who was waiting at the kerb.

Patrick answered. 'I like to be involved.'

As they approached the car she said, 'More like you like being in control.'

He looked at her unhappily. 'It's not that simple.'

About to slip into the car, she asked, 'Are you sure?'

He sat beside her and his rigid jaw and thinned mouth told her he was in no way happy with her comment.

He turned and fixed her with a lancing stare. 'It's my *responsibility* to be in control. I will not let down those who are dependent on me—in the workplace or otherwise. I will not apologise to anyone for doing my job.'

She was taken aback by the cold fury in his voice, but he had his mobile out and was speaking rapidly to someone before she could even respond.

CHAPTER SIX

A SET OF preliminary moss-green and off-white designs stared back at her from the laptop screen, as though willing her to make a decision.

Ever since Patrick had asked her what she was going to do differently with her business the question had constantly played on her mind. Time and time again she came back to the one major decision she had to make. Would she stop designing for the upholstery market in favour of specialising exclusively in fashion textile design—her true love?

And now she had to decide whether to submit these designs to Dlexa, a world-renowned upholstery textile manufacturer. Would she be crazy *not* to? It was a huge gamble to take. The upholstery business had often seen her through lean times. But it was also a distraction that ate into time she could be devoting to the fashion market.

So many times during the past few days she had been tempted to go and talk it through with Patrick, to get his advice. So much for her resolve to do this on her own…

Not that she had seen enough of him during the past few days to have such a conversation anyway. Their paths seldom crossed…and she had a sneaking suspicion that he had engineered it that way. Yes, they were both working incredibly long hours. And he was either out at meetings or locked away in his office at the chateau. Once or twice he had appeared in the kitchen while she was preparing a meal. But he'd always had an excuse to leave—something needing his attention elsewhere.

She tried not to let it get to her. Tried not to dwell on the fact that it was probably because she had said too much the other night. Asked too many questions. Tried to get to know him a little better.

At times she'd got a glimpse of a different man from the work-obsessed CEO the world saw. But as quickly as he opened up that fun and playful side he would shut it down again.

What did she expect, anyway? The man ran countless multimillion-pound companies. He wasn't going to have time to chat to her over a coffee.

She constantly felt as though she was waiting for him to appear, with a low-lying nervous anticipation she couldn't dispel. Each night disappointment sat heavily in her chest as she walked to her bedroom, knowing that yet another day had gone by without her seeing him for more than a few minutes. And in the mornings that disappointment was transformed into equally inexplicable excitement at the prospect of seeing him.

The designs for Dlexa would take at least another twenty to thirty hours of work to complete. Would it be worth the investment of her time? Her gut was telling her to specialise, to follow her dreams. But flashing in neon lights in her mind's eye was the total sum in her bank account, which had made her blanch when she'd checked it earlier today.

She needed a coffee.

His housekeeping staff had left for the day, leaving

behind, along the chateau's corridors, the smell of bees-wax and the air of contentment that settled on a newly cleaned and polished space.

In the kitchen she tackled the beast of a coffee machine. It still made her nervous. There were way too many knobs and buttons for her liking. But she was slowly getting the hang of it and its temperamental nature. Thankfully so, because it produced the best coffee she had ever tasted.

She was about to head back to the studio when she spotted a parcel on the kitchen table, wrapped in luxurious cream paper and thick gold ribbon. The card on top was addressed to her.

Intrigued, she opened the card.

Aideen,
We are sorry the sea ate your shoes. We gathered
all our treat money together to buy you a new pair.
Love, Mustard and Mayo
PS: We promise not to chew them when you return
to Ashbrooke. We hope you are enjoying Paris.

Inside the parcel, wrapped in individual silk pouches, she found the most exquisite ivory ankle-strap sandals. High enough to make her feel a million dollars, low enough for her to actually be able to walk in them.

They were stunning; if she had seen them in a store she would have fallen over herself to hold them just for a little while. But she couldn't accept them. Her pride had already taken a severe dent at the amount of help she'd had to accept from Patrick. It was humiliating to take so much and give so little in return.

And, given his remoteness in recent days, she didn't even understand why he was giving them to her.

She needed to go and speak to him—figure out why he was giving them to her and then somehow explain why she couldn't accept the gift.

She knocked and waited at the partially open door of his office. He opened the door with a phone to his ear and gestured for her to come inside.

He sat down behind his desk, his eyes moving speculatively to the package in her hand.

Her belly tightened and she turned away, inspecting the modern paintings hanging on the French Grey walls, failing to convince herself that his deep, authoritative and decisive voice had no effect on her. She tried not to listen to his conversation but was intrigued by the way he was able to quickly fire out the pros and cons of purchasing an office block in Rio de Janeiro. He ended the call with an order to proceed with the sale.

Her chest swelled with admiration. She wanted to be like that. Certain and unwavering in her decision-making.

His office was incredibly neat. The desk contained four different monitors, a keyboard, a ream of paperwork neatly stacked into a pile and nothing else. No empty cups, pens askew, or sticky notes scattered with random thoughts like on her own desk. No wonder he thought her messy. The guy was a perfectionist. Perhaps, to achieve what he had, he'd had to be.

'Take a seat.' He gestured over to two silver-green velvet-upholstered sofas that sat before the fireplace. He replaced the handset in its cradle before he moved over to sit on one himself.

She sat, and placed the parcel on her lap. For a moment she stared down at it, the shoe-lover in her reluctant to give it up. But then she placed it on the coffee table between them and pushed it towards him.

'Thank you for the shoes but I can't accept them.'

To that he simply raised an eyebrow.

A knot of tension grew in her belly.

'Giving me accommodation and a place to work for a month, flying me to Paris... You've been more than generous. I can't accept anything else from you—it wouldn't be right.'

'They're just a token from Mustard and Mayo.'

She couldn't help but say in amusement, 'Dogs who internet-shop? Now, *that's* clever.'

For a moment he looked as if he was going to insist, but then he leant towards her. 'Why don't you tell me why you can't accept them?' When she smiled, he held his hands up in admission and said, 'See? I *do* listen to you. This time I'm going to try and understand why before I try to persuade you otherwise.'

'It's not that I don't like them...they're beautiful...or that I'm not grateful.' She came to a stop and her heart was beating so wildly she felt light-headed.

She bent her head and inhaled deeply, clasping her hands. She squeezed her fingers extra-hard.

'I think I should explain...'

Was she crazy, telling him this? But she wanted him to know. So that he would stop ruining all her plans to be independent by giving her so much.

She glanced at him quickly, and then looked away from his frown and stared out of his office window, seeing the tips of the trees blowing in the light breeze.

'After I lost my business I swore I would never be dependent on or beholden to another person again.'

'What do you mean by "beholden"?' His tone was sharp.

She struggled to find the right words to explain what she meant. 'I mean…not indebted to another person. I don't want to feel that I always have to be grateful—that I owe someone else. That I have no right to voice my opinions. But it's not just that… I have to prove to myself that I'm not a failure. And accepting all your help feels like I'm cheating, somehow.'

He looked taken aback, and then he argued, 'You're not a failure if a business deal goes wrong. It happens to a lot of people. At least you had the guts to risk everything in creating a business in the first place. Not everyone could do that. And accepting the help of a neighbour is not cheating.'

He stood and paced the room, his jaw working.

'And I certainly will never—and I mean *never*—make you feel obliged or indebted. I am not that type of person.'

She flinched at the annoyance in his voice. She was making a mess of this. She needed to tell him everything. Then maybe he would understand.

'I'm trying to be honest with you. I want you to understand and I'm sorry if I'm offending you. Let me try and explain…then you might understand. My business partner…Ed. He was my boyfriend, too.'

Heat rose in her cheeks and she stopped as humiliation gripped her throat. She bit the inside of her cheek.

'Not only did he manoeuvre it so that I had no option but to walk away from the business, but he was also having an affair with our finance director.'

She jumped when she heard him utter a low expletive, and was taken aback by the dark anger that flared in his eyes.

'What an idiot.'

'I know. Him…and me.'

'No! The guy's despicable. Don't for one second think you were in anyway responsible.'

'But that's the problem. I was. I shouldn't have agreed to him owning a higher percentage share in the business. I shouldn't have believed all the lies he told me. I honestly can't believe I was so stupid. That's what I hate most— I'm now so wary of others. It's one of the reasons why I can't even accept the shoes. It's not just that they're way too expensive, but I keep wondering *why* you're being so kind and generous.'

He stopped pacing and looked at her with breath-stealing intensity. 'Because just maybe we are not all jerks. Some of us might actually have a heart and want to do the right thing.'

'I'm finding that hard to believe.'

'Don't let him have the power to change you, to make you unhappy.'

'I know… In my heart I know all that. But I can't stop these feelings.'

Across from her he folded his arms on his chest. A look of frustration joined his anger. 'You don't trust me, do you?'

Completely taken aback she gabbled nonsensically. 'No! Yes…I'm not sure… We don't really know one another. Oh, God, I'm sounding really rude. I didn't come here to insult you, and I'm sorry if I have. I just want you to understand why I can't accept anything else from you. It's not that I'm not grateful…call it pride, self-respect… I just can't. I hope you can understand?'

With a raised eyebrow and a quick shrug he said, 'I'm trying to.'

Part of her wanted to turn and run. This conversation had not been a success by any stretch of the imagination. She had insulted him and annoyed him and possibly even hurt him. She needed to try to make amends. Starting with showing some trust in him.

She inhaled a deep breath and began to talk. 'I'm sorry. I honestly didn't come here to insult you. I wanted to explain about the shoes. But I also came in the hope of some advice.'

His brow had creased with doubt but she forced herself not to stop.

'I'll keep it short. You said I should think about my business strategy. Well, there's an area of my business that brings guaranteed revenue, but it's time-intensive work and it's in an area I don't particularly want to specialise in. I'm thinking of not submitting work in that area again, but I'm worried about the revenue.'

'What's the worst-case scenario?'

'I lose revenue for a few months.'

With a quick nod he fired another question at her. 'Can you absorb that loss?'

'Just about.'

'And if the drop in revenue continues for longer?'

'I can always re-enter that market… It will take time to build my portfolio back up, but it's doable.'

He didn't ask any more questions, but instead walked back to his desk. After a while she realised he was waiting for her to speak. And she also realised she had her answer.

With a light shrug, she smiled. 'I think I know what I should do.'

He nodded. 'I think you do.'

As she went to leave the room he called after her.

'Are you certain about the shoes?'

Her hand on the door, she paused, and it was a while before she could turn around. After all she had said he was still being kind. But maybe he was also indirectly asking if she still didn't trust him.

Her heart turning over, she faced him. 'Maybe some time in the future?'

His eyes narrowed at that, and she fled down the corridor before either of them had a chance to say anything further.

Standing at his office window later that evening, Patrick spoke to his chief financial officer while staring out at yet another incredible dusk sky. This evening it was a riot of pink, lilac and lavender, with faint wisps of cloud to the forefront.

A movement on the terrace caught his attention. Aideen was out there, photographing the sunset. Wearing jeans and a silver and grey top, she had her hair pulled back into a high ponytail, exposing the delicate angles of her face, her full lips, the smooth jawline and long, slim neck.

Too distracted to concentrate, he ended the call early and stood watching her.

Their earlier conversation had been difficult. The shoes had been his way of saying he was sorry about everything she had lost in the flood...and for being so tetchy in recent days.

After their walk in the park the other night he had opted to keep his distance from her. He had revealed too much of himself. And he didn't like how good it had felt to be in her company. Her comment about being a good brother to Orla had only reminded him of how he had failed, and of all the reasons why he needed to keep his distance from Aideen.

But the shoes had unwittingly hit a raw nerve with her.

He cursed out loud when he remembered the raw pain etched on her face when she had described her ex's betrayal. No wonder she was slow to trust him. Not that it hadn't stung to hear her admit it.

But knowing what she had gone through strengthened his resolve that nothing could happen between them. He had to suppress his attraction to her. She had just come out of a destructive relationship. The last thing she needed was to be hurt again. And a messy relationship with him was a sure way for her to get hurt.

She needed practical support right now—not a lover. Not all the complications and misunderstandings and raw emotions and intimacy that went with that.

He opened the door from his office out on to the terrace and walked to where she was now sitting, on a wooden bench on the first tier of the terraced garden. The grass muffled his footsteps and when he called her name she looked up in surprise.

'I saw you taking some photos.'

Angling the camera towards him, she asked, 'Would you like to see them?'

He sat beside her and watched the images as she flicked through them on the viewfinder.

'They're beautiful. Will you use them in your work?'

'Probably. They will look great in silk.'

As she kept on flicking the pictures of the sky disappeared and a family portrait appeared in the viewfinder.

With a fond laugh she said, 'Welcome to my family.' She zoomed in closer. 'That's my mum and dad. My brother Fionn.' Then she flicked through another few photos until she found a close-up of a family of three. 'And this is my brother Gavin and his wife Tara, with their little girl, Milly.'

In the photo Gavin and Tara gazed down at their baby with utter devotion. Something kicked solidly against his gut. And kicked even harder when Aideen flicked on to a close-up of Milly.

'Isn't she so beautiful? I never realised just how much I would fall in love with her. The day Gavin rang to say she had been born…' She paused and shook her head in wonder. 'I honestly have never been so happy. You might even have heard my screams of excitement all the way up in Ashbrooke!'

Aideen's enthusiasm and love for Milly slammed home just what he was going to miss. He was never going to get to know Orla's baby. He coughed as a sharp pain pierced his heart.

She looked at him in concern and said, 'Are you okay?'

What was it about her that made him want to tell her? Was it that he was tired of holding in all the hurt and anger inside himself? Was it that she was so open herself?

'My sister Orla is expecting a baby. Next month, in fact.'

Her mouth dropped open in surprise. 'Really? That's fantastic. You must be so excited. Oh, wait until it's born. It really is the best feeling in the world. You wi—'

He cut across her. 'It's not that straightforward.'

'What do you mean?'

'Orla and I haven't been getting on.'

'Oh, listen—I argue with my brothers all the time. You'll be fine.'

Her exuberance and happiness were too much. How could he explain to her just how bad things were between him and Orla? How he had failed her? How she didn't trust in him? How she threw everything he did for her back in his face? It was easier to pretend that she was right.

He answered without looking at her. 'Perhaps.'

'Have you bought anything for the baby yet? I went on a crazy spurge before Milly was born. I bought her the most exquisite hand-knitted blanket in a shop in Mooncoyne. You could buy Orla's baby one, too.'

'I transfer money to Orla every month. She can buy whatever she needs.'

She swung forward on the bench to catch his eyes, horror in her own. 'Please tell me you're joking. You're Orla's only family. You *have* to buy her a present.'

He gave her blistering look. 'Now who's being dictatorial?'

She backed off, hands raised. 'Okay. Fair enough.' She paused for a whole five seconds. 'But still—you have to buy something for your... Is it a boy or a girl?'

Frustration ate into his stomach at her question. He didn't know, and it was humiliating and painful all at once. 'I don't know.'

'Oh. Does Orla know?'

He had no idea. To avoid answering her he looked at his watch. 'I have some calls to make.'

As he stood up she said with concern, 'It's gone eight thirty at night—do you really have to make calls now?'

He simply nodded, indicating that he did, but as he went to move away her hand reached out and stalled him.

'Will you just wait for a minute? There's something I want to say to you.'

He was about to argue, but there was a warmth to her eyes that had him sitting down beside her again.

He looked at her suspiciously and she knew she just had to come out and say what was on her mind. 'Can I be a nag for a few minutes?'

He asked warily, 'Can I stop you?'

'The crazy hours you work…'

Something shuttered in his eyes and tension grew in his jawline.

For a moment she was about to apologise for overstepping the mark, but she stopped herself in time. Maybe he needed to hear some of this.

'I know I annoyed you the other night, when I said you just wanted to be in control of everything. It wasn't a fair comment. I understand you have a lot of responsibilities, and I admire how hard you work and everything you have achieved. What I was trying to say was that I reckon you really need more of a balance in your life.'

He crossed his arms on his chest. 'Pot…kettle…black.'

He had a point, but that wasn't going to stop her. 'You're right. We both need to get a life. Stop working such crazy hours and start having a bit more fun.'

His jaw worked and he fixed her with a cool gaze. 'I have a life. One that I'm happy with.'

'But your life revolves around just work. You *must* need downtime. A way of relaxing, blowing off steam. Answer me this—have you dated recently?'

His answer was curt. 'No, I've been too busy with work.'

She rose a sceptical eyebrow.

'What about friends and family? Do you get time to see them?'

'Occasionally.'

'So basically your life is just work? That can't continue. You seem to be very hands-on with all your different subsidiaries—perhaps you should delegate more? That would free up your time and allow you to have a better balance. Time you could spend with those close to you.'

'Are you trying to tell me *again* how to run my businesses?'

His voice was ice-cold, and it stung to be on the receiving end of his displeasure. Who was she, anyway, to tell a successful billionaire that he needed more in his life?

It would be so easy to change the topic. But she was the only person in his life right now, and someone needed to say these things. And she cared for him—possibly more than she should.

Her heart thumped in her chest at his obvious irritation but she ploughed on. 'No, I'm not telling you. I'm just suggesting. Look, I know that you are super-successful, and that I lost my business last year, but that doesn't mean I can't have an opinion. I admit I might be wrong, but at least give it some thought.'

His gaze, rather astonishingly, slowly turned from furious to quizzical to mild amusement. 'I have to give it to you, Aideen. You're pretty tough underneath all that beauty and happiness. I have managing directors of multinational companies who would probably agree with you but wouldn't have the nerve to say so.'

She threw her eyes heavenwards, trying to ignore the pulse of pleasure his words evoked, telling herself he was only joking. 'Well, I can't see how pretending it's otherwise will help you.'

'You think I need *help*?'

He sounded incredulous. What did he think? That he was the only one who could help others? That he was the only one capable of being a knight in shining armour?

'You say you're happy, but my guess is that you could be happier…God knows, I know I could be.'

He looked at her quizzically. 'What do you mean?'

How could she tell him that she was sometimes lonely…sometimes scared about facing life on her own? It would sound so needy. And it would probably set off all types of alarm bells in his brain.

So instead she leant back into the bench and said, 'I miss being spontaneous—living life for the moment. I have been so bogged down in my business for the past five years I think I've stopped knowing how to have fun.'

Giddy relief ran through her body when he gave her a rueful smile. 'Spontaneity? I haven't had a lot of that in my life in a while.'

Something in his smile freed her. 'Let's do something *now*!'

'It's getting late…'

She laughed at the incredulous look on his face. 'Let's go clubbing.'

'I don't think there are many clubs in the village,' he pointed out with a laugh.

'We could go into Paris.'

'Yes, but I have calls I need to make…I won't be finished before midnight.'

'Cancel them.'

'I can't.'

She folded her arms primly and said, 'I told you that you don't know how to have fun.'

For a while he considered her with a smile. But in the

silence a tense awareness blossomed between them. His smile faded and darkness entered his eyes. He leant closer and her heart began to thunder again. She looked up into his eyes, barely able to breathe. He came even closer and his whole body seemed to eclipse hers.

His head slowed, moved down towards hers, and when his mouth was level with her ear he whispered in a lilting, sexy voice, 'You want spontaneity…?'

A deep shiver of desire ran through her. Every pulsepoint in her body felt as though it was thudding against her skin. Her body swayed closer to him, desperate to feel his strength and warmth.

Her throat had closed over. She barely managed to whisper, 'Yes…'

His hand lay against her cheek and with gentle pressure he turned her mouth towards his. Their mouths aligned and almost touched. She closed her eyes, suddenly dizzy with wonder. She squeezed her hands into tight balls. She couldn't touch him. Because if she did she was worried she would never be able to let go.

And then his lips were on hers and her entire body turned to jelly. His warm, firm lips teased hers with butterfly kisses and she gave a little sigh. He deepened the kiss. Her arms of their own volition snaked up to grasp the material of his sweater. Beneath her fingers his chest was hard and uncompromisingly male.

Her head swam. She swayed against him. His hard body was like a magnet. She longed to touch every part of him. She wanted more.

When he eventually released his hold on her and pulled away she looked at him, dazed, her senses overloaded.

With a lazy, sexy grin he asked, 'How's that for spontaneity?'

Without thinking, she breathed out in a husky whisper, 'Pretty spectacular, really.'

Her already flushed skin flamed at his obvious amusement at her answer.

Flustered, she added, 'And enough spontaneity for one night, I reckon. I think it's time I went inside.'

She got up to leave, but he placed a hand on her arm. His eyes were soft pools of kind amusement.

'Thank you for tonight...' For a moment he looked down, a hand rising to rub the base of his neck. When he looked up again he said with wry amusement, 'Thank you for the life coaching... You can pop the bill in the post.' And then, with his eyes sparkling, he added, 'And thank you for the kiss.'

It had been the most incredible kiss of her life. But this thing between them was going nowhere.

She gave what she hoped appeared to be a casual shrug, said, 'Goodnight!' and hightailed it up the steps to the terrace.

She walked briskly—first to the orangery, to return her camera, and then to her bedroom with a confusing mix of elation and worry.

It had been the most incredible, tender and emotional kiss she had ever experienced. But neighbours didn't kiss like that...and certainly not with such underlying passion and poignancy.

She lay awake for hours later, their kiss swirling in her brain.

They were only supposed to be neighbours—nothing more.

But they already knew more about each other than many close friends did. She had revealed more about herself than she'd ever done before. And slowly, bit by bit, he was confiding in her.

And, even though she knew they had no future, time and time again her brain wandered off topic and she dreamt of him kissing her. And of that kiss leading to a lot more...

CHAPTER SEVEN

DESPITE BEING ON a teleconference with his Northern Europe management team Patrick found himself zoning out of the conversation about a project delay and losing himself in memories of how good it had been to kiss Aideen last night. The soft fullness of her lips, the press of her breast against his biceps, the low purr of frustration when he had forced himself to pull away…

It had been a stupid and reckless kiss…but a large part of him didn't care. How could he regret something that had felt so good?

But how was he going to play it with her now? In truth, he wanted to throw caution to the winds and kiss her again. And possibly even more. But what of all the messy awkwardness that doing so would cause?

A movement at his office door had him looking away from his screen.

Dressed in navy jersey shorts and a white tee shirt, a pair of white trainers on her feet, Aideen smiled at him cheekily and waved two tennis rackets in the air.

Her long legs were toned, as was the rest of her tall, strong but curvy body. She brimmed with fresh vitality and health. She stepped into the room and he was unable to look away. An image of her brown eyes heavy with pleasure, the heat of her mouth last night, popped into his brain.

The sound of someone coughing had him looking back at the screen. Seven pairs of eyes were looking at him speculatively, no doubt wondering what had caught his attention.

He looked at his team, and then back at her.

He shouldn't. He really needed to finish this call.

'Elsa, take over for me.' He looked towards Aideen and raised an eyebrow, challenging her. 'And, Elsa? Please decide and implement whatever strategy you deem appropriate to get the project back on track. Update me only if there are any issues.'

Aideen was right. It was time he had some fun in his life.

He cut the connection on seven even more stunned looking execs and leant back in his chair. 'I was in the middle of a conference call.'

'You've been in this office since six this morning. You know what they say—all work and no play…'

He stood and walked towards her, doing his best not to allow the threatening smile to break on his lips. 'Are you saying I'm dull?'

He took unexpected pleasure from the blush that blossomed on her cheeks.

She swallowed hard before she spoke. 'No. Never, ever dull.' There was a hint of breathlessness in her voice and she blushed even harder.

'So what's with the rackets?'

'Well, as there's a tennis court worthy of Wimbledon sitting unused outside, I thought we should use it.'

He placed his hands in his pockets and looked at her

with playful sternness. 'Is this a not too subtle way of making me "get a life"?'

'You have me rumbled.' She grinned back cheekily. 'So, are you up to the challenge or are you too scared?'

When she put it like that there was no way he was saying no. 'Give me ten minutes.'

As she turned to leave she said, 'I must warn you, though. I was under-thirteen champion at my tennis club.'

He caught up with her out in the corridor. 'So you think you might be able to beat me?'

'I'll certainly try.'

'How do I put this nicely…? You don't have a hope.'

To that she playfully threw back her head in a gesture that said she wasn't going to listen to him and walked away. About to turn the corner, she turned around. 'Nice delegation, by the way.'

'And I did it without even flinching.'

She gave him a wicked grin and turned away.

She was right. He did need to delegate more. He had a talented and ambitious team surrounding him. And he was starting to suspect that he was holding them back by insisting on such centralised decision-making. He needed to empower his subsidiaries more.

He had once. When he had started out he had given them plenty of autonomy. But in the past few years, as the business had exploded in size, he had reigned them in. The truth was as his home life with Orla had become more fraught he had used work as a way of feeling in control, driven by the thinking that if he couldn't support her emotionally he would at least do so financially. By pulling the businesses back under his control he'd felt as though he was achieving something and he'd been able to bury the feelings that went with failure.

But centralised control wasn't sustainable. It had to change. But relinquishing that control wasn't going to be easy.

Two hours later he threw his racket up in the air in elation. Aideen stood at the opposite end of the court wearing a deep scowl.

'That was *not* out.'

'It was out by a mile. I told you I would win.'

'You didn't give me as much as an inch.'

'Like you did *me* any favours!'

She shook her head and stomped down towards the net. 'I didn't realise you were so competitive.'

'Aideen, in comparison to you I reckon I'm almost comatose.'

With a laugh she conceded, 'I hate losing.'

'So I gathered. Come on. I think we could both do with a drink.'

They walked to the kitchen and he prepared them each a large glass of sparkling water mixed with fresh orange juice. They took them out on to the terrace to drink, a light breeze cooling them down.

Across the table from him she stretched her arm in and out a number of times.

'Cramp?'

'I think I might have pulled a muscle on a return volley.'

'You *did* throw yourself about the court.'

At that she gave a sheepish shrug. 'I admit I can get carried away sometimes. I spent my childhood trying to keep up with my two older brothers. I couldn't help but develop a competitive streak.'

'Your competitiveness…hating to lose…was that one of the reasons why losing the business was so hard for you?'

'I guess. Despite my less than tidy ways, I've always pushed myself hard. I suppose my pride did take a dent. It was the first time in my life I failed at anything.'

Her words immediately resonated with him. His business success highlighted just how badly he had messed up with Orla. It made the success seem somewhat hollow when you didn't have someone to share it with.

She flexed her arm again, and said, in a thoughtful almost sad voice, 'I know I have to think about the future and move on. But it's really not that easy to just wipe away the past. To ignore everything that happened. To bury the pain. I can't help but wish that things had turned out differently.'

Something sharp pierced into him and he practically growled out, 'Were you in love with Ed?'

She blinked rapidly and her mouth fell open. Eventually she answered, 'I thought I was.'

A strange sensation of jealousy seeped into his bones and he had the sudden urge to punch something. He had never felt so possessive of a woman in his life. He needed to change the subject quickly—to distract them both.

'Try to forget him—and everything that happened. I appreciate it's hard, but it's vital you focus on the future. Tell me about your dreams, what you personally want to do in the coming years.'

She eyed him with a mixture of surprise and suspicion. But then she shrugged and said, 'Well, that's a big question.' For the longest while she paused, her brows knitted together in concentration. 'Nothing extraordinary, really. I've always wanted to visit St Petersburg. And travel to Dharamsala in India. Where the most incredible mulberry silk is woven. Afternoon tea in Vienna has always sounded like fun. Oh, and I want to learn how to bake a soufflé.'

'A soufflé?'

'They always sink on me—it drives me crazy.'

Curiosity got the better of him and he couldn't help but ask, even though he wasn't certain what answer he wanted. 'And family and relationships?'

She eyed him warily and it was a while before she answered. 'Check back in with me in a few years' time. Right now I'm not exactly in the mood to be in a relationship. All you men have a black mark against your names.'

'All three and a half billion of us?'

'Yes, every single one. Well, apart from my dad and my brothers.' She hesitated, glanced at him briefly, and then said in a rush, 'And possibly you if you continue being such a good neighbour.'

Trying but failing to ignore the reality check her words had caused, he answered drily, 'Glad to hear that.'

'So what about you? What's on *your* list?'

Like her, it wasn't something he had overly thought about. And yet it was a question that filled him with unexpected excitement. 'I want to continue on with the restoration of Ashbrooke. The east wing in particular needs conservation work. And there's an old bathing house on the grounds I want to restore, as well.'

'You really love Ashbrooke, don't you?'

'Yes, I do. I suppose I have a lot of emotional attachment to it because of Lord Balfe. His family owned the estate for generations and it was a huge honour that he was happy to sell it to me. There were several other interested parties, but he chose me. He spends most of his time in the Caribbean now—growing old disgracefully, by all accounts.'

'Do you see him often?'

'Unfortunately, no. Maybe I should buy a business in the Caribbean so I'd have an excuse to go there.'

'Or…an easier solution…you just take a holiday and go and visit him.'

She smiled cheekily at him and he couldn't help but laugh.

For a while they just looked at each other, the warmth and understanding in her eyes causing his heart to thump in his chest. A deep connection reverberated between them.

A slow blush formed on her cheeks and she leant into the table, her fingers drawing down over the grain of the wooden tabletop. 'What else is on your list?' she asked quietly.

His blood thundered in his ears at the strength of the connection he felt with her. He wanted to tell her about Orla and his dreams of them being close once again. But where would he even start to explain the jumbled up, contradictory one hundred and one emotions he felt for his sister?

Instead he said, 'I want to take part in the Isklar Norseman Xtreme Triathlon in Norway.'

'Now, *that* sounds impressive.' Her eyes sparkled with admiration, but the sparkle slowly faded. 'And relationships?'

What would she say if he told her he could never be in a permanent relationship? That he wasn't interested in being in one? That he was no good in relationships?

That he had lost everyone he had ever loved and never wanted to expose himself to that again?

It was easier to be non-committal rather than get into a debate about it. 'Some day, perhaps.'

She moved forward in her chair, a familiar look of determination growing. 'You won't meet anyone if you're stuck in your office twenty-four-seven.' When he didn't respond, she asked bluntly, 'Are you going to sacrifice the rest of your life to work for *ever*? Are you *so* determined not to let other people in?'

He gave a disbelieving laugh. 'I spend my days speaking to people on the phone. I travel. I speak to my staff.'

'Okay, let's call a spade a spade, here. Work conversations and travel don't count. You don't *really* have people in your life—meaningful relationships. And you want it that way. Plus, you've stopped knowing how to have fun.'

Thrown by the uncomfortable truth of her words, he chose to answer only her latter accusations. 'No, I haven't.'

'Prove it.'

'And if I don't?'

'I'll cook dinner for you tonight.'

'Am I supposed to be scared of that prospect?'

'Just imagine the mess I'd make of your kitchen.'

Despite his best efforts he winced. 'Fine. If you want fun, we'll go out tonight. I'll take you to dinner at one of my favourite restaurants.'

'You're on. But I'm paying.'

'No. It's my idea. I'll pay.'

She threw him a stern look. 'I'm sure you appreciate why I would want to pay.'

He breathed out in exasperation. 'I wish you would just accept my help.'

She looked at him with quiet dignity. 'I don't want to feel like a freeloader.'

Something pulled in his chest and he said in a conciliatory voice, 'Let's just go out and enjoy ourselves. By all means you can pay.'

Though she had insisted she would be paying for the meal, the moment she got back to her bedroom, fretting at the likelihood of jaw-dropping décor with matching prices at his favourite restaurant, she checked her online bank account's balance. Thankfully she wasn't yet in the red.

But it turned out that the restaurant was a traditional bistro, located in the back streets of St Germain. The menu proudly announced that it had been established in 1912. She guessed that the décor—Bakelite lights, simple wooden tables and chairs, tiled floors—hadn't changed a whole lot in all that time. It was utterly charming.

After they'd been shown to their seats by the maître d' she continued to look around. 'It's really lovely here.'

'This is one of my favourite restaurants in Paris. The cooking is excellent and the service friendly.'

Yes, and it was also very romantic, with its low lighting and small, intimate tables with a single candle on each. In fact they were surrounded by fellow diners who were totally engrossed in one another.

This was awkward.

She shuffled in her seat and looked away from the amused glance he threw in her direction.

She was saved from further embarrassment by the arrival of their waiter, who brought them a glass of champagne along with their menus.

Holding his glass up towards her, Patrick said, 'Here's to the success of Little Fire.'

Taken aback by the sincerity in his voice, and his support of her cherished dreams, she felt unexpected tears form at the backs of her eyes. She blinked them away rapidly and took a sip of her champagne.

She read the menu with both relief—she could afford the prices—and growing excitement. Every item on the menu was a mouthwatering classic of French cuisine.

'They have Grand Marnier soufflé for dessert—I'm going to *have* to order that.'

'Why don't you order dinner for both of us?'

She looked from him back to the menu and then back at him, taken aback and slightly horrified. 'But I have no idea what you like.'

He shrugged with amusement. 'I don't care.'

Ed would have walked over hot coals rather than allow her to order for him.

'Are you sure?'

He watched her with an assuredness and yet an intimacy that had her looking back down at the menu with a ricocheting heart.

'Absolutely.'

As she ordered she couldn't stop fretting that he wouldn't like her choices. She exhaled in relief when he proclaimed the Pinot Noir she had chosen perfect. But when his starter of rillettes and her warm artichoke salad arrived she pushed the food around her plate nervously.

'Aideen.'

She looked up at the command in his voice and her breath stalled when she looked into his formidable serious eyes.

'My food is delicious… Why are you so nervous?'

Giddy relief mixed with her trepidation, causing nervous energy to flow through her veins. She inhaled a shaky breath. 'I guess I'm waiting for an argument.'

'Is that what would have happened with your ex?'

'Yes.'

A tense silence settled between them. A quick glance told her that he was still studying her.

'How about we leave him in the past and you assume that I'm an okay guy?'

He said it with such quiet forcefulness that her stomach and heart did a simultaneous flip. God, he was right.

She lifted her head and met his gaze. 'You're right. And you're more than an okay guy.'

He gave a wry smile. 'I guess I don't have to worry about getting a big ego around you.'

With a cheeky grin she said, 'I compliment where it's deserved.'

'Are you telling me I have to work harder to earn your compliments?'

'Possibly.'

His eyebrow rose slowly and sexily and at the same time his eyes darkened. In a low, suggestive voice he said, 'I'll have to remember that.'

No! That wasn't what she'd meant! And why was she blushing? And why was her heart hammering in her chest? And did the couple next to them *have* to look so in love?

They spent the rest of the meal chatting about the countries they had visited, the movies they loved, the books they adored, but beneath all that civility a spiralling web of deep attraction was growing between them all the time. In every look, in every smile.

And the intimacy was only added to by her excitement at the amount of new books and places she had to try, based on his enthusiastic descriptions. It was as though a whole new and exciting world was opening up to her because of him.

'*Mademoiselle*, would you care to follow me to the kitchen?'

Confused, Aideen looked at their waiter. She'd only just noticed he was standing there, and said, 'Sorry...?'

'The chef is waiting for you.'

Perplexed, she looked towards Patrick, in the hope that he might understand what was going on.

With a sexy grin, his eyes alight with mischief, he said, 'Remember how you said you wanted to learn how to make a soufflé? Well, this restaurant is world-famous for them. You'll find no better place to learn.'

Dumbstruck, she stared at him. She leant towards him and whispered, 'What if I mess up? You've seen the way I work in the kitchen. This is a professional kitchen, for crying out loud. I might set off the fire alarm or something like that.'

'Maybe the chef will teach you how to work tidily as a bonus?'

She gave the waiter a quick smile and whispered impatiently, 'Patrick, I'm serious.'

He shook his head, amused. 'Go and have some fun. You're the one saying all the time that we both need to be spontaneous. Well, now's your chance.'

She sat back and took a deep breath. 'You're right.'

The waiter held her chair as she stood. She moved to the side of the table and leant over and kissed Patrick's cheek. 'This is the best surprise ever. Thank you.'

A while later Aideen returned to their table, triumphantly holding the biggest soufflé Patrick had ever seen, and smiling so brightly that the people at the tables around them burst into spontaneous applause. She took a playful bow, then sat and looked at the dessert, enraptured. The woman at the next table leant across and admired the creation, and Aideen enthusiastically described her experience in the kitchen.

He could not stop watching the delight dancing in her eyes, the warmth and humour with which she spoke to the other woman.

Two things hit him at once. First, the realisation that tonight wasn't just about helping Aideen and giving her support. He genuinely wanted to be in her company. He wanted to get to know her better. For the first time in years he had met someone he could talk to—a woman he deeply admired for her optimistic and determined take on life. And secondly the realisation came that he wanted her in his life as he'd never wanted a woman before.

Both things left him absolutely confounded.

CHAPTER EIGHT

ALL THE WAY home in the car they had chatted, and Patrick had teased her when she'd got Bernard to switch on the radio and then sang along to the old-time hits playing. He had declined her dare to join in, but Bernard had been a more willing singing partner, and by the end even Patrick had been humming along.

But now they were home that ease had vanished, and tension filled the air as they stood in the chateau's marble-floored entrance hall.

Silence wrapped around them and her stomach did a frenzy of flips when she looked up into the bright blue of his penetrating gaze. Dressed in a slim charcoal-grey suit and white shirt, he looked impossibly big and imposing.

Her insides went into freefall when his hand reached out and a finger trailed lightly against her forearm.

'I enjoyed tonight.'

Her body ached to fall against the hard muscle of his. To feel the crush of his mouth. But she didn't want to ruin what they had. Their blossoming...dared she say it?... *relationship* felt so fragile she was worried that taking it any further, complicating it, might pull it down like a house of cards.

So instead she gave him a big smile and said, 'It was fun. I don't think I've laughed so much in a long time.'

'Would you like a nightcap?'

She should just go to bed. They were on dangerous territory. She could see it in his blistering stare. This need for one another was a two-way street. Much as it pained her to do so, she needed to create a diversion—to call a halt to the chemistry fizzling between them.

'A nightcap sounds good. And I have a surprise I want to show you. I'll go and fetch it from my studio.'

'Now I'm intrigued. I'll fix us some drinks in the lounge.'

Walking towards the orangery, Aideen marvelled once again at the sheer scale of the chateau. What Patrick casually called 'the lounge' was a room at least five hundred feet square, with priceless parquet on the floor, littered with modern designer sofas and rugs, and with work from world-famous artists on the light grey walls.

As she reached for the surprise she had made for him on the trestle table, she hesitated and looked at it warily. Would he even like it? He could afford something encrusted in priceless jewels. Would he think this was laughable? Would he hate it? Her ex would have made some barbed comment that would have made her feel small and insignificant.

What was she thinking? She knew Patrick wasn't like that. He never intentionally hurt people. He was a kind man, with integrity. She had to stop letting her ex colour her judgement.

He watched her over the rim of his glass, desire flooding his veins, as she walked across the lounge floor to where he was sitting on a sofa; she looked incredibly beautiful.

Over cream wide-legged trousers she wore a vibrant lilac blouse, tucked into a thick band that displayed the narrow width of her waist.

Her hair was pulled back and twisted into a low coil at the back of her head, and he had spent the entire meal wondering what it would be like to press his lips to the pale column of her throat.

It was only as she drew nearer that he realised she was carrying something.

She stopped before him and gave him an uncertain smile before holding out a rectangular box. Then with a nervous frown she changed her mind and placed it on the beaten bronze coffee table in front of him before sitting opposite.

Covered in a pale blue and dark green silk fabric, in which the two colours ran into one another in layers, and the size of a shoe box, the box was too tempting not to open.

He sat forward and placed it on his lap. What could possibly be inside? He opened it up, fascinated. Inside it was lined in a rich dark navy velvet. And it was empty.

Confused he asked, 'What is it?'

'A memory chest for Orla's baby.'

He pulled the chest closer and made a pretence of inspecting it, his heart twisting at the reminder that he wouldn't be part of their lives.

In the periphery of his vision he could see Aideen's hands clasp her knees, her knuckles growing whiter and whiter.

'I was down in the village today and I saw the box in the little antique shop. It was originally lacquered on the outside, but I reckon too much handling and love over the years had damaged it beyond repair. When I saw it I thought it would be the perfect size for a memory chest for a baby. And it felt fitting to use a box that had been loved by someone before. The material I used to cover it was inspired by the sea and the land around Mooncoyne. I thought you might like to give it to Orla's baby...as a reminder of Mooncoyne, but also to keep up the tradition your dad started.'

He winced at her words, and she must have seen it, because at once she said with dismay, 'You don't like it.'

Seeing the chest had brought home just how much he hated the prospect of not being a part of his nephew's or niece's life. Anger towards Orla, and anger that they had lost their parents so young, had him saying crossly, 'It's not that. You shouldn't have bothered. It was a waste of your time. Orla will never accept it.'

'Why not?'

He put the chest back on the coffee table and reached for his brandy. 'It's too complicated to explain.'

She shuffled in her seat and he glanced at her. He looked away from the disappointment in her face.

She cleared her throat before she spoke. 'I know we're still getting to know one another...but I do want to help.'

He picked up the chest again and twisted it in his hands. Beneath the silk there was a thick layer of padding. No sharp corners that might hurt a baby.

'I'm guessing you spent hours making this?'

She tried to shrug it off. 'Not too long—just this afternoon. It was fun to do. But if you don't like it...'

His gaze shot up at the despondency in her voice. A wounded look clouded her eyes, but she gave him a resigned shrug. As though to say, *never mind.*

She had gone to a lot of effort. He wished she hadn't. But she deserved an explanation.

His throat felt peculiarly dry, and he wanted nothing but to get up and pace. But he forced himself to sit and talk to her, face to face.

'When my dad died Orla went from being outgoing and happy to an angry, rebellious teenager overnight. I was in my final year of university. I had already started a few companies on campus, and when I graduated—a few months after my dad died—I took them off campus and into my own headquarters. Orla moved to Dublin to live with me. We had no other family. From day one she fought me. She didn't like the school I selected for her. Some days I couldn't even get her to go. When she went out with friends she was constantly home late. Just to rile me, she started to date a series of unsuitable guys. Her school reports were appalling. When I tackled her about them she said she didn't care.'

Even remembering those days caused his pulse to quicken. He gritted his teeth and tried to inhale a calming breath.

'She had just lost her dad. School reports were probably way down on her agenda.'

His pulse spiked again. 'Do you think I didn't *know* that?'

She visibly jumped at his curt tone and he closed his eyes in exasperation.

'I'm sorry. That was uncalled for.'

She nodded her acceptance of his apology and waited for him to continue.

'I could see that she was hurting, but I knew her behaviour was going to hurt her even more in the long run. I had to stop her. I was, in effect, her parent. It was my duty to protect her, and I couldn't even get her out of bed in the morning.'

'But you told me before that you were only twenty-two.'

'That didn't matter.' He had been so full of dreams and ambitions that didn't involve a stroppy teenager. But he'd loved Orla, they'd had only one another, and he had given everything to trying to sort her out. Not that it had worked.

'Of course it mattered. How many twenty-two-year-olds are equipped to parent a teenager? It was a huge responsibility to take on.'

'What other choice did I have?'

She gave him a sympathetic look. 'I know. But don't downplay what you had to face. It was *huge*. Most people that age would have struggled. Many wouldn't have taken it on.' She paused for a minute, and then said in a quiet voice, 'It must have been a really difficult time for you both.'

'Yes, it was. I was getting pressure from her school. Work was crazy. I had to travel, so I employed a housekeeper—in truth she was a trained nanny, but I couldn't tell Orla that. She, too, constantly struggled with Orla. I used to come home from travelling, exhausted, to a sister who used to yell at me that she hated me. That I wasn't her dad and I should stop trying to act like it.'

'What did you argue about?'

'Everything. Her clothes, her going out, her curfew, the housekeeper… But the biggest thing was her refusal to go to school.'

'Did you consider moving her to a different school? Maybe she wasn't happy there?'

'After the fight I'd had to get her into that school there was no way I was moving her. It was the best school in Dublin. And she wouldn't even give it a chance. I told her she had to give it a year, but she wouldn't listen.'

'What do you mean, it was the best school in Dublin?'

'It was consistently in the top three for academic results in the entire country.'

'Was Orla academic? Are you certain the school suited her?'

He looked skywards. 'She would have been academic if she had applied herself. Instead she spent her days stockpiling make-up and texting on her phone. In the end I even moved us to a different part of the city, where she didn't have as many distractions. I confiscated her phone and stopped her allowance, but she still fought me all the way.'

'Maybe you should have given her some say in what school she went to. Included her in the decision-making. She had lost her dad, moved away from her friends…my guess is she was feeling pretty confused. Did you both talk through all that?'

'I was up to my eyes with work. And any time we spoke she ended up storming off, refusing to speak to me.'

'When I was that age most sixteen-year-olds I knew were pretty good at looking after themselves and knowing what they needed.'

She paused and rubbed her hands up and down the soft cream wool material of her trousers before giving him a tentative smile.

'I know this is easy for me to say, standing on the outside… Heaven knows, I'm only too aware how easy it is to get caught up in the messy dynamics of a relationship… how acute the hurt can be when it's someone we really care about… It can be hard to think objectively, to understand where we went wrong, how we could do things differently in the future.'

Again she paused, and gave him an apologetic smile, as though to forewarn him that he wasn't going to like what she was about to say.

She inhaled a deep breath. 'But maybe you should have allowed her to make some of the decisions herself... or made a joint decision. Not you deciding everything, controlling everything.'

His spine arched defensively at her words. 'I had to protect her.'

'Maybe she needed her big brother more than she needed a father figure... She was grieving for her dad. She would probably have resisted anyone who tried taking his place. I know I would.'

Some of what she'd said was starting to make him feel really uncomfortable. He hated remembering that time—how he'd floundered, the frustration of knowing he was losing Orla day by day.

As much to her as himself, he said, 'So it was all my fault?'

She moved to the edge of the sofa. 'No. Not at all. You were worried about her, and understandably wanted to do right by her. Protect her. But maybe you should have stopped and tried to understand what she needed, rather than what you *thought* she needed.'

'Well, she has made it pretty clear that now she needs me out of her life. Two years ago she left for Madrid, and now she rarely answers my calls. Before our dad died we were so close—she used to tell me everything. Now we have nothing.'

'Maybe the baby will bring you both closer?'

He gave a sharp laugh. 'I don't think so. She was over five months pregnant before I found out. And that was only because I flew over to see her. She admitted she hadn't planned on telling me. And she wouldn't tell me who the father is.'

'Why is that of any importance?'

She *had* to be kidding. 'Because he left her—the coward. And I would like to have a word with him and set him straight on parental responsibility.'

At that she smiled, and then her smile broke into laughter. He watched her, bewildered. And then he got it. He sounded like an old-fashioned controlling father.

He rolled his eyes. 'Next thing I'll be marching them both up the aisle, a shotgun in my arms.'

This only made her laugh even more. It lifted the whole mood in the room and gave him a little perspective.

'Okay, tracking down the father isn't going to be on my list of priorities.'

'Glad to hear it.' Her head tilted and she gave him a small smile. 'I really admire how you took on the responsibility of caring for Orla. You did your best in very difficult circumstances. My take on it, for what it's worth, is that if you stop pushing she'll come back to you. We all need and want family support. It's not something we naturally walk away from. And now that Orla is having a baby she needs your support more than ever before.'

He had to admire her optimism. 'I think things are too fractured for that.'

'You were the one who said you admired me for restarting my business. How about you try to restart your relationship with Orla? Think about what you would do differently so that you can have a better relationship with her.'

She made it sound so simple. 'I don't know...I don't want to upset her at this late stage of her pregnancy.'

'I understand that, but she needs you.'

'Orla wouldn't agree with you, I'm afraid.'

Even he heard the exhaustion in his own voice. He stared up at the ceiling. His little sister...pregnant. He just couldn't get his head around it. How would their dad have reacted? He would have worried, but supported Orla one hundred per cent. His dad had had unconditional love down to an art form.

Across from him, Aideen sighed. 'Patrick, I really think you need to cut yourself some slack. You were only in your early twenties. You were running several rapidly expanding multimillion-pound businesses and trying to parent a teenage girl. You did your best. Sure, you made mistakes. Haven't we all? But, as you've said to me, that's in the past. Focus on the future now. You have to think about the next generation in your family. Your nephew or niece will need you. Orla's baby deserves to have you in its life.'

His gut tightened. She was right. But what if he caused Orla more upset? What if they had yet another bitter argument? He would never forgive himself if something happened to her or the baby because of him.

He picked up the chest, the material smooth against his skin. 'I would like to keep this, if that's okay with you. Hopefully some day I'll get the chance to give it to Orla and her baby. It's beautifully made.'

He genuinely looked as though he loved the chest, and Aideen prayed that a time would come when he could give it to Orla. She could see how much the rift was hurting him.

'Were the arguments with Orla one of the reasons why you moved to Ashbrooke?'

'Partially... And in truth they prompted my move here to the chateau, as well. I love both houses, and I'm proud of the restoration I've carried out at Ashbrooke. It would have been terrible to see it fall into further decay when it's of such historic importance. At the same time, I *did* need to retreat and focus on my businesses. They were growing at a rate even I hadn't anticipated. But I also needed some head space after years of arguing with Orla. My apartments both in Dublin and in Paris held too many memories. Orla moved to Paris and lived in my apartment when she was expelled from school. It was pretty tense, to say the least—especially when I arrived to find she had moved two friends in with her.'

'You didn't tell me that she was expelled.'

'Amongst other things. She came to Paris to attend a language school, but she dropped out of there, too. She said she'd learn French faster working in a bar.'

She didn't understand why he sounded so exasperated. 'But that was *good*—she was taking on responsibility for herself and learning to be independent.'

'You didn't see the bar she was working in.'

'Am I right in guessing you didn't allow her to keep working there?'

'Too right. She was on the first plane back to Ireland.'

'How old was she?'

'Eighteen.'

She inhaled a deep breath. 'Were there any other options other than sending her home? She was an adult, after all.'

'She certainly wasn't *acting* like an adult.'

'Did sending her back to Ireland work? Did it help your relationship?'

He glanced at her briefly and then looked away. 'No.'

'Would you do anything differently if you had that time again?'

He looked thrown by her question. For a good few minutes they sat in silence, his gaze trained on a spot in the far distance.

'I would do a lot of things differently.'

His thumb travelled again over the silk of the chest, and when he looked up she realised the pale blue of the material was a close match to the colour of his eyes.

He held her gaze and said, 'You're the first person I've ever told any of this to.'

'What do you mean?'

'Exactly that. I never told anyone about the problems we were having.'

'Not the school or your friends?'

'No.'

'You mean you carried all of this on your own?'

'Orla and I only had one another. It didn't seem right to tell anyone else what was happening. It was private—between the two of us. Family problems should stay within the walls of a home.'

'But not something as big as this, Patrick. Not when you're on your own, with no one to ask for advice or just talk it through with. It must have been so tough for you.'

Bittersweet sadness caught in her chest. She was honoured and moved that he had told her. But she also felt a heavy sadness that he had been burdened with this for so long.

'You shouldn't have carried it on your own.'

A solemn, serious gaze met hers. 'I could level the same accusation at you.'

Emotion took a firm grip of her throat. 'You're right… It's hard to speak when you're hurting, when you're embarrassed and loaded down with guilt.'

'I'm glad I did tell you.' A smile played at the corner

of his mouth and he added, 'I never thought I would say this, but it's actually a relief to talk about it.'

It felt so good to see him smile. 'I'm glad, too.'

He considered her for a while, and her cheeks began to flame at the way his eyes darkened. An emotional connection pinged between them and her heart slowed to a solid throb.

In a low voice he said, 'I've been thinking over what you said about having more fun, and I've lined up a surprise for you tomorrow.'

Her heart began to race again, and to cover the wide smile of excitement that threatened to break on her mouth at any second she eyed him suspiciously. 'I hope it's not a triathlon, or something crazy like that.'

He shook his head with amusement, 'No, but I reckon you'd be pretty lethal in a triathlon—if the competitive way you play tennis is anything to go by.'

'You might be right, but I'm not the best of swimmers.'

'Really? You can't live by the sea and not be able to swim! When we get back to Ashbrooke I'll give you some lessons in the lough.'

Was he serious? He seemed to be. Mixed emotions assailed her at once, and a crazy excitement to know that he would want to do something like that. That there might be some type of future for them beyond Paris.

But what if she was wrong? Was she reading way too much into this? Was she crazy to believe and trust in a man enough to even *contemplate* the possibility of some type of future with him?

Her doubts and fears won out and she dismissed his suggestion with a laugh, praying it would mask the embarrassing frozen expression of hope on her face. 'Only if I can wear a wetsuit. The water is pretty cold in the lough.'

'Wimp!'

'I am not. Anyway, I have meetings tomorrow until four. Can the surprise wait until then?'

'Perfect. I'll collect you.'

She stood up and said happily, 'It's a date. Now I'm going to bed.'

Only as she went to walk away did she realise what she had said.

'Not that it's really a date or anything like that… You know what I mean.'

He, too, stood, and looked at her fondly, laughter in his eyes. 'Aideen…relax. And I would *like* it to be a date.'

'Would you?'

He pinned her with his gaze. 'Yes.'

His answer was such a low, sexy drawl that goose-bumps popped up on her skin. She gave him a skittish grin and before she embarrassed herself any further decided to make a hasty retreat. But not before she threw him another goofy smile.

As she walked out of the room she heard him say in the same sexy tone, 'Goodnight, Aideen. Sleep well.'

A delicious, deep shiver of anticipation ran the length of her body.

CHAPTER NINE

THE FOLLOWING EVENING at Issy-les-Moulineaux heliport, close to the Eiffel Tower, a helicopter stood awaiting their arrival.

As Bernard brought the car to a halt beside the impressive machine excitement bubbled in Aideen's veins. 'Where are we going?'

Patrick considered her mischievously as he contemplated her question. 'Now, if I told you that it wouldn't be much of a surprise, would it?'

'The helicopter is enough of a surprise for me… Oh, please tell me! I hate being kept in suspense.'

'No can do, I'm afraid. The good things in life come to those who wait.'

Bernard was waiting patiently at the door for her to exit, so she stepped out of the car. When Patrick joined her and they walked towards the helicopter she asked playfully, 'So is that your philosophy on life?'

He brought them both to a stop and stepped closer. He leant down. His breath was warm against her ear when he spoke and her heart did a triple flip.

'Sometimes the anticipation and the wait can be thrilling, don't you agree?'

Heat erupted in her body and she drew back to meet

his eyes, which blistered into hers. When she finally managed to speak it was in an embarrassingly squeaky voice. 'I guess…'

His gaze changed to a look of amusement and, taking her hand in his, he led her to the helicopter, where the pilot was waiting for them with the rear door open.

As the pilot made the final checks for take-off her mind raced. Was he confirming what she suspected… that he would like more with her? She had read signals so wrongly in the past. Was she getting this wrong, too? But the way he looked at her said she wasn't getting anything wrong. He looked at her as though he would like to bed her then and there.

For the entire forty-five-minute journey they played a game of 'yes and no' in which she tried to guess their destination. She was wrong on every count, and was rapidly running out of names. It was a good job she had listened in her geography lessons in school.

But when a baroque castle appeared in the distance, with its raked roof and tall chimney stacks, she whispered, 'Oh, my…it's Château de Chalant.'

Privately owned by the Forbin family, Château de Chalant was considered one of the most beautiful castles in France. It was never open to the public.

'What are we doing here?'

'Frédéric Forbin is a friend and business associate. I called him and arranged for us to visit the chateau.'

Flabbergasted, she could only stare at him, and then down at the manicured elegant grounds as the helicopter swept towards the chateau. As the helicopter landed, she saw a man waiting for them at the bottom of the steps leading up to a terrace that then led to double wooden front door.

'Is that Frédéric?'

'No, it's the chateau director, who is expecting us. Frédéric is away travelling. The chateau is of such historical and architectural importance Frédéric employs a conservation team, headed by the director.'

As they exited the helicopter she tried to dampen down the enthusiasm fizzing in her blood. She had studied the historic textiles of Château de Chalant while at university. Now she was going to see them first-hand! She wanted to babble with excitement, but forced herself to shake the director's hand calmly.

Then both men shook hands.

'Monsieur Fitzsimon, it is a pleasure to have you back at Château de Chalant. It's been a long time.'

'Good to see you, too, Edouard.'

There was a slight catch to his voice, but despite that Patrick looked totally at ease and in no way fazed, as she was by the grandeur of the chateau. Once again she was struck by how different his life was from hers—how used he was to mixing in the world of wealth and power.

Edouard led them into the vast entrance hall of the chateau, where two sweeping marble stone staircases, one at either side, led up to a wooden gallery that encircled the hall. Historic tapestries hung from the walls.

Unable to help herself, she walked to a sixteenth-century oak chair and exclaimed, 'Oh, wow! That chair is upholstered in Avalan fabric. I've never seen it in real life before; only in textbooks.'

The director looked at her in surprise. 'Not many people would recognise this fabric—are you a historian?'

'No, I'm a textile designer, but I have a passion for historical fabrics. I love how designs and patterns tell us so much about the period of history they were produced in, about the social norms and conditions.'

'Well, you're in for a treat this evening.' The director turned to Patrick. 'I will leave you and Mademoiselle Ryan to tour the chateau alone. If you need anything I shall be in my office.'

As they walked away from the entrance hall she asked, intrigued, 'Why did you bring me here?'

'This is the most beautiful building I have ever visited. I thought you would enjoy it. But now I'm especially glad that I organised the trip. I hadn't realised you were so passionate and knowledgeable about historical textiles.'

'I have a lot of hidden talents you don't know about.'

With a glint in his eye he said, 'Is that right?'

She mumbled, 'Yes…' and turned away, heat flooding her cheeks. She felt as though she was floating on air between the excitement of being here and her desperation to feel his lips on hers again, to be encompassed by his size and strength.

He was right. Anticipation was thrilling. But what if that anticipation led to nothing?

The first room he took her to was the print room. As Aideen looked around the room in astonishment he explained, 'It was a tradition for royalty and the gentry to collect expensive prints and paste them directly on to the walls.'

Some of the black and white prints illustrated faraway picturesque locations—the lakes of Northern Italy, Bavarian forests… Animal prints showed farmyard scenes of cows and sheep; another was of a spaniel, standing before a raging river.

She was blown away by the sheer extravagance of the room. Priceless print after print covered the entirety of the four walls. 'They're beautiful—what incredible detail.'

'This room was created by Princess Isabella—it's said Prince Henri of Chalant built this chateau as a symbol of his love for her, before they married.'

'That's so romantic.'

He didn't respond, and when she turned to him the air was compressed in her lungs. He stood in the middle of the room, his hands in his pockets, gazing at her intently. He wore navy chinos and a white polo shirt. His bare arms were beautifully carved with taut muscle, the skin lightly tanned with a dusting of dark hair.

She even fancied his arms. Was there any hope for her?

An awareness passed between them and she suddenly grew shy, giving him a quick smile before walking away to inspect other prints.

But he made for the door and gestured her to follow. 'If you think that's romantic let me show you something else.'

She followed him down the corridor until he stopped at a closed door.

'Close your eyes and I'll lead you in.'

She eyed him suspiciously. 'You're not going to play a trick on me, are you? Lead me down into the dungeon or something like that?'

His head tilted and he gave her a sexy grin that sent her pulse into orbit. 'As intriguing as that suggestion sounds… no, I'm not going to take you to the dungeon.' Then he gave her an admonishing look and said, 'Now, for once will you please try and trust me and close your eyes?'

She held her breath as his hand took hers. She heard the door open and then he slowly led her forward for about ten paces. She felt oddly vulnerable, and her hand tightened on his of its own accord.

All her senses were attuned to the solid strength of his hand, the smooth warmth of his skin, the torturous pleasure of being so physically close to him…

'Open your eyes.'

She gasped in astonishment. It was the most dazzling room she'd ever seen. It was like something out of a fairytale. Or a room she imagined might have been in a Russian royal palace.

She twisted around in amazement, shaking her head. The double-height rectangular room was a feast of gilded Baroque plasterwork. It was opulent and outrageous in its beauty. And so much fun she couldn't help but laugh.

'It's absolutely stunning! It's like standing in the middle of an exquisite piece of twenty-four-carat gold jewellery'

'It's called the Gold Room. Prince Henri commissioned it to celebrate Isabella's fiftieth birthday.'

She gave him a wistful smile. 'He really was romantic, wasn't he?'

He gave a light shrug and looked up at the intricate gilt stucco work on the ceiling. 'I guess when you find the love of your life you just want to celebrate it.'

A rush of emotion tore through her body. 'It must be nice to feel so loved.'

Their eyes met briefly and they both looked away at the same time.

She moved through the silent room, unexpected tears clouding her vision. The past year might have made her wary of others, but at the same time there was an emptiness in her heart. She wanted to be in love. Desperately.

With each passing day, as they got to know each other,

things were changing between her and Patrick. They now shared an intimacy, an ease with one another that had her thinking maybe they had something between them… something significant. Patrick telling her last night about Orla had been particularly moving, and also momentous. It was as though he had finally allowed her to step fully into his life.

Behind her, he called, 'Are you ready to see some more rooms?'

She nodded, but was slow to turn around. Was he feeling the same intensity she was? This need to connect on a different level?

An hour later her head swam as she tried once again to orientate herself in the vastness of the chateau. They had passed through room after room, all full of sumptuous furniture and historically significant textiles and antiques. And yet, somewhat miraculously, Château Chalant retained an air of intimacy. Was it because it had been built to celebrate love?

Eventually they found themselves back in the entrance hall. For some reason she didn't want their time here to end. She wanted to stay here with him a little longer.

With a heavy heart she said, as brightly as she could, 'Thank you for bringing me here—it really is a magical place.'

'The tour isn't over yet. I have kept the best room for last.'

Intrigued, she followed him into a vast, empty room with marble flooring. A bow window overlooked the gardens to the rear of the chateau.

She looked around, perplexed, taking in the ornate plasterwork on the domed ceilings and alcoves. Painted a silvery white, the sunlit room was a sleeping silent oasis, even in the tranquillity of the chateau.

'Why is there no furniture?' She jumped to hear her own voice echoing noisily around the room.

He had remained standing close to the doorway, while she was now perched on the sill of the bow window.

'It helps with the acoustics.'

What had been a whisper from Patrick echoed loudly across the room.

Trying it herself, she whispered, 'This is amazing.'

Again her voice barrelled across the room in a loud echo.

'It's called the Whispering Room. In days gone by apparently it wasn't accepted for courting couples to stand too close to one another, so young lovers would use this room to whisper messages to one another.'

'That's so sweet.'

'I sometimes wonder what they would have said.'

As he stood and watched her something broke inside her, and she whispered from her heart. 'They wished they could be together…they longed for the day they could be.'

For the longest while he stared at her. Had he heard her whisper? Maybe it would be better if he hadn't.

But then he whispered back, 'You're lovely.'

He said it so gently and with such sincerity she thought her heart was going to break in two. 'You're pretty special, too.'

'I like you, Aideen Ryan.'

Had she heard right? Had she imagined it? His smile said otherwise.

Through a throat thick with bittersweet happiness she whispered, 'I like you, too, Patrick Fitzsimon.'

He walked slowly to her, and although she was leaning against the windowsill her legs began to wobble.

He came to a stop before her and she looked up into his dazzling blue eyes. His body shifted towards her. His hand twitched at his side and at the same time her body ached with the need for his touch.

His head moved slowly down, her heart speeding up with every inch closer he came, until his lips landed gently on hers. His mouth moved against hers, slowly and lightly, and she thought she might faint because it was so tender and right.

When he pulled away from the kiss he brought his forehead to lie against hers. His incredible blue gaze held hers. It felt as though he was spearing her heart with the silent communication of the need of a man for a woman.

'Would you like a tour of the grounds?'

Dazed, she whispered, 'Yes, please.'

They made their way through the extensive gardens surrounding the chateau and a silence fell between them. She tried to keep her distance from him, but invariably found herself swaying towards him. As she walked along the gravelled paths, the late-evening sun warm on her skin, she bumped against him and he pulled her towards him, wrapping his arm about her waist. They shared a quick look and her insides tumbled to see the desire in his hooded eyes.

She felt drunk with happiness just being there…being with him. And every cell in her body was electrified by being so close to him. A lazy, intoxicating tendril of physical desire coiled around her body. Her skin felt flushed and a deep pulse resonated in her lips.

But that nagging thought that this was not reality, that

she did not belong here, continued to rumble at the back of her brain. Even as she tried her best to ignore it.

They didn't stop walking until they reached an extensive lake with a small island in the centre. They stopped on the pebbled beach, where a rowing boat lay beached to one side.

He went immediately to it and pulled it towards the lake. Holding it in the water, he called, 'Come on—what are you waiting for?'

She looked around doubtfully, wondering for a moment if it would be allowed. But then she rushed towards the water. She pulled off her ballet flats, held up her midi-skirt and jumped on board, giving a cry of laughter when the boat wobbled.

Patrick strengthened his grip on her elbow, and as she sat down he pushed the boat out further and in one fluid motion jumped on board himself. The boat wobbled even more, but as soon as he sat opposite her it steadied.

His oar strokes were long and even and they were quickly out in the middle of the lake. Other than evening birdsong and the swoosh of the oars in the water there wasn't another sound.

'This is my first time ever being out in a rowing boat.'

He looked at her incredulously. 'Seriously? How did you get to be…?'

'Twenty-eight.'

'How did you get to be twenty-eight without ever being out in a rowing boat?'

'Beats me.'

He continued to row and she tried not to stare at the way his biceps flexed with each pull of the oar.

'You'll have to have a go at rowing.'

'Really?'

'Climb over here into the centre. Try not to wobble the boat too much. I'll move to your seat.'

As she moved down the boat it began to bob precariously. She gave a little shout of alarm and gratefully grabbed on to his outstretched arm. As she fell forward she twisted, and ended up landing in his arms, her bottom firmly wedged in his lap.

His hand came to rest just above her waist, its heat on the thin cotton of her blouse sending a shiver of pleasure through her. His thighs, his chest, as they pressed against her, felt as though they were made of steel. Electric blue eyes met hers. Her pulse leapt. It would be so easy to lean forward, to kiss those firm lips again. To inhale his scent.

He gave a low growl. 'If you don't climb off me in the next five seconds I won't be responsible for what I do next.'

She leapt away—and instantly regretted doing so.

After he had moved to the stern of the boat she started rowing. The boat moved with ease and she thought with unjustified satisfaction that she had this rowing lark immediately sussed. But then they started going in circles, and she couldn't get the boat to go in a straight line. The fits of giggles that accompanied her attempts weren't much help.

Opposite her, he threw his head into his hands and then looked at her with amusement.

Time and time again he demonstrated the motion she should be using, but the boat still twisted. He suggested they swop places again but, determined, she refused to give up.

And finally she did it. The boat went in one direction. Straight back to shore. She didn't try to alter their course in case she started circling again.

As they neared the small beach he moved confidently to the bow and jumped ashore. Then he hoisted the boat on to the stones. He held her hand as she leapt off. She knew she was grinning at him like a fool but couldn't stop herself. She hadn't laughed so much in a very long time.

He watched her with a smile, and for a while she looked at him happily, but her smile finally faded as his stare grew darker. He took a step closer. Shots of awareness flew through her.

An intensity swirled in the air between them. Everything had changed since Patrick had opened up to her last night. She felt trusted. Her heart drummed a slow beat of deep appreciation, wonder, and attraction to this man.

Closer and closer he came, his intense blue eyes transfixing her. Her breath grew more rapid. Her lips pulsed with the need to feel his mouth on hers again. Her legs grew weak.

When he was no more than an inch from her, she was the first to give in. Her body swayed and she fell against his hardness. Her hands curled around his biceps. Against her thumb, which rested at the side of his chest, she could feel his heartbeat, which was pounding even faster than hers.

'I didn't ask before, so I should this time round. Can I kiss you?'

Her heart stuttered at his question. It was the sweetest thing anyone had ever said to her. Even if she'd wanted to there was no way she could pull away from him—from his warm breath, the overwhelming pull of his hard body, the dizzying inhalation of his scent.

She placed her hands on his shoulders, closed her eyes, and gave a small sigh of assent as she pulled his lips down to hers.

Whereas their earlier kiss had been slow and sweet, tentative and testing, this kiss was instantly intense, wild. Their hands explored each other's bodies with hunger. It was a kiss that might easily become a lot more.

She was quickly losing herself.

As one, they pulled away at the same time. As though they both knew it might quickly spiral into something neither wanted...*yet.*

She pressed a hand to her swollen lips and blushed. She had to hide how much he affected her. Because in truth she was close to tears...of happiness and despair.

'I'll tell you this much, Patrick Fitzsimon, you certainly haven't forgotten how to kiss in all that time you've been locked away in your office.'

He looked at her with amusement. 'Glad to hear it.'

But then dark need flared in his eyes and her insides melted.

'I want you, Aideen.'

Her heart felt as if it was going to burst right out of her chest. She so desperately wanted to say *Yes, please* and not give a thought to the consequences. But it wasn't that simple.

'Are you sure? Won't it...complicate things?'

His hand came to rest on her cheek and he gazed at her solemnly while his thumb stroked her skin. 'I like you. A lot. It doesn't have to be complicated. I promise you, no game playing. But if this is not right for you I'll back off.'

No! She didn't want that.

His touch, his scent, the magnetic pull of his body might be making her head reel so much that she could barely formulate a thought, but she knew that much. She didn't want this to end.

When he had whispered 'I like you' in the Whispering Room, he had looked at her with such intense integrity and honour it had been like a bomb detonating in her brain. And just like that she'd realised she was in love with this kind, generous, strong man. And, God help her, she knew she would happily take a few days in his arms over the alternative: never knowing what it would be like to be held by him.

Right now, to have loved and lost was definitely better than never to have loved at all. She didn't want to think about the future. Living in the present was all that mattered.

She scrunched her eyes shut for a moment, and when she opened them again she said, with a huge smile, 'Okay.'

It was as though a weight had been lifted off her shoulders. She had never felt so exhilarated in her entire life. To feel this good it must mean it was the right decision. Mustn't it?

All the way back to Paris she regaled him with stories of her encounters with fashion designers. He held her hand throughout, his thumb caressing the soft smoothness of her palm, and every now and again she would stutter and lose her train of thought as his fingers lightly traced along her inner arm.

Each time she shivered and her eyes grew heavy he wondered if her entire body was that sensitive. And his pulse moved up another notch.

When the helicopter landed Bernard was waiting to take them to his private club, close to the Eiffel Tower.

She gasped beside him when the maître d' of the club's restaurant directed them to their table in the rooftop terrace restaurant. And he totally understood why. Because, no matter how many times he came here himself, the sheer size and beauty of the Eiffel Tower this close up was truly impressive.

Their table, as he'd requested, was beside the low-level redbrick wall of the terrace, with her chair facing out towards the tower, he sitting to her side.

Once the maître d' had gone she stared at him, her huge chocolate eyes dancing in merriment, and then she put a hand over her mouth in disbelief. 'Oh, my God, I can't believe this place. It's incredible.'

'The club is one of the closest buildings to the tower.'

Their waiter arrived with the champagne he had pre-ordered and opened the bottle with a satisfying pop. He filled the flute glasses that already sat on the white-linen-topped table and retreated once he had placed the bottle in an ice bucket to the side.

She took a sip of champagne. And then another. 'Wow! That's the nicest champagne I have ever tasted. It's sharp, but with a gorgeous biscuit undertone.' She turned again to the tower and reached her hand out towards it. 'I feel like I can almost touch it.'

Then, as she looked around the rest of the terrace, he saw her expression grow even more radiant.

'This club is so impressive—' She stopped and blushed, and dropped her chin on to her cupped hand. 'Oh, dear. I must sound like the most uncultured date you've ever had.'

'You make a refreshing change from some of the jaded dates I've had in the past.'

She gave him a suspicious look. 'That's good...I think.'

If only she knew how many times in the past he had been left speechless by the cynicism and sense of entitlement of some of his previous conquests. 'That's *very* good.'

As they both leant forward to place their glasses on the table their arms touched and a silent energy bound them together. He moved closer and her lips parted ever so slightly. Hunger powered through him. He inhaled her scent. The scent that now lingered in the air of the chateau and one he looked forward to inhaling each day when he returned from his meetings.

Slowly their heads moved towards one another. Her head tilted to the side and passion flared in her eyes. Inch by inch they drew closer, and he had to stifle a groan when his lips met the soft fullness of hers.

When he pulled away he was amused by how dazed she looked, and said, 'You're the best date I've ever had.'

She blushed furiously and waved away his words, but her wide smile told of her delight.

A group of waiters arrived with the food he had also pre-ordered, earlier in the day. The surprise and glee with which she eyed the food had him smiling to himself in pleasure.

Once the waiters had departed she looked mischievously from the tiers of mouth-watering cakes to him. 'It's a bit late in the evening for afternoon tea, I would have thought.'

'You said you loved millefeuille.'

Shaking her head, she bent to inspect the three-tier stand. 'All the cakes I used to dream of when I was a student: opera cake, éclairs, *macarons*…even miniature tarte Tatin.' She looked at him, her throat working. 'Thank you.' She stopped as tears filled her eyes. 'This is so considerate of you…' And then she laughed. 'I'm actually lost for words.'

He gave her a smile. 'Then don't speak. Just eat.'

He poured her some tea while she selected a mille-feuille. He chose a raspberry *macaron*, filled with fresh raspberries and raspberry cream.

She closed her eyes as she ate the first forkful of millefeuille. And he almost choked on his *macaron*. She looked incredibly sensual, with her head tilted back, pleasure written all over her face. He glared at a man sitting at a nearby table who was also captivated by her, a powerful surge of possessiveness taking him by surprise.

Her happiness was increasingly becoming everything to him. It was as though he was plugged into her emotions and felt them as keenly as she did. When she was happy he was elated. When she was sad or upset his heart plummeted. He had never before felt so attuned to another person.

It was both incredible and awful at the same time. Incredible that he could be so close to another person that he felt her emotions. Awful because it would make saying goodbye all the more difficult.

As they ate they spoke about their past experiences in Paris, with the tower lighting up before them as the sun set. They both looked towards its graceful night-time beauty, but he quickly looked back at her.

Her eyes shone with happiness. She was curled into her seat so that her body was directed towards him, even though her gaze was still on the tower. Her lipstick had faded from brilliant red to a faint blush.

Unable to stop himself, he leant towards her and said her name gently. She turned to face him fully with a smile and his hand reached forward to brush a flake of pastry from her lips. At least that was what he intended to do.

He removed the pastry, all right, but his finger lingered on her lips, desire coiling in his stomach.

At first she stared at him in surprise, but then her gaze darkened. He lowered his finger but moved forward in his chair, wanting to be closer to her...

Awareness of his masculinity, of his raw power, flooded Aideen's body and her head began to swim at the heat and scent of his skin.

'I want you.'

It was the barest of whispers and she drew back a little, needing to search his eyes, to see if she had heard right. The hooded intensity there told her she had heard correctly.

Her throat was too dry to speak so she mouthed the words *me, too.*

His eyes darkened even more as they traced the movement of her lips.

Immediately he stood and held out his hand to her. Her insides had gone all funny and she worried that her legs wouldn't carry her.

Just as they were about to leave, the tower started its hourly light show, and as she stood watching the twinkling lights, enraptured, he held her from behind, his hands encircling her waist, his thumbs drawing lazy sensual patterns up and over her ribs.

In the back of the car she tried not to tremble as he held her hand. Silent, powerful restraint pulsated from his rigid body.

Once home, he threw open the front door and pulled her into the darkness, backed her against the wall.

He stood so close the heat from his body curled around her, and she gasped when his fingers moved to undo the top buttons of her blouse. Once open, he pulled it down to expose both shoulders. Slowly he left a trail of soft, knee-weakening kisses along her collarbone and the sensitive ridge of her neck, his fingers dragging down the apricot-coloured lace straps of her bra, leaving a burning trail of heat on her skin.

A deep moan of pleasure ricocheted from deep inside her. Her fingers scratched against the cool wall at her back, desperate to cling to anything.

'I want to make love to you.'

For the longest while she fought to answer him, her mind distracted as he continued to caress her earlobe, her neck.

The absolute gorgeousness of inhaling him… The bone-melting thrill of his large, muscular body being so close… The desperate need to touch every inch of him… To have his body crushed against hers. To have him make love to her.

Her hands clasped his face and drew him up to face her. Her breath hitched as his burning gaze met hers.

'I want you, too.'

CHAPTER TEN

A BUBBLE OF happiness and excitement burst in Aideen's heart and spread little beads of serenity throughout her body.

Beside her, twisted on to his side and facing away from her, Patrick slept, his breathing a slow and steady rhythm. The top sheet rested below his waist, and the beautiful, muscular expanse of his back was only inches away.

In the pre-dawn light she could just about make out the faint scar that ran for a few inches just below his shoulderblade. What had caused it? There was so much she wanted to know about him. So much more to fall in love with. Simple everyday events like him brushing his teeth, the order in which he dressed, shaved.

She moved closer and lowered her head against the hard muscles of his back, inhaling the musky, salty notes of his scent which always made her light-headed with desire.

Last night had been more exhilarating and tender than she'd ever thought possible. They had made love slowly and gently, with an intensity that had had her fearing her heart would split in two. With each kiss and touch she had tried to show him what he meant to her, hoping he would see just how much she loved his strength and dignity, loved his kindness and integrity.

Throughout he had whispered words of endearment to her, his eyes dark with passion…and also with the same amazement and wonder that had had her reeling, too.

And as she fell back to sleep, as she fell into a contented, exhausted pit of happiness, she wished she could stay there, in his bed, at his side, for eternity.

Two hours later the morning sun bathed the bedroom in a golden light. In their haste they had not got around to pulling the curtains last night.

Lying on her stomach, Aideen was sleeping, her skin still flushed from their lovemaking. He leant forward and touched his mouth against hers. Her lips broke into a smile and her eyes opened, drowsy and lazy with happiness.

She gave him a contented sexy sigh. 'Good morning.'

The huskiness of her voice evoked startling images of their lovemaking last night. Images that left him reeling in disbelief and with the desire to experience it time and time again. He lowered his head and kissed the warm skin of her shoulderblade. A ribbon of pleasure unfurled in him when he inhaled the fresh vanilla and floral scent that seemed innate to her very being.

Against the sweet scent of her skin he whispered, 'Good morning to you, too.'

She edged her hip closer to him as his hand ran over her back. Her eyes met his and they shared a look so intimate it felt as though the world had stopped turning.

Eventually he found his voice. 'Did you enjoy last night?'

She looked at him innocently. 'Best night's sleep I've had in a long time.'

For that, he kissed her hard, and he didn't stop until he heard her whimper with need. When he pulled away she protested, and then nudged even closer to him, the length of her body tucking into his.

A sexy wickedness flashed on her face. 'Okay, I'll admit that it was pretty mind-blowing.'

A deep groan erupted from the core of him. He pressed his mouth against the side of her throat. He ran his hand down over her back, his thumb bumping along her spine so that she wriggled, and she wriggled even more when the entire span of his hand moved down over the firm roundness of her bottom.

'Have I ever told you that you have an incredible body?'

Her giggle echoed off the mattress and her body shimmied beneath his fingers.

'As I recall, you said something to that effect several times last night.'

'Well, you'd better get used to it, because I reckon I'm going to keep you in this bed for a very long time.'

She gave a heavy sigh and smiled. 'That sounds like heaven. Being with you is incredible. I never want it to end.'

His hand stilled and his heart sank. He'd thought this was nothing but banter and teasing. But now her words echoed in his brain. They both knew this was never going to last. Didn't they?

He glanced at her again and the joy in her eyes had turned to disquiet. Her brow drew into a frown. She twisted on to her back, pulling the sheet up around her as she did so.

'What's the matter?'

He collapsed on to his back, too, and stared up to the ceiling. 'You know this has to end… I thought we were agreed on that?'

He felt her yank the sheet a little tighter about her. 'I know. But after last night…'

After last night? Panic and disbelief had him sitting up on the side of the bed.

Without turning to face her, he said, 'I have a conference call in ten minutes. I need to get ready.'

She didn't respond, and he walked rapidly to the en-suite bathroom. He flicked on the shower and immediately stood under the stream of as yet cold water, his mind too agitated to care that his body was protesting.

As the water pounded his scalp he closed his eyes and cursed silently. He felt as though he was drowning in emotions. Drowning in feelings he didn't want to have. Drowning in how mind-blowing last night had been. And not just physically.

Making love to Aideen had been different from anything he had ever experienced. At once he'd wanted to cherish her, protect her, possess her. In the act of love-making last night he had wanted their hearts and minds to fuse together as much as he had wanted their bodies to join. He had felt emotionally wrecked after it. As though he had exposed every part of himself to her.

Had he just made the biggest mistake of his life? He had never opened himself up to another person so much. He wasn't sure how to manage the vulnerability of that. And now she was saying she wanted it never to end.

Part of him understood that. God knew it felt so good, so right, to have her by his side. He drew strength from her. From her enthusiasm, from her sense of fun, and also from her quiet compassion.

But he couldn't ever commit to a relationship. Not with its demands and hurts and misunderstandings. Not when he already lost all those he had loved. What if he messed up in years to come and lost her? Just as he'd messed up with Orla? What if he failed her as he'd failed his mum and dad?

He was no good at relationships. In the end he would only hurt her. He didn't even know what to say to her now.

When she heard the bathroom door close Aideen looked down at her trembling hands and drew in a shaky breath. What had just happened?

She had spoken the truth—that was what had happened. And she had got it all wrong.

After last night she'd thought he might feel the same way. Even this morning, when he had looked at her with such affection, she'd thought there was more to this for him than just a casual affair.

Oh, God, she was so bad at reading men. First Ed. Now Patrick. How could she have got it so wrong?

He had looked horrified when she'd said she wanted it to last for ever. She had said it unconsciously. But it had been the truth.

Humiliation burnt deep in her stomach and her heart pounded in her chest. She needed to get out of here before he returned to the bedroom.

She wrapped the sheet about her and frantically picked her clothes off the bedroom floor. And then she ran down the ornate corridor to her own bedroom.

There, she collapsed on to the bed, her pulse pounding, her entire body trembling. Her skin was burning with embarrassment, but ice was flowing through her veins.

What was she going to do? She had sworn she would never fall for a man again, and here she was in love with a billionaire who was completely out of her league. A man who had run at the first notion of her wanting more from their relationship.

What had she been *thinking*? Talk about messing up on a spectacular scale.

She needed to get away. The humiliation was too much. She couldn't stay here. She couldn't pretend not to have feelings for him.

She winced at the thought of walking away. It might mean never seeing him again. Was she really ready for that? No. But there was no alternative.

An hour later, after an extra-long shower and generally delaying as long as she could, she walked downstairs. Patrick was nowhere to be seen, so she grabbed a cup of coffee, wrestling once again with the machine, and sat at the island unit, all the while rehearsing what she was going to say to him.

Not long afterwards he arrived in the kitchen, dressed in a slim-fitting navy suit. It showed the contours of his broad-shouldered, narrow-hipped frame to perfection, and for a crazy moment she longed to go to him, to wrap her arms about his waist, lower her forehead to that impregnable masculine strength and the power of his chest. Longed to inhale him. Soap… The sweet, musky tang of his skin…

He had no right to look so gorgeous and calm when she felt so distraught. But his calmness strengthened her conviction that she was going to leave here with her dignity intact.

He glanced at his watch. 'I have another conference call in ten minutes and then some meetings in Paris later. When I get back I think we should speak.'

His tone, his words, his stance were all shutting her out. He barely looked at her. Where had the warm and kind man of last night gone? Had it all been an act?

Horrible tension filled the room. Unsaid words, hurt and humiliation were thick in the air.

She wanted things to go back to where they'd been when they had woken, or to last night. To that carefree existence where reality had been suspended.

She didn't know what he was thinking. And the vulnerability that came with that cut her to the core.

Did he regret their relationship? Did he even regret answering the door to her that night of the storm? Did he wish she had never come into his life?

He was waiting for her to say something, but her throat was closed over and she was struggling to tell him what she had rehearsed. It was as though her heart was physically preventing her from saying the words logic said she had to speak.

He came a little closer and leant a hand against the island unit, his voice less brisk now, almost sad. 'I've always told you that I never want to be in a permanent relationship. I've never lied to you, Aideen.'

First Ed had cheated on her. Now Patrick looked as though he wanted to head for the hills. She had to understand why she wasn't good enough…why she kept getting relationships wrong.

'Why don't you want to be in a relationship?'

He looked totally taken aback by her question for a while, and then frustration flared on his face. 'I'm not interested…I don't want to be tied down. I want to be able to focus on work. It's not something I've ever wanted in life.'

Was it really that simple for him? Maybe it was. Maybe he didn't need love or affection.

She couldn't think straight.

Swallowing deeply, she said in a strained voice, 'I think we should call a stop to it all…it's becoming too complicated.'

A slash of red appeared on his cheeks and his voice was cool when he spoke. 'I don't want it to end, but if that's what you wish…'

Why couldn't he fight her a little? Had last night been nothing but a figment of her imagination?

She had to pull herself together.

All along she had said this would never work, and yet after just one night in his bed she had become delusional.

Now she knew for certain that this was never going to work. That this had been nothing but a brief interlude in her life. A magical, unbelievable interlude, but one that had to end. This wasn't her world. She didn't belong here.

She stood up and placed her cup in the dishwasher before turning to him. 'I think it would be best if I leave now.'

He moved closer to her, his hands landing on his hips. 'Oh, come on, Aideen. There's no need for this. Stay. I don't want you to go. Why can't we just enjoy each other's company for a while?'

'I'm not up for a casual relationship, Patrick.'

He looked at her in exasperation. 'Fine. I'll respect that. Nothing needs to happen between us again. You don't even have a home to go to. The cottage isn't ready.'

'I'll sort something out.'

'Stay at Ashbrooke.'

'You're not getting it, are you?'

'What do you mean?'

The sheer overwhelming impact of standing so close to his powerful, addictive frame but being so adrift from him emotionally had her blurting out, 'I can't stay in Ashbrooke. I can't be around you, Patrick.'

Heat fired through her body. Her cheeks were red-hot and tears burnt at the back of her eyes. She had said too much already, but she couldn't hold back the truth. The weight of it was physically hurting her chest.

'For the simple reason that I've fallen in love with you.'

Without meaning to do so he stepped back from her.

This was all going wrong.

She wasn't supposed to be telling him she loved him.

He didn't know what to say.

And in that moment he regretted ever opening up to Aideen. He should have kept his distance. He shouldn't have let her in. Look at what had happened as a result. He'd said he didn't want to hurt her. Judging by the pained expression on her face, he had done exactly that.

'I never wanted to hurt you.'

She gave a little laugh. 'I'm sure I'll get over it.' She paused and then stood up a little straighter, looked him in the eye. 'It was never going to work anyway. I always knew that. We are from different worlds. I don't belong in this world of wealth. I want a relationship of equals— one where I bring the same as the other person. That was never going to be the case with us.'

Though she looked as though she might crumble, she gave him a wobbly smile, her eyes brimming with tears again.

With a light shrug she added, 'This was never going

to be anything more than a brief interlude of happy madness. And even though I can barely breathe right now, knowing it's over, in my heart I know I will always cherish these weeks together. I'm glad I met you. And a part of me will always love you.'

Pain and shock had him sitting there and watching her walk away. He couldn't take it in, process all that she had said.

Both of them were agreeing that being together wouldn't work.

But if that was the case why did it feel as though he was being torn apart?

Less than ten minutes later he was still trying to process all that had happened when she reappeared in the kitchen, her suitcase beside her.

'I've booked a flight back to Ireland. When you return to Ashbrooke can you bring my files and paperwork from the orangery? I haven't had time to pack them. Perhaps you can ask one of your staff to do so?'

'I'll ask William to drop them off at the cottage.'

Part of him wanted to plead with her to stay. But this was for the best. Everything had spiralled out of control. He couldn't give Aideen the type of relationship she needed and deserved.

'I'll organise for my plane to take you.'

'No! Absolutely not.'

He was about to fight her, but then he realised why she would feel the need to pay for her own transport home.

With a resigned shrug of acceptance he said, 'I'll drop you to the airport.'

'I've already asked Bernard to take me.'

Fury shot through him and he said abruptly, 'No. *I'm* taking you.'

He had hurt her and let her down. The least he could do was see her safely to the airport. Say goodbye somewhere other than in the house where they had made love.

She looked away for a few seconds, and when she spoke again, he was taken aback by the pain in her voice.

'No. Bernard is taking me.' Tears shone in her eyes. 'I just want to go.'

'Aideen...'

Angry eyes flicked to his, and her voice was raw with emotion. 'I don't understand why you're fighting me on this. I can see that deep down you want me to go.'

'That's not true.'

'Yes, it is. You fled from our bed this morning. You're distancing yourself from me—burying yourself in work. Admit it, Patrick, you're pushing me away. Like you push everyone away.'

'I have never pretended that my work doesn't come first. It has to.'

'Oh, *please*... No, it doesn't. You just want it that way. At least admit that much to yourself.' She stopped and closed her eyes for a few seconds. When she reopened them they were filled with pain. 'Bernard will drive me to the airport.'

'I want to—'

She cut across him. 'Please don't make this any harder for me. I'm humiliated enough.'

He reached for her. Anger at his own bungling of this situation had him saying sharply, 'You have no reason to feel humiliated. I should never have suggested you come to Paris. This was all a mistake on my part. I'm sorry that I hurt you. That you have these feelings for me. But

I can't reciprocate them. Not with you. Not with anyone. I don't deserve your love, Aideen. Please remember that.'

She yanked her arm free and strode away from him.

He followed her out to the front steps, but she was already getting into the waiting car. Not once did she look back towards him.

CHAPTER ELEVEN

CYCLING HOME FROM MOONCOYNE, her front basket sparsely filled with the few food items she had forced herself to buy at the weekly farmers' market in the hope that they might kick-start her appetite again, Aideen heard the low cooing of a wood pigeon. Something about its regular familiar call reassured her. It told her that the world went on spinning even though it felt as though hers had ground to a halt.

Spring was in full bloom. The trees that lined the road were no longer stark grey-brown statues, reaching up to the sky, but lush green flowing bodies of movement and life. Waves of white cow parsley littered the hedgerows on either side of her, yellow buttercup flowers popping through at intervals.

Everything was changing.

It had been a week since she had returned from Paris. She had moved back into Fuchsia Cottage immediately, not caring about the dust or the noise as the builders carried out the renovations. It wasn't as if she was getting a lot of work done anyway. Thankfully their work was due to be completed by the end of next week. Hopefully then she would be able to give her work one hundred per cent of her concentration.

She had neither seen nor heard from Patrick since she'd returned. A part of her had hoped he might contact her. See how she was doing. Which was pretty crazy, really. He was probably just relieved to move on from what had been a disastrous scenario from his point of view.

He had visibly paled when she'd said she loved him. The panic in his eyes had told her everything she needed to know. Even now her cheeks glowed bright red at that memory.

In her first days at home she had wondered if she had made the worst decision of her life, becoming so involved, so intimate with him. In those long days and sleepless nights she had lived with numbing pain and an overwhelming sense of loss. And the haunting question as to whether her judgement had been all wrong once again.

But in the days that had followed, as her initial shock and gruelling pain had subsided a little, she'd found a clarity of thinking that had evaded her all the time she was with him.

She had been so overpowered, intrigued, in love with him, that when they'd been together she hadn't been able to think straight, think objectively.

Being with him had been like being awash with emotions that left no room for perspective. A perspective that now told her that it could never have lasted. He had said from the outset that he didn't want to be in a relationship. And she knew only too well that they were from different worlds. But when she had been with him all she had known was desire, longing, excitement, happiness. An itch to bury herself into his very soul, to know him better than she even knew herself.

Now that she was away from him, those emotions had lessened and she had finally got that perspective. Though her heart was physically sore, though she could barely eat or sleep, and though she sometimes thought she was going mad with her frustration, her wanting to be near him again, she didn't regret anything.

How could she when she had experienced such intense love and passion for another person?

Yes, she had wanted it to be for ever. She hadn't wanted it to end. But better that than never to have experienced it at all. How incredibly sad it would be to live a life never knowing such love existed.

In her heart she knew he had loved her in his own way. She had seen it shining in his eyes when they had made love. In the things he had whispered to her. But he hadn't loved her enough. And that was a fact she would have to learn to live with.

Now she had to start focusing on her work again. And hope that with time the pain would subside.

She neared the junction for the turning down to the road that led to her cottage and her pulse speeded up as she passed the wide entrance to his estate. But then she brought her bike to a sudden wobbly stop.

She dismounted, turned, and stared back at the board that had appeared on the wall. A sales board, to be precise, for a prestigious Dublin firm of auctioneers. And written on it, in giant capital letters, were the words FOR SALE: Historic House and Thousand-Acre Estate.

He was selling Ashbrooke!

What was he thinking?

She knew how much he loved this estate. Was he so desperate to put distance between himself and her?

She wheeled her bike over to the imposing twenty-foot wrought-iron double gates. For a minute she considered the intercom. Should she just leave it? It was none of her business, after all. But she could not shake off the feeling that he was selling for all the wrong reasons.

She pressed down on the buzzer and jumped when it was quickly answered. She instantly recognised his housekeeper's voice.

'Hi, Maureen, it's Aideen Ryan. I want to have a word with Patrick.'

'Aideen? Of course—come on in. I'll give Patrick a call to let him know you're here.'

The gates opened slowly and Aideen drew in a deep breath before she jumped back on her bike and started to cycle up the drive.

When she caught her first glimpse of the house, in all its magnificent grandeur, her chest tightened with a heaviness that barely allowed her to breathe. How could he walk away from this house which meant so much to him? She tried to imagine someone else living here but it seemed impossible.

The sound of fast-approaching horse's hooves on the drive behind her had her wobbling on her bike once again, and she came to an ungraceful stop when she hit the grass verge.

She twisted around to see Patrick, heading in her direction riding a horse. He was a natural horseman, confident and assured. Totally in control. And heartbreakingly gorgeous.

He pulled the horse to a stop a few feet away.

Heat and desire instantly coiled between them. Her heart thumped wildly against her chest as his eyes held her captive.

Memory snapshots of him making love to her had her almost crying out in pain, and she gripped the handlebars of the bike tighter against the tremble in her legs.

He dismounted and led his horse towards her. He was wearing a loose blue shirt over his jodhpurs. His eyes matched the blue of the sky behind him, but gave nothing away as to what he was thinking.

'Maureen rang to say you wanted to speak to me.'

No, *How are you? How have you been?* Instead this bleak, unwelcoming comment. It made her feel as though all the closeness and warmth they had once shared had been nothing but a mirage.

She couldn't show him how upset she felt, so she took a deep breath and tried to control her voice. 'I saw the for-sale sign.'

He frowned slightly and shrugged. 'And?'

'Why are you selling?'

'I listened to what you said. You're right. I *am* isolated here in Ashbrooke.'

She didn't understand. Bewildered, she asked, 'Where are you going to go?'

'Wherever my work takes me. I have property throughout the world. I'll move around as necessary.'

'But you *love* Ashbrooke, Patrick. I know you do. You love this house and this land as though you were born into it.'

His mouth twisted unhappily and he fixed her with a lancing glare. 'I thought you would be pleased. It was you who put the idea in my head.'

'No. My point was that you deliberately choose houses that enable you to be isolated. But you can be isolated in the middle of Manhattan if you really want to. I didn't mean for you to sell Ashbrooke. This is crazy.'

'I need to move on. It's nothing more complicated than that.'

'Isn't it? Are you sure our relationship hasn't anything

to do with it? Are you worried I might still hope something can happen between us? Because if that's the case, please believe me—I have absolutely no expectations. I know it's over. And I accept it's for the best. Never the twain shall meet, after all.'

He shook his head angrily and uttered a low curse. In that moment he looked exhausted. 'Aideen, I wish I could explain…but I can't.'

What did he mean? For a moment she considered him, wanting to ask what there was to explain. It was all pretty simple, after all. He didn't love her. End of story.

'Please reconsider selling Ashbrooke. Moving from here won't change anything. Selling a house won't stop you being isolated. You need to open your heart to others. My fear is that you won't, and you'll be alone for the rest of your life. And you deserve more than that.'

He threw her a furious look. 'Do I really, though? I hurt Orla. I hurt you. Why on earth are you saying that I deserve more?'

'Because you're a good man, Patrick.'

His hands tightened on the reins. 'And you're too kind-hearted and generous.'

She lifted her chin and glared at him. 'Don't patronise me. I know what I'm talking about. And maybe you should listen to your own advice sometimes. You told me once that I should believe in myself. Well, maybe you should do the same.'

His jaw clenched. 'I can't give you what you need, Aideen.'

'This isn't about me. Trust me—I wouldn't be here if I hadn't seen the for-sale sign. I want nothing from you. But I'm not going to let you make the mistake of selling the house you love because for once you actually allowed someone into your life.'

His eyes were sharp, angry shards of blue ice. 'That has nothing to do with it.'

'Are you sure? Because I'm not convinced. Are you going to reconnect with Orla and your friends once you leave Ashbrooke? What changes are you going to make to your life?'

His mouth thinned and he threw her a blistering look. 'Frankly, that's none of your business.'

She gave a tight laugh of shock and took a step back. Her heart went into a freefall of despondency. 'Wow, you *really* know how to put a person in her place.' Her throat was tight, but she forced herself to speak. 'And it *is* my business because I care for you. I don't want to see you shutting more and more people out of your life. You deserve to be happy in life, Patrick. Remember that.'

There was nothing else she could say. She turned and picked up her bike. At the same time his phone rang.

He gave another low curse and muttered, 'This number has been calling me non-stop all morning.'

As she pushed away she heard him answer it.

She pedalled furiously.

Seeing him again had brought home just how much she missed him. Would she ever meet another man to whom she was so physically attracted? Just from standing close to him her body was on fire. And her heart felt as though it was in pieces. Because emotionally she missed him twice as much. She wanted him in her life. It was against all logic and reason. But there it was. She wanted his intelligence, his kindness, his strength.

The sound of his voice calling her and the thundering of hooves had her looking around, startled. Patrick was racing towards her. He yanked his horse to a stop, but didn't dismount. He looked aghast.

'That was a hospital in Dublin calling. Orla has gone into early labour.'

For a moment she wondered why he was telling her, but then she saw the fear in his eyes. He didn't know what to do.

She dropped her bike down on the grass verge. 'Are you going to go to Dublin to be with her?'

He looked pale and drawn. For a moment she thought he hadn't heard her question. But then he looked down at her beseechingly. 'I don't know what to do. I don't want to cause her any upset.'

'Did she tell the hospital to call you and ask you to come?'

'Yes.'

'Well, then, she needs you.' For a moment she looked at the horse warily, and then she held out her hand to Patrick. 'Pull me up. We need to get back to the house quickly. While you get changed I'll organise for your helicopter to come and collect you.'

He looked at her, taken aback, but then nodded his agreement. 'Put your leg in the stirrup and I'll pull you up.'

He drew her up and sat her in front of him. It was her first time on a horse, and it looked like a long, long way down, but she couldn't think of that. Instead she tried to think of the practical arrangements that needed to be sorted out in order to get Patrick to Dublin immediately. She tried to ignore how good it felt to be so physically close to him again.

At the stables, a groom helped her dismount. When Patrick jumped off he hesitated, so she held his hand in hers and tugged him forward. 'Come on—there's no time to waste.'

They entered the kitchen via the cloakroom. 'Is the number for your pilot stored on your phone?'

'Yes, but I'm not—'

'No, Patrick. You *have* to go. Orla has never needed you more than now. I know you feel you have failed her in the past. That there is a lot of hurt and misunderstanding. But right now none of that matters. Orla and her baby are the only things that matter. She needs her brother. She needs your strength and support.'

For a moment he blinked, but then, as her words finally registered, determination came back into his eyes. 'You're right. Call the helicopter. I'll be ready in ten minutes.'

Aideen immediately made the call, and the helicopter crew promised to be at Ashbrooke within twenty minutes. True to his word, Patrick was back in the kitchen within ten. Wearing a dark red polo shirt and faded denim jeans, his hair still wet from the shower, he looked gorgeous—if a little distracted. She could feel the pumped-up energy radiating from him. She needed to keep him calm, reassure him.

'The helicopter will be here in ten minutes. Do you want to call the hospital again for an update?'

Instantly he took the phone from the counter and dialled the number. He spoke looking out through the glass extension, down towards the sea, his polo shirt pulled tight across his wide shoulders, his jeans hugging his hips, and Aideen remembered her first night here. How in awe of him she'd been. How bowled over she'd been by his good looks.

Her heart dropped with a thud and she felt physical

pain in her chest. Would she ever stop missing him every single second of every single minute of every single hour?

'She's seven centimetres dilated…whatever that means. She's doing okay, but they're worried as she's a month early.' His jaw working, he added, 'She has nobody with her. Damn it, she shouldn't be alone at a time like this.'

She walked towards him and placed a hand on his arm. 'She's going to be okay. She's in good hands, but she'll be relieved to see you. I bet it's pretty lonely, going through something so big all on your own.'

He inhaled a deep breath at her words and felt some of the tension leave his body.

'You're right.'

And then it hit him just how much he wanted Aideen by his side today. He felt as though he had been struck by lightning, the realisation was so startling.

'Come to Dublin with me.'

'No, I can't…'

'I want you to come—please.' His throat worked. Could he actually say the words he needed to say? After so many years of going it alone, to ask for help felt alien. 'I need your support.'

Aideen looked totally taken aback. Out of the window he could see the helicopter approaching. He looked from it to her, beseechingly.

'Okay, I'll come.'

He was about to lead her out to the garden when he remembered something. 'Hold on for a minute. There's something I need to bring.'

He sprinted down to his office and then straight back to the kitchen.

Aideen looked at the memory chest and then up at

him. She said nothing, but there were tears in her eyes before she looked away from him.

As the helicopter took off his pilot gave them their estimated flight time. He inhaled a frustrated breath and shook his head.

Beside him, Aideen asked, 'Are you okay?'

'No. If Orla had told me she was back in Dublin I could have been there much earlier. I wouldn't have been ignoring my phone all morning.'

'I can understand your frustration, but Orla wasn't to know that she was going to go into early labour. And, anyway, that was *her* decision. She's a grown woman, Patrick, about to have her own child. You can't control everything in your life. Today you just need to be there for Orla. Be the brother she loves, and trust that that's enough.'

Thrown, he was about to argue. But then he realised she was right. He had to stop thinking that the only way he could show his love for Orla was by taking charge and forcing her to lead the life he thought she should.

With a small smile he lifted his hands in admission and said, 'You're right.'

She gave him a smile in return and then looked away, her gaze on the endless patchwork of green fields that appeared through the window as the pilot banked the helicopter.

He longed to reach out and touch her, to hold her hand in his. His heart felt as though it would pound right out of his chest at any moment. Being so near to her but not being able to touch her was torture. But the hurt in her eyes was even worse. You could cut the tension in the helicopter with a knife.

Though his teeth were clenched tight, he forced them apart in order to speak. 'How is your cottage?'

She glanced at him warily, as though questioning why he was asking. 'Dusty and noisy...' She paused and held his gaze. 'But that doesn't matter. It's just really good to be home.' Then her gaze flicked away.

Why was the silence between them making him feel so uncomfortable? Before, he'd never had an issue with silence, but now it felt as if his heart was being ripped out to fill the void that sat like a physical entity between them.

He had to speak. Anything but this mocking silence which drove home much too eloquently everything he had lost: her humour, her warmth, her spark and her love of life.

'William will bring down all your files and office equipment once the cottage is finished.'

She nodded to this, her face impassive. But then she looked towards him with a frown. 'What's going to happen to William and Maureen and the rest of the staff?'

'It's part of my sale conditions that all the existing staff are retained by the new owner.'

'They're going to miss you—they're really fond of you.'

Were they? He had never stopped to think about it. But now he realised just how much he would miss them, too.

What was he *doing*? Was anything making sense in his life any more?

He looked back at her when he heard her clear her throat. 'I really hope your time with Orla goes well today. Please be patient. I bet Orla misses you desperately, but can't say it. Maybe for the same reasons that you can't say it to her.'

His mind raced at her words. Did Orla fear losing him, too? Was that why she always pushed him away? No wonder the harder he tried, the harder she pushed back.

He looked at Aideen in amazement. 'You might be right. So I just need to be there for her?'

'Yes!' With a small laugh she added, 'And for goodness' sake don't go ordering the midwives and doctors about. I'm sure they know what they are doing.'

'I won't.' He gave her a rueful look and added, 'My managing directors have a lot to thank you for, by the way. I thought about what you said about delegating more control to them and I've started doing so.'

She gave a small satisfied smile. 'And I bet the world hasn't come crashing down, has it?'

He gave an eye-roll. 'It's actually a relief to not be bogged down in day-to-day operations. I now have more time to focus on a strategic level.'

He paused for a minute, uncertain of where to take the conversation. There was so much more he should say, but he couldn't find the right words.

'How about you? What are your plans?'

For a split second she winced, but then she sat up in her seat, her voice unwavering as she spoke. 'I've had a lot of orders since Paris, and more than ever I'm determined to make Little Fire the most exciting bespoke textile design business in the world. And I'm looking forward to getting to know the people of Mooncoyne, I want to become part of the community. Get involved. I want to establish roots, to belong.'

Fresh admiration for her determination to succeed washed over him. But then a kick of reality came when it dawned on him that he didn't feature in any of her plans.

Which was only to be expected. And yet it twisted in his gut that they would soon go their separate ways.

It was what he wanted. What they had to do. Wasn't it?

CHAPTER TWELVE

His HELICOPTER LANDED on the hospital's helipad and within minutes they were rushing through the front doors of the hospital.

The receptionist at the front desk blushed furiously when she looked up to see Patrick, and garbled out directions to the delivery ward. As she left Aideen gave her an understanding smile. He had that effect on all women. Herself included.

He didn't wait for the lifts but instead took the steps up to the third floor two at a time. Aideen followed his frantic pace, glad she was fit from cycling around Mooncoyne.

Again there was a flutter of activity when he stopped at the nurses' desk. Then they were directed to a number of chairs dotted along the corridor outside the delivery rooms, while one of the nurses went into the delivery suite to enquire if Orla was able to see him.

She could feel Patrick's nervousness radiating off him. 'It's going to be okay.'

He looked at her for a long while and then nodded, the tension in his face easing a little.

The door of the delivery suite opened and the nurse came back out, beaming. 'They're ready for you,' she said.

Patrick looked at Aideen in amazement. 'Does that mean that…that the baby has been born already?'

Memories of holding her own niece for the first time, the tremendous wave of love that had speared her heart, caused a lump of happiness to form in Aideen's throat. 'Yes. You better get in there.'

'Will you come in with me?'

'No. This is *your* time with Orla and her baby.'

He hesitated for a moment. 'What if I say the wrong thing?'

'You won't. Just be yourself… And remember Orla is a mum now, well capable of looking after herself. She doesn't need you to make decisions for her—she just needs your support.' She paused and eyed him with amusement. 'And advice… But only if she asks for it.'

'Will you wait here for me? I'd like to introduce you to Orla.'

'I'll wait.'

He stood and moved to the door, but then turned and said, 'Thank you. For everything.'

She returned his smile, but after the door had swung closed after him it slowly faded.

From the delivery suite she could hear the murmur of voices. Earnest, but with no hint of argument. Maybe they would be okay. She willed them to be kind and patient with one another. To realise that they needed each other. She hoped they could forget the past and realise what a wonderful future they had before them.

Patrick would be a great uncle. He had so much generosity and integrity burning inside him. Along with strength and pride. He would be an incredible role model for Orla's baby.

The murmurs had given way to light laughter. Patrick now had a newly expanded family to fill his life.

It was time for her to move on.

She left a brief note for him on her chair, and then walked back down the stairs and out of the hospital. She would get a cab to the train station. In Cork, she would get a bus to Mooncoyne.

As she queued at the taxi rank she tried to ignore the excited families going in and out of the hospital. But when a young couple emerged, the dad proudly holding his newborn child, she had to turn away, tears filming her eyes. She could go and stay with her own family, here in Dublin, but knew that if she saw her mum she would instantly burst into tears.

She would go home and lose herself in her work.

The taxi rank was busy and the line shuffled along slowly. With growing impatience she willed the taxis to come. She needed to get home. She needed to be in Mooncoyne. She needed the silence and beauty of West Cork in order to heal her broken heart.

At last it was her turn. The taxi drew to a halt, but just as she stepped forward to open the rear door a hand clasped her arm.

Patrick.

She had been crying. He tried to draw in a deep breath, but his heart was pounding too loudly, his stomach flipping so frantically there simply wasn't enough room for his lungs to expand. He'd panicked when he had realised she had gone, and her note hadn't helped. She had said she wished him well, but would prefer it if he didn't contact her again.

This was going to be the most important conversation of his life.

What if he messed up?

What if he failed to convince her?

For a moment he hesitated, fearful of blowing this.

He had to pull himself together.

'Will you come for a walk with me?'

She looked back at the taxi and for a moment he thought she was going say no. But then her shoulders dropped and the wariness of her gaze lessened.

'Is this a good idea?'

He gave her a crooked smile and shrugged. 'I'm hoping it's the best idea I ever had.'

She stared at him in confusion, but then a faint hint of amusement shone in her eyes. 'Okay.'

He took her to a nearby park, where sunlight glimmered through the trees and cast dark dancing shadows on the grey tarmacadam paths.

He didn't know where to start, so he just blurted out everything that had been building in his chest, in his mind, in his heart, for the past week.

'I've missed you.'

She looked at him with surprise and hurt.

God, this was harder than he'd thought. He wanted her to understand but he couldn't find the words. He was usually articulate, forceful. But all of that was now lost to him.

Should he just take her into his arms and kiss her? Physically show her what he was trying to say?

That wasn't the answer.

He needed to start making things right.

'I'm sorry for what happened in Paris.'

Her head whipped round. In a rush, she said, 'No, *I*

should apologise. I said things that were too intense.' Pointing to the cute blush on her cheeks she added, 'As you can see, I'm pretty embarrassed about it all. I didn't mean to put you under any pressure. I guess I misread all the signs.'

He shook his head. 'No, you weren't to blame. Everything happened so quickly. The intensity of it all got to me. After focusing on nothing but work for so long I felt overwhelmed.'

Her mouth twisted ruefully. 'I guess what I said would have had most guys heading for the hills.'

A heavy sadness sat in his chest and his throat tightened with emotion. 'Not if they'd experienced what we had together. It was special... But I had believed for so long that I wasn't cut out to be in a relationship I couldn't see beyond that.'

She looked at him, bewildered. 'I don't know why you keep saying that you aren't suited to be in a relationship. Forget me, for one moment, and what we had. All I can see before me is a thoughtful, strong, honourable man who is deserving of love.' She shook her head in exasperation. 'You deserve to be loved, Patrick. I just hope in the future you can learn to let people into your life.'

He inhaled a steadying breath. He needed to let his heart speak and ignore the vulnerability and fear of exposing himself. The fear that she would say no.

'You asked me in Paris why I couldn't be in a relationship and I didn't answer you truthfully. It was a step I just couldn't take. Even now it feels like I'm about to yank out my heart and give it to you...which makes me feel pretty exposed.'

She looked at him, confused.

He took a deep breath.

'When Orla moved in with me I was frightened of losing her, like I'd lost my mum and dad. So I tried to protect her as best I could. But now, because of you, I understand that I took the wrong approach. I shouldn't have been so controlling, so protective. I should have included her in the decisions that had to be taken in the new life we were both suddenly facing.'

He inhaled a deep breath against the way his insides were tumbling.

'You were right about Orla. I have to let her decide what support she wants from me. I'll admit it will be hard to change, after years of trying to take charge, but I know I can no longer foist what I *think* she needs on her.'

His chest felt heavy with so many words still unsaid. He drew her away from the path and guided her to a bench under a giant chestnut tree. The wood was warm under his hands when he gripped the base of the seat tight. He glanced at her, and then away.

'That fear of losing someone is the reason why I swore I never wanted to be in love with a woman. In Paris, as we grew closer, that fear intensified. I was worried that if I fell in love with you I'd only end up losing you at some point in the future. And that thought terrified me.'

His jaw ached with tension and he had to work it loose before he continued.

'And rather than face that fear I refused to acknowledge what you meant to me. After we slept together all my feelings for you were exposed, and I panicked. I couldn't handle how I was feeling. How close I felt to you, how I wanted you in my life. And when you said you were leaving I didn't know how to ask you to stay.' Shaking his head, he added, 'At first I was angry at you for going. I wanted you not to love me.'

He gave a rueful laugh and looked towards the sky in disbelief.

'I was cross that you had fallen in love with me. As if somebody can opt in or out of falling in love. And then I tried to convince myself that perhaps you going was for the best. That if you stayed any longer I wouldn't be able to hide my feelings for you. And then I realised I was kidding myself—that I was lost without you. I missed you, Aideen, with every fibre of my being.'

He risked a quick glance in her direction and her look of compassion caught him off-guard. His throat tightened, but he forced himself to speak.

'For so long I thought I'd failed not only Orla but my mum and dad, too. That I had not faced up to my responsibilities. But now I realise I have to accept that I did the best I could in looking after Orla. That I couldn't do any more. I have to stop blaming myself.'

His heart raced in his chest and he squeezed his hands even tighter on the edge of the seat before he continued.

'Today, as Orla and I spoke, I could see for the first time in a very long time that we can have a relationship that works, one that's supportive and loving. And I realised that I have to stop worrying that I will mess up relationships… I have to let go of my fear of losing those I love. I also realised that if I let you go then I would really have failed. Failed you. And myself.'

Tears shone brightly in her eyes and his hand rose to capture her face. His thumb slowly stroked her skin. She was about to say something, but he spoke first.

'That first time I opened my door to you the night of the storm—when you fell into my arms and soaked me through—I looked into those startled brown eyes and deep inside myself I recognised you. Recognised that you are the one. But I was too wrapped up in feelings of guilt and fear to see it. The last thing I wanted to do was hurt you, so I kept telling myself not to fall for you. I hadn't reckoned on how you would worm your way into my heart. How my resilience would waver each time you smiled and laughed. I hadn't reckoned on the joy and fun you brought into my life. Just how mind-blowingly and crazily I would be physically attracted to you. How I'd lose my mind and my heart to you when we made love.'

His hand dropped from her cheek to hold hers. Blood pounded in his ears.

'I love you, Aideen. I don't know how, but in a matter of weeks you've turned my life upside down. I can't even pinpoint when I fell in love with you. Perhaps it was at every moment that you challenged me, whether it was on the tennis court or in how I chose to spend my life. Of course I didn't want to listen to you, but you loosened yet another chink in the armour I had wrapped around myself for years. Or maybe it was after I saw your delight went we ate at my club next to the Eiffel Tower. Until the day I die I will remember just how stunningly beautiful you looked that night.'

He watched her shocked expression, saw her hand pressed to her mouth. His stomach clenched.

He leant towards her and said in a low voice, 'Since Paris, all I can think of is our lovemaking…your soft whispers. I'm in love with you, Aideen Ryan.'

She said nothing, just shook her head, her hand still over her mouth. Didn't she believe him? Panic gripped him. Should he just stop? No. He had to tell her how much he loved her. How much he needed her in his life.

'I'm in love with your chocolate eyes, your smiling mouth, your messy chatterbox ways. There's so much I want to know about you. How you like to celebrate Halloween, Christmas, birthdays. What's your favourite flavour of ice cream? There's so much I want to experience with you. So much more I want to learn about you and fall in love with. To go along with how much I love your lips. The never-ending length of your eyelashes. Your constant daydreaming. The five tiny piercings in your right ear.'

That, at least, elicited a smile.

'In Paris I was convinced I couldn't give you the love you deserve. You had been hurt enough in the past without me adding to it. For so long I allowed my fear of losing those close to me to push people away. I was certain I wasn't capable of being in an effective relationship. I was terrified of taking that blind leap of faith—of telling someone you love them and all the vulnerabilities and uncertainties that go with that.'

He looked into her eyes, his heart thumping wildly.

'You helped bring Orla and her baby girl back into my life. My life was pretty empty until you arrived into it. My heart had shut down. I was tired of losing people I loved. But you kick-started it with a bang within hours of turning up in my life. That night of the storm I tried to shut you out, but you kept worming your way in with your warmth and humour.'

He shook his head and ran a hand through his hair.

'At first I thought helping you would be a good distraction from everything that was happening with Orla. But, in truth, now I realise that I wanted to make up for failing Orla so badly by helping you instead. I hadn't anticipated that it would actually be more about you helping me. As each day passed you became a bigger and bigger part of my life...until now I can't imagine a life with you. So much so that in the past week I couldn't settle to anything. I grew increasingly restless, and the only way I could think of distracting myself was by taking to the road again, by selling Ashbrooke. But the truth is I can't live without you. You have made me want to live life again—fully. You are the most beautiful, courageous, kind, funny, and tender woman I have ever met and I want you in my life…for ever.'

Her head swam with all his words. It would be so easy to give in to her heart, give in to the chemistry and attraction that drew her like a magnet to him. She wanted nothing more than to spend every second of the rest of her life with him, to know every single inch of him.

But they were from different worlds, and no amount of love would change that.

'I don't know what to say. Oh, Patrick… You know how I feel for you, but this is never going to work. We're too different. We're not equals. I don't want to be in an unbalanced relationship.'

The pull of his hand on hers forced her to look back up at him. Gentle eyes held her gaze.

'What are you afraid of?'

Her pulse pounded at his question and her throat dried. 'That you will have power over me. That I will spend my life feeling inadequate, unequal, that I didn't contribute my fair share.'

He pulled her closer until there was only an inch separating them. His beautiful gaze held hers with such compassion and warmth tears trickled down her cheeks in response.

'Have I ever done any of those things to you? Made you feel like you aren't my equal?'

'No…'

'Do you trust me?'

Her heart burst forth with the truth and she answered resoundingly. 'Yes, I trust you.'

'Will you trust me when I say that we *are* equals? That we are both bringing different but equally important things to this relationship? You are bringing empathy, joy, creativity...and you brought my family back together. What could be more important than that? You have a love for me that no one else can ever give me. How can any of those things be of less importance than wealth?' Before she could answer he said quickly, 'You *do* love me, don't you?'

She struggled to speak against the wave of emotions that churned in her body. She squeezed his hands, needing to clutch on to his strength in order to carry on. 'I love you with all my heart. You are kind and generous. More handsome than any man deserves to be. You make me feel like the most special person in the world. When we made love I felt an intimacy, a love for you, that was so intense, so real...it was almost frightening. I love you so much... But you have so much wealth, and I have practically nothing... It doesn't seem right. And I'm so confused.'

For a while he simply looked at her, deep in thought. His eyes grew sombre and determined. 'Are you saying that if I lost all my money in the morning you wouldn't love me?'

'No! Of course not!'

And then she stopped as a satisfied smile broke on his lips.

'So what *are* you saying?'

For the longest while she just stared at him, unsure. She trusted him. He had never tried to control or dominate her with his wealth and power. And if he was penniless it wouldn't change her love for him.

'I suppose I'm saying that I'm a little scared and daunted by all this.'

His head tilted to the side and he said gently, 'Being in love is a little scary…but I promise I will never hurt you.'

'Are you scared?'

'Of course! I'm scared of being hurt, too—of you not loving me as much as I love you.'

'But that would be impossible.'

'Would it? Are you willing to take the risk and be with me? I love you. I want you by my side always. I want to wake to your smile, sleep with you in my arms. I want to care for you, protect you, argue with you, grow old with you. I want to share everything I have with you. Because in giving, in sharing everything I have with you, I hope you'll see it as an indication of how much I love you. And in accepting me, and all that I have, you can show me how much you love and trust me. That you are willing to share my life.'

He dropped to his knees on the path before her and she could do nothing but gape at him, open-mouthed.

'Before this year is out I want to stand before our families and friends and ask you. Aideen Ryan, for richer or poorer, will you marry me?'

Dizzy, she closed her eyes for a moment. The sun warmed her face as she turned it upwards and her hand swept away the tears on her cheeks. A fiery intensity beat in her heart.

The sun danced beneath her eyelids and when she dropped her head she opened her eyes to the pale blue Irish sky. The same glorious colour as his eyes, which she then turned to. Eyes filled with love…and a little apprehension.

She could barely speak, her pulse was pounding so hard. 'I never thought I could ever love someone as much as I love you. With you I feel complete…I feel secure. I can be the best that I am with you. The world is more beautiful, more exciting, more intense with you in it. So, yes, I would be honoured to be your wife, to spend the rest of my life with you.'

His hands wrapped about her face and he gently drew her to him. Her breath caught at the power of the joy and love shining in his eyes.

He spoke in a low whisper. 'It has taken me so long to find you…to allow love into my life. I'm never letting you out of my sight again. Promise me that we will never sleep a night apart. That you will come with me wherever I go.'

Her thumb traced the lines of his lips and she spoke with light, teasing laughter. 'I promise… I will follow you to the ends of this world. But I'm warning you: I want lots of children, so you'll have a lot of uncomfortable nights in hospital chairs.'

At that he stood, and looked down at her with stunned joy. Then he pulled her up and, holding her by the waist, swung her around and around.

When he stopped they were both breathless with laughter. And then his gaze darkened. 'How about we start trying straight away?'

She inched forward and brushed her lips against his. 'Good idea.'

And then she was lost to his strength, his warmth. His love.

EPILOGUE

Eight months later

As SHE STOOD outside the double doors to the entrance of Ashbrooke's ballroom Aideen's fingers trembled where she held on to her dad's arm.

Behind her, her cousin and bridesmaid Kate fussed with the train of her dress.

To one side of the hallway a huge fir tree from the estate was bedecked in twinkling white Christmas lights. Through the windows beyond, fat flakes of snow fluttered down to join the heavy carpet of snow that already covered the estate.

Tomorrow—Christmas Day—she would wake up beside her husband. Giddy excitement raced through her at the thought, and she smiled quietly to herself.

She ran a hand over the delicate lace of her dress, her trained eye once again inspecting it. But there was no need. It was perfect.

She had spent weeks deciding on the design, and it had been handcrafted by a group of lacemakers who lived locally. It was a traditional Bandon Lace design, but with personal touches added—the shields that represented valour and honour on the Fitzsimon family crest, the three griffins of the Ryan crest representing courage and bravery. A seashell to represent Ashbrooke House. The sailing boat from the Parisian coat of arms. Symbols from all the places where she had fallen deeper and deeper in love with Patrick.

And on her feet were the ivory ankle-strap sandals Mustard and Mayo had bought her all those months ago.

With a nod, she signalled to her dad that she was ready.

The doors opened and once again she was dazzled by the ornate heavy gilt mirrored walls, the cherub-filled frescoed ceiling of the ballroom, and her heart leapt at its spectacular beauty.

Her family and friends beamed back at her and her already bursting heart exploded with joy. Her mum openly cried, while her two brothers tried to pretend they weren't.

Orla, holding baby Evie in her arms, looked from Aideen to Patrick with love and pride.

Patrick's best man, Frédéric Forbin, whispered something to him and he nodded in response.

When was he going to turn to her?

The dogs sat patiently at his feet, both wearing pale pink bows to match the bridal party. Behind him stood his large group of friends, including Lord Balfe, all of whom had travelled from around the world to be here. Friends who were once again part of his life.

And then he turned to her.

She wanted to run to him but forced herself to take the slow bridal steps. His hair was shorn once again, highlighting the sharp masculine lines of his face, the brilliant blue of his eyes.

Step by step she moved closer to her best friend. To the

man who made her feel like the most beautiful woman in the world.

With him, she was complete.

Before him, she'd felt as though she was a feather—floating through the air, happy, but never quite belonging, never quite understanding.

And now, because of him, she understood. That this life was about love. Giving love. But also receiving it. That was all that really mattered.

And tonight, at the stroke of midnight, she would give him his Christmas present: the news that she was six weeks pregnant.

* * * * *

LET'S TALK
Romance

For exclusive extracts, competitions
and special offers, find us online:

 facebook.com/millsandboon

@MillsandBoon

@MillsandBoonUK

Get in touch on 01413 063232

For all the latest titles coming soon, visit
millsandboon.co.uk/nextmonth

MILLS & BOON

THE HEART OF ROMANCE

A ROMANCE FOR EVERY KIND OF READER

MODERN

Prepare to be swept off your feet by sophisticated, sexy and seductive heroes, in some of the world's most glamourous and romantic locations, where power and passion collide.
8 stories per month.

HISTORICAL

Escape with historical heroes from time gone by. Whether your passion is for wicked Regency Rakes, muscled Vikings or rugged Highlanders, awaken the romance of the past.
6 stories per month.

MEDICAL

Set your pulse racing with dedicated, delectable doctors in the high-pressure world of medicine, where emotions run high and passion, comfort and love are the best medicine.
6 stories per month.

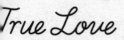

Celebrate true love with tender stories of heartfelt romance, from the rush of falling in love to the joy a new baby can bring, and a focus on the emotional heart of a relationship.
8 stories per month.

Indulge in secrets and scandal, intense drama and plenty of sizzling hot action with powerful and passionate heroes who have it all: wealth, status, good looks…everything but the right woman.
6 stories per month.

HEROES

Experience all the excitement of a gripping thriller, with an intense romance at its heart. Resourceful, true-to-life women and strong, fearless men face danger and desire - a killer combination!
8 stories per month.

Sensual love stories featuring smart, sassy heroines you'd want as a best friend, and compelling intense heroes who are worthy of them.
4 stories per month.

To see which titles are coming soon, please visit

millsandboon.co.uk/nextmonth